Suit and Suitability

Also in The Vintage Jane Austen:

Suit and Suitability

by Kelsey Bryant

For my grandmother, Irene Vogel.
Not only have you lived through the Great Depression, you
have given your family a godly heritage.
Thank you for always being so loving and supportive
in everything I do.

Historical Note

Many times while I was writing *Suit and Suitability*, I wished I could travel back in time to learn everything I needed to know about Ohio and New York during the Great Depression. But like all real-life mortals who don't have a time-travel contraption, I had to take the next best way to get there: books, websites, and movies. They weren't disappointing (usually!).

For reconstructing Canton, I found *A Secret Gift* by Ted Gup, various local history books at the Stark County Library and the McKinley Museum, and the museum's exhibits themselves, to be extremely valuable.

There really was a Players Guild in Canton, and McKinley High School's 1935 play really was *Secrets*, but there are no records of summer stock theaters coming to Canton that year. However, many actors got their professional start in summer stock, so I couldn't resist giving Marion that chance.

Two of my best sources about Broadway in the 1930s came from talkinbroadway.com and broadwayworld.com. It was astonishingly difficult to figure out the Broadway audition process back then, but two contemporary stories proved helpful: Edna Ferber's play *Stage Door*, the 1937 movie based off it, and the 1933 movie *Morning Glory*. Aspiring actresses have always captured the public's imagination!

For information on Hollywood, *The Golden Age of Cinema* by Richard B. Jewell was a fantastic main source. The 1930s was a dramatic time in theater history: on the East Coast, Broadway struggled, while on the West Coast, Hollywood thrived.

I referred to too many resources on the Great Depression to name, but at least one deserves special mention: *Daily Life in the United States, 1920–1939* by David E. Kyvig. My favorite source of all, though, was my grandmother, who grew up during that time and would have been just a few months younger than

Marion Dashiell.

The people of the Greatest Generation will always have my respect and admiration. I've enjoyed combining their story with Jane Austen's wonderful classic *Sense and Sensibility* (one of my favorite novels) to bring you *Suit and Suitability*. I hope it will not only entertain you, but also inspire you to trust in God's love and care for you. He will never leave you nor forsake you!

Many blessings,
Kelsey Bryant

✨✧Chapter One✧✨

"GUILTY."

The voice of the jury foreman was deep and emotionless, so uncannily like her father's that Ellen Dashiell could almost believe Dad was convicting himself.

The word plunged a knife into Ellen's soul. She watched her father's black-coated back for a dip or a sway or the slightest falter, but it was as straight and unyielding as always. Her own heart hammered and she pushed her gloved hands farther into her lap, forbidding them to tremble. Beside her, Mother and her youngest sister, Greta, put their arms around each other. On the other side of Greta, her other sister, Marion, gasped loudly. Around and behind them swelled the groans of their supportive friends.

The conviction followed. Twelve months in prison without parole and a twelve thousand dollar fine.

For something Oliver Dashiell hadn't done.

In a blur, the gavel thudded the bench; Mother jumped and squeezed Ellen's hand as if she were slipping. Sobs tumbled from Greta and Marion, and Dad's shoulders slumped for the first time.

Ellen could hardly bear it when he turned his long, chiseled face to his wife and daughters, gentled by the sadness in his dark brown eyes. She met his gaze and tried to lift the corners of her mouth, but they wouldn't budge.

"All rise!"

The full courtroom obeyed as the hulking black form of the judge departed through the door behind his bench. A murmur ran through the crowd. Mother's hand pulled out of Ellen's grip and shot toward her husband. He spun and captured it, pressing it to his lips before tugging her into an embrace across

1

the gleaming wood bar. Ellen glanced at her sisters; Marion clutched Greta's arm, giving their parents time together that would never be enough.

Then he tightly hugged each of the girls. When would Ellen feel his arms around her again, the solidness of his chest, the sturdiness of his shoulders? Her cheek brushing his soft, leather-scented business jacket? Twelve months. One year. It sounded like an eternity.

The wind was against them as they descended the courthouse steps, snapping at their skin and clothes with ferocious bites. Canton's brick and stone façades soared over them, every one impressing Ellen with her family's insignificance and aloneness. She glanced left and right to watch for cars as she and her mother and sisters crossed the street. Even the Gothic church behind them was stern and cold. Bells clanged over the traffic noise, clock towers proclaiming twelve noon like any ordinary day.

Ellen looked back at the gold-bricked courthouse, glancing at the angels trumpeting in the high tower. The trumpeters of justice? She'd always admired this palatial structure, but now it galled her.

Guilty.

The word throbbed in her mind. Guilty? Her dad? Guilty? Of embezzlement?

They threaded through the parking lot to their blue and black DeSoto sedan. Their battle with the February wind was almost won.

Leaving Dad behind in the courthouse was the hardest thing Ellen had ever done. Was he being taken to the jail next door that very moment? She relived hugging him, smelling his piney aftershave, feeling the steadying influence of his voice, eating up every detail of his handsome, fatherly face.

Daddy.

Mother climbed in behind the wheel, Ellen in the passenger seat beside her, and Marion and Greta in the back. Mother lifted her brown eyes to the courthouse after she started the car. Tears glimmered there beneath the light brown curls.

They got on their way. Marion was uncharacteristically silent, immersed in grief, while Greta groused about the unfairness of everything. Mother halfheartedly fielded her complaints as they made a beeline down Market Avenue North for home in Vassar Park. Past landmarks that reminded them of the way life was supposed to run: Sears. Loew's Theater. The Palace Theater. McKinley High School. The Canton Woman's Club.

"What'll we do now?" Greta asked as they left the business sector and wheeled by mansions of Canton's elite, whitewashed with snow. Her large, oak-brown eyes were magnified by the close fit of her red beret, pulled down over her ears, allowing only wisps of brownish-blond hair to escape. Far from looking older than thirteen—her goal—she looked ingenuous, like someone who needed protection. "Couldn't we have stayed longer with Dad somehow?"

"No." Mother sighed. "We couldn't have. It's been a long day; maybe you'd like a nap. Maybe we all would."

Ellen worried about Mother—she had always depended on Dad for everything from material needs to decision-making, like he had depended on her for comfort and encouragement. How would they live apart? Ellen had extricated Mother and the girls from the courthouse, out of the crowd and away from the reporters, because Mother had melted into inaction once Dad had been removed. Ellen could already feel the family responsibilities settling onto her shoulders.

"Someone could have invited us to their house, or come over to ours." Marion fluffed her movie star-blond shoulder-length curls. She succeeded at looking older than her age—seventeen—but it was all illusion. "I'm not sure that'd have really helped with the blues, but it'd have made us feel loved."

"Someone might turn up later," Ellen said, trying to believe it herself. Support from friends had been disturbingly sparse during the two weeks of Dad's incarceration. "Greta, I think focusing on our tasks will get us through the day. You and Marion have school tomorrow, and I'll be back at work…we can prepare and that'll help us carry on." She threw a pointed glance over her shoulder. "You could do the assigned reading you missed today."

Greta frowned. "Mother, do I have to?"

"Have to what?" Mother drove slowly, hunched over the wheel, her usual ladylike posture broken down by weariness.

"Read my assignments. I can't! I'll be thinking of Dad."

Mother sighed. She sighed almost as often as Marion, but not to advance drama. "You'll have a lot to catch up on tomorrow if you don't. But do what you want."

"I want to hear what radio shows are on weekday afternoons." Greta lifted a smirk, but dropped it because no one acknowledged it.

"Soap operas," Ellen responded. "That's why they're on during the day—schoolchildren wouldn't like them."

"You're just saying that because you don't listen to them," Marion countered peevishly. "There are good ones, Greta, and you can listen if you want."

Ellen didn't argue. Marion wasn't normally this contrary or snippy; the hard day oppressed them all. Useless fighting would worsen it.

"But I'll be sitting in my room thinking about Dad," Marion continued. "We have our own radio drama going on." A soft moan accompanied her sigh.

A drama was right. Huge changes were afoot, unwelcome, unforgiving, and unavoidable. Just how bad they'd be and how the Dashiells could weather them Ellen didn't know, but something Dad had said when he was first accused crept in to help her now: *God knows the outcome; He could tell us if He wanted to. But since He hasn't, it's clear that we're supposed to take it one step, one day, at a time. And that, Ellen, is how we'll get through this.*

The jury, pressured by the judge, had convicted him, despite the Dashiells' prayers. The decision had hinged on Green's testimony—Mr. Benton Green, president of Friar's Tool and Die where Dad was vice president, and…Dad's accuser. He was Ellen's boss, too, and she would be returning under his authority tomorrow. Hateful thought. Was God powerless?

Didn't He care? Why had He allowed this to happen?

Home couldn't come soon enough. The world was a mass of white, punctuated by trees. The evergreens were a welcome breach, having shaken most of the snow off their branches, but the deciduous trees stood gray and shivering. Ellen knew how they felt. A shudder traveled through her as the wind pounded on their long, boxy DeSoto, demanding to be let in. The sky was dingy white with domineering clouds. No amount of snow, softening the angles and curves of the landscape, making one think of purity, hearths, Christmas, and childhood fun, would ever make Ellen appreciate winter. What made it worse was the thought of how much more unbearable it was for her fellow Cantonians who couldn't afford enough heat—the families of workers who had been laid off and not hired again.

And now, just when the Dashiells had begun hoping they'd make it through the Depression without foundering, their lifeline had been cut. How would they manage without Dad and his income? Ellen's meager wages as a secretary at Friar's had only ever been enough for her personal needs and savings.

As Mother parked the DeSoto in front of 224 Cambridge Street, Ellen knew their days in the Elizabethan home they loved were numbered. Dad had told her and Mother to contact his uncle and aunt, who had already phoned the Dashiells days ago to offer sympathy and support. Although the Dashiells prized their self-reliance, Dad had quickly perceived his family would need help—and even a place to live.

"What! Leave Canton?" Marion's fork clattered to the table. The chicken and tomato-and-cheese rice that had been so appetizing fled her mind, driven out by Mother's world-overturning declaration the night after the trial. "Dad's convicted, he's getting transferred to the Pen, and now we're leaving Canton to stay with relatives we barely know?"

"Dad thought it best. But actually, we don't yet know if they'll agree. I haven't even sent my letter." Mother's troubled brown eyes looked to Ellen for support. "You remember the

Maddoxes, surely, Ellen? It's been years; we hadn't moved to Vassar Park yet. They came to a Christmas party. You must have been no older than ten. It's our fault for not seeing them as often as we ought."

Dim memories stirred in the shadows of Marion's mind. Loud laughter…frizzy hair…a funny mustache, or was it a beard? Uncle Melvin was a dentist. His wife was Jenevieve; she had something odd about her appearance, too. Was it tall hair? Decidedly not the people Marion would live with if she could help it.

Of course, Ellen, sitting straight and composed and eating rhythmically, though with even itty-bittier bites than normal, agreed.

"*I* don't mind leaving. I'm tired of Canton," Greta announced. Though her tone was brazen, her nose and eyes still flushed red from the tears she'd cried when Mother told them the news about Dad's transferal.

Dad was being taken to the Ohio State Penitentiary in Columbus. Tomorrow. Mother had visited him at the jail today, but the girls wouldn't see him again for eleven months. Their pretty house—its red bricks and half-timbering, garden and all, which Marion wouldn't give up for the world—was going back to the bank. And the world wasn't coming in exchange— instead, a dowdy country village called Cardinal Bush, thirty miles away.

"We'll live there only until Dad's release." Mother shored up her voice. Lately she had quavered and softened whenever she spoke of Dad, but she was strong now. "The only perplexing thing is what to do about Ellen's job."

"What about *Secrets*?" Marion demanded. She had been cast as the lead in McKinley High's senior play. It was a lovely play, a lovely role—portrayed on screen by the gorgeous little legend Mary Pickford herself! Oh, Marion would fight to keep it. "And the Guild?" Her voice rose.

"Marion, calm down. We must discuss this rationally," Ellen said.

Her plainspoken voice had the effect of a peaceful lake on

Marion's nerves. Somehow it always quieted her, no matter how upset she was. Marion inhaled deeply. "If you want a rational discussion, then I'd better lock my lips."

"You do that," Ellen concurred. "Mother, didn't Dad say I could live with Frances or an old school friend like Bess Norbert to stay on at Friar's? They might house me for a little rent or housework help."

Mother sighed. "Yes, though I hate to split the family even more."

"If I get a job, can I stay in town with Ellen?" Marion asked.

Mother frowned. "What about school? You *must* graduate, Marion. Dad insists on that."

"There's hours after school. Though I don't know what to do about the Guild. I won't give up acting..." Marion surveyed the various paths her life could take. How could she ever find happiness and accomplish her dreams now?

Ellen asked, "So, what ought we to do in the meantime, while we wait for Uncle Melvin's reply?"

"Dad said there's not much we can do until he replies," Mother answered. "He might have a place for some of our furniture, so we shouldn't sell all of it." Her face dropped to her hands with a little moan. "I wish Dad were here to help us."

"So do I, but he's not, so we just have to do our best," Ellen said quietly. Until now, Dad had been involved in every momentous decision any of his girls had ever made.

They went on to discuss the move. Dad had advised Mother about moving men and trucks, but she couldn't remember everything he said. She worried about the costs, about imposing on the Maddoxes, about Marion and Greta changing schools. Ellen attempted to allay Mother's concerns; Greta piped in questions fueled by her resilient, eager attitude; and Marion was silent, mulling over her future.

Though Ellen was outwardly tranquil as they continued talking and eating dinner, inside she battled worry. The Pen...the place where real criminals lived, crammed together like so many animals…murderers, gangsters, thieves…the place that had burned five years ago, snuffing out the lives of hundreds of prisoners locked in their cells…she didn't know of anywhere on earth closer to the description of hell. Her daddy was bound for it, the most upright man she knew and innocent of all wrongdoing. How could she have peace of mind ever again?

As a calming reinforcement while she washed the dishes, she pondered the letter Dad had written his daughters.

I never thought anything like this would happen to our decent, Christian, law-abiding family. But I asked God why, and the only answer I'm given is the verse in John: "In the world ye shall have tribulation: but be of good cheer; I have overcome the world." And before that it says, "that in Me ye might have peace." Tribulation definitely makes one turn to God, more than one ever thought was needed. Please remember that, girls. Terrible things have happened to our family, but I want you all to turn to God for help. He's the only one who can give it, because man fails.

Getting through the Depression, living a full life despite it, was Ellen's goal. Perhaps secretary work wasn't the way to do it, but as long as she could type and use her brain, she'd have bread to eat. She had thought, with luck, she'd be able to feed her family if ever anything happened to Dad. That was her plan until recently. Reality faced her now, raw and tougher than she'd bargained for: something had happened to him, and her plans for reaching her goal were quaking in the boxing ring. Maybe there was something else out there, past the Depression. But why kid herself? This had already lasted more than five years; it could last for the rest of her life, and moving up in life would be a pipe dream.

With Dad's good name snatched and his resources thrown to the wind, stolen from even his family, more than her foundation was gone. Her main encourager, the one who inspired her to work hard and build a successful life, was gone. A blow like this seemed impossible to recover from.

She prayed for Dad again. Would it do any good? When he was first accused, the Dashiells were confident he would be cleared. Why should they doubt God's provision? But then the false evidence kept piling up, and suddenly he was facing jail time and fines. Up till the last minute, they had hoped for acquittal, but with every passing moment of the last trial, the hope waned. And when the jury found him guilty, every hope the Dashiells ever held was snuffed out. Where was God then?

The last thing Ellen wanted was to give up on God, like many had, but right now her faith was shaken. She needed time to sort out how and why this had happened.

Now she couldn't even talk to Dad, who'd helped her sort these things out before. She hated to worry Mother, and Marion and Greta were far from ready for that type of conversation.

But there was Dad's letter…Dad only sought God the harder with all that had occurred. It ought to be Ellen's answer to her own doubts and questions. If Dad, bearing the brunt of catastrophe, kept pursuing God, then shouldn't she?

⧼Chapter Two⧽

ELLEN WAS NEVER KEEN TO SEE PEOPLE WHO DETESTED HER, but she cared much for duty; and if ever something was a duty, accompanying Mother on Saturday, two days later, to Cousin Louis Westwood's house fit the bill. Mother needed the support, Louis and his wife, Ida, needed to see the Dashiells weren't intimidated, and whatever was on the table needed as many rational minds to discuss it as possible. He had phoned several days ago to invite Mother over to talk about Granddad's will.

"I can't believe they're making you drive to *their* house when they've got something to tell you," Marion said as she fastened a favorite necklace of hers—a blue glass stone in a sunburst on a long silver chain—around Ellen's neck. "There. That tops everything off and you don't look like such a secretary."

Ellen glanced in her full-length bedroom mirror. Her dress was gray, circled with a narrow black belt, with a rippling collar, buttons down the bodice, and shallow pleats in the skirt. Conservative, correct, and boring by Marion's standards, it was one of the nicest she owned. She grinned. "What's wrong with looking like a secretary? They have to look nice; not gorgeous like an actress, but dolled up all the same. Haven't I been doing my job?"

"Sure you have!" Marion laid her hands on Ellen's upper arms and slid her chin onto her shoulder; brown-eyed and fresh-looking, one blond, one brunette, they stared into the mirror side by side. "But there's a secretary look and there's a dinner date look. I'm going for the dinner date look. Ya need jewelry for that."

"And you have more experience there than I do." Ellen smirked. Boys from school and the Players Guild asked Marion out at least once a week; young men from Friar's never asked Ellen out. They felt she was above them. Though Ellen didn't feel that way, she was still glad they never approached her because she baulked at dating a man who didn't interest her. Having fun with male peers was great, but it was all too easy for them to get the wrong impression from one's attention.

"It's to your advantage," Marion said. "I'm the costume queen, don't forget; people would come from miles around to get my advice…if they only knew who I was." Marion desired mainly two things: one, that she'd either catapult to Hollywood or at least gain a scholarship to acting school; and two, she'd be admired for the ingenious costumes she devised for the stage and maybe earn the silver screen that roundabout way.

Marion was certainly prettier than Ellen, but Ellen didn't much mind. Marion's goals depended on her looks, and Ellen's did not.

"Well, thanks for your help; it's time for us to go." Ellen twirled away from the mirror and snatched her purse.

Marion blocked her path to the door. "I'm dying to know what Louis has to say about the will. Are we about to inherit a lot of money, maybe enough to pay Dad's fines and all the bills, with glorious cash left over to pay for things like acting school? Common sense tells me I'm dreaming, but that romantic part of me…I'm overwhelmed with hope!"

"Judging from experience, I think common sense is correct. That romantic part of you will get you in trouble someday." Ellen half-smiled and sidestepped her sister.

Ridgewood was a ritzier neighborhood than Vassar Park; one step out from Canton, it was at least one step up in class, with red brick roads, spacious lawns, and large, strongly individualistic houses. The Depression had raided here, too, however; several mansions had the empty, haunted look of homes longing after their owners.

Mother parked the DeSoto on Twenty-third Northwest Street, and she and Ellen looked at each other. "This may be a silly question, and I keep dismissing it, but do you think there's any money for us from the will?" Mother asked in a defeated tone.

"I...I wouldn't depend on it," Ellen replied. She paused. "Ready?"

Mother sighed. "As ready as I'll ever be."

The Westwoods chose Ridgewood on the prospect of a novel and fashionable house built just for them. Mother's father, older brother, sister-in-law, and nephew had all moved there in the late twenties, selling Mother's childhood home on the formerly classy Tuscarawas Street in the center of Canton. The old place was still grand, but the Westwoods had had enough of living in the middle of "Little Chicago" after a neighbor was burglarized. Ellen thought it odd that all the Westwoods lived together while Mother was only ever marginally included since she'd married Dad. He was "beneath" them. Mother's brother and sister-in-law had since died, and two months ago, so did her father; there remained only Louis and his bride of two years.

The house, though built of sand-colored brick, forced one to think of a castle, boasting two stone chimneys, and stone arches over the doorways and windows. It was strangely paired with terracotta roof tiles. Marion liked it because it was so fantastical, like something in movies about eccentric millionaires. Ellen wondered how the Westwoods could have been responsible for its design. They weren't millionaires, nor were they eccentric or even imaginative.

A short, plump, silver-haired housekeeper opened to their ring. Mrs. Foss took their coats and led them across the gleaming hardwood floor to the parlor, through an arched doorway just down from the foyer and opposite the wide, sweeping staircase.

"Aunt Augustine," Louis said in his thin voice as he pushed himself out of his wingchair. He took his pipe from his mouth. Everything about him seemed smaller than it should—he himself was barely as tall as Ellen and his aunt, who were both five foot six. Pale skin with mousy brown hair completed his wispy appearance. He looked at Ellen, a question in his beady brown eyes. "And Ellen?"

"Oh, Ellen, we didn't know you were coming!" Ida exclaimed, her voice rich and smooth as she rose in mild surprise from the floral davenport on which she'd been half reclining. She was an inch taller than Louis. "It's a fortunate thing we didn't serve lunch; we'd never have thought *you* were coming."

Ellen absorbed with a smile the accusatory, icy blue gaze narrowed her way; getting offended wasn't worth the trouble. She and Mother returned the greetings and sat on the davenport that matched Ida's. Ida dropped her elbow to the arm again, and her head to her palm. Her lavish brunette curls glistened.

"Are you feeling okay, Ida?" Mother asked.

"Oh, a bit under the weather. I hardly ever get colds, so it's strange."

"You don't mind if I keep my pipe, do you, Aunt Augustine?" Louis asked.

Small talk came naturally to Ellen and Mother, so the four of them managed to keep awkward silences at bay, though Ellen could never shake the air of discomfort. She felt herself tiring as she strove for subjects that had nothing to do with Dad, Granddad, finances, or how long it had been since they were together.

The parlor, though architecturally modern, was populated with Granddad's stately furniture. Ellen had only fragmentary memories of it, wrapped with the sense of inferiority and sternness she'd felt as a little girl.

"Louis, perhaps you ought to tell them what you and Granddad discussed," Ida said after about ten minutes. Her full red lips affected a gracious smile. "I'm sure they're dying to know."

A glint of worry flashed across Louis's face. He pried his pipe from his teeth. "Yes, well, swell idea, dearest. Aunt Augustine, I was there when Granddad died; that is, I spoke with him a couple hours beforehand. And, well, you know he had a will, and you weren't included at the reading of it because you weren't in it. But he did give me some, er, instructions regarding you, and I want to honor them, in honor of his memory, and, well, because you are my aunt."

Mother caught Ellen's eye and cleared her throat. "Louis, why did you wait this long to tell me?" She sounded sad, almost apologetic, anything but critical; even Ellen would have been more forceful.

"Well, I..." Beady eyes wide, Louis took Ida in his gaze.

"We have been busy, very, very busy." Ida swooped to the rescue, her voice a little more animated than usual. "Granddad had a lot of affairs needing attention. And then you know how the holidays are; my big family demands a lot of our time. Between that and business and keeping a home running, we haven't been free to do anything else since Granddad died. But we should have tried harder to contact you; you must forgive us on that account. Then the trouble with your husband came up, and we didn't want to bother you during that dreadful time. You noticed Louis phoned you just as soon as that was over."

Mother and Ellen nodded, but although Ellen tried to believe Ida was sincerely sorry, nothing in her tone suggested remorse. Rather than assert that they had been wronged, the most dignified thing to do was let it go. They waited for what Louis would say next.

"Granddad exhorted me to...take care of you and your daughters. He was upset that things had gotten so cold between you that he couldn't see you one last time before he...went on."

Mother caught her breath. Ellen grasped her hand, trembling in its glove. "Was he?" It was both a question and a defiance. Mother's voice, fighting sorrow and resentment, was barely above a whisper.

Louis paused. "Yes, I do believe he was. So, as per his instructions, and now, with your husband...with Uncle Oliver in jail, it is really necessary for me to step up and assist you. I'm afraid it can't be financial, there's not quite enough for that, but I'd like to assist you in other ways. For example, I can help you find another place to live if you aren't able to keep up with house payments; I can help you find customers if you start up some sort of business...anything to help you support yourself."

So that was it. Ellen hadn't known what to expect; financial help had been on her mind, but she hadn't allowed herself to hope. Thus disappointment didn't really describe what she felt.

"You were his sole heir?" Mother asked.

"Yes." Louis looked at his wife, then at the Persian rug, finding his nerve in one place or the other, for when he glanced up he met Mother's eyes without wavering. "But I got a lot of instructions, you got to believe." He smiled thinly and restored his pipe to his lips.

"Would you ladies like some refreshments? I've got cookies and coffee with the ring of a bell," Ida said, rousing herself to reach for the coffee table.

Proudly refusing hospitality wouldn't do any good, so Ellen agreed when she saw Mother hesitating. Ida rang her shrill silver bell with a flick of her wrist, and shortly Mrs. Foss ambled in and crossed her hands over her expansive black dress.

Ida made her request; Mrs. Foss nodded. "Yes, missus. And missus, I think Mr. Shepherd is outside, waiting in his car. Do you want me to invite him in?"

"Everett? Already? Gee, the silly boy must know he's early— that's why he's out there shivering." Ida chuckled. "Motion to him from the door before you bring the coffee."

With the entrance of another guest, the uncomfortable discussion would be over. That brought a *phew*—but also a sarcastic *great*—to Ellen's mind. She wanted to talk about how Louis proposed helping the Dashiells.

"It will be a pleasure to meet one of your friends," Mother ventured.

"What? Oh, yes. Everett is an old friend, or rather the son of an old friend of my family's." Ida settled back into her couch, sounding bored. "He moved to town a couple of weeks ago, hoping for a job, and wouldn't you know, he just got one."

"That's quite a feat. He must have exceptional skills." Mother nonchalantly reached up to pat and fluff her brown curls.

"I don't know how exceptional they are, but he's an

accountant and the son of a *former* businessman." Ida fixed Ellen with a friendly, yet haughty, gaze. "Ellen, would you have guessed he's been hired at Friar's Tool and Die? You still work there, don't you?"

Ellen started inside, but she manifested nothing except primly raised eyebrows. "Has he really? I still work there, yes, and now that you mention it, Mr. Green did say he was looking for an accountant. He didn't advertise, though." She didn't mention that the former accountant, Virgil Howard, had been fired for not catching the embezzlement. She, however, suspected that Virgil had helped frame her dad; but she had no proof.

Ida shrugged. "Louis and my father put in a good word for him."

At that moment Mrs. Foss reentered, a young man several steps behind. "Here you are, Mr. Shepherd," Mrs. Foss said cordially.

"Thank you." Everett Shepherd's soft voice was more youthful than what seemed to fit his age, which Ellen estimated to be twenty-two or twenty-three. He was of average height, slim but not stringy, with a somewhat pinched-together face that also managed to be pleasant, even endearing. His dark brown hair was parted on the side and slicked up into waves, and he wore a black suit and maroon tie with gold dots.

"Hello." He strode into the room focused on his hosts, but stopped short when he caught sight of the Dashiells to his left.

Louis arose and went to shake hands as Ida said, "Come sit down, Everett. Coffee is on its way."

"Thank you." Everett glanced at the Dashiells on the opposite side of the room from the Westwoods as he crossed the rug in the center, giving them a slight nod and a movement of the lips—probably an inaudible "How do you do"—before easing into the wingchair that matched Louis's. Did he feel the tension in the room? Did he feel intrusive? Or was he always that bashful and uneasy?

After a couple of pleasantries, Ida asked him, "Have you heard from your parents lately?"

"No." Everett shook his head slowly.

"No news is good news, wouldn't you say?" Louis said.

"Absolutely."

Ida raised an eyebrow. "There isn't any reason to think otherwise. They were in good health when you saw them last, and they probably haven't done anything new. They can't do much these days, can they?"

"Being rather limited, er, monetarily," Louis added with a smirk.

"*Ahem*," came Mother's none-too-discreet cough.

Ida and Louis looked their direction as if they really had forgotten them. Ida gave her husband a nudge with her eyes. "Everett, this is my aunt and cousin, Augustine and Ellen Dashiell."

Everett nodded at them again. "How do you do? It's an honor to meet you." He paused. "I'm really sorry that I, uh, interrupted your visit."

"We've just wrapped up our main conversation," Ida assured him. "We're going to have refreshments, and then they'll be on their way."

"It's nice meeting you as well, Everett," Mother said with a big smile, and Ellen echoed her. Ellen could sense Mother's motherly favor already creeping toward him, like a hen who wanted to cover a stray chick with her wing. It must be the shyness that drew her—yes, the shyness and the boyish, unhardened face.

"Where does your family live?" Mother asked.

"New York—City, that is. We didn't always live there, so that's not really home." Everett's sentences were halting. "I mean…" He stole another glance at Ellen; every one of his glances toward her seemed furtive thus far. "I was born in Ohio."

"Oh! So you are a Midwesterner. Then coming here should make you feel at home. Where exactly?"

"South Vienna, a small town near Springfield. But you probably haven't heard of it?"

"No, but it sounds idyllic," Mother encouraged.

"Ah, coffee! Here you are, Everett. Time to get you warm," Ida said as Mrs. Foss brought a laden tray. "Help yourself to the cookies. There's *amaretti* from the Italian Bakery, just natural with coffee. And then there's plain sugar cookies."

Ida poured Everett's coffee, piled four cookies onto a plate, stood, and placed it all in his hands as he moved to the edge of his seat. Only then did she serve the rest, but without noticing his worried look as he puzzled out how to get what was sitting tantalizingly in his palms into his mouth. When he tried to balance his cookie plate on his knee, Ellen spoke up.

"Ida, could he scoot his chair over to your parlor table?"

When Ida realized what she was talking about, her brows knit in mild annoyance. Everett's ears turned pink, but he acted grateful and relieved once he was ensconced beside the table.

After finishing their treats and a bit more small talk, both Dashiell women rose.

"We'll have to invite you over again sometime." Ida's smile slid smoothly onto her face. "Have a safe drive home."

"Let us know if you need anything." Louis stood, prepared to show them out.

Only Everett looked genuine—genuinely bewildered to know what to say as he courteously arose. Contrary to Ellen's expectations, no one had told him they'd be seeing each other at Friar's Monday morning, so she spoke up herself.

"Ida says you've just been hired at Friar's. Congratulations. I work there as well."

Everett's eyes widened. "No—you don't say? Wow. What do you do?"

"General secretary, receptionist, and a bit of bookkeeping."

"Why, that's—that's swell. I'm the new accountant, so I guess we'll be...er...seeing something of each other."

Ellen smiled brightly. "Yes, I guess so."

In the car, mother and daughter allowed their deflated spirits to show. Mother's shoulders slumped, which was becoming habitual when she sat. "They seem to have a pretty good idea of where we're headed, but they're not going to help," she said.

"It appears so."

18

Mother sighed.

"The Maddoxes will help us," Ellen hurried on. "I'm sure we'll hear from them soon."

᭒᭒ᷟChapter Three᭒ᷟᴥᷟ᭒

ELLEN CROSSED HER ARMS, PULLING HER COAT TIGHTER AS IF that would somehow make it a thicker shield against the wind. If only buses could be heated. She left the house just warm enough, but the bus ride sapped it away, leaving her with nothing on the three-block walk from the stop to Friar's.

The streets sported some activity. None of the shops were hubs, but enough were open to give the impression of a healthy town, obscuring the scars of dead businesses. The rising employment over the past few months had steadily vivified Canton; it was doing better than many other places she heard about. But would it ever be *prosperous* again? Head bent to the cold, Ellen's eyes were raised to smile or nod at the people she passed. She was determined to maintain a cheerful, friendly pretense. Canton might write her off completely otherwise.

Friar's Tool and Die was a two-story brick box the color of sooty clay, dutifully gridded by windows, though nothing brightened the gloomy workrooms. Chimneys stuck out the roof like too-small feathers in a hat. Not a glamorous place to work, but at least Ellen, one of only three women here, could feel more feminine by contrast.

Her desk and two lobby chairs facing it were the first things beyond the entrance. The desk wasn't much to look at: just a slim office piece topped with a black phone, evenly fanned stacks of paper, a miniature pot with a paper flower Greta had made, an antique blue china inkwell from Marion, and Ellen's pride and joy—a big, black, fancy Royal 10 typewriter. Behind stood an orderly line of white filing cabinets, also her prize, because she was responsible for their flawless organization. Two enlarged photographs decorated the walls: a black and white image of the building in its early years—1909, wasn't it?

—above the lobby chairs, and a colorized birds' eye view of 1920s Canton to the left of her desk.

Spartan, but clean. Home with its four females wore plenty of frills, but here Ellen could focus on the organizational tasks that filled her days and helped structure her life.

After she hooked her coat and hat on the coat rack in the far right corner but before she left the room to check in with Frances Lundberg, a stream of cold wind gleefully rushed inside with the opening of the front door.

"Hello!" She wore a cheery smile as she turned to the new arrival—a coworker?

It was Everett Shepherd. His eyelids seemed droopy as he blinked at Ellen, but his smile tugged up in return. She noticed for the first time his eyes were green. "Hello…again."

Ellen was glad she had put so much effort into her smile; shy Everett needed all the optimism he could get, this being his first day on the job and all. "Mr. Green will want to see you first off." She picked up the phone. "I'll let his secretary know you're here."

"Okay." Everett tucked his gray fedora under his arm, pocketed his gloved hands, and idly surveyed the little room.

"Miss Lundberg? The new accountant, Everett Shepherd, is here."

Ellen smiled at Everett and opened the door at the back that led upstairs to the inner offices. "Right this way, please."

"Oh." Everett lurched forward a step and caught himself on the desk. "Sorry, I'm a little clumsy this morning. I overslept."

"Still not completely awake, huh?" Ellen asked sympathetically.

"No. It's, uh, been a while since I've had to wake up early for a job." Everett grimaced as he reached Ellen. Putting his hand on the door's edge above her head, he said, "Er, allow me."

"Oh! Why, thank you." Chivalry was certainly welcome here. Ellen proceeded, Everett followed, and up the dim stairs they went.

What would working with and under this new accountant be like? She felt comfortable with him; his quietness didn't unnerve her because she was quiet herself. He was amiable, and even more than that, he was courteous. If easygoing but proficient Virgil Howard had to be replaced, Everett was a decent choice.

"Careful, these are steep," Ellen said as they hiked the stairs. A bit farther on, "I guess we have a couple of outside acquaintances, don't we."

"Yeah, it's kind of…nice," Everett replied.

"How long have you known Ida and her family?" asked Ellen.

"Ever since I can remember."

"Old friends?"

"Yeah." Everett paused. "My dad and Claude Bingham went to school and college together, and they stayed in touch."

She wasn't well acquainted with Ida's family, but the few times she'd seen or heard about them, they'd struck her as being…well, like Ida. How had someone as genuine and sweet as Everett Shepherd gotten along with them? Well, if he could tolerate the Binghams, he'd operate admirably under Benton Green. Everyone who worked directly for Mr. Green had to possess a measure of tact and restraint to *keep* working for him.

Ellen's distrust of her boss after Dad's impeachment had definitely affected her forbearance. She'd liked him pretty well before—he was a sound businessman and, despite his demands and impatience, was generous and humorous, with a joke for everyone. He'd even pushed through hiring her at the company when Dad had doubts about nepotism. But now she couldn't help but burn under a feeling of betrayal whenever she saw him. He had begun treating her rather coldly, too, even before she'd changed her mind about him—back when she thought it was all a mistake.

She worried about her job.

But she ought to say something to Everett before they arrived outside the big office, to put him more at ease. He was so stiff; he had to be hiding a quaking heart.

"He'll be friendly, I'm sure," Ellen said. "He'll certainly give you a chance. It sounds like you know what you're about, and you were recommended by a trusted peer." She smiled. "All of us here will try to make your job easier."

Everett gave a quick nod. "Thanks."

Ellen let him into the office. He didn't try to hold the door for her this time. At her desk a few inches from the swing of the door, Frances Lundberg looked up sharply from behind large, round, black reading glasses. She prided herself on her appearance: immaculate, unromantic, unimaginative, "the opposite of a movie star floozy"; and she seemed to summon its inherent power of respectability as she scanned Everett up and down. Poor guy. Ellen wished she'd had time to urge Frances to be easy on him. He didn't need putting in place.

"Miss Lundberg, this is Everett Shepherd," Ellen said.

"The new accountant, huh?" Frances sniffed, folding her hands on her desk. Her short blond hair rippled smoothly with finger waves. "Well, well, you're rather young."

Everett's ears bloomed pink.

"I'll let Mr. Green know you've come." Without taking her intense blue eyes off him, Frances plucked up her phone to contact the inner office behind her.

"Send him in," barked Mr. Green's distorted voice.

Frances smirked at Everett as she cradled the phone. Everett tried to smile back. "You heard him; you can go in." She jerked her head toward the solid oak door. Everett mumbled thank you, slipped past her desk, and entered his new boss's lair.

Ellen wasn't aware she was standing still for so long watching him until Frances asked, "Anything the matter?"

Ellen shook her head. "Are you going to put him through the wringer?"

Frances cracked a genuine smile. "Don't I always?"

"Yes, but…he's different."

"What, is he already a milquetoast?"

Ellen fought a grin. "No, but I'm afraid you'll make him one if you're not careful."

"Aw, if he's a man, he can take it. Besides, I have a sort of grudge against him already—Virgil Howard was a perfectly good accountant, and a family man, and it's a crying shame he was sacked."

"It's not Mr. Shepherd's fault."

"Technicalities." Frances sniffed again and shooed the thought away with a wave. "Don't you have work to do?"

Ellen smiled and turned to leave. "I always do. But you know what I mean, Frances? He's nice, and we might as well be nice back and make the best of it."

"We'll see. I'll give him a year; then maybe I'll warm up to him."

"You do that." Ellen's smile grew and she departed. She gave Frances a week.

Ellen was filing paid orders when Everett emerged into the lobby about twenty minutes later. After exchanging welcoming half-grins, Everett said, "I guess you're supposed to show me my office, the bookkeeping room, the records, and so forth."

"And you'll meet your other bookkeepers, too. Let's go back into the hallway—that's how to get there."

Their short trek felt heavy with unspoken reflections, but Ellen expected that of a quiet fellow. He'd probably relax after a few weeks.

To Ellen's consternation, the bookkeepers, Hilda and Joe, weren't that friendly to him, either. Hilda was a single mother of three, and Joe was married with six children; she'd have expected their maturity and Christianity to carry greater weight. But perhaps, like Frances, they had no compassion for a single man who got a family man's job, and under such messy circumstances, too. How long would Everett have to work with a shadow over his career that he hadn't even cast? Injustice happened all the time, but did her closest coworkers have to perpetrate it?

Mr. Green wanted Everett to audit last year's accounts first, so Ellen gladly left Hilda to assist him while she returned to filing. Actually, her feelings were mixed; leaving him in a cold room with a colder companion spooned in some guilt, but not crossing her eyes over mounds of figures was certainly sweet.

Light bookkeeping here and there was fine, even enjoyable for a change of pace, but working hour after hour with numbers was not her idea of a swell time.

The morning passed rhythmically, most of it consumed with typing copies of memorandums to the various department supervisors. Typing alone in utter silence was bliss. Ellen didn't see Everett until a little after noon, when he came out the hall door, trailing Hilda and Joe by a few minutes.

"Hello." He stopped at the corner of her desk. He had already donned his coat and fedora and draped his striped maroon scarf around his neck.

"Hi. Going out for lunch?"

"Yeah…though I don't really know what's nearby."

"Well, Hilda's gone home; she works only half-days." She felt a flash of guilt. But Hilda couldn't type, so she couldn't do Ellen's job, and now Ellen herself had a family to support. "Joe doesn't eat at restaurants. He brings lunch from home but doesn't like eating it here, so he goes to his church's basement. What kind of food do you like?"

"Do you go anywhere?"

Ellen smiled. "I eat lunch at my desk. Mr. Green goes to Bender's on occasion, and there's also the Courtland Hotel, and Philadelphia. He rotates among them. They're all downtown, though, and they're kind of…pricey."

"Good to know. Oh, and to answer your question, I'm not picky about food. So long as it tastes good, I guess." Everett half-grinned and drew his gloves from his pocket.

"There's a sandwich shop down the street," Ellen said. "I know the owner; he goes to my church. You might go there, if you're okay with sandwiches."

"Sandwiches—oh, they're fine! The best, actually. I'll try it." Everett turned to leave, then, hesitating, met Ellen's eyes. "Can I…can I get you anything?"

Ellen turned up a little smile. "No, thank you." She perched her fingers on Royal 10's keys; she had one more memo to type. "My paper sack is at my feet, and it's got a sandwich, too. Thank you, though. It's very kind of you."

Mr. Green went for his meal soon after Everett left, and five minutes later, right on cue with Ellen stacking the last memo and swiping up her sack lunch in the same motion, Frances burst into the room. She didn't always eat in with Ellen, but it was fun when she did, two or three times a week. They could discuss current news, library books, recent movies, and the vagaries of secretarial work. Frances was forty-one but young at heart and unconcerned with the typical matters of middle-aged women. She lit up like a light bulb on topics like Agatha Christie and Hercule Poirot. Ellen enjoyed Agatha Christie, but preferred classics like *A Tale of Two Cities* and *The Scarlet Letter*, heavier fare that withstood decades of opinion. Maybe she was a snob, but why read unless one expanded one's mind? That was her brand of enjoyment. Entertainment came from cinema and radio.

Today, Frances took only two bites of her sandwich before launching the conversation on an atypical course. "So, is your dad keeping his spirits up? Has he thought anymore about appealing?" Frances was fiercely loyal to Dad, her favorite boss. Her steel-trap mind had groped for evidence of Dad's innocence ever since his accusation. If the evidence had eluded her, there wasn't much hope for anyone else to find it.

Ellen took a bite of her egg salad sandwich and chewed while deciding what she should say. "He's doing all right. He doesn't let on that he's feeling depressed, though you know he has to be. We're worried about him, of course. As for appealing…he hasn't mentioned it."

Frances harrumphed. "He ought to, in my humble opinion. But that takes money, and where are you supposed to get that now? His pay was slashed so much you don't have much savings left, do you?"

It was funny how much Frances knew about the Dashiells' finances, but she'd known them for so long it made sense. "We spent it on lawyer fees."

"Of course." After a moment Frances spoke again. "If there was a good chance he'd win, we could raise the money for appealing." At Ellen's open mouth poised to protest, she held up her hand. "The workers like your dad, Ellen. I think enough of them would be willing to help him out, if it means clearing his name. There's your church folks, too."

Hope didn't balloon in Ellen's heart; she only felt more defeated. This promise of what could happen *if only* wasn't any good—the *if only* needed to be tangible. There had to be new evidence. There had to be enough money. There had to be a lawyer who could prove Dad innocent.

The egg salad seemed dry now, and she had trouble swallowing. Quickly she downed some water. "Thanks, Frances. That's encouraging. But we'd have to present something new. Otherwise we don't have a chance."

Frances's eyes narrowed—at the situation, not at Ellen. "That's what I'm working on."

Ellen didn't think it would ever be found. She had heard the ins, outs, ups, downs, of all the evidence and what it supposedly proved, and she saw no loophole. All they had to go on was Dad's character-backed word that he hadn't done it. She was characteristically inclined to look at the positive, but now it seemed no positive existed.

Around four o'clock, the beginning of Ellen's final hour at work, Marion thrust open Friar's front door and entered the cheerless little lobby, only slightly less chill than the gray and white street and not nearly as colorful. How Ellen could work day in and day out in such a place, Marion hadn't a clue. She ought to marvel at her for the feat, but the more natural response was to pity the poor girl.

"Hi, Ellen." Marion took off her dark blue hat and fluffed her blond curls as she approached the desk. "How are ya?"

"Hi! I'm fine." Ellen peeled her fingers off the typewriter and, interlacing them, gave them a rest on the desktop. "What are you doing here?"

"I didn't want to go all the way home to let one of you know I've got a Players Guild thing tonight. It was impromptu, 'cause one of the fellas has a friend from a stock company who's staying over for the night, and he's agreed to watch some of us do readings and give us tips about the job. Isn't that wonderful?"

"Sounds like it," Ellen replied. "What time will you be home?"

"Nine or so; maybe later. We're meeting at the Jewish Center, as usual. Six o'clock, but there's no telling how long it'll last."

"Right; you don't have to tell me actors are never punctual." A little smile crossed Ellen's face.

"We're trying to let everyone know, so I have to go find Grace, another student, and a couple of people from the Guild. Just the people who might actually have a future, you know."

"In...acting?"

Marion nodded. "Yes. Steve won't have time for everyone. Tough, I know, but theater takes only the cream anyway." She raised her eyes to the door in the back of the room. A *casual* inquiry couldn't hurt, or make Ellen suspicious. "Before I fly, since I'll be home so late tonight, how has your day been?"

"Oh, fine. Nothing out of the ordinary, except the new accountant, of course."

"How did that go? Is he fitting in and catching on?"

Ellen's lips twitched for a tenth of a second. Hesitation: something must not have gone right. "Yes. Like I said, he's shy, but he knows what he's doing. Good workers always fit in right away."

If Marion dallied just a little longer, maybe he'd make his entrance through that door. "Beautiful. Say, 'sister, do you have a dime'? Or maybe more like two quarters? I'll pay you back. Some of us are eating at Taggarts, and I'd rather eat there than have Grace offer me something at her place. I don't want to take advantage of her; I don't think she gets enough to eat as it is."

Ellen got to her feet and padded over to the coat rack in the corner, behind the door. "You're not going to spend *all* of it, are you? Fifty cents for a meal...besides, how are you going to pay me back?"

"I'll clean a house or something. And no, I'm not going to spend all of it. Who knows, maybe one of the boys will treat me. It's just backup."

Ellen's back was turned as she fiddled with the coin purse in her coat pocket. At that moment, the door Marion had been watching so assiduously swung full-out and into her sister. She'd never before seen the guy whose eyes and mouth were as wide as Mickey Mouse's, so he had to be Everett Shepherd. He slammed the offending door and gabbled, "I'm so sorry, I'm so sorry!" as Ellen faced him, similarly startled, but with a twinkle replacing the shock in her eyes.

Marion could no longer keep her giggles locked up. Everett looked at her for the first time, his mouth shut now but his eyes still huge. Marion managed to corral her laughter and said with a grin, "Sorry. Oh, you two! That was hilarious. Couldn't have staged it better."

"No, I guess not." Ellen fingered her elbow, which had taken the brunt of the hit. "Marion, this is Mr. Shepherd. Mr. Shepherd, my sister Marion." A smile was welling up, so she pinioned her lower lip with her teeth.

"It's a pleasure to meet you, Mr. Shepherd." Marion held out her hand.

Ears turning pink, Everett advanced to take it. "It's an honor…the pleasure's mine."

"Ellen tells me you're having a swell first day."

"Why, yes, I suppose I am." Everett clasped his hands. His eyes seemed to have trouble meeting hers.

"I hope it continues. I really have to fly now. It was so nice to put a face to the name. I heard my mother and sister met you at the Westwoods'."

Everett nodded and smiled. He had a nice one, sweet and unassuming and natural, not the kind that tried to impress with a strong jaw or white teeth. He seemed like a fellow their family would adore. It was about time someone like that showed up at Ellen's job. She might need help cultivating a relationship with him.

"I'll see you later, Ellen. I hope we'll meet again soon, Mr.

Shepherd." Marion perched her hat on her hair and tilted it so the brim hung just above her right eyebrow. "Does this look good, Ellen? You could really use a mirror in here, you know."

"As long as the wind doesn't knock it off, it looks pretty. There's a mirror in Miss Lundberg's office if you don't believe me."

Marion shook her head, blew Ellen a kiss, and exited stage left.

ꙮꙮꙮ Chapter Four ꙮꙮꙮ

"I WISH HE'D ASK YOU OUT ON A DATE." MARION BRUSHED HER slightly damp hair in preparation for rag-curling it overnight. She stared at the blue wallpaper, seeing things that were not there. All three girls were in Ellen's room, where they often congregated before bedtime. "Maybe he's not the One, but he's sweet and could give you some nice times. I'm tempted to say you'd better ask him here to dinner, but that's much too forward. That's the trouble with these shy guys; it takes them forever to ask."

"I'm not sure I want him to do it anyway," Ellen remarked nonchalantly. She was sitting in bed across the room with her nose in a book. If she'd only look up, Marion could give her a dramatically shocked expression.

"And he's not really that shy; he's just that way with me," Ellen continued, flipping a page. "He's reserved, but he talks to the others fairly easily, even Frances and Mr. Green."

"Ah. I know his type." Marion gathered her collection of cotton rags and a bottle of setting lotion into her lap. "He doesn't know what to do when faced with a pretty girl. He gets nervous."

"We've had some good conversations." Ellen's placidity was undisturbed.

"Oh? Like how business is doing? Or perhaps something scintillating, like politics?"

Ellen finally looked at Marion. "As a matter of fact, a little more personal than that. He's not a wood board. He just doesn't show his feelings. I don't either, you know, so it's fine with me."

"Okay then, I'll take your word for it. He's nice, no doubt about that." Marion smiled and wound the batch of hair she'd just slicked with lotion. If she hurried up these curls, she'd have time to devour more *Captain Blood* while her mind still perked. She was going job-hunting after school tomorrow, starting at the Palace Theatre, so the curls were essential; but satiating herself with a swashbuckling adventure novel put her in a happier state of mind and gave her sweet dreams.

"Ellen," came Greta's muffled voice from where she lay heaped at Ellen's feet. Marion had thought she was asleep.

"Yes, dear?" Ellen's voice was unperturbed as her eyes floated up from her book, *The Christian's Secret of a Happy Life*, which she'd started reading a couple days after the trial.

"I wanted to ask Mother but I don't want to worry her—more than she already is," Greta began, her head still pillowed on her arm. "But what if we move to Cardinal Bush and the kids there find out about Dad? Do you think they'll treat me the same as the kids here do?"

"Do you mean unkindly?"

"Yeah. Snobbish, calling me a Chicago dame, telling me to go back to the slums with the rest of the hoods." Greta spoke bitterly. She was the type to stand up for herself, which had made for some interesting drama at school.

"You can hide things you don't want people to know," Ellen said. "Not lying, just not confiding in those you can't trust. I don't think the kids in Cardinal Bush will ever find out where Dad really is. Just tell them he's away working, because that *is* what he'll be doing in jail."

"But some kids are sneaks. Someone will find out sooner or later and it'll go *everywhere*. What'll I do then?"

"Tell them to hold their tongue if they value their lives and vacate your presence with sniveling obeisance, and if they don't get that, say, 'Can it and scram!'" Marion put forth with a serious face.

"Behave with dignity and say, 'I'm sorry, but I don't want to talk about it right now.'" Ellen raised a dark, slender eyebrow at Marion. "Most of all, don't let them see that it bothers you, because your reaction is what they're after. You remember Mother telling you that?"

"Easy for you to say. You're not in school anymore," Greta huffed.

"People still look at me strangely. They don't say anything in so many words, but they're thinking the same as the kids."

"Just think of how the grownups are at church," Marion added. "What isn't spoken or done is just as powerful as what is."

Ellen closed her book, her finger holding the spot, and stroked the cover. "If we end up going to Cardinal Bush"—they still had yet to hear from the Maddoxes—"we'll have a new name to make for ourselves, a new reputation to establish. If we do it well, people will not only believe there's nothing wrong with us, they'll also believe what we say about Dad. We're building his reputation, too."

"If no one in the whole town knows but us, maybe none of the kids *will* find out," Greta mused, her words drifting. She jerked awake. "Uncle Melvin and Aunt Jennie don't blab, do they?"

"Not that I know of. They're family, so they have a reputation to protect, too." Ellen opened her book and her eyes sought the words they'd fed on earlier.

"We can impress on them the need for discretion," Marion said, twisting up her last rag with a rush of anticipation as she recalled where she'd left Captain Blood. Not long now. "Mother may have already done that. It'll be fine, you'll see." Nevertheless, she hoped, yes, and expected, too, that she wouldn't have to go to Cardinal Bush to find out for herself.

The next afternoon, the call finally arrived. Mother motioned to Ellen, who had just entered the front door, all bundled up for walking from the bus stop after work, and they shared the earpiece.

"We're overjoyed to help you—" Uncle Melvin was saying.

"Absolutely thrilled, more like it!" came Aunt Jennie. "It's the bee's knees to help you, dear."

"All four of you can come, though of course Ellen ought to

keep her job. That's what I would do if I were a century younger than I was. Of course now I'd not be opposed to retiring," Uncle Melvin said.

"Our big old house has stood empty for so long with just the two of us," Aunt Jennie inserted. "We had four whippersnappers ourselves, so it would be like gathering four more back home."

Greta skipped down the stairs, caught sight of them, gasped, and crowded close to catch the conversation.

"Soon as you and your darling girls get things settled and can come out, why, out you must come," Uncle Melvin continued. "I don't have a truck for moving, but I've a sedan—a Graham—serviceable old thing, hardly ever breaks down; we could fit some boxes in. Your littlest can sit on the roof or hang out the back if she had to."

Greta chuckled.

Teary-eyed, Mother showered them with thanks while relief sent chills traveling Ellen's spine. "May we call you back about particulars once we've made plans?" Mother asked. They gushed yeses.

After she hung up and the three embraced in a triangle, Mother rubbed her forehead. "What *will* we do with all our furniture?"

"We could loan it to friends." Ellen started for the kitchen, the others following. Marion was not yet home, probably sidetracked on a job hunt. Ellen proceeded to explain her ideas, down to which friends could take what piece.

"Will it all be well taken care of, I wonder?" Mother's eyes rested on the china cabinet in the dining room, a large, illustrious piece that was the only antique she and Dad owned.

"We can give our favorite things to our most trusted friends," Ellen replied. "Frances can take the china cabinet with all its china, I'm sure. She'd think it English and quaint."

Greta leaned on the breakfast nook table and giggled. "Boy, Uncle Melvin and Aunt Jennie sound like screams. They might actually be kind of fun to live with."

"Even if they want you to ride on the roof of their car?"

Ellen quipped, her mind unburdened enough for only that one joke. She was already formulating the telephone conversation she'd have with them that evening. "Mother, I'll start making notes on what we ought to discuss when we phone them back."

The front door opened and the sounds of Marion echoed from the foyer. Greta jumped up. "I wonder if she found a job?" She darted into the dining room to meet her.

The two returned as Ellen settled at the table with paper and pen. "Did the Maddoxes call?" Marion asked.

Greta grinned and planted her arms akimbo. "Tell us your news first."

Straightening, Marion delved her hand into her limp blond curls. "It's not exhilarating in the least. I didn't get anything. I tried the Palace and the other theaters first, of course, but they weren't looking for so much as a ticket agent, though I did notice the Palace has a stupendous lineup of shows and I'm more determined than ever to stay in Canton for that. Though a lot of good it'd do me if I don't have any money!"

She dropped her hand to her hip and unfurled the fingers of her other hand one by one. "I tried Sears, Woolworth's, Bon Marché, McRory's, even an office. I don't remember which office; it's all Greek to me. But they'd all be dreadfully boring, so I'm almost glad I didn't find an opening."

"You just have to keep your eye out for ads, and don't be afraid to take something small, because that's how you build experience," Ellen said.

"Just remember, factories are out of the question," Mother said.

"I don't want any of that, shop or factory. I want to act. I could be in a summer stock company to start with; I know I'm good enough for that. I just have to have the chance." Marion tugged out a chair and collapsed at the table with a huff. "I don't know why getting an acting job should be so hard for me! And now I'm faced with having to disappear into a dinky, nothing town in the middle of nowhere—I bet the high school doesn't even have a drama program. What'll *that* do to my future?"

"There'll be time, dear, you're only seventeen—" Mother began, turning from the cold chicken she was cutting and still holding the knife.

"*Only* seventeen? If I'm really going to have a future, I should have been in a movie ages ago. Shirley Temple, Rochelle Hudson, kids like them will have futures."

"You've gained a lot of experiences acting for the school and community—" Mother tried again.

"Yeah, I know; and Steve, that fella from the summer stock, said I was good. But none of that means anything unless some bigwig sees me, and how can he unless I'm somewhere I can be discovered? Heavens, if I leave before I get to play Mary in *Secrets...*" The golden flash in her eyes glittered out a brighter, happier light. "If I can ever get a lead in something the Guild puts on, it'll get me noticed." She gripped the edge of the table. "If I could just get a job, though, I could bypass that and go to acting school once I can afford it, and then I'm guaranteed to find a real, paying acting job." She sat back. "But I have to have a job to get a job. It's a vicious cycle; I'm in a vortex."

At the rate she talked and thought, Ellen could see why.

"Marion," she spoke gently yet firmly, "you're overexcited and you won't get anywhere like that. What you need is to have some tea, sit in front of the grate, write down your goals, and find the clearest route to reaching them."

Marion's flaxen head dropped with a sigh to the cushion of her arms. "Will you help me, Ellen? My mind's so full I can only get myself to the grate, if that."

"One thing at a time, or you'll drop *my* mind into a vortex." Ellen put a smile in her voice. "I need to write down what we're going to discuss with the Maddoxes."

Marion's head flew up. "So they did call! Tell me all about it. It'll divert my worries for a bit. Greta," she changed into a snooty accent, "you may fetch me my tea and pull a chair up to the fire for me."

"What fire, milady?" Greta returned in the same accent.

"The one that treks from the cellar into the hole behind the grate in the wall, of course," Marion sniffed and waved her hand.

"Aw, take care of it yourself. Now, do you want to hear what the Maddoxes said or not?"

"Well, Mother, shall we begin?" Ellen tipped the point of her pen to the sheet again. She wanted the Dashiell women to sound like they knew exactly what they were doing.

Ellen and Frances were discussing the move at Ellen's desk when the door to the offices opened and Everett slipped in. Frances threw him a glance but not a smile. It had been more than a week since Everett had started working, but Frances had contradicted Ellen's prediction and not warmed up to him. The only explanation seemed to be that she didn't trust him; perhaps she saw him as a spy, or a traitor, or some other villainous type from a detective novel. But wasn't Frances too intelligent for that?

"Well, I must be on my way. The hour's ticking. Have a nice lunch." She encompassed both Ellen and Everett in her goodbye, plopped on her cloche, and swept out the front door. In an instant, she was back. "Ellen, I don't think I'll forget, but write down 'Frances's cousin,' just to be certain. I'll return early and give him a call right away."

Ellen jotted the note, then looked up at Everett, who had wandered to the lobby chairs in front of her. She wasn't ready to tell every acquaintance about her family's move, but she'd rather confide in Everett than not, especially since they talked more easily now, albeit about less important things. "My family is loaning Miss Lundberg our china cabinet, you see," she explained. "Her cousin has a truck that we hope can transport it."

"I see." Everett stepped before a chair and softly cleared his throat. "May I eat in here?"

"Of course. I'm glad of the company." This was the second time he'd stayed in the office to take his meal, claiming that eating out every day would cost too much. She'd felt sorry for him and his excuse for a lunch—a smooshed bologna sandwich whose bologna wouldn't stay between the bread—but enjoyed their conversation, though at times the long silences seemed awkward, particularly in contrast to Frances's oratories.

Everett seated himself and self-consciously pulled something from his paper sack. A bologna sandwich that looked a little neater today.

From before, Ellen knew he wouldn't start eating until she did, so she turned from Royal 10 and lifted her lunch to the desk. "You can scoot your chair to my desk, if you want." She smiled. "It's more like a proper meal that way."

Everett gratefully complied. She closed her eyes and whispered grace. When she finished, he was looking at her. "Would…you like to do that together next time?" he ventured.

"Why…yes." Ellen was only a little taken aback, but praying together would be pleasant and companionable.

She unpacked her food. Everett wouldn't ask about the china cabinet—he was anything but nosy—but she'd like to tell him more. "My mother and sisters are moving out of Canton."

Everett's hand froze on its way to his sandwich on her desk as he raised startled eyes. "Oh?"

"We're disposing of some belongings so we don't have so much to move," Ellen continued conversationally. "The china cabinet is Mother's prized possession, so it has to go to somebody we trust greatly."

"Certainly." He still didn't twitch.

"I'm not going with them that I know of," Ellen said. "I have my job, and the only reason I'd move is if I didn't have it anymore. So I'll be looking for someone to board with. Quite a change living away from one's family, isn't it? Of course, mine will only be thirty miles away, but for me, that's a great distance."

"Where are they moving to?" Everett asked, finally picking up his sandwich.

"Cardinal Bush, a little town in Portage County." She lowered her voice, though everyone in that part of the building was most definitely out. "They're going to live with my dad's uncle and aunt."

Everett stiffened, as he always did when Dad was mentioned, but took his first bite. A moment later he said, "If you don't mind me asking...how is your dad?"

This direction was unexpected. "Well..." Was that a waver in her voice? She steeled it firmly. "He's not here in town anymore, so that's partially why we thought it justifiable to leave. He's...been transferred to the state penitentiary."

Everett's whole sensitive face fell into crushed sorrow, as if it were *his* father who'd been shipped there. He actually looked...handsome. Now, how could she be thinking that at this moment? "No, really?" he grunted.

Ellen nodded and glanced downward, catching sight of her dish of baked beans but finding less appetite than before. Why did sharing all this with Everett, as opposed to anyone else, rip all her wounds afresh? She'd been managing fine. "Only my mother can see him, every once in a while. They have strict visitation rules. We're praying they'll let him out on parole, and it may happen in a few months. Though the judge said he wasn't eligible for it, we're hoping he'll relent on reports of good behavior or something."

"It could happen," Everett murmured. "I hear...some people tell me that it's all a mistake, that he's not guilty. Isn't there a way to prove that?"

Frances and the bookkeepers had been talking with him: good. "No, not that we've found yet. Money is missing from the company's bank account, and it's my father's word against Mr. Green's and Virgil Howard's." She didn't want to get emotional, but Everett should know all the facts, including some of her feelings. With a carefully maintained tone, she said, "We don't understand how this happened. Mr. Green and my father were partners, friends even. My father is a God-fearing man, and I can't see him even imagining stealing from his company, let alone wanting to and carrying it out." She hesitated. She had never fancied that the walls had ears, but now they seemed to crowd forward to hear. *That's silly.*

She continued, "If my father isn't guilty, the only explanation seems to be that it was a frame-up. Why, we don't know. If it was a misunderstanding, it could have easily been explained if he'd been asked."

Their eyes were locked while she spoke, lunches forgotten; he'd taken her cue in ignoring his food. Having spoken, she let her gaze slip. There. The ugly facts had been presented, and he could now draw his conclusions about Dad and Mr. Green.

Everett cleared his throat. "It is very odd indeed." He made half his sandwich disappear in silence, staring at the crack where her desk met the wall. "It's an awful business. I can see why it has you sore. I hope it gets cleared up."

It wouldn't be fair to ask whether he thought Dad was guilty or not, but it was tempting to attach a lot of importance to his sympathy. Did it mean he believed Dad's innocence? Or was he just being his usual agreeable self? Oh to add, *It'd be worse if he were guilty, because his betraying us would be far more terrible than Mr. Green's betraying us,* but that was presuming too much upon Everett. She wouldn't force people to listen to her woes. She'd said enough for now.

Gradually they worked away from the sober conversation until lighthearted chat came as effortlessly as any between two young people, and for that Ellen was pleased. She and Everett both tended to be too grave. But on the whole she felt very uncomfortable. The atmosphere in the room was too heavy, the walls too close. For once she felt how Marion did about this place.

The morning after her conversation with Everett, Benton Green summoned Ellen to his office. He was letting her go. Frances would take over all secretarial duties. He appealed to dwindling funds, but the unbendable glint in his dark brown eyes told her the real tale: there were deeper reasons. He had been waiting for this.

After he told her she could work until Friday to finish her projects, she walked out of his office feeling as if the world outside had collapsed and this building was next. The carpeted floor seemed to be quaking, the outer door she pursued wavering. Hadn't she prepared herself for this possibility? Hadn't misgivings flashed her plenty of warnings after Dad's conviction? Why was she so shocked?

Frances's presence in the room made only a vague impression on her; the sound of Frances's voice may have meant she was asking a question. Somehow Ellen opened the door without fumbling. Some clarity came to her as she faced the long, night-like hall. Frances wanted to know what had happened, did she? Well, Ellen couldn't tell her. Mr. Green would have to. Frances's explosion of temper would be something to see. Ellen had work to do, and such a limited time to do it in. Four days! How could she get everything done? *Just make it down the hallway, down the stairs, to your desk. You'll know what to do then.*

Her hand sought the railing she usually ignored as she descended. One footfall at a time. This job had been her stability, and for Ellen Dashiell, where there was stability there was life. Even though working here had been painful because of Dad, day after day had worn off the pain until it was almost a balm. It had become a victory that she could keep working and earning wages from the place that had betrayed him. Now she, too, had been betrayed.

At her desk, she allowed herself only an instant's immobility to consider what it would be like to never sit there again. Would Frances ever use it? Hilda? Who would greet the few visitors? Answer the phone, type the memos, file the orders, dispatch the mail? Business had been picking up. How would Frances handle it all?

Well. Benton Green would just have to deal with it. Too bad for Frances, but Benton Green had it coming. Maybe he would have to do some of his own paperwork or take his own orders. Serve him right! Stooping to the level of a secretary would give him a much-needed new perspective. He could see what he'd lost, and then have to waste the money and time hiring and training a new secretary. Ellen took a blank sheet of paper from a drawer, sucked in a deep breath, let it out, and proceeded to tear the sheet into thin, even strips, feeling a tiny satisfaction with each *rip*. The pile of paper curls on her desktop—her destructive handiwork—made her feel in control of herself again. She could return to her files without putting them in danger of a similar fate.

She worked feverishly until she was done and sitting at her desk again, just as Frances stormed into the room.

"I'm leaving! I swear I'm leaving! This is the last straw. He's loused it up big time now, sister, and I won't take any more of his baloney. Come on, we should leave, *now*." Frances, red-faced, her hair an electrocuted mop from how she had mussed it, planted her palms on the desk and leaned into Ellen's face.

Ellen was calmer now, and besides, seeing others angry always made her forget her own beef as she sought to pacify them. "You didn't tell him that, did you?"

"I managed to restrain myself until he shut his door, then I went kablooey."

Good. Frances had high passions, but at least she had long since mastered the art of restraint in the office. "I don't want you to quit your job, Frances. You'd lose everything. As for me, look, he'd *win* if I walked out now. He'd have thrown me out sooner if he could. I'm staying here until the last possible moment and wringing every cent I can out of him, because I'm going to need it."

Frances's breathing slowed. "Attagirl, Ellen. Attagirl. Keep a cool head." She straightened and ran her hands through her hair. "But he just can't do this to you! There's gotta be some accountability."

"Dad's gone; why should I still be here?" Ellen said quietly. "That's how he sees it. He's wanted to get rid of me ever since he got rid of Dad." She wouldn't say that unless she were absolutely certain.

"Will you look for another job? Or will you move with your family?"

It seemed vain to look for another job when Canton's well of good positions was always dry. But could she let Marion down? If Ellen didn't stay in Canton, then neither did her sister.

If there was nothing, there was nothing, and Marion would just have to accept it.

Before they left work that day, Frances gathered all the office workers in the privacy of the bookkeeping room and dropped them the news. Hilda and Joe were disgruntled, but they were more sympathetic toward Ellen than angry with Mr. Green. As far as they were concerned, jobs were continually in danger and none were safe, so Ellen's was no exception.

Everett's eyes widened, but he said only, "That's awful," and looked away from Ellen and Frances. He usually stared into space when he wasn't otherwise occupied, but Ellen had discovered that he also let his gaze drift when he was upset, as if unwilling to let anyone perceive his irritation.

"I will be giving Ellen a going-away party at my place after work on Friday," Frances announced before they dispersed. "You had *better* come." She wagged her finger at each of them, particularly Joe and Hilda. "Even if it's just for a few minutes, a bite to eat, and a chance to give her a proper farewell."

When Frances had gone upstairs to retrieve her things and the bookkeepers had left, Everett followed Ellen to her desk and regarded her silently as she straightened some stacks of paper and covered Royal 10. Then he spoke. "Does this mean…you're moving away with your family?"

Ellen smoothed the typewriter's cover. "Perhaps. I may try to find another job, but I don't hold out much hope. There won't be another one that will pay so well and give me funds for room and board. I feel sure of that." She looked up at him. "I'd have to be well established in something for me to split from my family."

Everett nodded, rotating his fedora in his gloved hands.

"Who knows? Maybe there's a position in Cardinal Bush. I haven't asked my uncle and aunt because I didn't think I was going."

"It sure'd be nice," Everett said. He went on rotating his hat. "God will look after you, don't you think?"

The simple words cast calm over her still churning mind. For the two months since the trouble had begun, she had puzzled over what God was doing amid all this turmoil. She hadn't found a satisfactory solution. But Everett's gentle statement did more to satisfy her than all those hours of anxious searching. God would look after her and her family. She had to meditate on that truth awhile and pray that it would sink in.

"You know, you're right. He shall."

They stood quietly for a moment, then Everett cleared his throat. "It occurred to me that you may need help moving. I'm only one person, but if you could use the assistance…"

Ellen smiled her first true smile of the day, her heart lifting with unusual buoyancy. Trust Everett to be chivalrous. "That would be swell."

He nodded quickly. "I guess you can just keep me informed and let me know when you need the assistance." He started to turn. "Oh, do you, er, have my address or any way to contact me without having to go through your cousins? That might come in handy."

"Right, I think it certainly would. I wouldn't exactly want to return here, either, to find you. Here, jot down your address and phone number, if you'd like."

Everett did so on the scrap of paper she pushed forward. "Well, I'd better beat it…are you going to be okay? I could walk you to your bus stop or…"

"Thanks, but I'll be fine. I have a tiny bit left to finish up here, and I don't want to keep you. The days are short enough as they are."

"Okay, if you're sure." Everett turned one last time at the door and tipped his hat. "At least you'll be back in for the rest of the week. That's gotta make you feel better."

"It does. I get a whole paycheck that way, and that could make a big difference in the near future."

Everett left, and Ellen, almost unwittingly, kept her eyes on the door for a long minute. She'd just gotten used to working with him, had been finding it quite nice in fact…goodness, why did she have to get torn from four good coworkers like them? Friends, every one of them. Would they miss her? Only time would tell how *she'd* cope with the loss of her job.

ᏧᎾ Chapter Five ᏒᎾᏮ

MARION SLIPPED SLOWLY, PURPOSEFULLY, FROM ROOM TO ROOM of the house, her footsteps echoing on the wood floors and every door opening and closing with a heightened click. The emptiness was eerie, like her childhood memories had been burglarized and she was left with only their ghosts. Her room seemed a stranger, all of its furniture gone: her little-girl vanity, her bookshelf, her dresser, her reading chair.

It had been a dream house, this Elizabethan. She, Ellen, and Greta had squealed in delight when they saw it for the first time seven years ago. It was out of a fairy tale. Its maples, elms, and oaks were woods, its flowering plum trees enchanted brides, its gardens fairy courts, its yard a lawn where energetic imagination knew no bounds. Inside, the girls each got their own room, like true princesses, and the number of rooms felt mountainous. Four bedrooms, two bathrooms, a cellar, an attic, a kitchen, a laundry, a dining room, a living room! Everything was bright and new. What she wouldn't give to go back to those days.

The house had lost its fairytale luster as the years wore on, but something of its old spirit revived as she viewed it bare, like the very first time she saw it. She would never despise it again. Not that she ever had...but anything less than admiration and appreciation seemed like spite now.

She would never call it home again. When Dad returned to them, they might not return to Canton, and even if they did, how could they get this house? They couldn't afford it anymore. If things ever transpired to reinstate the Dashiells as masters of 224 Cambridge Street, Marion would be long gone...to Hollywood.

Leaving Canton wasn't leaving all of her dreams, was it?

Surely she could find someway to further her plans in Cardinal Bush?

"Marion! Everett's here!" Greta hollered from downstairs.

Marion was about to climb into the attic. "Just a second!" She clambered up the narrow staircase, opened the door, and peeked inside. It was frigid, but she simply *had* to live every ghostly memory of this house one last time. The attic had been the best of indoor playgrounds. There was the hexagonal window, unattainably high in the peak of the roof, letting in light but tantalizing her with the promise of a neighborhood vista she could never see. She'd always wanted Dad to put a ladder beneath it, but he had never gotten around to it, and now she'd never see...there were a lot of nevers, weren't there?

She hurried back down, all the way to the foyer where boxes piled on top of boxes. Everett Shepherd, Frances Lundberg, and Joe whatever-his-name-was, from Ellen's work, were in the room attacking the stacks. Bob and Noble, sweet boys from school, must have taken an armload to the car. Conspicuously absent was Cousin Louis, who had thought sympathy was help enough. Or maybe Ida had told him so.

This was real, it was happening, there was no turning back. That was the melancholy thing about it. She had looked forward to this solid place being the foundation she could always rely on during the ups and downs that shaped any artist's career. Now what did she have?

They crammed all the boxes and small pieces of furniture into the two cars and the truck that were moving the Dashiells to their new life. What didn't fit they put into Joe's car for Frances to keep until they could get it from her. All the big pieces, which had helped form the home's character, were loaned out...all except the piano. That was staying for whoever would live there next. The Maddoxes had a piano, but it'd probably be old and wheezy.

They said their farewells, Mother locked the house, and everyone took their leave under a gray March sky, surrounded by a gray, unornamented world of dingy grass and barren trees. The atmosphere couldn't have been better.

Because Everett had to drive the more unwieldy truck, Ellen was driving his green Oldsmobile. "You're quiet today," she remarked as Marion settled next to her and slammed the door.

"What can I say? We're leaving our home; I'm melancholy."

Ellen nodded as she pressed the button to ignite the engine. "You're not even going to joke about my driving?"

"No. You'll do fine. All you need is practice." She stared at the dream house while Ellen pulled away, following Mother and preceding Everett. "Everett's a special fellow for letting you drive his car. The boys I know would shoot themselves first before they let a girl drive their car."

Ellen half-smiled.

Neither talked much as they wove out of the edges of Canton and into the countryside. It had been a long while since Marion had been outside Canton, and the fields, despite their grayness, looked quaint and peaceful, especially when they contained a farmhouse or red barn. Misty hills were a somber backdrop. Nothing could be less exciting, but as it matched her mood, she liked it.

The miles wore away as they traveled northeast. After thirty minutes, they turned off the highway onto a smaller one, loosely walled by trees with bristly networks of branches shivering in the wind.

"We should be almost there," Ellen said, breaking a ten-minute silence. "The town itself comes first, and the Maddoxes live a mile past it, on their own road."

"I'm glad we're seeing the town first. They can make no pretenses when they're describing it to us," Marion replied. "I still think we all should've come up here for an afternoon, instead of just Mother."

"You girls had school. Anyway, what would we have gained by you saying you did or did not like it?"

Marion sighed. "We'd have moved no matter what I wished. Still, it's plain awkward to land on someone's doorstep and say, 'Glad we're moving in! I do remember ya, I really do, it'll just take me a few days.'"

"You're good with new people."

48

"Not old people."

"Well, here's your chance to learn. Besides, they're not that old."

"Old enough to not like me."

"Well, make them like you. You know how to behave."

Marion puffed at her bangs. "You're going to make this argument go on forever, aren't you?"

"No. Because look…I think that's Cardinal Bush ahead of us."

It was just a tiny, dilapidated house on the left, but like a beacon fire, there was another farther along to the right. Two houses together promised more to come. Sure enough, beyond them was a collar of woods on either side of the road, and beyond that arose a whole neighborhood.

Since first impressions said a lot about an unfolding drama, Marion scrutinized what was inevitably becoming her milieu with every inch they drove. The houses were modest and though at a glance their flat character felt identical, each had eccentricities to set it apart once she studied them. The omnipresent trees suggested the neighborhood had been cut out of the woods, though they were thickest to the left. It looked as though a genuine forest was back there, behind the houses. Marion smiled. Woods were good for the soul. Maybe whoever owned them was either permissive or oblivious and let people stroll there.

After their car bumped over intersecting train tracks, roads branched off in both directions, the left ones into the mystery of the woods and the right ones into a tamer, more jumbled life where the houses stood closer together. The business part of town began abruptly with a diner on the right and continued while houses still framed the left a ways, and then the whole show was given over to commerce.

Though not busy, the businesses seemed healthy enough. At least they were all open and operating. A drugstore, a five-and-dime, another diner, a grocer, a post office…the usual. Centered in the small downtown strip—she was being genuine when she thanked God—was a movie theater. A tiny affair, but was it open? Yes! The marquee quietly proclaimed *Bright Eyes.* That Shirley Temple film had been released way back in December. Of course Cardinal Bush only offered a second-run theater. *It's better than none.*

The only other places of interest were several churches, a large school, a puny, neglected-looking library, and a corseted, uptight, two-story building, "Community Center" spelled out on its brow. Nothing appeared too promising as an acting venue, but you never knew.

"It's bigger than I thought," Ellen commented unoriginally as trees reconvened around the thinning buildings at the edge.

"A mile more, huh?" Marion said. "I wonder if they live where there's lots of trees. I like these woods."

"All they and Mother said was they live on a private road in a Victorian house."

"People don't always know what's important to mention. But at least the house ought to be interesting."

The road curved left. On the right was a gray field with smallish trees cropping up in mushroom-like groups, presenting a peaceful view, if dull. *Poor place; if everything wasn't so shrouded in late-winter gloom, I'd have a much better impression,* Marion thought. May and June would do the trick. The trees on the left pressed in close to the road, and then ahead, Mother turned into them. Marion nodded, satisfied.

The lane they turned onto really didn't hold them long, but the trees enchanted it, somehow lengthening it. When they turned right onto a narrow, climbing dirt track, the world outside the trees was gone. This must be the private road. At the end a clearing on the top of a low hill opened up, and then they saw the house.

Marion was speechless. It was as gray as the world, gray on the siding and roof and even the dirty white trim. It was one of those structures with so many details, mounding and building and springing off each other, it'd take years to memorize them: a covered front porch, a side porch, two chimneys, a turret, a tiny balcony, a sliver of a window in the peaked roof, bay windows, carved swirls, a stained-glass window...

It was eccentric and out-of-date, and laughably delusional to think it belonged in 1935. It looked abandoned by all but the barn in similar condition on the far side of the clearing.

Ellen opening her door broke the spell over Marion. "It's old," Marion laughed as she followed. "It's hard to believe anyone lives here."

"There's their car." Ellen waved to the barn wherein sat the rickety maroon Graham. "I'm glad we persuaded them not to come help us, if that's the car they had to drive."

Suddenly the house came alive. The front door flapped open and out flew a lady in a flowered red shirtwaist dress. She had iron-gray hair done up in a tall, puffy knot, black eyes that sparkled like the night sky, an aquiline nose, and a wide, buoyant mouth that hid her teeth enough to keep up her respectable, matronly appearance. Her long string of pearls almost took it away again, and when she squealed, the appearance went up in smoke.

"Oh Gussie! You're here! And your girls, your girls. Oh Gussie, they're beautiful." Aunt Jennie Maddox, the brightest thing on the lot, enveloped Mother in a hug. She transferred to Greta next. Slight little Greta was actually the same height as her, but she disappeared behind the wideness of the red dress.

Marion braced herself as next in line, and just before Aunt Jennie absorbed her the front door opened again and released a tall, barrel-like man, thick-limbed and solid, but moving with a gliding ease, unlike his wife's bounce. He had fuzzy, dark gray hair, large, irregular features, and blue eyes full of something... mischief, probably, given the quirk of his mouth. He must have thrown out the facial hair in the years since Marion had last seen him. His suit was brown, and at his side slunk a tall, slender, white and mahogany dog.

"How ya doin'?" He reached Mother in several strides and pumped her hand. "Good to see you, good to see you. Hope the journey was good. Sweetheart, you're loaded for bear. Sure you couldn't have done with our Graham-6? I bet your boat rode too low in the water to be safe and sensible."

"Well, I...think we did all right," Mother managed, returning her hand to the security of its twin.

Uncle Melvin gave each of the girls a vigorous handshake while the dog sat out of the way, polite and regal, and Aunt Jennie hugged Everett with the question, "Why, who is this? That nice young man you said would be helping you?"

"What's your name, chap?" Uncle Melvin asked as he turned to him.

Everett looked like a rabbit wishing to bolt. "Everett Shepherd."

"How wonderful of you to help my nieces. Wonderful. And you'll be here helping an old man out, too, eh, with unloading the cargo and so on? Wonderful!"

"What's your dog's name? You said you had a Russian wolfhound but you never said his name," Greta asked, taking a step toward the stoical animal.

"Why, his name is Sport. Looks like one, doesn't he? Like an athlete! It has a nice ring to it, good for the memory." Uncle Melvin rested his large hand on the dog's head. "Come and pet him; you know you want to, and Sport here won't mind."

Greta smiled and stepped forward slowly, sticking out her hand knuckles first. Sport's absurdly long nose nudged it with a jerk and he looked up into her face with a pondering gaze. When Uncle Melvin removed his hand and she petted the dog's silky white head, his muscles relaxed, but he still regarded the newcomers gravely. Animals were Greta's thing; they would be best friends in no time.

"Gussie—" Aunt Jennie scurried to Mother's side again. "Gussie, I think I know which girl is which. I can tell by the look of them. Shall I try and see if I'm right?"

She looked over the girls with a warm, triumphant smile; it seemed rather silly at that point. Her teeth showed, mostly white and good, but two were missing on the sides and one was broken. "Greta's simple, because she's the youngest and looks it. Marion's the actress, so that must be you, dear." She beamed at Marion, then swung around to Ellen. "Ellen is the secretary —and the only one left—so that is you, my dear."

"You're right!" Greta exclaimed, her small hand still

caressing Sport's ears.

The smile deepened and more teeth showed, but Marion had to acknowledge it wasn't so silly anymore; it was kind, likable, confident. The glittery black eyes weren't obscured by her cheeks; they shone intelligently. It wasn't easy to distinguish between Ellen and Marion based on their ages, and they'd changed so much since they were little and Aunt Jennie had seen them last. Anyone who could read people at a glance like that was worthy of respect. She was keen enough to pick up on Marion's starlet hairstyle.

"Now. Have you had lunch? I have a great big pot of soup that Melvin and I didn't dent at all when we ate at noon."

"Yes, thank you, we've eaten," replied Mother. "One of our friends brought sandwiches for all of us movers."

"You must be so tired. I'd think you'd want to come in and rest before you took another step."

"Well..." Mother consulted Ellen with leaden eyes. She was tired. She'd been working like Cinderella for weeks now, and the lull of the drive must have allowed it to catch up with her.

"It would be a good thing, yes," Ellen spoke up. "But not too long. We don't have Ev—" Her words cut off; she glanced at Everett. "Mr. Shepherd for very long."

They must not be on a first-name basis yet, Marion realized. Either that, or Ellen didn't want to strike a match to a waiting bonfire of speculation, which described most relatives—especially elderly ones.

"How about an hour? Soup or tea or coffee would warm you up in this gray chill," Aunt Jennie said, already edging toward the house.

"A catnap would revitalize you," Uncle Melvin offered. "It sure would. I use one every day, and it works wonders on a busy day full of appointments. Half an hour is all."

"I'm afraid once I'm asleep, there'll be no waking me," Mother said with a half-smile that looked more like Ellen's than her own.

"Gray chill" didn't exactly describe the outdoors, which was far colder than a "chill" to Marion, but it did describe the house. The coffee and tea did the Dashiells and Everett good, but during their respite and while they unpacked the vehicles and piled boxes in the parlor (it *was* a parlor, since it was Victorian; Marion refused to call it anything else), drafts chased them from entrance hall to parlor to dining room and the wood floor was ashen with age and dust. Marion would have expected a cheerful, blazing type of house to belong to the Maddoxes, but perhaps it was too much to keep up in these times. As it was, only the parlor fire filled the bill. Sport wisely remained there, lying on the dark green rug, once he realized everyone would keep returning to the room no matter how often they left it.

They finished at dusk. Aunt Jennie, who had bowed out of helping once the small boxes were moved, had a large supper ready by then. All afternoon she'd crowed about the beef and potatoes and green beans she was roasting, which candied carrots "just like Christmas" and the vegetable soup from lunch would accompany marvelously. Following would be a cherry cobbler that would only go in the oven once they sat down to eat, so it would be "piping and runny" when they were ready for dessert.

She and Uncle Melvin compelled Everett to stay. Aunt Jennie reasoned, "So you won't faint on the way home," while Uncle Melvin assured him, "I don't share my food lightly. Consider it a supreme compliment and gesture of goodwill that I'm pressing you to stay." Because aromas had been drifting from the kitchen for at least two hours, Everett didn't object.

After Uncle Melvin said grace and they all filled their plates, Aunt Jennie said with a satisfied sigh, "I'm so glad to be in my dining room again. We haven't eaten in here since Christmas. But now we can use it every day!" She clapped her hands. "It is pretty dull and drafty, but some living will enliven it." She smiled at Greta as if at a baby. "Especially with children and young people."

"She's alone an awful lot in this house," Uncle Melvin said, vigorously sawing his two hunks of beef into bite-sized pieces. "Just Sport and the chickens—and the garden, when it's growing. She does laundry for folks because she has a machine, but she's pretty far out of town to get many customers."

"Only a mile, but when you don't have a car, it isn't easy to carry loads of clothes," Aunt Jennie added helpfully. "*I* walk into town whenever my ankles and knees are holding up, because I have so many friends to visit." Her voice sounded a tad boastful, but lots of friends were a good thing...too bad Marion had left hers in Canton.

"Well, now we have a car to share," Mother said with a smile.

"Oh, I wouldn't dream of making you drive me around!" Aunt Jennie exclaimed.

"But it's the least I could do with you taking us in," Mother countered. "Please let me help wherever I can. I'd feel so ashamed if you didn't."

"We're all here to help you," Ellen said.

Marion gave her sister a sideways glance.

"Well, all right then. It will be great fun for me to have a car. We've only ever had one, except when my son Mel still lived with us and we shared another. As for you helping with other things, that would be swell, Gussie. But I can't have you working as slaves; no, I can't. I know I've let the housework slide since it's hard on my knees and back, but you must promise never ever to overwork yourselves, ever."

Mother smiled. "We promise."

"How are you getting that truck and your car back at once, my boy?" Uncle Melvin asked Everett, sitting to his right...and to Ellen's left. Uncle and aunt, who had assigned chairs, already seemed to have caught on to how things might stand there.

Everett had visibly relaxed with the Maddoxes, though questions shot his way still caught him off guard. He paused and looked at Mother before answering. "The farmer doesn't need it right away, so I was going to come up with a coworker next Saturday."

"If it's all right with you to leave it here that long," Mother hastily added.

"Of course! We have more room than we know what to do

with, inside and out!" Uncle Melvin replied. "The Graham will like the extra companionship; the truck can tell it what farm life's like." His chuckle came out as a snort as he curled a hand over Everett's forearm resting on the table. "Actually, son, it's nice for me to have a truck outside my home. I've always wanted one."

Aunt Jennie rat-a-tatted her fork on her plate. "Melvin, we must tell them now."

Her husband cocked his large head and furrowed his thin brows.

"My dears," Aunt Jennie put her palms on either side of her plate and jutted her face forward, "my dears, we wanted so much to make you feel welcome that we've planned a welcome party for you next Saturday."

Marion's wasn't the only Dashiell jaw to drop.

"So soon?" Mother asked faintly. She gathered her wits and fluffed them up to sound resolute. "Really, you don't have to go to that fuss. We'd much rather slip into your life quietly and unobtrusively. We hate causing lots of work. We feel guilty enough as it is disrupting your house like this."

"Piffle!" Uncle Melvin popped a cube of beef into his mouth and slid out his words around it. "We love parties. With you, we found the perfect excuse to have one."

"We haven't had one in ages, not since last summer at least. Family parties, yes, but not gay neighborly bashes. Oh, it will be so much fun! We'll get to introduce you to all our friends at once; won't that be expedient? Well, the invitation list is limited...this old house will only hold so many, after all, and you also can't meet *everyone* exactly at once. We've just invited the people we think you'll get along with best. Mostly the younger set." Aunt Jennie pointed her beaked nose toward Everett. "So you coming back on Saturday will be perfect! You and your friend can join us for the party, and maybe help these ladies not feel so overwhelmed."

Everett's green eyes were wide and he looked first at Ellen, then at Mother, and finally at Marion as if their approval was needed. Evidently Aunt Jennie thought nothing of *his* level of social comfort.

"I suppose nothing we can say would change your mind and save yourselves the trouble?" Ellen asked.

"Nothing. We've already had a few R.S.V.P.'s." Aunt Jennie's teeth showed themselves in a beam.

"It's...a good thing it's a week away." Ellen tried to smile. "You'll need help getting ready, of course, and that should give us plenty of time."

"Now that you say it, I guess it would be a good thing to spruce up the house a little, though I hate to put you to work your first week here...no, no, the guests will just have to take us for what we are. They're all friends, and what do friends do, but love you for who you are?"

"Within bounds, of course, but I certainly doubt anyone will be offended by a dirty house, if it really is all that dirty," Uncle Melvin chimed in—or rather, clanged in.

"I shouldn't worry about it. If we get some cleaning done, we get it done; if we don't, we don't. I'd much prefer having yummy food, fun games, and a good mood for stimulating conversation."

"I like that philosophy," Marion said with a grin.

Aunt Jennie and Uncle Melvin laughed and pretended to applaud her.

"This party will more than make up for all that's happened to you, you'll see!" exclaimed Aunt Jennie.

On Sunday, Marion explored. She actually found the house interesting. Misshapen little rooms populated every floor; even the cellar and attic were divided. Their furniture and décor were a fascinating study if one felt curious and nostalgic.

Marion and Greta shared a room while Mother and Ellen shared the one directly across the hall. The wallpaper in both, though yellowed, was striped with pretty red tulips, and the furniture, though rickety and scratched, was an achingly sweet vestige of a more romantic era. Marion and Greta's window overlooked the vegetable garden, currently a brown rectangle in the middle of the grayish clearing. A scraggly little apple tree stood by like a big sister.

As for the house's *special* features, the balcony was closed off since Uncle Melvin didn't trust the floor. The turret had been abandoned to spiders and dust and Marion couldn't see much out of its windows besides the surrounding moat of trees. Its highest window, a luminous diamond, promised more, but it was unreachable...just like the attic window at home.

ভ্ড৺Chapter Six৵৻ঀ৸

THEY'RE GOOD SOULS, THEY REALLY ARE, BUT THEY MIGHT HAVE asked us first, Ellen thought as she filled the mop bucket from the kitchen sink. It was Monday morning; Greta was at school, Uncle Melvin was at his dental office, Mother and Aunt Jennie were grocery shopping, and Marion and Ellen were readying the great gray house for the party. Nothing Aunt Jennie could say, or Marion for that matter, could make Ellen feel less duty bound to alleviate Aunt Jennie's responsibilities.

"Despite what she says about the house," Ellen had told Marion, "I can tell it hurts her to let it go like this. She's too quick to laugh it off. I also found her knocking down cobwebs with a broom in the upstairs hallway last night."

Ellen hefted the bucket from the sink and wobbled into the parlor, where Marion was plunking keys at the out-of-tune piano. "You're going to make me wish I had started at that wretched school today," Marion said.

"You should have, it's not wretched, and," Ellen swiped her finger across a shelf of books, "you should have been done dusting in here by now. You'll be in my way, dear."

Marion sighed. "Mopping goes much faster than dusting. Why don't you help me out? You gave me two rags. And as for school, I don't think I even need to bother going. Sure I transfer easily enough, but what difference will three months make? They don't have drama, I've learned all there is to learn at high school, and right now I need a job to raise money for acting school. Therein lies *my* future."

"So that's your rationale for staying home? Here you made Aunt Jennie think you're a martyr."

"I am—to my cause. C'mon, before you knew about this party business, didn't you want to go job-hunting this week,

59

too?"

"Marion." Ellen took one of the rags Marion had left on a chair and sprinkled it with water from the bucket. She rubbed it carefully over the nearest lampshade. "You made your promise to Dad."

"I don't remember promising."

"You did. He took it as a promise, at least."

Marion stood motionless at the piano, her back still turned to Ellen. Would she listen? Ellen felt like sighing herself as she caressed the round, fragile body of the lamp with her rag, freeing pink flowers and green leaves from a mist of dust.

"Dad wants us to succeed and prosper, doesn't he? I don't need a high school diploma to become an actress earning that all-important salary. I do, however, need acting school, and to get there I need money, and to get money I need a full-time job. School has the ornery habit of getting in the way of things like that. Believe me, if I could, I'd just pursue my acting dream without a thought of money, but I'm told that's impossible. Unfortunately, I don't have a Daddy-Long-Legs."

"No, but you do have a daddy who wants you to succeed, and part of succeeding is getting a high school diploma." Ellen dusted the side table where the lamp sat. "Don't you know you're far more likely to get somewhere, even a prestigious college with acting courses, with a diploma? You could get a scholarship that way. That's more than likely what Dad envisioned for you."

Marion finally swiveled around to face her. Even in the dimness of the room, Ellen could see a glimmer of tears in her eyes. "If I could've stayed to play Mary in *Secrets*, I'd have been awarded one. I know it. That'd have solved all our problems." She gave a wry little laugh. "I misspoke myself. It'd solve one half of my problems."

"That's right, always put things in perspective," Ellen said. "But really, you don't know if you'd have gotten one."

The glimmer was escaping her eyes now and tracing down her cheeks. "Oh, Ellen, what am I to do? My dreams seem so unattainable, and Daddy's case is so hopeless, and..." Marion brushed her fingers violently under her eyes. "And here I am blubbering."

Ellen crossed to her in three steps and folded her trembling body into an embrace. Marion relaxed into her. "Crying won't do any good, true, but patience and hard work will. And trust." She hesitated. Would Marion receive her words? "Trust in God. He has a plan for your life, and you just have to find it and be at peace with it." Marion stiffened ever so slightly. "And…to a lesser extent, you can trust Dad, too. He's got good reason to want you to graduate. Lots more jobs are open to you with a diploma than without. You could earn enough for acting school. As for Dad's problem, wouldn't it make you feel closer to him, and that somehow you were helping him, if you followed his wishes and graduated?"

Marion returned the embrace, hard. As they parted, she sniffed and blinked her eyes dry. "If you put it that way, yes, it would make me feel closer to him."

Ellen half-smiled. "There you have it."

Marion looked around the room. "You put in that bit about patience and hard work for your benefit, didn't you? I guess I'd better help you all I can today, since I'll be at school tomorrow."

"You'd better!" Ellen flapped her dust-rag in Marion's face.

"And tonight I am practicing that piano. It needs exercise. To think, I left a princess of an instrument pining away in an empty house on Cambridge Street in Canton."

The girls set about their work. Ellen felt a little more cheerful, but something about their exchange nagged at her: Marion had stiffened when she spoke about God's plan. Stiffening at the thought of God was never a good sign.

Ellen herself had finally found peace, for the most part, in their circumstances. They were far from the perfect norm their lives had been, but God had not abandoned them. She was coming to understand that even if things fell further, they didn't need to fear, because they were His children. His provision thus far filled her with thankfulness. But oh, how she prayed for Dad's acquittal and for a job.

The week passed rapidly. Despite Marion's resolution, she

got cold feet when Tuesday morning came, and it took all Mother's and Ellen's pleading to thaw her reluctance and get her to finally go.

As for Ellen, the housework and planning gave her much needed industry and satisfaction. It would have made her crazy to sit around idle or comb Cardinal Bush in vain for a job. She wasn't used to scrubbing floors, Hoovering carpets, or polishing brass, so the exertion put her to sleep instantly each night without time to brood.

The new sensation of soreness helped distract her, too. Of course, repetitive chores promoted thoughtfulness, but she directed her mind to think hopefully about the possibilities of the near future...and the books she read during downtime. Most of the Dashiells' library had come with them, and the Maddoxes had two bookshelves in the parlor.

She prayed while she scrubbed the kitchen from ceiling to floor on Friday, the day before the party. "Thank you, Lord, that Greta likes school, and that the kids are nice to her. And thank you that she has the woods, and Sport, and the chickens." Ellen smiled as she washed the top of the icebox. Sport—quiet, cautious, and aloof—had fallen in love with Greta. The Dashiells had had a mutt once, but he died when Greta was ten, leaving her inconsolable for weeks and restive for months. She hadn't been the same happy girl since. They'd always assumed it was the preadolescent years, but Greta's drastic attitude improvement now that she had Sport made Ellen wonder if it wasn't all tied up in a dog's companionship.

No, Ellen wouldn't need to worry about Greta.

Marion's attitude, however, had plummeted to a new low. "Lord, please help Marion to trust in You and seek Your will for her life," Ellen prayed. "And help her to find contentment here."

She understood Marion's feelings. Cardinal Bush's senior class was small, so Marion felt excluded and awkward. These kids had been together since kindergarten and watched schoolmates drop out one by one depending on their goals, so what remained was a determined core of students dead set on college and careers. No sense of humor or passion. They'd never understand her, Marion decided. She halfheartedly beat Cardinal Bush for a job, but mostly with Ellen in mind, because Ellen hadn't had time to look for herself. Besides that, she explored the woods and the house with Greta.

"As for Mother," Ellen turned to the stove to continue her cleaning and praying, "thank you that she's taking these changes courageously, and help her to keep relying on You." Mother didn't like living in someone else's musty house, getting grime on her clothes from cleaning, or doing strangers' laundry, but she locked her dismay within and cultivated gratefulness.

Raised in a privileged home, she had dived into hardship when she'd married Dad. They had to swim, without lifelines, to the surface of prosperity again, but they'd stayed there until now. No doubt Mother remembered what it was like and pulled from the same reserve of strength to rise over this new plunge. Then, she'd had her husband, and God. Now she had her girls, a poor exchange for their father—but God was, if possible, even more present than before.

They had so much to be grateful for.

Ellen approached the party like any other job assignment, and on Saturday morning she surveyed the state of things with her usual feeling of fulfillment at a job well done. Only last-minute foods needed to be prepared now. But, breakfast first.

Aunt Jennie ambled into the kitchen in her diamond-figured cotton blanket robe and slippers while Ellen rummaged around collecting cooking utensils. The kitchen had been Uncle Melvin and Aunt Jennie's preferred living room. Until the Dashiells had come, they'd even spent cool evenings there in comfy chairs pulled up to the radio. The grate gave off the best heat and the walls hugged in the oven's warmth.

"Good morning, dear. Dressed already? Ah, I should introduce you to the practice of staying in pajamas on Saturday mornings. It does wonders for one's rejuvenation. Now, shall we have quiche?"

"Quiche would be lovely, except aren't we in rather a rush to prepare the party food?" Ellen asked. When Aunt Jennie had made quiche last Sunday, they'd had to wolf it down and barely got to church on time.

"There's no rush. Is your cousin and his wife coming?" Aunt Jennie opened the icebox and pulled out three eggs. "Hold that thought; is Greta up yet, or shall I gather the eggs?"

"Not yet, but I'll rouse her. I'm sure she'd hate missing out —"

"No, no, I'll go. You've all made me shamefully lazy. The small task and brisk air will do me good. Before I go out, answer my other question, won't you, dear?"

"They aren't coming, I'm afraid. They recalled a prior obligation." When Mother invited them, Louis had said he and Ida *might* be able to attend, but on Friday he'd called back with their apologies. He "remembered" the Binghams were having them over for dinner Saturday night.

"But that nice young man still is?" Aunt Jennie huffed on her coat over her thick robe.

"Yes, he is."

"It's too bad your coworker couldn't come, and that school friend of Marion's. I should so much have liked to meet them."

"We were certainly disappointed, too." Ellen took down plates from the china cabinet. She missed Frances even more than she'd expected, so she had a hard time keeping cheerful when Frances told her she was sick. *I wonder how they're coping at Friar.* Lillian, Marion's friend, couldn't come without Frances as guardian, so Everett was coming alone with Frances's farmer-cousin, who was anxious to reclaim his truck. Marion was already in a heavy sulk, so the disappointment added only a drop to her bucket of woes.

Saturday and its work passed smoothly. After dinner the pies were prepared and popped into the oven while Mother, Marion, and Ellen assembled sandwiches and Aunt Jennie mixed her chopped bacon biscuits…it was vital that they be served hot from the oven.

"You can't have a party in wintertime and serve cold foods,"

Aunt Jennie opined. "Cold drinks, either. No, we're having coffee, hot chocolate, and hot apple cider. Yum, doughnuts are scrumptious with cider, aren't they? Pity we can't have doughnuts, but I haven't enough grease right now."

Marion's forkful of mushroom and mayonnaise filling leaped onto the tray instead of onto the bread she was spreading. Her eyes bounced between the clock and her companions. "Golly, we wouldn't have enough time, either! It's two thirty; can't I go dress now?"

"Why yes, yes, we should all get dressed. It wouldn't do to be late to our own party, would it?" Aunt Jennie smiled. She shooed at Marion, her spatula spotting the floor with batter. "Go up, dear. I'm sure you have loads to do, you like to get dolled up so much. We'll join you in a jiffy."

"Make sure Greta is getting ready," Ellen called behind her. Ellen had already arranged her hair by curling and rolling it under at the nape of her neck, so all she had to do was change clothes. She always pinned back her hair and seldom curled it, but Marion was shamelessly persuasive when it came to decking out for parties.

Marion had rag-rolled her hair last night and it still swirled wonderfully despite all her fuss about the contrary happening. The poor girl was desperate to look flawless today, though in her own words, "I don't need to impress anyone special. I just like to look my best for whoever's around!"

Ten minutes later, the rest of the cooks hurried upstairs for their transformation. When Ellen had donned her teal-blue lace dress, pearls, and black high-heeled pumps, she knocked on Marion and Greta's door. "Need any help in there?"

"Yes! I need ribbons in my hair!" yelled Greta. "I can't tie them right, and Marion's too busy."

Ellen sighed internally…so she wouldn't be down before the first guests arrived. Greta had two mint-green ribbons to give her straight, brownish-blond hair some semblance of style. She was going to be a pretty young woman, but she was growing so fast she looked lanky in her pale-green, white-polka-dotted party frock.

"How do I look?" Marion asked breathlessly, smoothing her skirt and touching the diminutive curls she had formed around her face. She'd done herself up with a bit of makeup besides her normal lipstick, and she glowed like a rose in her satiny pale pink dress.

"Beautiful," Ellen replied, adjusting the loops on Greta's last bow. "For someone who's not trying to impress anyone special, you're pretty impressive."

"You look too grown up," Greta complained. "I look like such a kid next to you."

"You are a kid." Marion turned back to the vanity mirror.

"So are you!"

Marion looked back with a mischievously smug smile. "Not anymore. For all practical purposes I've graduated."

"Which doesn't mean you're completely grown up. So don't get cocky." Ellen half-smiled. "Now be down just as soon as you can," she added and made her escape.

Marion would have said she'd timed her descent perfectly, because right in the foyer, talking with Aunt Jennie, stood Everett Shepherd. They looked up at her as a step squeaked.

"They wanted to get the truck out of the way before other guests came." Aunt Jennie beamed, glancing between Ellen and Everett. "Your farmer friend is already gone, the unsociable creature! He could have at least warmed his insides with some coffee. Well, we have Mr. E. to ourselves now for a little while, don't we, Ellen?" She wagged her finger at Everett. "Now, now, don't get your hopes up about the food. All the guests must have fair game at it."

Everett gave a small smile. "It does smell very good in here."

"The pies and biscuits are baking now. Fresh and hot from the oven!" Aunt Jennie clasped her hands and abruptly rotated and waltz-stepped into the dining room. Ellen watched, then returned her eyes to Everett, who produced another small smile. His smiles were never contrived; they were spontaneous and welled up from his calm pool of feeling while his green eyes shone with a warm, gentle gleam.

Ellen caught herself, realizing they had been staring at each other for who knew how long. "We're entertaining in the parlor," she said, spinning on her heel to lead there. "How was your drive?"

Minutes later, people trickled in to the booming welcomes of Uncle Melvin and Aunt Jennie—two couples the Maddoxes' ages; one of Greta's teachers and her daughter, Greta's age, whom they had all met at church; and one couple and one single woman around Mother's age. Arriving later would be a young lawyer named Calvin Bradley.

The Maddoxes had given the Dashiells the scoop on every one of these favored friends. It was only a matter now of sorting them out, making pleasant conversation, and remembering what *not* to say of what the Maddoxes had told them. Ellen was skilled at that, but she worried about her mother and sisters. *Though Marion sure is aloof just now. She's spoiled for youth and for theater people. She shouldn't be a problem.*

Marion and Everett started out the party sticking so close to her Ellen felt she had extra shadows. Great. She was no sparkling conversationalist herself, but she did endeavor to speak to everyone, slipping politely to each unengaged person. It was harder with two dependent shadows. Soon, however, Everett got absorbed in a discussion with the talkative, middle-aged Mr. Henry, and then he seemed confident enough to be on his own with any chattery person who'd have him.

While Ellen and Marion stood side by side attending to Mrs. Henry, Aunt Jennie's strong, stifling arms wrapped across their backs and clutched their shoulders. "How about some music, ladies? I know where we can get some, hmm-hmm-hmm."

Surely she's not going to ask Marion? Ellen watched her sister for a reaction which was slow in coming.

It came when Aunt Jennie said, "Marion, the piano's right over there," and loosed Ellen while pinioning Marion's shoulders. She nudged her around and Ellen was treated with a full-on view of Marion's expressive face: soaring brows, furrowed forehead, wide brown eyes, and open, curled lips.

"Surely you can't mean!" Marion exclaimed. "Why, Aunt Jennie, that thing isn't—" She veered away quickly. "I'm not fit to play that thing. I'm all out of practice."

"Piffle. You serenade us every time. Go on, Marion. Live music is just the thing! We haven't had someone play at a party of ours since our Gloria got married and left!"

"I'm all sorts of sorry, but I have to refuse." Marion dug her heels into the carpet as Aunt Jennie pushed harder. "Did you hear me yesterday? It sounded terrible!"

Ellen applauded her tact. At Greta's age Marion would have tossed her head and blurted out the truth with a malicious gleam in her eyes. Ellen tried to assist her. "We can bring the radio from the kitchen, Aunt. I'm sure Mr. Shepherd or Uncle Melvin wouldn't mind doing it."

"Marion sounds lovely to me. Now go." Aunt Jennie gave Marion a final shove.

Marion faced Aunt Jennie gravely, threw a glance at Ellen, and sighed. In an undertone, she said, "Aunt Jennie, your piano isn't fit for company."

Aunt Jennie widened her eyes before her lips split with an eruption of laughter. "Now that is really nonsense! You make it sound like the radio."

Marion stiffened with shock. "Aunt, are you tone-deaf?"

Aunt Jennie chuckled again. "Maybe I am. Now go." She shooed with her hands.

Marion shared one more hopeless glance with Ellen, then shrugged, sighed, and went to what she certainly considered her doom of the day. As if she were already not having a good time.

"Maybe you could sing instead," Ellen suggested quietly before she was out of earshot.

With the air of a martyr, Marion collected some music she'd brought from home and proceeded to coax out "Tumbling Tumbleweeds," a calculated choice, seeing as the country character was forgiving to the piano's tone. *She's probably thinking of how Cardinal Bush feels like the middle of nowhere, too,* Ellen realized. Then she played "We're in the Money" and really, it didn't sound bad because she pounded with such energy and feeling.

No one stopped talking—or, in a much smaller number of cases, attending to talkers—except Ellen, Greta, and Greta's new friend Violet. The younger girls stood transfixed beside the instrument while Ellen excused herself from conversation with Mrs. Henry and Aunt Jennie to retrieve a tray of cookies and sandwiches from the dining room to offer around.

She could actually hear better in the relative quiet across the foyer where the food was kept. On her return a knock clunked against the front door. Balancing her tray, she opened the door, smiling and saying welcome.

"Hello. Sorry I'm late," said the young man, smoothly doffing his fedora.

"You must be Calvin Bradley. I'm Ellen Dashiell. Don't worry; the Maddoxes said you needed to come late. We're just pleased you arrived." Ellen stepped back to let him in, impressed by his sturdy, responsible-looking face and tall, straight, gentlemanly bearing. He looked like a welcome addition.

Calvin Bradley was the son of a now-deceased friend of Dad's who had always lived in the area, and the Maddoxes, loving both Bradleys, had more or less adopted the son. He was the only lawyer in town, specializing in property law as well as consulations for bigger affairs that made villagers feel out of their depth.

He glanced toward the parlor as he entered, head slightly cocked. Marion had started to play—and sing—"I Only Have Eyes for You."

"We're having some music," Ellen explained with a half-smile. "Let me put this tray down and I'll take your coat and hat."

"No, no, I can get it myself, thank you," he said in a hushed voice, working off his black coat. He kept an ear tilted toward the other room. "She makes that old instrument sound almost nifty. Her voice is golden."

"That's my sister." Ellen waited for him to hang up his things. "Cookie or sandwich? There's other food in the dining room."

He didn't answer at first, because Marion was trilling out the most lyrical part of the song, where the title words danced. Then he took a sandwich and thanked Ellen with a smile.

Ellen moved into the parlor and started the rounds with the tray. How interesting that this man was so struck with Marion's singing. *He and Marion will probably get along well. Maybe the evening will pick up for her.* She grinned to herself as a particularly off-pitch chord pierced the song. *On the other hand, she might be mortified to know that someone who appreciates music is hearing this.*

Marion soon brought the song to a close, ending with off-key notes, and dropped her hands to her lap. "That's it, I'm finished," she told Greta and Violet.

Ellen came up to them with the tray. "You should just sing something."

"Aunt Jennie wouldn't like a performance without her precious piano."

"She's not paying attention."

"Then why bother even singing?" Marion waved her hand behind her, dismissing the rest of the people in the room. "No one else cares."

"Just sing, Marion. People will listen if you do, and you'll make up for…this." Ellen touched the piano top.

Marion sighed. "No one informed me I'd be entertaining." She rifled through her music.

"Sing 'I Got Rhythm'!" Greta suggested.

Marion glared at her. "What a silly notion. That's much too theatrical. Ah, here we are. 'You're Getting to Be a Habit with Me.'"

Greta wrinkled her nose.

Marion stood at the other side of the piano from the girls and faced the room, her eyes casting disparagingly over her oblivious audience, though Ellen saw Mother, Everett, and Calvin Bradley looking Marion's way. "Here goes nothin'," Marion sighed and proceeded to sing her song from memory.

She sounded every bit as good as a singer on the radio, and though Ellen might not have a well-trained ear and know much about pitch and rhythm, she was critical when it came to both her sisters' abilities. Marion's voice was soprano, sweet yet soulful—rather a mix of Annette Hanshaw and Ruth Etting. It made a good impression wherever she used it.

Sure enough, she had everyone's attention by the end of the song, and they applauded when she fell silent. She'd gotten so absorbed herself that she was smiling.

"Yoohoo, Ellen, Marion! Come meet Calvin Bradley!" Aunt Jennie called after a pause.

The dreamy sparkle left Marion's eyes and she looked toward Aunt Jennie, seated on a couch across the room. The newcomer stood beside her, gazing at Marion.

"I met him already. He's nice," Ellen murmured as she and Marion made their way. "He enjoyed you even when you were on the piano."

"Is he tone-deaf, too?" Marion whispered back.

"That isn't what I meant," Ellen gritted, wishing she could explain; but Aunt Jennie was already calling out introductions.

⌒◉⌒Chapter Seven⌒◉⌒

"ELLEN, MARION, THIS IS THE CALVIN BRADLEY YOU'VE HEARD so much about," Aunt Jennie exclaimed, pinching the man's suit coat sleeve.

Actually, you didn't talk about him much at all, Marion noted to herself, but she smiled sincerely and said as she shook his proffered hand, "As if we'd be meeting any other Calvin Bradley! It's a nice, distinctive name."

He wasn't bad looking, in a mature sort of way. His dark eyes searched hers with a confident, gentle gaze as he summed her up, which she met fearlessly, seriously. He had a mild, proper air about him. He wouldn't be a lively conversationalist, but perhaps a polite and well-informed one who'd actually let her talk about something interesting—if she talked with him at all, which, given the people in the room, she was likely to, even if she wouldn't otherwise seek him out. He was tall, strong-jawed, broad-shouldered like an athlete, and dressed smartly in a dark gray suit, light blue tie, and black shoes. The poor fellow's dark brown hair, however, was combed over to hide a receding hairline. *How old is he? Thirty? They probably said but I sure don't remember.*

Aunt Jennie introduced the sisters.

"I had the pleasure of being welcomed inside by Miss Dashiell," Mr. Bradley said, the unconscious motions of his head and hands slight and smooth. They matched his soft-spoken voice. "I highly enjoyed your music, Miss Marion."

"Why, thank you! Glad you did. I wasn't at my best…or rather," Marion was suddenly aware that sounded conceited, "I was feeling pretty low about how I did."

"You needn't have, I assure you," Mr. Bradley countered.

"Oh, he was taken with you all right," Aunt Jennie chirped

with a broad smile. "I'm sure he didn't hear a word I said! Even his hello was slow to come out."

"An aficionado of popular music?" Marion asked.

Mr. Bradley shrugged, his head tilting a little to meet one shoulder. "I enjoy any and all music. Never learned to play anything, to my chagrin."

"That's too bad." Sympathy stole into Marion's voice of its own volition, though she couldn't say she felt it. She wasn't one to empathize with someone right after meeting him. Nevertheless it was there, and his gaze seemed to intensify toward her because of it.

"I don't mean to sound cliché, but it's never too late to learn," Ellen spoke up. "Though I would guess you're far too busy right now with your work."

"I am, fortunately."

"Yes, most fortunately! Business activity is a blessing these days," Ellen said.

Marion squinted. What was it that Mr. Bradley did? *I better keep my ears open so I don't embarrass myself—or, more likely, Ellen.*

"Calvin has helped us before," Aunt Jennie said. "I don't know all the ins and outs and details of what he did exactly, but he helped us greatly; didn't you, Calvin? What was it exactly?"

"Well, it had to do with the tax difficulty over your husband's office. But I don't think any of you would wish me to go into the details." Mr. Bradley smiled.

"Oh, Ellen has a head for business, so she'd probably find it fascinating." Marion rubbed her upper arms. "But it gives me the shivers! Awful that money is what makes the world go round when it's one of the most complicated things on earth."

"Try law," Mr. Bradley said wryly.

Law! That's what he did. Disgust made a wave across her face. "You're right; that *is* worse. I haven't had a lot of experience with it, thank heaven, but I've had enough to know it's not only complicated, it's downright ridiculous!" Vehemence crept into her voice.

"Oh, you poor dears." Aunt Jennie brushed crumbs from the purple skirt of her dress. "Calvin knows all about your misfortune; your Uncle Melvin and I told him. He was in an outrage over it, a perfect outrage! You can't imagine this mild-mannered man in a perfect outrage, can you?"

Mr. Bradley glanced away uncomfortably and returned his gaze to the group with a quirked grimace. "I wasn't aware I had been so voluble. But I did feel some...confusion over how— wait, forgive me, you may not wish to talk about this."

Ellen exchanged a look with Marion. Marion shrugged and chuckled. "It sounds as if you know everything already, and we've been over it enough that...that the 'misfortune' doesn't throw us into a fit anymore."

"It's still not something you'd wish to discuss at your welcome party, however," Mr. Bradley said, his voice weighty with understanding.

"No, I guess not." Marion shrugged again and swept a hand through her blond swirls. "What should we discuss? I'm game for anything to do with music or the stage!" She arched her eyebrows at Mr. Bradley. "You like music; what's your opinion on movies and the stage?"

"I like both, in moderation. I don't see many plays, but I catch the movies I'm interested in when they come here."

"What type of movies do you like?" Marion asked.

"The usual, I guess: crime, action, adventure...comedy... Westerns."

"No romance?"

"That could be sprinkled in with no harm done."

"You sound well rounded."

"Marion here is interested in becoming an *actress*," Aunt Jennie said. "I haven't seen her act, but if her voice is any indication, she'd be the bee's knees onstage."

Mr. Bradley nodded, his gaze searching Marion's face again. Really, this guy knew how to give a look, didn't he? It wasn't admiring, as far as she could tell, and it was all above-board and respectful, but it made her uneasy, because he seemed to be looking for something...and whatever it was, no doubt she didn't have it. As deep and complex as she felt herself to be, she was still just a teenager, and Mr. Bradley made her aware of

2

her age somehow. Though, come to think of it, he probably didn't realize quite how young she was.

"Have you acted before?" he asked.

Now, I'm not so dippy I'd aspire to become an actress without knowing what's involved, Marion mutely remonstrated. "All the time, in high school and the Players Guild, the community theater at Canton. Not before that; I wasn't introduced to acting much before junior high. We weren't allowed to see movies."

"Which is a fine thing, because back then you couldn't know what movies were decent and what ones weren't," Mr. Bradley said. "Now with the Code finally being enforced it's much 'safer'—I'm sure your family's happy about that."

"Oh yes. I never got to see as many movies as I wished. But now the theaters are a field of daisies, and I can run wherever I wish." Marion grinned. "So long as I heed the Legion of Decency's Motion Picture Guide. My parents insist upon it. What movies are you looking forward to seeing, Mr. Bradley?"

"I'm afraid I haven't been to the theater lately, so I don't know what's in the previews."

"What! How come? Calvin, have you been overworking yourself?" Aunt Jennie threw up her hands. "Why, that's precisely why you were late today! You'll go stark crazy if you don't take time to relax. That's the trouble with him, girls; if he has a staggering workload, he never takes a break. Foolish young man. You know if you ever need friends to help you unwind, you're welcome here."

"Thank you for that. But don't mind me; I enjoy my work, although taking telephone calls and filing papers does get tiresome."

Barely suppressing a gasp, Marion widened her eyes as she glanced at Ellen. If that girl didn't speak up, her bigmouth little sister would just have to speak up for her.

"Oh? No secretary?" Ellen questioned.

Bull's-eye.

"No. I've been able to keep up with everything until recently, and then I'm too set in my ways to hire one. My office is small."

Aunt Jennie's whole face came alight. "Calvin! You need a secretary? Why didn't you say something before?"

"I—" Mr. Bradley paused, confusion wreathing his features.

Marion chuckled. "Aunt, I think he just said he *didn't* want one. But I agree with you, there is a difference between wanting and needing." She ignored Ellen's nudge.

"Well, when you decide you can't take it anymore and go to hire someone, come straight to me and I'll get you that someone." Aunt Jennie patted Mr. Bradley's arm and exaggeratedly winked at Ellen. Mr. Bradley's glance hopped among the trio, and when he raised his eyebrows slightly and rested a knowing look upon Ellen, it was obvious he understood.

"*If* I decide so, I shall come to you first," Mr. Bradley said to Aunt Jennie.

Swell! Now, how could they make him fall for his need? Ellen wasn't going to promote herself; she was awfully fond of the "wait and see" technique. Marion always seized the moment.

She was new to this job application business, but if it was anything like acting, one had to thrust oneself out there. She mastered a coyly serious look. "Mr. Bradley, I hope it doesn't seem too forward of me, but Ellen is quite the secretary. It's her passion. She was a secretary for two years in Canton. I know you aren't ready yet, but when you are, look no farther."

Ellen, trying to appear dignified and not too vexed, said, "Now that we've beat that dead horse enough, Mr. Bradley, perhaps you'd like some more of my aunt's delicious refreshments?" She held forth her tray. He selected a cookie and Ellen moved on.

Marion remained standing with Mr. Bradley while Aunt Jennie chattered with her new neighbor, Mr. Henry. When Everett approached with an intrigued look on his face, Marion took it upon herself to introduce the two young men.

"He works with money," Marion finished, readjusting her mask of disgust. "Money and horrid figures. At least money buys you things; figures just sit on a lined page and glare."

Mr. Bradley chuckled, his half-eaten cookie waiting politely in his hand. "I agree with you, Miss Marion. Figures don't sit well with me, either. I'm certainly glad, however, that they have attracted Mr. Shepherd's attention."

Everett smiled indecisively.

"Were you interested in math as a boy?" Mr. Bradley asked.

"Yes, a lot, actually. Numbers were always easier for me."

"Easier than what?" asked Marion.

"Say, um, words. People."

"Ah. That's understandable. People are complicated—if you don't like the study of human nature, they'll always and forever be hard to harmonize with." Marion nodded to punctuate her point. "Me, I'm captivated. I can't get away from people, at least if they're fictional, and even if I hate them. They're endless founts of fascination."

Mr. Bradley brushed crumbs from his hands. "I, too, prefer people. Being a lawyer, you could say I'm obligated to."

"I bet you meet a lot of people you could hate," Marion joked.

"Hmm. Could, I suppose…but try sincerely not to. If I kept a closet of wrongs, the door wouldn't shut. And then where would I be?"

He was pretty good with words; this was genuinely entertaining. "Your closet wouldn't be serving its purpose," she returned.

"Yes. The wrongs would spill out. But really, I shouldn't have such a closet."

"Ah. I guess not. But do you?"

He hesitated, his gaze jumping on and off her face. "Yes. I shouldn't, but I do, and I ought to try harder to get rid of it."

He was scrupulously honest. How peculiar for a lawyer. She didn't need to know that he nursed a painful grudge against someone—but he couldn't lie and say he didn't. Perhaps she shouldn't have asked, however fun a sustained metaphor was.

"I guess that's the right thing to do, yes," she agreed, gravity she didn't feel laced in her expression and voice. This party was too distracting to give him her full attention, but she knew what she ought to feel and thus it came out. "I'm afraid I don't forgive very easily. But we've been abominable, ignoring poor Mr. Shepherd. If we don't watch out we'll be prime examples of why he prefers numbers over people."

She was gratified to see she produced a smile, small but sincere, on Everett's glum face. She continued, "Numbers can get you into all sorts of trouble, too, however, especially if they're attached to money. Money is the root of all evil, don't they say?" Alluding to the "misfortune" again felt like a pinprick to her heart. She had ignored it earlier, but for some reason it affected her now.

"The love of money is the root of all evil is what the original says. Evil never proceeds from objects, but from people," Mr. Bradley observed. In his soft-spoken voice, what needn't have sounded serious was somehow authoritative and compelling. Marion wasn't sure what she thought of his way of speaking in general. It didn't match the lighthearted, almost frivolous atmosphere; he obviously didn't know how to take a party. Yet what was the disgrace in making weighty statements? At least he felt things.

"You speak truly," Marion said with a smile.

Just then Ellen walked up to their small circle, her tray gone and in its place a glass of apple cider crowned with a wisp of steam. Since no one broke the lull that had descended, she asked, "Does anyone want hot drinks?"

They all set off together and convened as a somewhat youthful foursome in the dining room.

"It certainly is quieter in here," Ellen remarked as she poured Mr. Bradley's coffee. Marion poured apple cider for Everett and hot chocolate for herself.

"And easier to talk," Marion seconded. "Mr. Shepherd, I don't believe you and I have yet had a good discussion on film and stage and story. You say you prefer numbers to people, but does that extend to fiction and make-believe? Do you like reading? How about when you were young?"

"Well, I…liked the radio, and still do, a bit more than films. And Westerns and adventures were my only reading fare for a while, until college." He ventured a smile. "Does that meet your approval?"

Marion bestowed a glance on Ellen as if directing the question to her as she answered. "I don't know that my approval really matters, but I'd say it sounds like you appreciate entertainment to a respectable degree. I like adventure and historic romance, so I won't judge you for liking the lighter fare. I don't think it's really lighter, in fact. How can it be, when the characters suffer so much? When they are such heroes and heroines? If anything, we should emulate them. They represent the pinnacle of human struggle, and if they gain a victorious end, we should take note and be encouraged. If they don't— why, we still might learn from them. They connect us to all those who suffered before us."

Captain Blood in her favorite book was the epitome. Convicted of treason through an unjust trial and sent to Barbados as a slave, his situation resembled Dad's. His ultimate vindication bolstered her courage that things would turn out right for Dad.

"You speak truly," Mr. Bradley said...and grinned slightly. "Laudably. And if people really took that from the movies and other entertainment, we'd be a stronger race. But I fear most go only to be amused and forget about their troubles. It takes a powerful actor to reach across the divide and help them in their own lives."

There now, he actually did have something interesting to say! It certainly was better than she'd expected from the afternoon. "That, sir, is my dream. To reach across the divide and be an actress who touches hearts." She put reverence into her tone.

Mr. Bradley studied her for a moment, then looked down. "I do hope you fulfill your dream; but unfortunately, experiencing grief and loss is, I feel, what brings that realism to one's acting abilities." He looked up again and turned up one corner of his mouth.

Why is he smirking like that? Is he laughing at me? Does he think I'm too shallow and inexperienced to be a good actress? Marion raised her chin. "I do my best to imagine, watch, and read to express grief and loss and other strong emotions, but I believe talent plays a large role." She mirrored his smirk. "My hope is to get by without experiencing that, but if it goes into my art, then so be it."

"That's probably too much to hope," Ellen said, flatly and heartlessly pragmatic, taking away from Marion's dramatic moment.

"Yes, it is," Mr. Bradley agreed.

Marion still felt irked with him. "It isn't as though I haven't experienced *any* heartache. Think of my father." She'd been doing all right; truly she had been. But the pin pricked again, and the pain stayed longer. Somehow the injustice done to Dad, and the thought that her grief in the matter was being dismissed, made her angrier and sadder than she'd been in a while.

He must have noticed her sharp tone; he hesitated and then changed the subject to how they were getting along in Cardinal Bush. *That* was boring. She didn't have much good to say, and didn't relish describing her woes to someone like Mr. Bradley, so she let Ellen talk. His eyebrows rose in mild surprise when he learned Marion was a high school senior, and the conversation scooted to her again when he asked what she and Greta thought of the school, the world he'd known for twelve years of childhood.

Marion glanced at Ellen and Everett while she and Mr. Bradley went back and forth. *Everett and Ellen need some time to themselves, not standing here listening to us jabber.* How to get them alone? "Yeah, Mrs. Guest is still there, and boy is she hard. Say, is it nippy out in the sun? How about stepping outside for a bit?" Bingo. Ellen and Everett hated the cold; they wouldn't set foot outside.

It worked...the two of them remained in the dining room while she and Mr. Bradley left for the foyer. They got as far as the coat rack when Aunt Jennie appeared in the parlor doorway like a grinning genie.

"There you are! Come, Calvin; the men are talking up a storm about politics, and I know you get deliciously riled up about the government, so do please join in. Marion, you could learn a thing or two by listening to them. It's an educational experience."

Whew. It succeeded even better than she'd expected: she didn't have to be alone with Mr. Bradley. Her mind could wander in the parlor with that lousy debate going on over her head. Mr. Bradley was decent and at least halfway interesting, but he was too serious and thought her callow. She'd think more highly of him if he'd give Ellen that job…

ᒐᕉᖾ Chapter Eight ᕉᖾᒐ

"I'M SURPRISED IT TOOK HIM THIS LONG, BUT HE IS A HARRIED lawyer," Marion remarked upon hearing that Mr. Bradley had finally called Ellen on Wednesday. After school she and Greta found Ellen in the dining room re-pasting peeling wallpaper corners. Mother and Aunt Jennie were in the cellar hanging a customer's laundry. "I also think he didn't want to look like he was being pushed around by a bunch of females. Well, the joke's on him, because once we knocked it into his brain, he realized he can't do without you."

Ellen, on her knees, smoothed down a piece of the gold and green Victorian paper. "I don't think he was concerned about his ego. He just needed time to consider it. He is one busy man, you got that right—I'm not going to the office for a proper interview and introduction to the job until Friday, because he'll be in Canton arguing a case tomorrow. Aunt Jennie managed to invite him over for supper tonight, though."

"I wonder what we'll talk about. Tooth stories? Property law? Dad's case?" Marion slid into a chair and started unfastening her pinned-up curls.

"You said he likes movies and music," Greta said. "But anyway, Ellen, what is there to eat? I'm starved!"

"Bread and butter. One slice only, though, and don't load up on the butter. We're having a big, fancy meal tonight because of Mr. Bradley."

Marion waved her hand as Greta darted away. "Mr. Bradley is *mildly* interested in movies and music. He's not enthusiastic enough to suit me or make for a really swell conversation. His head's in other matters."

"He has good taste," Ellen observed, moving to another spot.

"I do wonder their motivation for inviting him over. Is it just to talk about your job? Or are they wanting Mother to get to know him, for some ulterior reason?" Marion donned her teasing look, even though Ellen's back was turned. "I thought they knew about Everett, but—"

"Oh, you're the limit," Ellen said placidly. "No one's making any matches. They'd invite him even if we weren't here, because that's what they do. They're hospitable and they like him."

"He's too old for you anyway." Marion shook out her hair as she laid the last pin on the table. "And don't you forget that."

"He is only twenty-six, not that that changes anything."

"Twenty-six! I thought he was thirty if a day."

"I can see why you thought so, but I have it on authority from Uncle Melvin and Aunt Jennie."

"Some people age quickly. That happens to the serious-minded."

"I don't think it's a matter of aging so much as naturally looking mature for his age. He's not a factory-worn worker who's had a harsh life."

"It's his mind that ages him."

"His mind?" Marion could hear Ellen's eyebrows reaching up even if she couldn't see them. "So everyone who looks older than they are has been 'aged' by something?"

"Yes! Take me, for example. When I wish to look older than I am, I use makeup. That ages me."

Ellen chuckled contemptuously.

"I'm being perfectly serious. Some people need exterior things, like a tough life or makeup. Other people need a mature mind."

"Which do I have? Or don't I look older than I am?"

"You do; your mature mind ages you. If Mr. Bradley were a younger-minded person, you and he might actually be suited for each other. But he's not, and that's glorious for Everett." Marion briefly wondered if Everett might have been jealous of Mr. Bradley when they'd met on Saturday.

"Who's the matchmaker now? You watch too many movies and read—and act in—too many romances "

"I only think about this because I care for you! I don't care a fig about other people's prospects. Unless they're fictional, of course." Marion giggled.

Greta returned and settled into another chair at the dining table. With the advent of the Dashiells, both that room and the parlor had become less formal and more an extension of the close-knit kitchen. "Ellen, who do you think is handsomer, Everett or Mr. Bradley?"

"What kind of a question is that!" Ellen stood up and very meaningfully, or so it seemed to Marion, kept her face away from the table as she sought for more flyaway wallpaper.

"On the contrary, it's a very good question." Marion exchanged a grin with Greta. "Well done, little sister."

"I haven't considered it. And besides, a man is more than a handsome face. Now, don't you two have something more important to do than interrogate me?"

"I'm eating," Greta said. "And then I'm going for a walk with Sport."

"What else did Uncle Melvin and Aunt Jennie say about Mr. Bradley? Entertain us, Ellen. We need a diversion." Marion realized she'd probably missed a lot of background on this man, a life story Aunt Jennie had narrated to Ellen and Mother while she was at school. So what if he wasn't all that interesting to her? She'd be spending the evening with him, so she'd better know as much as possible.

"Only if you promise to stop your nonsense."

"Promise."

"But it's going to get boring now," Greta complained.

"Cut that, let her talk. Go on, Ellen. 'Once upon a time, a very serious-minded baby was born...' Take it from there."

A shake of Ellen's head reiterated her sentiment that Marion was "the limit." "I hope you don't look at this as a gossip-fest, because it's not."

"Fret not. I only want to know about him so he doesn't feel like such a stranger tonight. It saves me the trouble of asking."

Ellen paused, then set out on the course Marion had determined for her as if it were a tightrope or a gauntlet.

Marion could always tell when Ellen was unwilling to talk; the words halted more than they strolled. "Aunt Jennie told me they've known Mr. Bradley's father since he was a boy. He was only a year older than Dad."

Ellen began carefully circuiting the room, on the lookout for more paper corners to paste. "It certainly would have been nice to know him now. Can you imagine the stories he could tell?" She knelt to inspect something and hesitated. "He died three years ago from a heart attack. Mrs. Bradley died ten years ago from tuberculosis. Their son has been alone ever since...no siblings. He's always been studious; college was a matter of course—he got his law degree at Ohio State and came back here to open up a practice four years ago. The Bradleys are an old family in the area and people from Canton to Akron come to consult. He's good at what he does."

Marion examined her fingernails while she waited for more. It didn't come. "Is that all?"

Greta licked butter and crumbs from her fingers and jumped up. "Wow, that was a scream. I think I'll go for my walk now. You and Marion can keep talking about Mr. Serious-mind's life story."

Greta shipped off, and Marion pinioned Ellen with a glare— of course, the exasperating girl's back was turned again. "He's lived a dull, average life...or did you just make it out that way?"

"Most people live dull, average lives. Think of mine."

"Phonus balonus! You are not dull, Ellen. How could you be? You're my sister. The sister of a star in the making."

People other than her family would think her horribly arrogant...and they would be justified. She sounded arrogant— and it wasn't entirely a simple joke, though she hoped her family viewed it as such. It would never do to speak that way in front of anyone else. It was a habit she'd formed to shore up her confidence; no one else knew how insecure she felt at times. Admitting it made her dreams recede. But repeating her dreams aloud, even half-jestingly, somehow assured her they'd become the gorgeous castles they appeared to be from a distance.

No, she would not be living a dull, average life.

Marion twined her leg around the chair and slipped out and up without bumping the table. "I guess I'm all caught up on Mr. Serious-mind. He's appearing at six? I should get semi-ready, decide what I ought to wear and everything. How old do you think I should look tonight?"

"Why don't you borrow something of Greta's? That should really suit you, the way you've been acting," Ellen replied without missing a beat.

"Ha ha," Marion intoned. Some people thought Ellen funny-boneless, grave, and yes, even dull...but Marion knew better.

The evening arrived and proceeded to pass, noisy but tedious. Uncle Melvin joshed a lot with Calvin Bradley about work, town, and the nation, as was his default with other men; Aunt Jennie ensured the talk always returned to the Dashiells' sorry state of affairs while Mother tried to direct it elsewhere; and Mr. Bradley, Ellen, Marion, and Greta hung on for the ride.

Marion watched for signs of preference in either Ellen or Mr. Bradley, but there were none to be seen. Ellen was her polite, attentive self and Mr. Bradley was *his* polite, attentive self. *It'd never work. They're too alike. At least Everett needs her and admires her. Of course, you can never tell what those painfully correct and preoccupied types like Mr. Bradley are thinking. It might take him months—or years!—to realize the merit of what's right before his eyes. Ellen's not showing any emotion either. Of course, she hasn't showed any emotion with Everett yet. But I'm pretty certain she prefers him...she's worked with him for weeks and they're most definitely friends.*

The best part of the evening came in the parlor after supper when Uncle Melvin and Aunt Jennie begged Marion to play piano and sing.

"You liked that the other evening, didn't you, eh, old man?" Uncle Melvin clapped his hand to Mr. Bradley's shoulder. "Want to hear it again, I'd say."

"If Miss Marion is willing," he returned quickly.

Marion would have preferred a less eager response, but she was in the mood for musicality. "I'll sing, but I'm not touching that instrument. I'm," she hesitated, "not feeling up to it. It's easier for me to just sing."

"Whatever you're up for, dear," Aunt Jennie said. Her twinkling gaze danced between Marion and Mr. Bradley. "I'm sure Calvin appreciates anything you can give. You ought to have seen how enthralled he was the other night. Stars-in-his-eyes enthralled."

Marion froze at the edge of the sagging davenport, about to shove herself up. *Hold a minute. Surely she's not thinking Mr. Bradley and me...?* No, she was joking, and this time she must realize the joke had no basis in reality.

Marion sang a popular tune, then Greta piped up, "Can we *all* sing something, like a glee? That'd be fun!"

"I only know hymns, and old love songs from a century ago when I was young," Aunt Jennie said. "I'm game for those! Old love songs would be the cat's meow, don't you think, Calvin?"

"Hymns are the extent of my repertoire...well, hymns and songs that ain't fit for mixed company!" Uncle Melvin chuckled and winked.

"Hymns would be lovely!" Mother exclaimed. "Do agree, Marion, please. It's been so long since we've had any kind of sing-along."

Mother's plea was what did it for Marion, and though hymns weren't nearly as fun as the other songs waiting in the air, they made her feel cozy and nostalgic, and yearning for Dad. The Maddoxes were terrible singers, Mother, Ellen, and Greta were tolerable, but Mr. Bradley's mellow baritone harmonized like Dad's. Good for him; his talents weren't all tied up in the dead-serious things of life.

That would have made a fine finale, but the Maddoxes pressed Mr. Bradley to stay, so instead the evening dragged on. Marion hadn't gotten to relax with a book, radio, and a refreshing swallow of alone time all day—always a challenge to grab here—so her impatience climbed steadily during the last interminable hour.

They were talking about cooking.

"What did you have for supper last night, Calvin? Surely

more than a sandwich?" Aunt Jennie asked.

"I had stew."

"How many nights in a row have you had *that?*" Aunt Jennie pressed.

"I'll wager he concocted it on Sunday and has eaten it every night since," Uncle Melvin said. "What you need is a woman, Cal. At least a housekeeper, but it's time you got a permanent housekeeper, I'll say." He chuckled and slapped his hand down on his knee. "Get married, you know, Cal. Get married. It's time, don't you think? Best thing you could do."

Mr. Bradley nodded politely. "It will be the best thing, when I meet the right woman."

"Ah! Beautiful. That's the way to look at it." Aunt Jennie crossed her palms over her heart and fluttered her eyelashes. "And you'll meet her soon." She pointed at him. "Just don't hermit yourself up so much, and it will be easier. See? We've already helped you by introducing you to two eligible girls; though one *may* be taken." Her glittering eyes swung to indicate Ellen.

Marion panicked for her sister. Aunt Jennie's tongue needed to be jammed before she humiliated her, in front of her new boss, too! "Aunt, you're shameful. Feeding Mr. Bradley unfounded gossip?"

"It isn't unfounded gossip, and I merely thought I should warn him." Aunt Jennie winked at Ellen. "Perhaps you thought he'd think *you* were the one taken, hmm, Marion?"

"For all he needs to know, I *am* taken. We're both taken."

"She is right, Aunt; we aren't here to make matches. That's a thing of the past," Mother's voice broke in. It was about time. "Girls don't like being talked about like that. Especially my girls. They both have ideas of what they'd like to do without worrying about marriage just now."

"Nonsense! They're just playing coy, don't you think, Melvin?" Aunt Jennie planted her hands akimbo and sat forward. "Calvin, what do you think?"

"I think my opinion doesn't apply at the moment," Mr. Bradley said softly.

Marion suddenly lost patience. "It certainly does not. Your presence just might not, either." She crossed her arms and heaved herself backward into the davenport. She was done talking. Finished with it. Mr. Bradley was twenty-six years old and a dull lawyer! He considered her a silly child. How dare Aunt Jennie insinuate such a thing?

Talk was cumbersome for some time, at least for everyone but Aunt Jennie and Uncle Melvin. Marion sat silent about ten minutes. Mr. Bradley had long overstayed his welcome. Pressure or no pressure, if he really wanted to leave, he could have and should have. Her face was not silent, however; many statements her eyes stabbed with scorn and her mouth refused to laugh at; any questions directed her way she pretended not to hear.

Finally her brooding could take no more of the talky room. They'd seen her angry, and ten minutes was long enough to make her point. Waiting until Mr. Bradley was speaking, she announced she was going to bed and bade everyone a careless goodnight.

After several minutes of lying in bed trying to read, Marion felt her mood shifting. *I was insufferable, wasn't I.* Oh, well, did it really matter? *I bet it does. Ellen's going to be working for him, so he'll probably not forget what I do.* She'd gotten that alone time, but it was ruined by remorse. It wasn't too late…Mr. Bradley was just getting up to leave from the sound of it…but no. She would *not* go back downstairs. She wanted to impress on those people that *she* would not be imposed upon, even if others were amenable to being kept up late and humiliated.

She got the feeling she was being spoiled and juvenile and confirming just what Mr. Bradley believed her to be…and also plain wrong toward him. But she didn't want to turn introspective and condemnatory just now. Ellen would accomplish that for her if—no, when—she cornered her.

"So how was your first day?" Marion asked Ellen as she and Greta strolled into Calvin Bradley's law office late Friday afternoon. After coming home from school and finding nothing else to fill the idyllic early April day, they gallivanted back into Cardinal Bush with Sport to see Ellen.

"It went very well." Looking as prim and self-assured as if she had been there for years, Ellen sat behind a slender desk in the bare little front room, her hands folded atop the blotter. The room was a sort of foyer in the bungalow-style house that had been converted into the law office. "How was school?"

"Good! I got an A on my test." Greta skipped to the window for a glimpse onto the porch where she had tied up Sport.

"Wonderful. So was it as hard as you thought?"

Greta faced the room again, satisfied. "Nah, not a bit. I think I over-studied."

"I don't think there's such a thing as over-studying," Ellen cautioned. "Don't get cocky; the next test may be harder. They'll certainly be hard in high school." After glancing at the doorway to the inner office, she caught Marion's eye with solemn intensity. She beckoned Marion over with two crooks of a finger.

Marion stood before her desk, feeling like a student facing the principal. "What?"

"Are you going to apologize?" Ellen murmured.

Marion sighed. Ellen *and* Mother had rebuked her for Wednesday night and the worst of it was she knew she was wrong. "Does he even care? I sure didn't notice that he did on Wednesday," she whispered back, aware that Greta had sidled nearer.

"He casually mentioned he thought you must have been tired. I...took the liberty of apologizing for you. But something from you would be far better."

Marion sighed again. "Is he in there now?" She tipped her head left, toward the office. Ellen nodded. Marion took a step. "He's not busy?"

"Not too busy."

Marion patted her hair, straightened her back, strode to the doorway, and, looking in, softly tapped the frame.

Calvin Bradley was half-covered by a gargantuan desk to

Marion's right. It was literally the size of the Dashiells' dining table that they'd loaned somebody-or-other in Canton, but solid as a box, squatting without any feet on the edge of a dusty Oriental rug centered in the spacious room. Two Windsor chairs faced it. Bookshelves with curved-up shelves, looking like smirking mouths, lined the walls except where windows, on the far left, let in light and where a closed door stood opposite Marion. The books were faded, chunky specimens of the type that dissuaded one from opening them. The office must have been the house's former living room.

He glanced up at her knock and rose. "Hello," he said gently, though it seemed not from offense, but uncertainty. It cratered any resistance Marion had erected against him.

She stepped forward to the desk, well aware that there was a new buoyancy to her feet, and with a subdued concern she hoped reflected in her eyes, she began. "How are you? Well, I trust. Say, I don't like beating around the bush when there's something to be said. Do you mind? I was abominable Wednesday evening, and I have no reason for it other than I felt you were eating into my alone time. I'm one of those silly creative sorts that need time to themselves in order to make decent company." To be completely truthful, she'd need to add "in groups I think are tiresome" but she was not about to lay *all* her psychology before him. That'd take the rest of the day and the night and he'd still not understand her…and thus would perish any respect for her, if he possessed any at all.

He was about to speak, but she held up her hand. "Almost finished. I am sorry for how I acted. I was also taking my frustration with Aunt Jennie's insinuations," an inconvenient heat flared in her cheeks, "and extending it to you, which wasn't fair in the least. Do you think you can forgive and forget?"

"Of course," he said. "Your sincere apology means a great deal. I remember how long schooldays are."

With a little sigh Marion let her shoulders relax. Her face cooled. "I'm quite relieved." *He still thinks I'm childish, though.*

"I hope we can all be friends. Your sister…she's quite the employee. She helped me clean up the place today, and still had time to start on the secretarial work that has piled up."

"That's Ellen for you. Well, I don't want to take up any more of your time. I hope you have a pleasant rest of your day." Marion backed away with measured steps and a smile, careful not to let it become too bright so as to cheapen the moment. Too big of a smile spelled insincerity onstage and in life. "Until we meet again!"

"Good day." Mr. Bradley raised a hand in farewell and, still on his feet, watched her leave with that searching gaze of his. He used it on the other Dashiells, and probably on every new acquaintance or whoever elicited his interest, but she seemed to evoke it the oftenest. *I'm a puzzle to the uninitiated.*

Reentering the foyer area and closing her eyes, she rolled her shoulders and ran her fingers through her hair. *What a relief that turned out well.* She didn't care if some people tasted gall when they looked at her, but since Mr. Bradley was respected by the rest of her family, she was glad to have his good opinion.

Ellen gave her a smile of approval, then told her Greta had gotten antsy and was out with Sport. "Are you going home now?" she asked.

"May as well. It'll be getting colder quickly with the sun going down." Marion glared at Ellen and lowered her voice. "I might not have come today if I'd known what you'd have me do."

Ellen stared back at her gravely. "I'm sure you feel better about yourself. You ought to, at any rate."

"Sure I do, but that doesn't mean it wasn't hard. Eating humble pie is never appetizing." Marion turned to the front door.

"Dad always told me that you grow every time you admit you're wrong and really believe it," Ellen said. "Well, I'll be home by five thirty. Uncle Melvin will fetch me."

They said their "see you later's" and Marion left, a pang in her heart at the mention of Dad. It had been more than a day since he'd last visited her mind, and she hated herself for it. He ought to be in her mind at least as often as she saw him back in the days when everything was whole. She'd never thought about him as much as she should have, never appreciated him like she would have had she known he'd be taken away so soon. And here Ellen had to go coupling him and his wise, pithy sayings with that hunk of humble pie…it was a day for self-mortification and regret. And even though the westering sun was bright and nature was arousing new life to flush the landscape with color, Marion seemed to be wearing gray-tinted glasses. There really were a lot of things to be depressed about. Dad, school, Cardinal Bush, no theater, no friends, living with relatives, embarrassing oneself in front of holier-than-thou lawyers.

That wind was cold. If another freeze came, all the fragile life would be swept into oblivion.

Marion and Greta walked on the dead grass alongside Main Street, the sidewalk not yet beginning. Mr. Bradley's office was on Main Street several blocks past downtown, from the Maddoxes' side of things, where the houses on the outer rim started morphing into businesses.

The townspeople were friendly, greeting the girls as they passed; even those in cars waved. Greta warmly responded, but Marion was never ready when a greeting came, and always offered a return too late. She was usually like that, lost in her own thoughts.

What was it that Ellen had said, or rather Dad, about growing every time one apologized and meant it? How did that work? Wouldn't it be better just to do nothing wrong—wasn't that the real growing up? The question was how to get there.

Downtown, interesting tidbits filled the signs and storefronts, with people scurrying on foot, on bicycles, by car. Even Marion could acknowledge its intrigue. The cinema was the central and largest object. Opposite was a small square, the real center of town, where a statue of the founder tried to compete with the draw of movie land. What would she do without the cinema? It kept its film offerings fresh, changing them out at least twice a week.

A car horn honked beside them. Marion's eyes darted to the street as a rusty blue roadster glided away in the other direction.

The big lug.

"Was that honking at us?" Greta asked. "Who was it?"

"A boy from school."

"Ohhh? Somebody mooning over you?"

"He's a big lug. He's the only senior fella who doesn't already have a girl, so he thinks he and I are a pair. It took him a while to get enough guts to chase after me, and now he won't leave me alone."

"You're so pretty, though. I thought all the fellas would be mooning over you," Greta protested.

"Small-town fellas are loyal. Most of the couples have been paired off since grammar school." Her senior class was impenetrable; she responded in kind. She was a stuck-up outsider, and that was all right with her. Besides, a friendship wouldn't last long because she didn't plan to stick around to cultivate it.

And then all high school boys were immature, she'd realized lately. They were really just overgrown kids who wanted to look good, dodge responsibility, and have things their way. Their desires grew with their skeletons, but nothing actually changed.

"What's his name?" Greta asked.

"I'm not going to tell you. I'll not have you teasing me about him."

"Aw! But teasing is fun. Isn't it, Sport?"

"Sport has the smallest sense of humor in any dog I've ever met," Marion retorted. "Don't appeal to him if you're talking teasing."

The girls made it through the rest of town and finally out into the country, the longest part of their walk. But the most peaceful and, with spring luster coming on, the most enjoyable.

Boys. My future. Growing up. Acting...oh, how I want to act! "Come on, Greta!" she said aloud as Greta stooped yet again to pick a flower. "I'm cold."

"I want to ask Uncle Melvin or Aunt Jennie what this one is, too. I haven't seen it before; have you?"

"No. Let's go! Look how far ahead Sport is getting. He wants home."

Greta had unleashed the sleek, slender dog once town was behind them, and he hadn't stopped the three times Greta and Marion did to pick flowers. His white and mahogany fur rippled in the wind like a girl's hair and the curl at the end of his white tail bobbed back and forth as he trotted on. He *was* beautiful, and chic. Aristocratic. Imagine Uncle Melvin having a dog like that! Sport vanished beyond the trees as the road curved into them. Soon the trees on the right would give way to the field and the lane into the woods would appear on the left. The rumble of a car drifted from that direction, the first that would pass since they'd left town.

Brakes squealed. A strange, muffled *thump* sounded amidst the deafening screech. Then the growl of a car, a roar; and around the curve careened an unfamiliar, dark green coupe. The girls scurried off the road and watched its fast-disappearing tail.

"What happened?" Greta asked in the profound silence after it was gone. Suddenly the area beyond the curve, behind the trees, loomed large in Marion's mind. She and Greta gaped at each other in horror.

"Sport." Greta's wide brown eyes gazed at Marion. Then she turned and shot off, pelting down the pavement and shrieking, "Sport!"

ᔕ᥆᠊Chapter Nine᠊᥆ᔕ

"It might not be...!" Marion called, a fist of fear clenching her stomach. Oh, if that dog...that poor thing...how on earth was she to handle this? Had the car just driven on? Who would do such a thing—leave a poor hit dog lying in the road? Maybe they'd missed! Marion found herself running, her Oxfords bogging her feet to the road, holding her back so that the distance stretched unattainable.

Athletic Greta, acres ahead of her, disappeared around the curve, and Marion heard a gasp. A moment later she rounded, too.

The white and brown rug that was Sport lay on the right side of the road, Greta kneeling over him. "He's hit, he's hit," Greta sobbed.

Marion went to them, but before she could get a good look the grumble of another motor sounded in the distance, and she pivoted both ways in terror to see where it was coming from. "Greta, we need to get out of the—"

A black roadster sped toward them on the left side of the road. Good. Out of harm's way. Say! Maybe they could help—

The brakes squealed before she even raised her hand, and the machine rolled to a stop a few feet away. A man in a beige trench coat and fedora threw open the driver's door and jogged to them. "Heavens, what happened? Is it hit?"

"Yes!" Greta cried.

The man—a young man with a honeyed voice and regal profile—lifted his fedora, ran his hand over his bronze-blond hair, and replaced it. "Where can I take him for you? Is there a vet here? Do you live nearby?"

That man was gorgeous. Marion's stomach did a double flip and with the stress of everything she almost felt woozy. *Pull yourself together, you idiot!* "Greta, don't touch him!" she snapped the first order she could think of, though it didn't seem logical even to her. Logic was beyond her at this point.

"He's whimpering, he needs me! I think his leg is broken, and maybe his ribs. Oh, I should never have let him off the leash!" Greta's voice was wavering, battling tears; she didn't look at Marion behind her.

The man did. His eyes were green, his eyebrows low and solid, his side-parted hair slicked back to reveal a widow's peak. His face was oval but firm and strong at the jaw with a faint cleft in his chin. Why did he have to be gorgeous? Between the dog and him, she could never hope to reason.

"So some stinker hit your dog and just drove on? Lowdown!" The man punched his palm. "We need to get him to the vet, though I'm not sure you're supposed to move something in this condition, are you? Perhaps I should muzzle him?"

"We don't need to muzzle him, not if I'm here!" Greta exclaimed.

His complete focus on the situation brought Marion back to it. "I honestly don't know. I've never had to deal with anything of the sort before. We don't live far; less than a mile down that dirt road you just passed. His owners will know what to do."

"I'm his owner, Marion! At least, I'm responsible for him." Greta jolted with the force of her words as she stared down at Sport. "I should never have let him get that far ahead of us!"

"If I take him right to the vet, maybe moving him won't be so bad." The fellow shoved his hands in his pockets and gazed expectantly at Marion.

Marion's cheeks heated. *I hope it's not showing!* She wished she could put her cold hands to them. This nippy breeze wasn't helping her appearance. *Idiot! What about Sport?* "We've only lived here two weeks, so I don't know if there's a vet or not."

"There's one in Canton. Can't we take him there?" Greta twisted to face her, eyes still wide and horror-stricken.

"That's thirty miles away, Greta!" Her equanimity was really jumping ship now, panic taking its place. What to do, what to do? "There's got to be somebody nearby who knows how to take care of this. Even a doctor or nurse. Goodness, even Uncle Melvin might be able to do something! Let's just get him home." Mother was home, Aunt Jennie was home, maybe even Uncle Melvin. The first step seemed to be just getting herself out of being in charge.

"Okay, right. We'll load him and take him there, and we don't have to take him out again till we know what we're going to do." The man ran to the passenger side of his roadster and opened the door. "I've got a blanket to carry him with. I'll unfold the rumble seat and you two can ride there. Here, I'll open the top, too." He came with the blanket and knelt beside Greta, gingerly touching Sport's head. The dog whimpered but didn't even flinch. The leg he lay on top of jutted at a crazy angle, and a dark red circle formed beneath him.

"You'll get blood on your car..." Marion protested weakly. It was a flashy, shiny machine trimmed with mirror-like chromium. The seats must be new leather.

The man waved away the thought. "Not with the blanket down."

"Of course," Marion said with a delayed nod of comprehension. What a sweetheart.

With pounding heart, Marion helped the man and Greta move Sport onto the blanket. Blood...she had better not touch any blood...or get it on her favorite, blue coat... Each girl grasped a corner while the man took two. This close to him, Marion smelled his woodsy cologne.

Slowly, as if carrying a huge, hot pot of soup, they bore the wilted Sport to the car. The man tried to grin. "He's a big, muscular fella."

"He's swell. I adore him," Greta said, panting. "It's okay, Sport. It's okay."

Once they settled Sport in the front seat, Marion could breathe again. The man shut the door and swept to the back by the rumble seat. "May I assist you?" He helped them climb up and over. "Sorry it's such an unglamorous seat. I swear to you I don't usually make my passengers ride there." In another moment he was behind the wheel and starting the motor; he clipped a sharp U-turn, rushed down the road, and took a precarious left on the lane. They glided along, noticeably less jarred than when in the DeSoto or Uncle Melvin's Graham, and not two minutes later Marion remembered just in time to shout, "There's our driveway!" He made the turn smooth as water and they screeched to a halt in front of the house.

The embarrassing house. *Stop thinking about your image, Marion. You're a little fool.* "Here we are. Fiddlesticks; my uncle isn't home yet. Just a moment, I'll get my aunt or my mother." If only Ellen were here. Marion didn't trust even Uncle Melvin to forge his way through this crisis as painlessly as Ellen, unless he had the necessary medical knowledge, which she doubted.

"Oh my, *someone* got a ride home with a handsome stranger!" Aunt Jennie heaved out of her porch rocking chair, leaving it frolicking behind her. "Is that the Parrington boy? I mean nephew?"

Marion's face burned, and it was almost satisfying to rebuff, "Aunt Jennie! Sport is hurt. He was hit by a car!"

"What? Hit! Oh, Lord have mercy!" Aunt Jennie's smiling face collapsed into alarm as she puffed down the stairs. "If only Melvin were here! Gussie! Gussie!" She climbed back up and threw open the screen door. "Gussie! Come quick! It's Sport! Oh, I don't know what to do!"

There they were, a bunch of incompetent females and one indecisive but gloriously good-looking and attentive male. The women went back and forth about what to do, the young man's concerned gaze following the movements of the frantic discussion.

"I think you should take him to Mr. King." Mother's seemingly final verdict was the man on the other side of town who Aunt Jennie said was skilled with animals. "The more experienced, the better."

"The vet in Akron, though," Aunt Jennie wouldn't let one of her opinions drop, "he absolutely can do something!" Her other opinion was that they should wait for Uncle Melvin. "It's only twenty miles from here."

"Ma'am, my aunt uses the vet in Akron. She thinks he's first-rate. If you're not certain, I'll take him there. We can't afford to waste another minute." The young man was leaning his tall, lithe form against the passenger side door, drumming the top with his fingers. Oh, to know his name! If this argument would shut up...but even if it did, how on earth should Marion ask at a time like this?

"I wish my husband were here! He could go with you."

"One or two of you ladies would do the trick." The young man's eyes met Marion's. A thrill danced through her.

"I'll go," Marion found herself saying.

"Me, too!" Greta exclaimed quickly.

"It's too difficult for you, Greta," Marion retorted.

"I'm closer to Sport than you are." Greta had stopped crying, but her words trembled again.

"I'll go, girls," Mother said. Logically, she *should* go, as the most capable adult present, though no doubt she was wishing Ellen or Uncle Melvin were here; but Marion was irritated. Perhaps she was *trying* to prevent Marion from getting to know this young man. *Silly!* Marion chided herself. *You've just been silly this whole time. If that's her intention, she's only being proper and protective.* But that didn't curb her resentment.

Then Greta pleaded to go, and by the time Mother persuaded her to stay—which entailed impelling her into Aunt Jennie's arms to keep her from climbing into the rumble seat after Mother—Uncle Melvin rattled up.

"Another delay?" the young man groaned. He was just about to start his car.

Because Sport was his baby, Uncle Melvin made short work of the ladies' protracted decision. In five minutes he and the young man had sped away in the roadster with Sport, leaving four anxious, disconsolate women.

Eventually they headed for the porch. "Aunt Jennie," Marion said while Mother was comforting and cuddling Greta, "you know that young man? He's somebody's nephew around here?"

"I should have known you'd want to know." A pinch of Aunt Jennie's spice came back and she smiled as she hiked up the steps behind Marion. "I've only seen him once, but his aunt Bertha Parrington lives out Uniontown-way. If he's who I think he is. I've heard—" Marion held the screen door for her and she eyed Marion slyly—"I've heard he's some sort of actor. In the movies, even."

Marion's heart quickened, but she was reluctant to trust Aunt Jennie. She got stories wrong all the time. "Is that so?" Marion tried to sound nonchalant. "Well, it will be nice to find out. If he is an actor, he might have some tips for me. But what is his name?"

Aunt Jennie winked. "Truthfully, dear, I don't know his name. Wilkins sounds familiar, but I can't wager on it."

"He does seem nice. He seems quite the hero, actually," Mother remarked from behind them.

"Yeah, he really helped save Sport. At least, I hope he helps save him," Greta sniffled.

"In that humdinger of a car," Aunt Jennie added once inside, patting Marion's arm.

Oh, dear. Putting up with teasing was not going to be fun. *I need to keep it casual. Like Ellen. She almost has them convinced she's not sweet on Everett.*

"But that poor dog. Oh, Gussie, girls, you don't know how much that dog means to Melvin! Why, he's had him seven years, since he was a little pup. Oh, he was the cutest thing. He hunted with him sometimes. Oh, if that pup dies…"

That made Greta crumple again. Aunt Jennie was weepy. As Marion imagined that she could be riding in the open roadster with the man possibly named Wilkins, cold be disregarded, she was snappish to everyone. Only Mother was able to maintain any equilibrium—she even remembered to phone Mr. Bradley and ask him to bring Ellen home, in absence of Uncle Melvin's services.

When Ellen arrived she restored things to order with her infectious composure. "Really the only thing we can do right now is pray and carry on normally. I'm starved, aren't you? And Uncle Melvin will need supper if he doesn't eat out."

Marion would be superfluous in the kitchen, so she lounged

on her bed, tired from her long walk and trying to find interest in her new library book, *Scaramouche the Kingmaker*. It was another Rafael Sabatini, sequel to *Scaramouche*, her second favorite Sabatini. *Captain Blood* was her first. But the romantic Scaramouche, a flat, invisible figure formed of silent words on a page, was no match for a flesh-and-blood hero every bit as charming and dashing.

An actor, hmm? Lolling on her side, Marion stared toward the rectangle of light on the opposite wall, the last vestige of day to reach inside her window. *Wilkins? I've never heard of him, or seen him, but of course a big actor wouldn't come to Ohio. But still...an actor! A movie actor! He might be bigger than I know. He could tell me lots. This could be my big break. And oh, what a break! He's something.* Marion shivered, remembering her thrills blended with the cold-fingered wind as she stood outside with him. He had looked at her keenly, hadn't he? Especially when he'd suggested one or two of the ladies go with him?

The covers of *Scaramouche the Kingmaker* were slipping out of her grasp; she let them close and left the book resting on her pink patchwork coverlet. She nestled her bent arm under her head and settled into the pillow. If only she could talk to him again, without this poor, tragic business hanging around them like a dismal mist. She would have to be ready when he drove up with Uncle Melvin—and hopefully a mended Sport. Greta could help her stand sentinel. While everyone else was hovering over the dog, Wilkins would fall back to give them room and she could speak to him...start out by thanking him for rescuing Sport, laughingly ask his name and wonder if Uncle Melvin had told him hers, mention that her busybody aunt thought he was an actor, offer a demure insider's joke about the theater, answer his question that yes, she did act! Oh, she wasn't very good, but she loved it anyway. Loved the adventure of becoming someone else, the glamor and excitement and teamwork of producing a play; wondered if movie acting was as different as they said. She'd come across as sweet, sincere, but sharp.

Maybe he'd fall for her.

If he wasn't already on the ground at some other girl's feet.

Which, given his age and appearance, seemed very, very likely. That was the trouble—all the fellas who were already *men* were also already taken.

Maybe two hours later, in the middle of a supper starring chicken and dumplings, Greta's and Marion's attuned ears heard tires churning the dirt drive. With an identical cry they sprang from their chairs, covering a span of the faded rug in one leap. Greta was out the door first only because Marion suddenly realized she didn't want to appear childish or coarse by bursting outside in such a manner.

It was dark, of course, and the light from the doorway only reached so far, but Greta ran to the car anyway. The sky was clear, and the moon and stars shone cold and distant. Marion stepped off the porch, willing her eyes to adjust rapidly. A hulking black shadow rose from the back of the car.

"How is he?" Greta asked.

"He's still with us, darling, still with us…though I often had to wonder while the vet was working on him," Uncle Melvin replied, standing outside the passenger door. "He's cleaned up, his hip is set—it was fractured—and he's got a broken rib, but that'll mend if the old boy's careful. You'll help him be careful, won't you, Greta? He's just as inclined for action as his dear old master. He won't be able to walk for days; just lay by the fire or stove and be waited on. You'll be a good little nurse. And then he'll want to get up but he shouldn't, you know. The doc gave explicit instructions he wasn't to be allowed up for anything if we're to keep that hip in place."

Marion walked slowly toward the car as he spoke with his hand on Greta's shoulder. The driver's door of the car opened and shut.

"I take it you could use some help getting him inside?" came Wilkins's query.

Marion could make him out well enough now. Her breath caught as she saw him smile at her. At Uncle Melvin's affirmative, he circled to the passenger side and the two men cradled Sport's blanket-wrapped body between them. They proceeded as carefully as any hospital stretcher-bearers, Uncle

Melvin stooped to accommodate Wilkins's somewhat shorter height, until they deposited Sport by the kitchen stove on a nest Aunt Jennie threw together.

After watching Sport settle his head on a bunched-up portion of the blankets, Uncle Melvin clapped Wilkins on the back and seized his hand. "How can we ever thank you enough? You saved this chap's life, and that's no exaggeration."

"Thank you," Greta piped up, a little shyly for her. She was sitting cross-legged on the linoleum floor and stroking Sport's head.

"I think you've said it enough." Wilkins flashed a grin at all of them, but his eyes seemed to rest longest on Marion. He swept off his fedora. "Being properly introduced to everyone would be terrific, though. You told me so much about all the ladies, but I don't believe *they* know me from Adam."

Marion's heart palpitated; she was relishing this. The handsomest guy she'd ever seen, who might very well be an actor, standing in their pitifully unrefined kitchen and asking to be introduced to her. Pretentious and snobby could not be used to describe him.

"Haha, that's right!" Uncle Melvin sent a lopsided grin around the room. "Everyone, this is John Wilkins, or better known as Wilkie St. John. He's visiting his dear old aunt Bertha Parrington—"

"Ha! I was right!" Aunt Jennie crowed.

"For a little while. She's not up on her game health-wise, so he's cheering her up."

"Oh, the poor dear! What's the matter with her?" Aunt Jennie asked. "She must be quite old by now. She's your great-aunt, isn't she? She must be! Why, how old are you?"

Marion wished they would all just leave the room. There were more important things to discover, and less impertinent ways of going about it. Wilkie's *age* was significant, yes, but anyone could see he was young enough to be interesting. What she really needed to know was where he came from and if he acted.

"Oh? You know her?" Wilkie's tone bore the slightest hint

of offended reproach, but it was too subtle for Aunt Jennie to taste.

"Not too well, but I've heard enough about her from the gossip chain. Uniontown isn't *that* far from us. She's very wealthy, I know."

Wilkie laughed sarcastically. "The most important thing to know, huh? So yeah, she's my great-aunt, but she's an old dear. And yeah, she is wealthy, but she's got a good heart." As his glance flitted across Marion's face, his left eye seemed to blink more fully than his right. A wink?

The barrier restraining her words collapsed. "I know you don't want more thanks, but it was really swell of you to stop and use your valuable time to help us. You even ruined your blanket for the poor dog."

"Ah, blankets can be replaced; a dog girls cry over can't be." Wilkie waved his hand, though his smile showed he was pleased with her words.

"I'm Marion, by the way," she added, since no one else was introducing themselves as he'd requested.

If only they were alone, she could pepper him with questions, and they could wing some marvelous repartee. But her family was already gaping at the two of them as if they were movie characters about to kiss. They knew she was attracted to him—it was impossible for her to hide something like that: her eyes sparkled too much, she leaned too far forward, and she touched her hair and face too often. If it were only her mother and sisters she wouldn't mind. She hated concealing what she was passionate about. But Uncle Melvin and Aunt Jennie were another matter. How they acted could scare or repel Wilkie so much he'd dismiss her friendship. And then he would be gone—poof!—an angelic visitation, nothing more.

How could she prevent that?

Fortunately Mother spoke next. "I'm the mother of these girls, Augustine Dashiell, and the niece-in-law of the Maddoxes. I'm pleased to meet you. I haven't had my chance to fully thank you yet, but if there is anything we can do for you, we'd consider it the highest honor to do it. My youngest daughter would have been devastated if Sport had died." She was so strong and dignified, it was like Dad was in the room. "You must be dead-tired; have you had supper? Feeding you is the least we could do."

"No thanks; we ate in Akron. But you're a peach to offer."

"How about something sweet?" Aunt Jennie pressed. "I can whip up bread pudding in less time than it takes to say 'Jack Robinson.'"

"She's a queen of a cook, old boy," Uncle Melvin said.

"I don't doubt it, but you forget I have an aunt who's worried sick about me." Wilkie chuckled. "I phoned her from Akron and she begged me to come home as soon as I could. However, would you permit me to call on you tomorrow? I want to see how the pooch is coming along. You'll all be home, won't you?" He looked at Marion.

She nodded as Uncle Melvin, Aunt Jennie, and Mother chorused a tangled "Of course!"

"Come for lunch." Aunt Jennie beamed.

"I'm afraid I can't. And I can't stay long, either; perhaps that bread pudding would be ready for me at four in the afternoon?"

"Yes! It will be extra moist and rich and rummy, because it's your thank-you," Aunt Jennie said.

"Pile in extra currants or raisins or whatever it is you use, because this old boy wouldn't let me pay him for fuel," Uncle Melvin directed.

"Now I really need to scram, but first, I haven't had the pleasure of meeting you yet, sister." Wilkie looked earnestly at Ellen, content to be obscured by the others, standing against the dining room door. "He told me your name, sure, but to hear it from your own lips would be charming."

"Ellen," she answered with a half-smile and a placid sheen to her gaze. She donned that maddening mask whenever she met someone new so no one could tell what she really thought of them.

"Beautiful. You damsels have the names of princesses. Well,

I'm off. I don't know which was the greater pleasure, rescuing your pooch or meeting yourselves, but it was all a joy and I wish you the best. You, too, Sport. See ya, kid. Don't get down; he'll get better, you'll see."

Greta managed a bright smile.

They all trailed him to the door, Uncle Melvin and Marion at his heels. Aunt Jennie would have been there, too, if she hadn't ceded the space to Marion with a large, wise smile. If Uncle Melvin would stop just inside with everyone else, Marion could sashay out to Wilkie's car under the moonlight and give the young man one more word to leave an impression lasting until tomorrow.

Uncle Melvin's stride didn't slacken as they crossed the porch. Marion slowed, then halted and sighed. It wouldn't do to follow them. What would Wilkie think she was, a ravenous farm girl? So it was Uncle Melvin who accompanied him to the car, spouting pleasantries and wisecracks that reverberated into the singularly unromantic night. The moon was behind a cloud, making the blackness dull and bleak. *Silhouette*. What a pretty word, and a prettier picture. Maybe Wilkie would glance back and see her silhouetted in the gold rectangle of the doorway...

She waved as the roadster swooped away, seeing a knight on horseback and a grateful, rescued maiden fluttering a handkerchief. Ridiculous, but emblematic and powerful. He hadn't just saved Sport, or Greta; he'd rode into Marion's life in a swift, black set of wheels and destroyed her lethargy and depression, granting her hope, even if it was unfounded. Until tomorrow, then.

ᘓᘏᘓᐧ᳐Chapter Tenᐧᘏᘓᘏᐧ

MARION'S MOST JOYOUS DREAM OF THE NIGHT BEFORE CAME true Saturday afternoon when Wilkie singled her out for a talk. She had tried everything she could to catch a tête-à-tête, from waiting outside for him when he first arrived (Greta fouled that up by watching from the window and squealing his arrival to everyone in the house) to asking if he wanted to walk around the "grounds" (desperate, considering what inhabited the so-called grounds—the chickens). But all it took was Wilkie sitting beside her on the parlor davenport, resting his elbow on the back, rotating toward her, and asking a question that was blatantly hers and hers alone to answer. He ignored Uncle Melvin's and Aunt Jennie's attempts to distract him and simply went on talking with her for several minutes. It was glorious.

"So you act. High school, stock, amateur?" The pupils in his moss-green eyes quivered as he gazed at her face. "Movie?" He smiled. He had a wide mouth, and when he gave his small grin, the long corners quirked at the ends. Even that small smile was radiant with life and fun.

Here was her moment. "High school and amateur, but I'm hoping to get into stock. I *really* hope to work my way up or go to acting school, whichever happens first, so that—well, so I can make it as big as I can. I love acting and want to do it for the rest of my life."

"I knew there was something special about you." Wilkie nestled closer to the davenport. "Do you have any talent, or is it all ambition?" His mouth corners upturned again.

Marion grasped for words but couldn't find them. Finally she blurted, "It—it could be all ambition. But I feel that it comes naturally to me…it's like breathing. Playing a role is as real to me as my own life; maybe even more."

His smile split apart. Somehow it gave him the face of a little boy. "You're probably pretty good then. Better than me, definitely, because my life is more real to me than my roles."

Marion felt two spots of heat in her cheeks. Had she said the wrong thing? Was it normal and admirable to feel the way she did about acting? Was she misjudging her feelings? No; she knew her feelings, and they didn't lie. But…"You make me wonder if I really have any talent." She affected a giggle. "Maybe I've got it all wrong, and real actors divide their dual lives better than that."

"Nah; every actor's different. You've got it just right."

"So what pictures have you been in?" Marion asked. Wilkie had verified Aunt Jennie's rumor, but they hadn't dwelt on the subject long enough. He was a genuine Hollywood actor. Marion trembled with anticipation; every movie he'd made was another world he'd visited and helped bring to the laypeople who so desperately needed a break from their own. Hearing about them was like hearing the wonders a traveler had seen.

"I had a line in two." Wilkie rattled them off, then put on a Bronx accent. "Dat ain't bad, babe, when ya tink how new I am." He transferred to his normal voice. "I haven't been out there long—just two years, and they're making me work up the ranks. I've also played a manservant who didn't talk, and I was an extra in four others." He listed them, concluding with, "Have you seen any of 'em?" He searched her face eagerly.

"No." Marion pouted. "Not a one! How maddening."

Wilkie laughed at her expression, a musical chuckle that made her wish to be carried away on its waves. "Aw, too bad. Oh well, I'm in the sea of extras; there's no distinguishing me from all the other Joes."

"I hate that I haven't seen you in anything. Are you in something upcoming?"

"Well…don't let this get out—I don't want to be hounded around here—but yeah, I sure am: *Les Misérables*. It's premiering this month. After it was wrapped I cut loose to visit my great-aunt here. A long overdue visit, you might say."

Marion dropped her jaw. "*Les Misérables*! Heavens, you're in one of my favorite stories of all time! I can't wait to see it. Do you have lines?"

"Alas, no. But filming alongside so many stars, how could I complain? You'll have to watch close if you want to spot me; don't blink."

"I shall be looking for you as if I were in a ship's crow's nest looking for land." Hopefully she didn't sound foolish in trying to be funny. She had never felt so unsure of her remarks before. "Sorry, I've just been reading Rafael Sabatini. I like romantic things like that."

"So do I," Wilkie said, his eyes focusing on hers for a long second. Then they casually drifted away. "Say, did you know there's talk of a remake of *Captain Blood*? Warner Brothers will film it this summer."

"What! Hot dog! That's the best news I've heard in years! Who are they casting?"

"They're taking a chance on some no-name from Australia. We'll see how he does." Wilkie interlaced his fingers, his left arm still at rest on the davenport.

"Yeah—he better be good. He better be extraordinary, to do Captain Blood justice. I remember they made it a couple years after the novel came out, but I was too young to see it. I think it was about ten years ago. But to see it with sound! Now that's something grand." She snowballed Wilkie with a few more questions about the movie whose plot she already adored; about the stars mostly, because that comprised all he really knew. He answered with dancing eyes and half-smiling lips.

"Basil Rathbone. I saw him as Mr. Murdstone in *David Copperfield* earlier this year. He was quite the villain," Marion said.

"Would you like more bread pudding, Wilkie? How about more coffee?" Aunt Jennie interrupted.

Never before had Marion talked with anyone so on fire as her with love for the movies. They were the only two in the room; characters, plots, actors, and sets were the only things that existed, pulled from memories and experiences whose only purpose was to create this effervescent, all too brief dialogue.

And now it was broken by Aunt Jennie's useless question. The meddling biddy was a cow who couldn't stay out of the corn.

"I think, since he's been content this last half hour, you could have waited a few more minutes to ask," Marion said frigidly.

"Marion—" Mother began.

Aunt Jennie and Uncle Melvin started laughing. Aunt Jennie said, "Someone's touchy! Well, dear, it is rather rude to shut people out of conversation like that, and I don't like being shut out, rules of etiquette or no. Surely, Wilkie, that isn't *all* the pudding or coffee you wanted?"

"Indeed it is, believe it or not. Don't get me wrong; it was very good. But I don't want to spoil supper. My aunt likes me to stuff myself at her meals. She gets offended otherwise, so I can't afford to eat another bite or drink another drop."

"You're excused then." Aunt Jennie smiled indulgently; her smiles seemed a little silly when bestowed on Wilkie.

"Oh, am I? Good, because I need to leave." Wilkie poised to hop up from his seat. "Thank you, it's been a swell visit, getting to know you and all."

Marion frowned. He was leaving already! Her heart flamed in rebellion and frustration. "Do you have any idea how long you've been here? Not nearly long enough for a polite visit." She smiled teasingly, but her tone stressed her disapproval. Yet she couldn't really blame him; the parlor of a Midwestern farmhouse and its inhabitants were not grand prize winners in the fascination competition. They probably ranked one hundred out of a hundred, compared to those creative types in the top ten he was used to in California. It would have been different if they—Uncle Melvin and Aunt Jennie, that is—had been a willing audience; every actor valued an audience, on and off stage. But they'd hardly let him talk. Marion knew only that he was born near Akron and moved to Detroit when he was a boy, grew up there and in New York City, and achieved Hollywood two years ago. His age was still a mystery, as were all the consequential events of his life.

"Then I'll have to come again. If you can bear that." Wilkie stood and stretched his arms above his head, then fastidiously straightened his well-cut jacket. "Besides, I want to see how the pooch is getting along."

"He'll like that," Greta spoke up, leaning forward on the piano bench she'd pulled into the circular sitting area. Her brown eyes looked like a pleading puppy's. "Don't forget to stop and see him before you go."

Of the Midwestern farmhouse inhabitants, Ellen seemed the only one who wasn't smitten with Wilkie by the end of that visit (he probably had them smitten by the end of his *first* visit, in fact). Actors and movies never enthused her, so Marion supposed a live actor made no difference. Not that she understood the flat-minded old dear, but she could accept and forgive her. Especially since Ellen was the only one Marion would tolerate being in the same room with her and Wilkie, if by any chance she ever had her wish.

"Yes, please do come again," Marion said softly, rising with him. The others got up, too, drowning out anything she might have murmured next with their farewells and tail-end jokes. Wilkie went to the kitchen to gently rub up Sport's ears and long snout as they all followed and talked. Marion kept back in the dining room, her whole body giving in to a sulk as she leaned against the foyer doorway, not even setting foot near the kitchen. What was the use in meeting him, if she was only ever going to see him in this—this—*environment?*

They all trooped out again, past Marion and into the foyer, chattering and chuckling. She sidestepped along the wall farther into the dining room rather than be carried with them. Wilkie, last in line, took a big step backward and flattened himself against the wall beside her.

"Hello, wallflower," he said.

"Come to join me? Were you transplanted or something?" Marion returned.

"Somehow I don't think you're a real wallflower. Say, do you have a place you like to hang around in town?"

Marion's heartbeat quickened. He was really, genuinely desiring to see her again, not in this stuffy, crowded old pen, but alone? He was really that interested in her? "I don't, actually." How she wished she did. "I've been here so short a time I haven't found a good spot." An image flashed in her mind. "But I have seen a café on Main Street, downtown, that looks pretty swell…we could meet there, and if we don't like it, we can find someplace else." She blushed when she realized she had given away where she thought he was leading with his question. For shame! So eager and naïve. What if he hadn't meant he wanted to see her again?

But he smiled his beautiful smile. "That's swell. Monday, after you get out of school? What time would that be?"

"Three thirty. I can make it there by three thirty." Happiness swept over her like the wave of a lake; she felt completely lost in it.

"See you then." He smoothed the blond hair beyond one temple and turned to go.

"Yeah. See you then," she managed. Faintly, she realized after it was out.

Monday afternoon couldn't come quickly enough.

"You and he *must* talk about the acting business some more," Mother said to Marion as they washed dishes after supper that night. "He could tell you so much about what you'd be in for. I don't think Aunt Jennie or Uncle Melvin would object to having him over again, maybe for supper. That's all it would take, just a few hours one night to give you some advice."

"Mm. Yes, he could." Even though Mother was speaking of Wilkie, Marion found it hard to concentrate. Her mind already brimmed with thoughts and plans; added drops only spilled over unheeded. Did Mother say a few hours one night? *Hopefully I'll see a lot more of him than that.*

"It is so fortunate that he popped up out of the blue," Mother continued. "I'd been…praying for some direction for you, knowing how upset and listless you've been lately."

Mother had prayed for this? For someone like Wilkie to come into Marion's life? No; that wasn't what she said. It was for direction. But God might have answered that prayer with Wilkie. *Maybe my life truly is following a plan.*

"I worry about you, a Christian girl going off to Hollywood," Mother said quietly, dragging the dishcloth languidly over a sudsy white plate. Marion's attention snapped back to the room, to Mother. "I know how gifted you are, but one hears stories...and actors have always had this disreputability...I'll cut right to the chase—I don't know if you can withstand the temptations, Marion."

She felt as if Mother were speaking in a dream, her words unclear, her meaning slippery.

Mother finally looked at her straight on instead of in little stolen glances. "Aren't you going to say something?"

"I...don't know what to say." Suddenly she did. "I can't give it up, Mother. I can't." She fought impassioned panic. "What else do you expect me to say? I've wanted it for so long."

Mother looked down at her dishpan, her profile disclosing her trembling lip. "I know. But now that you're graduating, and you're so close to going away—"

"I don't have the money for it though."

"But you'll start working toward it. Before you know it, you'll be setting out. You'll be at school pursuing this thing and you'll feel there's no turning back."

"I already feel that there's no turning back."

Mother met and matched her gaze once more. "Maybe there are good things for you in Hollywood. Or professional theater. I'm not saying acting, or rather, acting as a profession, is wicked; if we thought that, we should most certainly have quenched your ambitions long ago. But there are more important things in life than acting. Things you ought to, you *must* clutch harder and closer than your dreams."

An ill, unnerving sensation roiled in Marion's stomach. She couldn't listen any longer. She whirled to leave, but Mother grabbed her wrist with an unfamiliar strength, perhaps born from the laundry she'd been conquering alongside Aunt Jennie. Marion was shocked enough to stop; Mother had never laid a hand on her before.

"Do you understand what I mean, Marion?" Mother's voice was strained.

"No, I don't!"

"Your faith. I mean your faith. Please don't go until we can talk about this rationally. Oh, how I wish Dad were here." Mother sounded near to tears, though her eyes weren't shimmering yet.

Mother was pretty heartbreaking, especially since she had invoked Dad. Marion hated grieving her...certainly she could be adult and stay to hear her out. She relaxed, and Mother liberated her wrist.

"I...I think I owe you an apology. I haven't been a very good example." The shimmer appeared in Mother's eyes. "Somehow I didn't train you up very well in...caring about what God desires and demands of us. He's our Father, you know, and our Friend, and it'd be a sorry sort of business to lay Him aside for anything, even one's dreams. Do you understand what I mean?"

"How would I be doing that by going into acting?" Playing difficult wasn't her aim anymore; she genuinely wanted an answer. Not that pleasing God was her driving force in life— she might as well be honest with herself—but she didn't want to purposefully offend Him.

"Giving in to temptations. Drinking, smoking, frivolity, playing unsavory characters, losing your belief in God, falling into im...immorality. You'd be putting yourself in danger. So many things could happen to you in a place like that."

"There are decent people there."

"But many who are not. It's them I worry about."

"I won't fall into the wrong crowd, Mother. I wouldn't feel comfortable with them."

"Resistance wears down over months and years."

Marion paused. "I don't see how it can when I'm determined not to. I'm a very determined girl."

"It's hard to explain how it can happen because it's such a subtle process," Mother said, absently folding the rag. "But it does happen all the time. People change to be like the people around them. They can't help it." She sighed, and her voice held a tremor. "I don't want it to happen to you. Dad wouldn't forgive himself, either."

Marion thought for a moment. Actors frequently got a bum rap, no mistake, but those she'd met were all decent, upstanding, and friendly. Wilkie was just such an example. All those scandals in New York and Hollywood couldn't be the rule—like all news, only the bad came to the surface. Gossip columnists would call it the cream. If one wanted to live decently in Hollywood, one could. How should it be different than anywhere else? She opened her mouth to spell out her reasoning but then Aunt Jennie swept in.

"You two are taking an awful long time cleaning up in here," she declared, holding open the swinging door and surveying them. "I'll help. I feel lazy and slave-driver-like enough as it is letting you do all the work."

"You were supposed to be relaxing in the parlor with your knitting." Though her back was turned to Mother as they both faced Aunt Jennie, Marion could hear the forced smile in Mother's tone.

Their discussion was over. A relief—yet not. Mother's badgering was stopped, but on the other hand Marion hadn't convinced her of anything. This conversation would happen again. And it would unfold no differently, unless she could get Wilkie on her side when it occurred. Mother seemed taken with Wilkie; she might listen to him. So—all Marion had to do was avoid being alone with Mother until Monday night, or, rather, alone with Mother and Ellen. Wherever serious discussions cropped up among the family, Ellen would be in the middle of them. Marion frowned as she resumed drying the dishes Mother handed her. Ellen would no doubt side with Mother, and then Marion and Wilkie would be hard pressed. Ellen or Wilkie…who would win an argument?

Marion stayed in the parlor with her book that night after the kitchen was tidied; if she went up to her room, Mother might follow. They were a cozy bunch, chattering as noisily as if it were a party. Hadn't Aunt and Uncle ever considered silence to be golden? She had to use all her powers of concentration to read *Scaramouche the Kingmaker*, but then Ellen said something about Mr. Bradley and Dad's case, and slowly she lowered her book to her lap.

"He was very interested in it and felt that the trial hadn't proceeded correctly." Ellen, too, had had a book, but now she'd switched to crocheting. Her hands moved expertly, tightly working together to make spider-webby white yarn twist on and off her hook. "He wanted me to ask you, Mother, if he could look into the case a bit more. Even though his experience is in property law, he's interested in all kinds, so he wants to learn about embezzlement through a real-life case. He said it should be okay with Dad's lawyer to discuss it if you give your approval."

"Is he really quite interested?" Aunt Jennie asked, looking at her husband with expressively tall eyebrows.

"Oh, ho, ho," Uncle Melvin chortled. "That means he's going to try and get involved and solve that case on his own. He never takes a simple academic interest in a thing; his time's too precious to him for that, and he cares about folks. I'll level with you: he must really fancy you gals to take up your case like this."

"I'll say. It's so sweet of him, isn't it?" Aunt Jennie rested her knitting needles. "And then I can't help but think it's some loyalty to his pop, too. Clarence—that's Calvin's father—would stop at nothing to help a friend, and goodness, were they friends, Clarence and your dad." She smiled and let out a blissful sigh. "He's such a noble young man."

"Sounds all conjecture to me," Marion sniffed. She had told herself she'd stay out of it, but calling Mr. Bradley "noble" for wanting to study a case was taking his merits too far.

"You've been touchy about him ever since Wednesday," Aunt Jennie accused in a playful tone. "You'd better watch out, because that touchiness is liable to make us believe you're in love. If it doesn't lead to love itself." She giggled.

"Well, of course I give my approval," Mother stepped in, finally. "I should love to have him look into it. Who knows?

Maybe he'll see something no one saw before. He is extremely astute. What do you think, Ellen?"

"I think it's a sound idea. Fresh, knowledgeable eyes on a case could help if we're looking for grounds to appeal," Ellen said.

"As if he needs another serious subject to occupy him." Though she smiled, Aunt Jennie shook her head and set her needles to work again. "I'm beginning to believe not even a sweetheart will slow him down."

"True, true. I agree. Poor thing will be alone all the time, and while away her days pining for him…or maybe she'd have an active life of her own, and then, well, how would they manage? Beats me. Perhaps they—"

"Hush, hush, Melvin!" Aunt Jennie nearly shouted. "That's enough out of you. I take back what I said. Calvin *will* settle down when he meets the right one—" she shot Marion a significant look—"and they *will* manage wonderfully. He's a wonderful man, and a good, hard worker, and his wife will never be in want."

Though she may be bored, Marion added silently. Perhaps she was being unjust, but in contrasting Wilkie and Calvin Bradley, she had realized exactly how much Mr. Bradley was wanting in the arena of charm, intrigue, and vivacity. A zest for life; that's what he lacked. She hoped for his—and his future wife's—sake he'd find it someday.

Maybe after Monday the Maddoxes wouldn't even tease her about him anymore! Now wouldn't that be the "cat's meow."

ᒲᘓᕈᕈ Chapter Eleven ᘓᕈᘓᕈ

"HIYA, BABE. HOW YA DOIN'? WHADDAYA WANT TA DRINK?"

Grinning, Wilkie sprang gracefully to his feet, his chair sliding back without a sound. He stepped in front of Marion and swept out the chair across the table from his, changing his accent to one of utmost gentility. "My dear."

Five minutes late—she'd underestimated the distance between school and Main Street Grill—but that was okay, because a lady should never be kept waiting. If she showed up first, she might appear overeager.

"Thank you. I guess having to play proper people in all those movies taught you manners?" Marion returned his grin as she sat.

"You could say that. But I have my Midwestern upbringing to thank for being *receptive* to the lessons." Wilkie pushed in her small, black metal seat. "So, what can I order for you? My treat."

Marion waved her hand vaguely. "Oh, I don't know. I'm not very hungry. What do they have? I've never been here, you know." She giggled, then stopped abruptly. A schoolgirl giggle! Inexcusable! What must he think of her? She got positively loony whenever she was around him, and that had to stop. She reined in her wits. If this was going to go anywhere, if she was to gain anything from this friendship, she had to mature, not the other way around. *It's like playing a grown woman. Make him see you as fully adult as you feel.*

"On second thought, I'd adore coffee. It's nippy out." Marion lightly rubbed her upper arms.

"Coffee at a fine restaurant, my, my, my." Wilkie shook his head even while he caught the eye of an incoming waitress. As he requested two coffees, he quirked a grin at Marion and

119

added, "Bring two doughnuts while you're at it, won't you, toots?"

"This restaurant is nicer than I expected," Marion remarked, perching her elbows and folding her hands on the shiny cream tabletop. The floor, cream-colored tile spotted with green diamonds, could almost be called fancy. "I'm used to larger places in Canton, you know. But this is darling, and a lot quieter." They were the only customers at the moment. Teenagers didn't come here...which was why Marion picked it. The last thing she needed in her high school world was well-founded gossip.

"So you prefer the big city to a country hamlet. Me, too." Wilkie propped his chin in his left hand and hunched over the table, gazing at her like she was the most fascinating phenomenon in the world. "More social whirl, more opportunities, more of the high life. More of *life*, I tell you."

"Certainly more opportunities. It's pleasant and quiet here, but I'm getting bored. I'd come here to escape, but certainly not to live," Marion agreed.

"You're right, I feel awfully rested here...almost restless, but not quite. Not yet. I can give it a little time. So do you have a chance to act here? Any theater to boast?"

"No. That's what makes it not so hot here."

Wilkie straightened like a pole and his green eyes shone with an electric light. Beautiful. "You can fix that, you know." His voice was nimble. "You know how? Start something, babe. Start your own theater or club or what have you. You can be director, lead actress, costumer, all rolled into one brown-eyed blonde." His gaze locked with hers, and together they raised the energy of the moment. "Tell you what, I'll help you. I'm gonna be here a few weeks yet, and you and I can start this together, and you can keep it going when I'm gone."

"Say, that's swell! I mean, I don't want to think of you as gone yet, but I adore your idea. But...well, how *shall* we find someone with talent? We can't open the floor to just anyone."

"Got any friends? We could start there."

Marion hesitated. "Nobody to speak of." Should she have

tried harder to make friends? Wilkie might have…

"Don't blame yourself. Small-town cliques are tough to break in to." Wilkie dismissed the folks and her qualms with a flick of his wrist. "So we start fresh. That may be best, actually, 'cause then you don't get on the bad side of all your friends when you tell them they can't act."

Marion chuckled. "I still want a drama club though. How can we make that happen without getting a bunch of terrible and angry actors?"

"We can't. That's how other amateur groups have to do it, to find the folks that really are good. And sometimes they have to take the good with the bad, if they don't have a big enough pool to draw from. I say we place an ad in the paper and see what we get—if we want, we can turn them all away, but there's bound to be somebody with something worthwhile."

"That's not fair. You get to leave after a few weeks while I have to stay."

"Then I'll make all the casting decisions—and hence all the enemies. Fair enough?"

"I'll be left with a huge responsibility if I want to keep it going."

"You can do it, kid. I can tell your dedication's going to carry you far. You may get out of here before they pelt you with rotten tomatoes."

"Oh, I hope so." Marion sighed. "You were joking, though. But I *do* hope to leave after I graduate. I love my family, but I *must* act. It's insatiable, and I'm going wild not doing it. I'm tired of just playing me and I want someone else's life—a new character to become. You know how it is? It's my food and drink, to make myself someone else. To help bring a whole different world to life. Even if it's helping with costumes and props."

"Yep. You've got it bad." Wilkie leaned away from the table as the waitress brought an aromatic tray of coffee and doughnuts.

Marion cupped cold hands around her thick, white mug and pulled her eyes away from the alluring ginger-brown doughnut.

Lunch and supper seemed miles away in either direction. "Tell me everything you did, Wilkie. How you got started, how you became professional, how you're living it now. I want to know everything."

"A quiz? I thought I skipped those by avoiding college." Wilkie took a sip of his coffee, but his eyes twinkled.

"No. It's an essay, a speech. While you speak, I'm going to eat my doughnut without worrying about talking with my mouth full."

Wilkie laughed, took a big bite of his fried piece of heaven, and chewed with his mouth open. Crumbs spilled out as he drawled, "Wellll darlin', I reckon ye're in fer the long haul."

Nibbling daintily at a broken-off chunk dipped in coffee, Marion just simpered at him.

Wilkie swallowed and patted his mouth with a napkin. "Now I suppose I ought to put on my serious professor face," he pulled down his eyebrows, looking akin to Mr. Veith, her math teacher, and his voice descended to a gruff decibel, "and tell you that each person's experience is different. This is true. But there are general principles," here he steepled his fingers, "that everyone must follow, and this is where I went wrong."

Marion choked back a giggle.

Wilkie resumed his normal tenor. "My grandmother was a chorus girl before she settled down and married my grandfather. That's where I got it. The bug. The bug that, when it bites, bites you right where it hurts and doesn't let go till you're dead." He illustrated by pretending to bite his doughnut. "Or at some such time; I exaggerate. She took me to plays and films before I was old enough to protect myself. She told me I could be an actor, so that was what I wanted from the time I was six right on up to when I was seven. That was when I wanted to be a policeman. That soon passed, however, and I wanted to be an explorer. Then a pilot—Lindbergh, you know. Then a politician. A millionaire. At last, in my freshman year of high school, I returned to acting, because then I could be them all—and more."

Marion was adoring this…adoring *him*.

"Our high school drama class wasn't much, even though it was New York, New York, but it was something. My grandmother coached me when she graced us with visits from Detroit. She died when I was seventeen, so she wasn't there to back me when I told my people I wanted to go to acting school." Wilkie assumed a stirring, dramatic cadence. "The papers sentencing me to four years of prison—my dad's alma mater—were drawn up; the money was collected and about to be paid to the jailers. 'We have enough,' Dad declared; it was true, even with the Depression we had enough. And then—salvation." Wilkie pressed his hands together in a prayer gesture and rolled his eyes to heaven. "Our bank failed, the money was gone, I was free. I hightailed it to the theater district and tried to find an acting school who'd take me as a charity case, but they slammed their doors in my face. I interviewed for roles; more slammed doors. I interviewed again, again, and again, and finally—" He took a deep breath and let it out with, "I was given a bit part in *The Stuarts*, at the Rose Theatre. My first paycheck. It was the making of me!"

Marion beamed and her hands fluttered with the motion of a butterfly in a burst of tiny applause.

"During a dry period when I was nigh unto dying of thirst, a mentor-friend of mine, Hugh Snodgrass, made the timely and genius suggestion that he and I ought to interview for a movie, being made right there in New York. Long story short, as soon as I realized I only had to act for a few minutes, and I was paid more for those few minutes than for months of stage work, and when I saw myself on the magical mirror, the silver screen—mostly for that moment of magic—I loved movies more. It was Hollywood or bust. I was eventually in enough shows to pay for my train ticket, and off I tramped, just under two years ago now."

"Wow. That's wonderful." Half of Marion's doughnut was left, and she nudged it around her plate. Here was her chance to speak; why was she nervous? *Because he's the first Hollywood actor I've spoken to. But that's a ridiculous reason.* She fixed her gaze on Wilkie and smiled. "For me, it's movies, too. I love the stage, never want to leave it completely, but I want to try movies. They're more magical because their sets look like the real thing on screen. More people see you, too, so you have a better chance of becoming a household name. Someone who lasts in the memory. That sounds vain, but really, it's a noble thing to aspire to. Immortality. But just doing what one loves is enough to make it worthwhile."

Wilkie nodded as he sipped his coffee. "The money is good, too, when you're earning it, and the company—they're screams, all of them. You never lack for fun. Doing what you love and living the perfect life along with it—what more could you ask?"

"Nothing!" Marion confirmed. "Say, tell me about the name Wilkie St. John. When did you come up with it?"

"Before my first audition for a play. 'John Wilkins'—that sounds like a doctor's name, or a professor or somebody's, and it's the most boring and forgettable name you'll ever come across."

"I don't know; John Smith is very boring but we don't forget *him*, the famous explorer. And then there's John Wilkes Booth. Now *that's* a pleasant association, and also unforgettable."

Wilkie shrugged and wagged his head. "Truth is, I don't like John Wilkins and never thought it fit, so when I set out to reinvent myself, I was highly original and turned my name upside down and made it catchier."

"Do folks remember your name now?"

"They do."

"Do you recommend a stage name for me?"

"Hmm. Marion Dashiell. It's quite a pretty name. Think it suits the persona you want to show?"

"I don't know. I haven't thought about it that way before. I only wanted a change because, like you, I feel like I'm reinventing myself."

"It sounds proper and pretty. French. Sweet. Likely to grow into a respectable old dame."

"You're good at this! Well, I guess that's a nice persona to have. I probably couldn't ask for more. Not greatness, like Lillian Gish or Mary Astor."

"And why not? You deserve it just as much as they. Keep Marion; I like that. It's classic and it grows. But tweak the Dashiell. Dash—that's strong, great. You need to keep it. But what do you have to hook it to?"

"My mother's maiden name is Westwood. How about Dashwood?"

"Marion Dashwood. Splendid! It sounds loveable. Is it just me, or does it have a familiar ring to it, as if it's been used before?"

"It's quite possible, given how many women are in this world." Marion grinned. "But it's perfect! It sounds romantic and strong and lead lady-ish. And it doesn't completely replace my past, because I love my family and don't want to sound as if I'm breaking with them. They'd be sensitive about that."

Wilkie raised his coffee mug. "To a new name and a new destiny!"

"To a new name and a new destiny!" Marion couldn't help a giggle as she clunked mugs with him, but hopefully she sounded at least somewhat wise and mature. Like she knew just what she was getting into.

They talked awhile after that, till Marion realized she ought to go. She felt well armed for whatever serious discussion she and Mother might have that night. Wilkie had assured her that though Hollywood was rough in places, if a girl was careful and hung with the right crowd, she and her virtue would be safe. Especially if she had a trusty man watching out for her.

"I'll drive you," Wilkie offered.

"Thanks! But drop me off at the junction? I don't want them jumping on you if you were to come to the house."

He agreed, and on the way they revisited the drama club idea. They decided to modify the plan and invite only people who seemed like a good fit with the two of them, and to make it a much smaller affair than Wilkie with his grand notions had originally imagined.

"Why, even just the two of us can get hold of a two-person play and have fun!" Marion said as they neared the lane where Wilkie would deposit her. She added to herself, *I'd prefer that.*

Aloud, "And the audience? The audience could be anybody and everybody, so long as it was somebody."

"Yeah. All you need for an audience is people, and we know *those*." Wilkie made a dramatic U-turn and parked in the lane broadside, stirring Marion's memory back to the day they'd met, when this black Ford DeLuxe roadster had shown its muscle carrying the injured Sport. Was it really only three days ago?

Wilkie hopped out and hurried to open the passenger door for her. "Well—I'll be seeing you around, I guess," he said as they stood facing each other, the roadster between them and the main road.

"Yes. Don't wait too long before dropping in. We must get our club going, if we're to do anything with it before you leave."

"Oh, I might be staying longer than I'd planned at first." Wilkie thrust his hands into his pants pockets and whistled tunelessly.

"Really?" Marion gasped. She was too pleased to care how elated she sounded.

Wilkie laughed. "Really. My great-aunt would want it, and since I've no pressing engagements in Hollywood, and I'm not spending any money, I might as well."

"Oh, that's wonderful! When shall we see each other again? I must know."

"I'll drop in when I have a free afternoon. Be patient." Wilkie smiled his big, handsome smile and walked around to the driver's side. "In the meantime, you have loads of work to do: make friends and convince them to come act with us. I'll find the play."

"I'll do my best!" For his sake, she would.

To her satisfaction Marion found no other talent for the drama club that first week, so she had Wilkie to herself. He visited twice, Wednesday and Friday, and then on Saturday Marion's family left them alone in the circular, top turret room so they could read a play—a four-person play called *Underhanded*.

Midway through, Wilkie suggested they get Ellen to make it easier on them, and Marion had to agree. The myriad lines were getting out of hand.

Ellen entered the dusty room, furnished with only an ancient couch, her face passive and accepting; but Marion could read *What am I getting myself into?* in her eyes.

"It's a lot of fun, but the characters interrupt each other so often and the lines are so interwoven that we're getting mixed up. Bedlam is fun to a point, but we *are* trying to be serious about this play," Marion explained, escorting Ellen to the couch. "Your character sits for most of it, so you sit yourself right down here."

"What is it about?" Ellen asked, accepting Marion's copy of the script.

"It's based off a dime novel, about a guy and girl who are trying to solve a mystery about a break-in into an old lady's mansion. You're the old lady, Mrs. Higginbotham," said Wilkie. "It was the smallest-cast play I could find among my great-aunt's collection. She has two copies of several playbooks for just such an occasion."

"She has everything, doesn't she?" Marion remarked. "You've mentioned books, art, cars, cats, birds, music, jewelry, antiques...is there anything she doesn't collect?"

"Friends. Relatives in good standing. She hated my grandmother, her sister-in-law, the former chorus girl. She loves me, and while I'm not entirely sure why, I'll bask in it while I can. I'm her heir, you know."

"You don't say! Well, you must stay in her good graces. She doesn't mind you acting?"

"Well..." he stretched out the word, "she's not overly fond of my choice of professions, however fond she is of me. It's little better than being a bum, in her opinion, and twice as sinful. But she has no children and doesn't like any other family member, so as long as she keeps liking *me*, I'm safe."

"How safe are you? What would you do that could alienate her?" Marion asked.

"Oh, I don't know. Commit a crime. Argue with her. Marry a

girl she's not keen on. Things like that."

"I guess using the roadster she lent you to transport a poor, bloody dog wasn't one of them." Marion smiled.

"Nah; but she did—*ahem*—'require an explanation.'" He threw his voice into a high pitch.

"Excuse me, but where are we in the play? Am I supposed to chime in somewhere?" Ellen asked, the corners of her mouth curving toward a half-smile as she opened her playbook.

Marion glided to stand beside Wilkie, opposite Ellen. "Oh yes! Ellen's time is limited. And she's nervous enough as it is without us drawing this out. Now then, act one, scene one." She tapped Wilkie's right shoulder and his arm snapped out, holding their book open in front of them.

"Now then." He cleared his throat and pretended to put on glasses. "Are you ready, my dear Mrs. Higginbotham and Judy?"

Acting against a skilled actor like Wilkie filled Marion with a sense of indescribable, passionate belief in the reality of the character she played. Even though Judy had cliché lines and actions, all felt real because they came from a real person, a girl who nursed an infatuation for Fred but wasn't sure if he returned it or just paid her attention out of generosity. The transformation from Marion to Judy was as refreshing as a bath, and as convincing as if she'd studied the part for months.

They made it through. Ellen left much to be desired in the way of acting, but at least her reading was precise and rhythmical.

"You're a swell addition," Wilkie told her. "Now all we need is one more person to make this really work." He furrowed an eyebrow at Marion. "If someone will do her recruitment job next week like she ought to and get one more person, preferably a fella, we'll have a good enough troupe to put on this show in earnest."

"Two more persons," Ellen hastened to say. "Don't count me. I'm just helping you for today."

"Is your kid sister any good?" Wilkie asked.

Marion shrugged. "She overacts. Maybe when she's older she'll have some skill, but not now. Say, how are Everett's acting skills? If we can get him to come next Saturday, you'll join us, won't you, Ellen?"

Ellen paused. "I don't think acting is his thing any more than it's mine."

"He might surprise us."

"Who is this Everett fellow?" Wilkie wondered.

Ellen answered composedly, "A family friend I used to work with in Canton."

"He took the place of the old accountant, the one who was fired for you know what," Marion added. On Friday she had spilled the sad story to Wilkie, since he'd earned her trust from the very first.

"If you haven't found anyone more promising, we'll give him a run-through. At least he'll be comfortable with you," Wilkie said. "Well, I'm afraid I ought to be off now. I'd love to act this out with you again, but my great-aunt will be wondering where I am. I pledged myself to be on hand for her bridge party tonight."

"Won't that be boring?" Marion clasped her hands. She wouldn't plead outright—that wouldn't be mature—but every word and gesture henceforth would be an entreaty for him not to leave so soon.

"Sure it will. But remember? I'm supposed to stay in her good graces." He winked.

"Wait, please. Do you see that window far up there?" Marion pointed to the small aperture just beneath the slope of the turret roof, a luminous, pearly white rectangle. "Are you tall enough to stand on the couch and look out of it?"

"I'm flattered you think me that tall, but I'm afraid I shall look like a midget beneath it, my dear girl," Wilkie replied in the character of Fred.

"Are you certain?"

"Very. Why are you so intrigued by that window? There's a perfectly good one facing the other way."

"But I want to see out of *that* one. I bet it looks over Cardinal Bush. I'm a sap for views, especially when they're hard to get to. I can't stand being kept from a view. In the attic at our house in Canton, there was a tall, tall window we couldn't look out of, and Dad never got around to making me stairs or a ladder to reach it."

"I didn't know you still cared about that," Ellen said.

"I started caring again once we were leaving. But oh well, that's in the past; it's this one I'd love to see out of now."

"Why don't you ask our uncle?"

"Are you kidding? He's not fit to climb these stairs, let alone rig up a ladder."

"I'll do it for you," Wilkie spoke up. "I'll get you that view."

"Truly? You're wonderful, Wilkie!" Marion felt the stars dancing in her eyes. "I think there must be a ladder here somewhere, and if we could just get it up the stairs...not today, of course, but perhaps next time?"

"How about when Everett comes? Another man will be just what the job calls for."

Down in the foyer at the bottom of the stairs, the three of them met Uncle Melvin and Aunt Jennie welcoming a guest— Calvin Bradley.

"Ah, there they are!" Aunt Jennie exclaimed. "I told you you'd see the girls sooner rather than later. How timely! Why Wilkie! Are you going already?"

"Calvin, old boy, have you met Wilkie St. John?" Uncle Melvin tugged Mr. Bradley forward by his arm and reached out for Wilkie's, as if he were introducing two dolls to one another. "Or should I say John Wilkins? Folks with two names ought to be ashamed of themselves for the muddle they put other folks in."

Mr. Bradley shook his head and said without smiling, "No, I have not had the pleasure." He put out his hand, but it looked as though he forced it forward.

This is odd. For goodness' sake, why should he be so cold? Marion wondered. Mr. Bradley wasn't outgoing, but she had never seen him stiff like this. She started. *He must not like Wilkie. He must be jealous of him! But why? It's not because of either Ellen or me, is it?* Boys got jealous over girls, she saw it all the time, but that was in high school—and the movies, to make the stories more interesting. But staid, old-before-his-time Mr. Bradley?

"Wilkie, this is Calvin Bradley, your rival," Uncle Melvin said, moving his hands to each man's nearest shoulder.

The gazes of Marion, Ellen, Wilkie, and Mr. Bradley rocketed to him in varying degrees of wide-eyed horror.

"Yes, you have a rival, Calvin." Aunt Jennie chuckled. "It will be a struggle, I'll say, because Mr. Wilkie here is an actor. A movie actor."

"I know of him," Mr. Bradley said, his voice flat.

"You do! Well, you *are* a lawyer, so you have your ways," Aunt Jennie responded. "You haven't seen him in a *movie*, have you?"

Wilkie appeared surprised, too, as he regarded Mr. Bradley with a cocked eyebrow and a slightly open mouth. "I have not had the pleasure of meeting *or* hearing of you. More's the pity, since you're a lawyer. Lawyers are swell people to know."

"Your people used to live around here, I understand, and you've been here for visits?" Mr. Bradley said.

"True! I guess you must've heard something of my escapades, then. Say, I'd love to stay and help you warm the air with some chatter, but I've got to scram. My great-aunt is expecting me." He snatched his coat from the rack without waiting for Aunt Jennie or Uncle Melvin, but snapped his fingers as soon as he had it on. "Oops! I forgot to check on the pooch. Where's the kid? Is she with him?"

"Her mother took her to a friend's house. She had hard work to convince her to leave without disturbing you up in your attic," Aunt Jennie replied with a smirk.

"I tell you, you have all these girls wrapped around your finger, Wilkie, old boy." Uncle Melvin slipped his long arm around Aunt Jennie's thick waist. "Go see Sport, because that's the first thing Greta will ask about when she gets back and finds you gone."

Marion trailed Wilkie to the kitchen where Sport reclined on his bed—still on strict bed rest. After patting and pep talking the dog, Wilkie turned to Marion.

"Have I told you often enough how superb your acting was?

Probably not, because I really can't say it enough."

"Aw, you're sweet." Marion waved a hand in dismissal, but she felt she would burst with joy. "You bring it out of me somehow. And you're not bad yourself." She smiled coyly.

"You'll get somewhere, babe. Don't give up, no matter what life does to you."

With someone like Wilkie to encourage her, how could she give up?

ᎯᏫᎤᏋ༄Chapter Twelve༄ᎤᏋᎯ

WHEN ELLEN TOLD AUNT JENNIE AND UNCLE MELVIN THAT Everett hoped to visit next Saturday, the two exchanged grins, then insisted Everett should come Friday evening for a dinner party and only leave when absolutely necessary on Sunday evening.

What Ellen wouldn't give for privacy! Everett was just a friend, after all, and this wild conjecture would repel him. She needed a friend...none of her high school girlfriends were coming forward; Frances only phoned once a week or so. She never thought she'd lose Marion's companionship, at least not yet. Even during their busiest times at home in Canton Marion flooded their leisure with chatter. But somehow Wilkie took up more of Marion's time than a whole acting troupe.

She worried about that, though Mother didn't seem to mind.

Ellen did have Mother. They talked more than ever about Dad, Marion, Greta, themselves; about the past, present, future; about plans, trivia, dreams. But they never went for an enjoyable outing together.

She was astonished at her yearning, as if starving for food, to go to the movies, to go bowling, to play volleyball, to hike in the woods, with a friend. She dared not admit, even to herself, how much she anticipated Everett's visit. She had never considered herself a people person before. *It's petty to feel this way; you're just bored. The trouble is you've caught up what Mr. Bradley and Aunt Jennie were behind in and now you've only a normal workload.*

To her surprise, Everett agreed to come Friday night until Saturday, but he needed to be in Canton on Sunday.

Before they hung up, Ellen said, "I think it's my duty to warn you that Marion has a new friend who's an actor, and they've cooked up something they may try to involve you in." She

133

shook her head and smirked as she pictured Marion and Wilkie interacting as their characters.

"Thanks for the warning. Is it something I'd want to get out of?"

"How are your acting skills?" Ellen asked.

"Oh. Not very good."

"Neither are mine. They may settle for your reading skills, though."

"I don't have those, either."

"Maybe they'll leave you alone then." *If she could get out of it, they'd be free to do something else, such as bowling. Though that may look like a date. However—not if we take Greta.* "They found a four-person play to dramatize, and they need two more actors, so pray they find them."

"Sure will."

The Maddoxes also invited Wilkie, Mr. Bradley, and Mrs. Cavendish and Violet, Greta's teacher and friend, for the Friday night supper. They'd all scrape elbows around the dining room table, and knowing her aunt and uncle, Everett would be seated next to her and Marion would be in between Wilkie and Mr. Bradley.

Lord, please don't let it be an embarrassing night. I've tried so hard to be circumspect, as has Everett, and he certainly doesn't deserve to be humiliated, Ellen prayed as she crowded place settings onto the table for the evening. The plates were mismatched china, so she had to arrange them carefully to still look pleasing.

Beyond the clanging and chatter in the kitchen, she heard an engine putt-putting in the driveway. Five o'clock. Folks wouldn't start arriving until six—Wilkie, however, could arrive any time. He probably never consulted a clock.

He had lifted Marion from her gloom, that was certain, and he genuinely seemed to like her. He was exceptionally nice, courteous to everyone, and, from his stories, seemed to behave even in Hollywood. Ellen couldn't label him with any serious faults. He wouldn't be around too much longer anyway, or so he said—though, two weeks ago, he was supposed to be leaving now. Sometime during the first week of their acquaintance that had changed. Now, he was leaving—when? He ignored dates like he ignored clocks.

Marion thought the world of him; whether Ellen and Mother should be wary was one of their many topics of conversation.

"Maybe Dad could have the heart to boot him out, but I don't. He is so friendly, and he's helping Marion so much! Try as I might, I can't find any harm in him," was Mother's conclusion.

Ellen herself had given Marion a caution every now and then, which Marion either laughed off or nodded at maturely. It was the mature nods that settled Ellen with enough peace to trust Marion. At the same time, she wished she could know Wilkie's mind. Did he realize how far Marion was falling for him?

The three house-vibrating knocks on the door with the bottom of his fist was Wilkie's characteristic knock. Ellen left her stack of place settings on the table to answer him. Marion scurried downstairs, not clothed in her good frock yet, but with her hair and makeup done.

She skidded to a stop in front of Ellen and Wilkie. "I'm glad you got here early! We can run through the play—right after I dress. Help Ellen until I come down again."

"Yes, ma'am!" Wilkie dipped his head with the motion of a horse, then looked to Ellen. "Your orders?"

Ellen shrugged as Marion trotted upstairs. "I'm setting the table, but you can come watch."

"And talk? But that's a given." Wilkie chuckled and followed her.

Ellen just shook her head with a grin he couldn't see. But actually, she could use this rare moment when they were alone to ask him some questions. Mother and Aunt Jennie were busy, Uncle Melvin wasn't home from the dental office yet, and Greta was off in the woods. But now that she had him, the questions she'd wanted to ask seemed rude at worst and pointless at best. If he wasn't being foolish at the moment, his goodwill and cheerful spirits always suppressed her uneasiness about his intentions. She could imagine Marion's whine if she found out Ellen had interrogated him.

Maybe if she took the course of asking about Hollywood?

Ellen slid the top plate off the stack and into place on the table. "Wilkie, please don't be alarmed if I seem like I'm prying. I'm Marion's sister and I just want to know, plainly, what she's in for if she pursues the acting business." She straightened the setting's silverware. "Do you know anyone like her in Hollywood? Would she be safe there? Would she...still be Marion, or would she change?" She looked up and across the table at Wilkie.

His eyes met hers. "She'd be all right. You have my word. A sweetheart like her doesn't spoil."

"Are you sure, though? She's more impressionable than she believes."

"I'm positive. That girl's principles are going nowhere. She'll find other good folks to help her."

Ellen nodded. Wilkie hadn't wavered when he answered. Could she trust him? One half of her wanted to cry yes, the other no. He had swept into their lives so quickly, yet he fit them all like a glove—gallant to Marion, endearing to Mother, heroic to Greta, gracious to Aunt Jennie, chipper to Uncle Melvin, brotherly to her. He hid nothing. Though Ellen didn't always approve of his gaiety of character, to be just, his only fault seemed to be flippancy.

Marion entered, lopping off any other queries Ellen might have made. She was ready in record time, arrayed in her best pale pink satin.

Wilkie turned to her with a laugh. "You look gorgeous. I haven't seen that dress before."

"It's a special occasion."

"I'll have to make more special occasions so you wear it more often."

Marion's face, as she would put it, was "all flowers and sunshine."

"Say, where are we all sitting? Is Mr. Sour-face still coming?"

"Who's Mr. Sour-face?" Ellen demanded. Flippant

impertinence, surfaced again.

"Oh, Ellen, it's just a nickname between the two of us." Marion cut Wilkie with a dagger-like look. "For Mr. Bradley. You're around him more often, of course, but as for us, we never see him smile. So he's Mr. Sour-face."

"Wilkie has only seen him twice, and you not much above that."

"But not to smile or chat happily in the course of a whole Sunday night dinner? When all around him were laughing people? That's a sour face."

"Poor fellow. Everyone speaks well of him, since he's a lawyer and all, but everyone forgets to speak *to* him," Wilkie added.

"That's what comes of being dull, I guess." Marion shook her head, sighing theatrically. "Well. Shall we go up and read the play?"

"Wait one minute. You aren't being fair." Ellen planted a hand on the back of a chair. "Mr. Bradley is—"

"Is kind and generous and good. I *know*. And he's your employer. Don't forget *that*, Wilkie." Marion giggled and clipped out of the room in a pink cloud, Wilkie at her heels.

Ellen glided to the doorway after them. "This discussion isn't over, Marion." *Dad's firm guidance would be welcome right about now...*

On Saturday, Everett did take Ellen—and, at Ellen's suggestion, Greta and Violet—to a larger, nearby town to go bowling. The spirit of lighthearted competition refreshed Ellen as much as she'd thought it would, and Everett was much more at ease away from the Maddoxes'.

After competing all together, Greta and Violet bowled their own game while Ellen and Everett sat at a table drinking Coca-Colas that he'd bought.

"Old folks like us need a tonic after so much exercise," Everett joked in response to her thank-you as he sat, eyes on his curvy brown glass.

Ellen chuckled. "Would you like to play another game after we're rejuvenated?"

Everett looked up and his slow, boyish smile emerged. "Yes."

Ellen took a sip and decided to jump right into a worthwhile conversation. They shouldn't let their paltry time together go to waste. "How are things at Friar's? I know you don't like to go into detail when Uncle Melvin asks, but I'm hungry for details."

Contemplating his drink, Everett bit his lip absently. "Uh… much the same. There aren't really any details to add." He glanced at her, calculations going on behind his green eyes.

"Aren't there?"

"Well…unless I ought to tell you about my, er, venture." His ears went pink.

Ellen raised her eyebrows at him, one corner of her mouth quirked up to smile. "Nothing illegal, I hope?" She was expecting him to laugh, but instead he flushed even more.

"No, no. It's…it's *anti*-illegal, rather." He took a deep breath. "You see, I've been closely watching Mr. Green. And…looking through his papers. It's suspicious. He just bought a yacht, and from what I know of Friar's finances, he shouldn't have the money to do that." Everett's last words mumbled as his chin dipped to his chest. "Mr. Bradley suspected him first, and suggested I keep an eye on him."

Ellen's gaze was stuck on Everett. She was silent for a minute. "I don't know if I understand. You mean he might be the real embezzler and framed my dad?"

"Yes."

"Mr. Bradley thought of that?"

Everett nodded, a sudden ashen cast crossing his face but leaving again.

"Wow. I suppose somebody did it, and it wasn't Dad." It made a lot of sense, really; among other facts, what Ellen knew of Mr. Green's character meant he was at least more capable than Dad of such a thing. This information might lead somewhere… "You have to be very careful when you snoop, don't you?" She half-smiled. "It's brave of you."

Everett looked up quickly with another blush. "It's nothing much." He shrugged, attempting nonchalance, but she could detect his surprised pleasure at her praise.

"It's probably best to not discuss this further, I guess," Ellen said. "Not here, at any rate. But thank you for what you're doing. I'm extremely grateful that you and Mr. Bradley are taking such interest in the case. Your support is a blessing."

"I wouldn't do anything less. And Mr. Bradley is really the one you should thank. He first suggested I dig around."

"But you risk discovery every time you 'dig around.' You're sort of a spy behind the battle lines." Ellen realized her hands were ice cold from squeezing her glass. She relaxed her hold and grinned. "I sound an awful lot like Frances. I don't read or watch much intrigue, I really don't."

"I know." Everett grinned back easily, a contrast to his previous rigidity.

They talked about lighter subjects for a while, then transitioned cautiously yet earnestly into spiritual matters after the Coca-Cola vanished from their glasses. What rich, unhurried, and meaningful conversation they could have, and this was no exception—Ellen had missed it even more than she'd thought.

The second game of bowling was forgotten until jolly, expectant Greta and Violet descended upon them, full of vivacity from the lanes. With exchanged smiles and no protests, Ellen and Everett rejoined the action. After all, playing could forge links in the chain of friendship just as strong.

The weeks passed quickly and amiably for Marion…and, it seemed, for Wilkie. Warm, vibrant spring arrived in earnest. With the passage of winter came the sense to Marion that she was no longer a displaced migrant, but a purposeful pioneer of a whole new life. She had Cardinal Bush instead of Canton, a rickety old farmhouse instead of a suburban palace, the Maddoxes instead of Dad, a four-person play instead of McKinley High's *Secrets* and all the Guild theater she could wish for, and Wilkie instead of goofy high school boys.

Only the last was better, but she could make do and find fulfillment because of it. Because of him.

She found Irma and Bill, juniors at school, for the other two parts in *Underhanded*: Mrs. Higginbotham and the butler, Walters, who turned out to be the crook who burglarized his employer. They were fun sidekicks, and because they were dating didn't complicate Marion and Wilkie's friendship.

One idyllic Saturday morning late in May, the whole crew— Marion and her family, Wilkie, Everett, and Mr. Bradley—were getting set for a day trip to Turkeyfoot Lake, a beautiful recreational park at the other end of a thirty-minute drive. She and Wilkie were on the couch in the turret room discussing the play and waiting for Everett's and Mr. Bradley's arrival, while the others were cleaning or cooking or otherwise being productive downstairs.

Wilkie fingered the collar of his diamond-patterned pullover. "Are you suffocating? Let's open a window."

"You have yet to put that ladder you promised me under the high window," Marion tossed out, adding a sly twist to her coy smile.

"Why, we ought to do it today!" Wilkie grabbed hold of the lower window's sash on the opposite wall. "We'll have the manpower." Grunting, he heaved up the reluctant old glass. "If you ask nicely, that is."

"Oh, please, Wilkie, I would be ever so indebted to you if you would lead your men in emplacing my ladder. You should be my hero."

"Sensational. All right, we'll do it. Just as soon as the others get here. And whaddyaknow? Here comes unsuspecting victim number one. Everett's an obliging fellow. He'll do it."

"I'm surprised Mr. Bradley isn't here yet," Marion said. "Well, perhaps I'm not—he's always early, unless he nails himself to his desk. Which is all the time. So he's actually never early."

"That doesn't make sense," Wilkie countered. "How do you know he'd be early if he's never been early before?"

"He has the personality for it: serious and exacting."

"Hmm, you got me there. I can't argue against logic!"

"Let's go down and get Everett." Marion started for the door, leveling a look over her shoulder at Wilkie. "You don't need anyone else to help, so no excuses!"

Below, everyone scurried around, readying things for the outing, except Ellen, who was loitering in the foyer with Everett. On the stairs, Marion's breath caught on a wisp of sentimentality because they looked so perfect together, Everett a few inches taller and broader and his hair a shade darker, and both their expressions tranquil yet happy. They were standing closer than she'd seen them stand before, though patently unconscious of it. She felt shameful for interrupting them, but when Uncle Melvin whooshed in from the dining room, her and Wilkie sweeping down was only a slightly bigger crash.

The foyer now noisy as the surf with greetings, it took everyone a moment to hear the phone ring. Ellen's secretary instincts sent her rushing to the kitchen to answer it.

She returned looking sober. Mother and Aunt Jennie trailed her, curiosity poised on their faces. "That was Mr. Bradley. He won't be joining us—"

"That is bad news," Aunt Jennie inserted.

"He won't be joining us right away, that is. There's some business he must attend to, and he expects to be on his way in an hour. He said to go ahead; he'll meet us at the lake."

"Calvin is always shorting his fun." Uncle Melvin dug his hands into his gray hair. "He needs to relax one of these days, or he'll run himself ill, poor fellow."

"Hear, hear! I'd go to his office, or wherever he is, and drag him bodily to the lake if I could catch him," Aunt Jennie declared. She and her husband bantered awhile over what they could do to "help" Mr. Bradley before she finally said, "Well, the food is almost packed. We'll be ready to go in a jiffy." She and Mother bustled off.

Marion and Wilkie slipped out to the porch to wait.

"Are we sure this isn't a big ruse of Mr. Sour-face to avoid fun?" Wilkie chuckled. "Though he doesn't seem like the inventive sort."

"That's for sure. It must be real," Marion said. "Though why whatever it is has to be done *today* may be his own invention."

"He must be all kinds of glad to get out of a pleasure trip," Wilkie said.

"He gets to do his dull duty; that's always a joy to him." Marion giggled. She respected Mr. Bradley most of the time, she really did, but it was so entertaining to poke at him because he was such a solemn person. Good thing Ellen was out of earshot; it nettled her worse than anything.

"Say, I have an idea to throw our own monkey wrench into the plans. But we'll have to be quick—no ladder moving today." Wilkie smirked with an enigmatic shift in his eyes. "Want to hear it?"

A few minutes later, amidst a lot of bustle, the group piled into two cars, Marion and Wilkie into Wilkie's roadster. Ellen thought she'd ride there, seeing as the Maddoxes' Graham would be crammed with baskets, a dog, and five other people. It was too bad to leave Everett alone in the crowd, but he was getting used to them, and accompanying Marion and Wilkie was only proper and prudent.

Vroommm! Just as Ellen straightened from loading a basket, Wilkie's engine sprung to life. She spun around but before she thought of shouting or holding up her arm, the black Ford was darting down the driveway. She stared after it.

"What's the matter, Ellen?" Mother asked, about to climb into the other side of the big car.

"Didn't they think to have someone ride with them?"

"I would desire an explanation from them as well!" Aunt Jennie exclaimed, posted outside her door. She puckered her lips. "Rude little lovebird darlings, very inconsiderate."

"Well...perhaps I shouldn't have, but she asked me so quickly..." Mother put her fingertip between her teeth. "And sweetly."

"What did she ask you?" Suspicion trickled into Ellen's

mind.

"If Wilkie could take her to his great-aunt's for the day. Apparently this was the only day they could go, so Wilkie suggested it out of the blue."

"Who'd want to miss a jaunt to Turkeyfoot Lake? They're off their nut!" Uncle Melvin said. "To a stuffy old lady's house? They should have their heads examined. Maybe I could do it under pretense of cleaning their teeth."

"I don't know what they were thinking." Mother spread her hands.

"Young people will do nonsense." Aunt Jennie beamed, shook her head, and fiddled with her hair bun. "Shall we be going? We're having a late enough start as it is. We don't want to miss any more of the day."

"I'm sure she'll be fine, Ellen," Mother said, more resolutely than Ellen believed her to be. "Wilkie has talked about taking her there, so today is as good as any."

"But why skip the lake? Marion has talked of it for days." Ellen felt other qualms, but with Everett behind her and the family right inside the car, she didn't want to mention them now. She couldn't help but think Dad would have said no. She'd speak to Mother later.

ᏕᏅᏬᏉ Chapter Thirteen ᏬᏉᏅᎶ

"OH, THAT HOUSE—IT WAS JUST WONDERFUL! TO THINK THAT someone in Ohio farm country could have a beautiful mansion!" Marion gushed the next morning. Uncle Melvin was not yet awake and Aunt Jennie was cooking in the kitchen, so only the Dashiells sat around the table with coffee or hot chocolate.

Marion had come home late. Mother and Ellen had been getting worried, but she laughed it off and assuaged their consternation ever so slightly with her fine mood.

"Telephone next time," was all Mother said.

Ellen wanted to be harsher, but she couldn't usurp Mother's role. Striving to stay completely respectful, she questioned Mother's response when they went to bed in their shared room, but Mother only said she'd talk to Marion further the next day.

Father God, You know I'm trying to do all I can within my bounds. You'll take care of the rest, won't You? In fact, it's all in Your hands, Ellen had prayed that night.

She also pondered Mr. Bradley's disappointment when he arrived at Turkeyfoot Lake and Marion wasn't there. She knew him well enough to see it—the way he scoped the group assembled by the water and asked where Marion was; the barely perceptible frown that draped his face when Ellen had explained.

Greta was eager for details from Marion in the morning. "Tell us more! And then I'll tell you all about Turkeyfoot Lake."

Marion regaled them with descriptions of Mrs. Parrington's house and grounds, Aunt Jennie shouting questions or remarks now and then from the kitchen. "It's a little out of date, but its bones are strong. Wilkie will know just what to do with it," Marion finished. "It has the most wonderful views from the upstairs bedrooms."

"So is he going to keep it or sell it? What about Hollywood?" This time Aunt Jennie popped her head past the door.

"Oh, he thinks he may keep it. He likes Ohio."

Ellen's heart skipped a beat as she took another sip of tea. Wilkie had never said anything admiring about Ohio before. Did his seeming change have something to do with Marion? She might as well ask herself straight out—was he genuinely in love with Marion? And thus wanting to keep a foothold in Ohio to please her and her family?

Marion was too young, Wilkie too unstable. True, she wanted what he had, and if she was to go off to Hollywood, it was best to do it with a husband and protector. But…Wilkie? Perhaps, if they were determined to marry, they could put it off a few years until Marion received more theater education… Ellen stopped. *What am I doing?* Speculating wildly, upsetting herself. This was the silent version of what Aunt Jennie did. Why was it that girls, no matter how sensible, always extrapolated a marriage out of a hint of romance?

Ellen started as Marion's mug clinked—she had set it firmly on the table. "Mother, may I stay home from church today?" she asked in a rush. "Wilkie wanted to take me to a service his church is having tonight, so we thought we might work on the play this morning instead. We know afternoon is set aside for the big dinner and family time."

While Ellen felt her spine go rigid, Mother stiffened entirely. "I don't think that's a good idea," Mother said. "Skipping church is not a small thing."

"But I'm going tonight."

"I don't know anything about Wilkie's church. What denomination is it? Is it a special service, or do they always have a night service? Why must you go tonight, and not this morning?"

Marion's tone rose in pitch, on the defensive. "It's a guest speaker, specially here to talk to youth. Wilkie thought I'd like it."

Mother relaxed a little, and she spoke in her normal, gentle way. "Oh? In that case, might Ellen and Greta wish to go, too?"

Marion hesitated. "It's...well, Ellen maybe, but Greta is too young."

"I am not! Why do you always say that?" Greta demanded.

"It's for older youth. Kids on the verge of bigger things besides high school."

"I can handle it anyway," Greta said.

"Well, Greta, Marion is right; it may be a message you wouldn't get much out of. But Ellen, shouldn't you like to go?"

Ellen hesitated. She usually did enjoy church speakers. "Perhaps I would." She glanced at Marion to judge her feelings.

"Oh, Ellen, must you?" she burst out, leaning forward. "It's not that I mind your company—it's just Wilkie and I so much like doing things just the two of us." She sighed. "I sound horribly selfish—who am I to forbid you from coming?—but...you understand, don't you?"

"Yes, I do," Ellen replied. She understood, but didn't like it. Marion was becoming far too attached to Wilkie. She was infatuated, and how were they to know where it would lead? If everything could simply be laid out in the open, Ellen would feel much better. But she couldn't force herself on Marion, not with the girl's state of mind.

"Thank you." Marion leaned back, relief rushing out in her voice. "So, may I go, Mother? And stay home this morning?"

"You may go, but...I don't think it's appropriate for you to be here all by yourself with Wilkie," Mother pronounced with some effort. "Have him come this afternoon, for dinner. You can be excused early from the table and rehearse then."

Marion's face fell, her gaze dropping to her mug, but she nodded eventually. "I'd better ring him, then—but you know, Mother, we're perfectly trustworthy. I don't see why I can't stay home!"

"Call him, Marion, and you can have the afternoon with him."

"Then he won't need to go away and come back," Ellen added.

"And we can *all* see him," Greta threw in.

Marion rolled her eyes, but went obediently to the phone in the kitchen.

Oddly enough, Wilkie did not come for dinner, claiming his great-aunt wanted him, but he came in the mid-afternoon. Aunt Jennie and Uncle Melvin were napping, so the house was subdued when he arrived. It matched his mood—he was strangely quiet. He and Marion went straight to their turret room.

That did not last long. Not ten minutes later, while Mother was dozing on the davenport in the parlor and Ellen was trying to stay awake over her book, footsteps hammered the stairs, softly in the turret, loudly on the main staircase, quickly and relentlessly. Mother gave a little snort as she awoke while Ellen set down her book and strode to the doorway.

Wilkie was hurrying down the last few steps.

"Wilkie? What's the matter?"

He landed, propelling across the foyer, only stopping to grab his hat. As he laid hold of it, he looked at Ellen, his face drawn in pain. "You'd better go to her."

"Marion? Why?"

Her voice seemed to soothe his flurry to be gone. He put his hat in the crook of his arm, hugging it to him, and faced her. Mother joined them as he explained, "It's a crying shame, but not a disaster. Only I can't convince Marion of that. See, I'm leaving for New York tomorrow, so I can't see you anymore for the time being. And because it's so sudden, I have to pack today and demolish all our carefully laid plans." He sighed and smiled sadly. "I've loved every minute I spent with your family. Make sure you remind Marion of that."

"Leaving? When will you be back?" Mother's mellow voice was nearly strident.

"That's just it; I don't know. My aunt's going, too. We're visiting family. She may just stay in New York awhile. And then I'll have to get back to Hollywood sooner or later. Believe me," he quieted, "if I could, I'd..." But whatever his claim may have been died before it lived. "Well, you understand, don't you? My aunt's a demanding person; if I could, I'd stay here."

"But must you really leave now? If you need a place to stay, I'm certain the Maddoxes would say you're more than welcome here," Mother said.

"Aw, you folks are swell. I've seldom been happier anywhere else, and that's the truth as if an angel would say it. I—" He looked up the stairs and seemed to forget what he was saying. "I can't stay. But thank you. I'd better go—I'm sorry. I feel awful scramming like this. I wish she hadn't cried. Would you say goodbye to your aunt and uncle and the kid? The pooch, too; he's the one who started all this. Though seeing your sister walk down the road might have been enough." A grin straggled out and he stepped forward to shake hands with Ellen and Mother. "I'll never forget your kindness."

"Come back someday," Mother said.

On a peculiar impulse as their hands met, Ellen nodded, adding, "We would love to see you again."

Wilkie grinned wider. "That means a lot coming from you." He spirited his hat to his head without the usual flourish and backed toward the door. "Goodbye." And then he was gone.

"How disappointing! How could he desert us so suddenly? Can't he stand up to his aunt's whims, or make his own decisions?" Mother cried. "I'd better go see Marion. I can only imagine the lather she's in, poor dear."

For the next couple of days, Marion was a shadow of herself. She went to school only because Mother and Ellen persuaded her to. She hardly spoke. Graduation might as well have been years away instead of weeks, considering the amount of interest she gave it. She read and slept in the turret room and complained of headaches.

She finally talked to Ellen on Wednesday when Ellen visited her quiet lair. Sunset filtered through the high window, spotlighting Marion reclined on the couch.

"I'm glad you're here," Marion murmured, arm thrown over her eyes. A book was propped open against her knees.

"I wasn't sure you would be," Ellen ventured.

Marion sat up, scooted over, and closed the book. "Sit."

Ellen sank into the depleted couch, noting that Marion had been reading *Captain Blood*. After a moment Marion said, "I'm glad I have you, Ellen. You and all the rest of the family." She sighed. "I just wish Dad were here."

"Well...we love you," Ellen said. She and Marion hadn't been this near each other since Marion had cried in her embrace when Wilkie left. Affection warmed Ellen's veins and she slipped her arms around her sister, pulling her closer. "If there's anything you want to talk about, Mother and I are here for you. I wish Dad were here, too."

She desperately wanted to ask if Marion and Wilkie had come to any sort of understanding or definition of their relationship, but then again, could Marion have confined such a thing to herself? And would asking her imply that Ellen didn't trust her? Now that Wilkie was gone, Ellen wanted to treat Marion with all the sensitivity she needed. And need it she did —so far she had been positively raw with this untreated wound, refusing any salves or bandages.

But Marion ought to talk. If the salve could come from her own hand...if she could surrender some of the pain... "Are you sure he didn't tell you when he's coming back?" Ellen asked.

"He was utterly vague. As far as I could tell, he's not coming back." Marion's voice was soft and caressing.

"Did he leave an address or telephone number?" Ellen had wondered this long before, but couldn't have asked until now.

"Yes. And he took ours. But he didn't promise to write to me." Her eyes drifted to the floor, a dirty wooden vacuity. "I'll write to him." After a moment Marion shifted to look at the window high above them. "Funny how he never managed to put that ladder up for me. Oh, well. He'll do it someday; or else, maybe it doesn't even matter. I saw a swell view from his great-aunt's house, and that was lovelier than this would be."

They sat in silence until they were called for supper, both thinking deeply but unwilling to open their mouths. Ellen was afraid to probe, and she assumed Marion still wished to hide the full extent of her thoughts. How unlike her.

Would she ever be her normal self? Had they seen the last of Wilkie? What exactly did Marion mean to him? Only God knew, and though she tried to trust His power, Ellen hated unknowns...fictional mysteries were well and good, but in one's own life they were a nuisance.

ᏋᎧ᷈ Chapter Fourteen ᏋᎧᎧᏮ

ELLEN AND MARION SETTLED INTO THE STIFF TRAIN SEATS after they could no longer wave goodbye to their family on the Cardinal Bush platform.

It was late June. Once Marion had graduated, she begged to return to Canton, and Mother hadn't the heart to say no. As for Ellen, returning was more of a duty than otherwise.

How had she agreed to this? It started with a conversation with Mr. Bradley at the office over a week ago. He'd asked, rather hesitantly, about Marion's plans after graduation.

Ellen had explained, "She's going to Canton to look for a job. But really she wants to go back to acting in the Players Guild. She hopes to get a scholarship or earn enough money for acting school. She'd love to go where there are scouts or professional auditions because she feels she's talented enough to be a professional now, but acting school would almost guarantee that."

They talked about how Ellen would miss her. "But when she's not acting, she's languishing. I don't want to see that, either," Ellen said.

Mr. Bradley nodded. "She's the type of person who must climb as far as she can possibly go." He spoke softly, as if even more thought than usual resided behind those words.

Ellen wasn't surprised. Marion meant something to him; she wished she knew what. A simple, brotherly soft spot? A reminiscence? Love? Perhaps all three. Even though he was stoical, he must be hurt by the way Marion treated him—civil, dismissive, flippant.

And then Mr. Bradley had done something that really did surprise Ellen: offer her a two-week vacation at half-pay if she wanted to accompany Marion. The only reason she finally consented was because he declared he himself needed a vacation. He wished to relax: visit a friend or two and lodge at an inexpensive lakeside hotel. Nature, particularly water, was his escape.

Even today, en route, she was still mildly dazed that she had such a thing as a vacation at half-pay. All the work, all the clients, were left to fend for themselves. It was a strange, never-before-tasted relief—tasting so strange it almost wasn't a relief.

She sighed quietly. Canton. So soon? The past trouble had seemed years old in Cardinal Bush, but Canton gusted it right to her memory's doorstep again. The heartaches it would rekindle...could she overlook them and move on? *If I could completely master my feelings, I could pass over anything that life throws me. Isn't there a Bible verse about that? 'Keep thy heart with all diligence'? If I don't let things affect me, then the hurt is already solved, even before it penetrates.*

Friends—dear ones, like Everett and Frances—awaited her there, and focusing on them ought to help drive off the bad memories. Ought to. And then, to see Marion happy...that was worth anything.

The palatial antique china cabinet confronted Ellen and Marion as Frances Lundberg welcomed them into her ground floor apartment, her open front door a handbreadth from nipping it. Recollection stole Marion's breath. A beloved piece of their home...she had forgotten it was here. In came swooshing images of home, and she was standing in their dining room, cocooned by the yellow wallpapered walls and white, green, and yellow floral rug. The rug had been a meadow in Marion's eyes, the walls sunlight shafts.

Ellen's and Frances's exclamations made the old world flee, and the memory of all that had happened between then—*home*—and this moment was with her again. Why did things have to change? It wasn't just change...it was deterioration.

Wilkie wasn't deterioration, but Wilkie *gone* was. She'd written him a letter about her temporary move, then left

Mother with exacting instructions to telegram her if he ever came and to have Uncle Melvin lock him in the turret room until she got back.

Now Marion had to somehow live without him—but only for a time. He'd be back as soon as he could, and she'd be more than ready. For now, acting with all her might was the one way to bear living. *Underhanded* was a beautiful dream because she had acted it with Wilkie, but with no Wilkie, she, Irma, and Bill had dropped it. Marion's friend Lillian, who had invited her back to Canton, had told her a summer stock company was coming, and every Cantonian with a spark of desire to act was aflame at the possibilities. They might be hiring, or someone from the company might see a rehearsal or show put on by the Players Guild.

If I'm chosen, Wilkie, I will find you again, or help you find me. I promise. Marion gazed into his eyes as if they were really before her. She felt listless, and she wasn't even sure she could rally enough to act with a Wilkie-sized hole in her ambition, but it was the only thing she knew to do.

Marion and Ellen were staying at Frances's, because of all their friends she had the most room. They spent the rest of that first Saturday afternoon settling in.

"I'm certainly glad there are oodles of friends wanting to see you," Frances told Ellen as the three of them sat on her pink sofa to rest and chat before they made supper. "Or else I don't have a clue as to how you'd occupy yourself. You'd probably go volunteer to clean someone's house or serve at the soup kitchen."

Ellen smiled. "Or I'd read. I haven't had much time for reading of late."

"What you ought to do is come haunt Friar—or rather, Mr. Green," Frances said. "It'd put some fear into his body. Either that, or give him someone else to be angry at. He's been angrier in the past few months than ever—because his one secretary can't accomplish everything, and he's having to do some of his own legwork."

"Oh, no, are you bearing the brunt of his irritation?" Ellen asked.

Frances chuckled and patted her hair. "It's a trial, but it keeps life exciting. I argue back at him, and I've won some ground—because he's doing some work on his own, you see, like opening and reading all his mail and composing his own memos. Say, I've been dying to ask—that fetching young lawyer, did you send him in? He asked some questions, said he was curious about the 'recent embezzlement scandal.'"

"Do you mean a tall young man with dark hair? That's Calvin Bradley," Ellen responded.

Marion scrunched her forehead. *Fetching young lawyer? Mr. Bradley? I guess I can see that from Frances's perspective.*

"We didn't exactly send him; he's interested in the suit because he thinks justice wasn't done," Ellen said.

"We really hit it off after I found out he's on your dad's side. He's your new boss, isn't he? Jeepers, you've got a swell one."

Marion couldn't help but chuckle, considering this was Mr. Bradley Frances was talking about, but it felt wry. Everything felt wry nowadays.

"Well, Marion, are you eating with us tonight? Your friend doesn't need you *immediately*?" Frances asked.

"No, she can wait until tomorrow. I said I'd call her if I could come, but I'm dead tired. I'll probably spend all day with her after church anyway, so I better rest up now."

"Dead tired? What'd you do today? Pack at the last minute?"

"As a matter of fact, yes." She hadn't felt motivated *at all* to do it, even though she was supposed to be dying to return to Canton. But instead it killed her to go.

"Before you left the first time, you were a top that couldn't stop spinning." Frances studied her. "As soon as you got to one spot, you'd be off to another."

She was getting nosy. Nosiness was unbecoming in a friend, even a very old one like Frances…besides, she wasn't so much Marion's friend as Ellen's. "Being tired will do that to you." Marion added a pinch of sharpness in her tone to ward the lady off.

"It will also put people out of sorts," Ellen said placidly.

Marion darted her a glare, but Ellen just raised her eyebrows brazenly.

"Now, now, I sure don't mean to criticize." Frances leaned across Ellen's lap to pat Marion's knee. "You're quite allowed to possess whatever level of jazz you wish."

"Thank you," Marion couldn't help but snap, but she shut up afterward so she couldn't offend again. *Things will be peachy from now on if Frances doesn't ask anything more. The definition of "peachy"? Being left alone.*

Even though Ellen was delighted to reconnect with Frances, the weekdays dragged, especially since her habit-dependent mind couldn't grasp why she had to stay behind when Frances was going off to Friar's.

After Saturday, Marion was hardly around. Everett came for dinner on Sunday; Bess Norbert took Ellen out on Monday; Ellen phoned Mother on Tuesday. Besides that, she cooked and cleaned while listening to radio shows she never knew existed, and heard about Marion's and Frances's affairs at each day's end. But she felt idle, even when hermited in Frances's apartment reading or doing handwork, two things she'd counted on to make her vacation satisfying.

Wednesday morning promised change—when Cousin Louis phoned. "How are you, Ellen?" His reedy voice was slicked with oil.

Ellen was instantly on her guard. "Fine, thank you. How are you?"

"I'm well, I'm well. Ida and I heard you were back in town, and we thought it really...really, er, propitious. We had just been thinking of you and wishing we could invite you for dinner sometime, but it'd be such a lengthy drive from...from where you live. But now that you're here, how should you and Marion like to come for dinner—oh, tonight, if you can manage it?"

"Thank you most kindly, Louis. But I'm afraid tonight is too short notice. I don't know what Marion is up to, and it'd be impolite to walk out on our hostess without more warning. Would Thursday, perhaps, be all right instead?"

"Perhaps. Let me ask Ida." Ellen found herself listening to silence for a full minute before his voice returned. "No, I'm afraid that wouldn't do. It's tonight or nothing." He sounded abrupt, as if giving a deathly serious ultimatum.

Ida-infused dialogue. That's more like it. Ellen sighed internally. "I'll try to phone Marion and Miss Lundberg and see what I can arrange."

She got a hold of them, and, though they protested, gained their consent. Before long, that evening had been promised to the Westwoods.

"You'll be happy you came," Louis said during their second conversation. "Ida's youngest sister will be here, and you're sure to get along famously." Once again, he spoke with confidence —no doubt Ida was in the room.

As the sisters rode the bus that evening, Ellen's thoughts returned for the umpteenth time to Ida's sister. It was evidently important to the Westwoods that she and the Dashiells meet. Ellen fought to withhold judgment, but she was dubious. Every member of the Bingham family she'd met—Mr. and Mrs. Bingham, two of their sons, Ida herself, and another of their daughters—had a proud, intolerant air, and the personality of the youngest, only twenty years old or so, might be even worse.

Meet her with an open, generous mind, else you'll be cold from the beginning, and that's no way to treat anyone, Ellen admonished herself. She hoped Marion would behave.

Several blocks from the bus stop, the lavish house loomed over them as if to intimidate them. An arch ushered them into a covered walkway to the front door.

"I don't think you and I have ever been here by ourselves before," Marion remarked. "It's a thrilling place, don't you think?"

"Not particularly," Ellen answered. "Unless you mean thrills of the cringing variety."

Marion chuckled. "I'm glad to see *it* once more. The people, though? Hardly."

Louis acted as his own doorkeeper this time; the housekeeper and maid must be busy with the kitchen. "Hello," he managed with a forcedly bright smile. "How are you?"

"Very well," replied Ellen, walking into the dim, spacious foyer. June made the outdoors shine even at this hour. "It's a fine thing to see Ridgewood in early summer. The trees and grass are lushly green and there are so many blooms out." She surprised herself with her own congeniality; she hadn't been sure she could muster it.

Louis relaxed slightly at her words. "Yes. Well, Ida and Leona are in the parlor. We were afraid you'd be late. I understand dinner is nearly ready."

"Ellen and Marion! You're late; you must have forgotten where our house is," Ida tsk-tsked from her perch on the floral davenport as the three of them entered. Her deep voice attempted playfulness.

They were *not* late—but Ellen dismissed what was probably just Ida's version of a joke.

In front of the other davenport stood a petite, pretty young woman with fair skin, hazel eyes, and natural, brunette curls springing from a widow's peak. She wore a fashionable mint-green dress and white shoes, and her hands, chest-high, squeezed each other in her eagerness. "Ida, introduce me, why don't ya?" Her tone was excitable and high-pitched.

"I was getting to that," Ida snapped. "You don't have to stand, you know; you're not a man or an inferior."

"I don't care. Just introduce me." The girl took one dainty step forward.

Ida rolled her eyes. "This is Ellen, the older of the two, and this is Marion. Girls, this is my youngest sister, Leona Bingham. She's fresh from graduating college and finds herself in want of companionship. You're close in age, if nothing else, so we thought you'd do."

Ellen's thoughts abruptly braked. Was *that* Ida's purpose for the whole occasion—to find her little sister companions? But why them? Didn't college girls have plenty of friends? Unless there was some ulterior motive to coupling the girls, the

Binghams must be desperate to resort to Ellen and Marion.

"Um, should they sit down, Ida, or is dinner almost served?" Louis asked.

"They can sit; Mrs. Foss will fetch us when it's served, and it's nothing to hop back up again," Ida replied, snuggling further into her arm of the davenport.

Leona sat and patted the wild floral cushion beside her. "I'm awfully glad to make your acquaintance," she said.

"As are we to make yours." Ellen half-smiled as, with a glance at Marion, she took the proffered seat. Marion joined her while Louis dropped into what Ellen assumed was his favorite wingchair. He picked up his pipe from the table beside him, but Ida frowned at him.

"You're better off waiting till after dinner," she said. Louis grimaced but put it down again and began to tap his knees.

Is he always this nervous, or is it just with us? Ellen wondered. He had been nervous on the phone, nervous during her last visit...

"Ellen, Ida tells me you didn't go to college, but you took the vocational course at McKinley and became a secretary. But then you lost your job and moved—do you have another job where you live now?" Leona asked, her tone quieter but still chirpy.

"I do, as a matter of fact," Ellen replied. Louis and Ida looked startled for an instant. "I'm a secretary for a lawyer right in Cardinal Bush."

"How were you able to come to Canton, then?" Ida asked.

"He gave me two weeks' vacation while he took one himself."

"Nice boss," remarked Louis.

"And Marion, how do you keep yourself occupied?" Leona continued. "Are you a student?"

"I just graduated high school," Marion said. She hesitated. "I'm visiting friends in Canton, perhaps all summer."

"Do you have plans for the future?"

"Yes, of course." Marion sat straighter. "I'm an actress, and I plan to do so professionally."

Leona raised her brows, but her hazel eyes did not glint with admiration. "Why, isn't that fine. Actresses are so popular these days!"

Marion remained silent, doubtless detecting the undercurrent of incredulity in Leona's voice.

"I do adore a good picture, and a play. The drama club put on great plays at Western—Western College for Women, where I attended, you know. My high school had a lot of talented girls, too. That was in Columbus—I didn't attend high school *here*, you know. Have you been in many plays?"

Leona questioned Marion, who gave unwilling answers, for another few minutes. Ellen popped in here and there to smooth over Marion's part of the conversation, but Louis and Ida did not deign to participate, as if they were parents supervising their children's playtime. By the time dinner was served, Leona seemed to have realized Ellen was the more promising conversationalist, and the two of them chatted affably, if superficially, over the elaborate and satisfying meal. Ida and Louis talked between themselves and Marion made silence her companion. Either Marion was in one of her moods or something about Leona had repelled her, but she spoke only if spoken to, though mercifully she looked attentive.

Over dishes of cherry cobbler and whipped cream—or, as Ida and Leona called it, crème Chantilly—Leona said, "I adore dessert, don't you? It reminds me of fashion. I adore fashion. Clothing and things can be such confections if you whip them up right!" She eyed Ellen's and Marion's outfits for the dozenth time. "Of course, it's rather tough in these times to dress well, but one does what one can. I pride myself on dressing well with limited funds."

Ellen didn't risk looking at Marion, though she felt the sting for her. Fashion was eminently important to Marion. Her frock tonight, cream with colorful flowers, was tasteful and nothing to be disdained; she had even updated it by adding seams to the midriff. It wasn't her fault she *truly* had no money to help her wardrobe.

Ida made a rare breech into the conversation. "Limited funds? Leona, don't make yourself an idiot. Father gives you plenty of money."

"But Ida, everyone's funds are limited nowadays," Leona whined, "compared to what they were. That's what I meant."

Ida pinioned her with a glare; Leona looked to her dessert. "If that's really what you meant, be more careful with your words. In fact, your mouth would be better off if the word 'money' and any of its synonyms never came out of it. It isn't ladylike, unless you really know how to use them."

Leona raised her eyes to Ellen's across the table, her look a mixture of pitiful and exasperated. It was actually a practiced look; she must be used to Ida's harangues. Though she had been rude about the Dashiells' appearance—unless it was a blunder—anyone who was Ida's victim deserved sympathy, so Ellen conveyed it in her return glance.

After a moment Ellen asked, "Do you like sports, Leona?"

"Oh yes, I do enjoy a few. Tennis, mainly, though I'm not very good." She giggled. "Do swimming and bowling count? I like those. And I love watching a football or basketball game, if I know the boys on the teams. I went to plenty near Western at Miami University and it was such fun. Do you like sports?" By now Leona had gotten into the habit of only looking to Ellen for response.

"Yes, quite a bit. In high school I was very active. I'm only ever able to go bowling now, however."

"We must remedy that!" Leona exclaimed. "Why, I would adore playing tennis with you or swimming somewhere together. I needed a chum, and now I've found one."

"So all they wanted was to snag you for their baby sister?" Frances demanded when she, Ellen, and Marion talked that night back in her living room. "They're vultures; they don't treat you like people. How could they even be related to you? You're some of the most decent folks I know."

"Well, you know the difficulties Mother had with her father and brother. I'm not sure what made Mother so sweet and them so...hard," Ellen replied. "But I don't think our cousin had much to do with the Leona affair. In fact, I think he was somewhat embarrassed about it. He seems embarrassed whenever he has to deal with us."

"He'd probably rather we didn't exist. Then his conscience would never bother him," Marion inserted.

"Marion," Ellen warned. But she might very well be correct.

"So this Leona will be keeping you busy, won't she." Frances poured herself more tea from the teapot on her end table. She had a cup or two every night while she read Agatha Christie or other British detective novels. "Or at least you, Ellen." She grinned at Marion.

"Yes, I'm glad I frightened her off," Marion said. "Besides being a ninny, she's someone I don't have time for. She doesn't even believe I can act. What would induce someone to doubt another's ability like that? Jealousy? Inexplicable dislike?"

"It may be jealousy. Or maybe she knew girls who dreamed of being actresses, and nothing ever came of it, so she doesn't take the dream seriously," Ellen suggested.

"That's no excuse."

"No, but you still can't blame her; she hasn't seen you act. She'll think differently once she does. I'll make sure to invite her to something."

"Don't trouble yourself."

"Has she gotten you committed to doing anything with her, Ellen?" Frances asked.

"Yes, actually. Tomorrow. She isn't wasting time, knowing I have only a week and a half. She'll be driving me to Brookside out at Meyers Lake and we'll play tennis. She'll lend me an old sports dress of her sister Jackie's. We'll go to lunch afterward."

"Well, I'm glad you'll be busy. Just don't dare go out for supper again. Evenings are *mine*. Do I need to reiterate that? Better yet, jot that down in shorthand and put it in your mirror. Oh, and have her drop you off at Friar's, why don't you? Mr. Green will be out tomorrow and I want you to see the place and say hello to everyone. We've missed you awfully."

"I don't think I want her to do that...Mr. Green knows her father, and if she tells her father, Mr. Green will—"

"What on earth could he do to you now? Not a thing. He wouldn't dare come after you here."

"It's you and the others I'm worried about."

"Don't be. We'll pretend we didn't know you were coming, which will be the case for everyone except me."

"Don't lie about it, Frances."

"Who said anything about lying? Don't worry. You're perfectly safe coming, and it won't even be uncomfortable since Mr. Green's not there."

"Do go, Ellen. It'll be good for you to see your crowd again, and think about how much more peaceful, if boring, you have it now," Marion said. "Everett would love it."

That turned the heat on in Ellen's cheeks; did it show? She didn't trust herself to contradict Marion. She'd probably sound foolish and get teased.

For some reason—perhaps because she had more leisure and had seen him in so many different situations—lately Everett had been entering oftener and staying longer in her mind. They hadn't made definite plans to see one another after Sunday, and she felt anxious to see him soon. They were in the same town, after all; distance couldn't come between their friendship now.

"Tomorrow won't be much of a vacation day, then." Ellen chuckled. "I'll be busy morning, noon, and night."

"You wouldn't like it otherwise," Frances said.

ᕼᕼᕼ Chapter Fifteen ᕼᕼᕼ

"It's a beautiful day, isn't it?" Leona asked as Ellen climbed into the dark-blue roadster in front of the house containing Frances's apartment. The neighborhood was an old one, near the roughened middle of town, so Leona had left the engine running and honked to summon Ellen. The top of the roadster was down and her eyes darted every which way. "All set? Well, let's get out of here." She pulled away from the curb. "How do you feel safe living here?"

"I think the neighborhood only *looks* questionable," Ellen replied. "It's actually very quiet, and the residents are pleasant."

"Oh." Leona sounded skeptical.

"Thank you for inviting me today. It's so kind of you, especially since we've just met," Ellen said as the car extricated itself from the tight, residential streets and merged onto a larger one.

"Think nothing of it!" Leona said brightly. Now that she was in a surer place, her neck and shoulders relaxed and she sank back into her seat. "I was frightfully dull after graduation, and all my friends live elsewhere. My family is tired of me. But I'm all kinds of glad they introduced us. You're a swell girl and I feel like we've known each other ages. You're a much better listener than any of my old friends, and you're so much nicer than anybody in my family."

That gave Ellen a trickle of alarm. She was hardly confidential with even her mother and sisters—would Leona start confiding in her and expect the same in return? Ellen detested almost nothing more than insincere relationships, but her tact and desire for peace tended to subject her to them. What sorts of things would Leona divulge? Gossip? Family affairs? School scandals? *Whatever it is, it's really nothing to be alarmed over. The thing is to just be guarded.*

"Well...thank you." What else could Ellen say?

"So of course I want to spend time with you," Leona continued, giving her head a shake to displace the brown curls blowing into her face. They batted about behind her in the wind; she looked pretty and fresh in the summer morning. "Maybe that's selfish of me. But if you benefit as well, then it's not."

She smiled so ingenuously...perhaps her mind really did only reach that far. If she wasn't exactly a stimulating companion, at least she might be harmless. Spending time with her would be worthwhile if it helped Leona's loneliness.

"Selfishness is sometimes difficult to identify," Ellen remarked, "and always a struggle to fight. But when two people enjoy the same thing, I think the question of selfishness can be put to rest." It was true. Ellen's arms itched to play tennis again; they felt straitjacketed in their tight, blue sleeves.

A few minutes later, Ellen deemed it the best time to ask Leona if she could drop her off at Friar's after lunch.

"Why, what an odd request. But you and your friend know best, of course!" Leona was silent for a moment. "I wish I could stick around, too, since I know someone who works there. But I promised Mother I'd be home at one. We have another engagement, though why she should care whether I'm there or not is mystifying to me."

Brookside Country Club was west of Canton in the middle of woods and fields, a little beyond Meyers Lake. The hilly, tree-wrapped countryside enveloping the route was pretty and the girls kept a conversation rolling, but the short drive felt long to Ellen. Any time could be lengthened by discomfort.

Leona had a membership at the club and paid Ellen's fee— Ellen hadn't known there'd be a fee, so she thanked her a good deal, feeling very self-conscious.

Ellen changed into the pretty, slightly worn white sports dress that had belonged to Jackie Bingham—"Jackie got a new one because she'd had this for several years, but it's too large for me," Leona explained—and the two of them collected rackets and balls and commenced their first match.

As soon as they stepped onto the court, Leona's cheer and chattiness burgeoned. "I'm serving first. You don't mind, do you? You're such a sweet girl!" She threw up the ball and hit downward with all her might. "Oh, that dratted net. I really loused that up, didn't I?" She giggled. "Let's call this practice and not keep score yet."

Every volley was accompanied by Leona's commentary.

"There! It's yours!"

"Fiddlesticks! You got it!"

"Ha! Got it!"

"Oh, you!"

"Dreadful ball!"

"You'll be a dear and get that, won't you, Ellen?"

"I'm pooped. How about a rest?"

They'd been at it only fifteen minutes, but Ellen consented. She wasn't breathing any harder than normal, for the game had only just started picking up. Fortunately the longer Leona played, the better she was. Ellen could say the same of herself, though she already felt anxious for a harder match.

Leading Ellen to a glass table under the covered patio where they could see tennis pairs on other courts, Leona perched in a chair. "Ellen, could you be an angel and fetch us some water? You seem less tired than me. Just go inside and ask for a pitcher of ice water—oh, and two tumblers—and it will be so refreshing."

When she returned, Leona poured the water, chatting amiably, "I used to play often, but I was so busy during my last semester I haven't played since last fall. No—make that summer. How long has it been since you've played? Surely not more than a few months?"

"Actually, I believe it's been two years."

"Indeed!" Leona peered at Ellen with slightly narrowed eyes, showing the same incredulity with which she'd regarded Marion's acting. "Well, you must have been something! But you've probably stayed active. I've just been studying and making the social rounds all year. Dancing doesn't keep one as fit as one should think."

Ellen nodded nonchalantly. Even though she'd been confined to an office ever since high school, she walked often, and that *could* count as being active.

They rested for a few minutes before Leona suggested taking up their rackets again. It resembled a game this time—they kept the ball bouncing longer because Leona steadily progressed.

"Oh goodness, Ellen, I'm pooped this time for sure." Leona doubled over, hands to knees, as the ball bounded beyond her. "But jeepers, wasn't this fun? I'll improve next time. I just need to regain my agility."

"Great fun!" Ellen agreed sincerely, dashing the sweat from her forehead and remembering to go up to the net so she could shake Leona's hand like a proper match. Leona mirrored her.

"Ugh. Our hands are slimy." Something about the way Leona snickered and wiped her hand on her snow-white skirt made Ellen sense she was speaking only of her. "I feel messy, don't you? Let's clean up."

Leona led the way to the powder room and then to a sleek tea room within the country club building.

"How nice! This place has a lot of amenities," Ellen commented as she and Leona entered the tea room and proceeded toward the lunch counter.

"Oh yes, it's great fun to belong here. What should you like? This is my treat, too, you know."

Small sandwiches, fruit, crackers, drinks, and other snacks were the only things served. Ellen was hungry—if she were Marion she would have said ravenous—but she wasn't about to order the number of things it would take to replenish her energy.

"I know this isn't much of a lunch, but my engagement requires me to eat something there, so I don't want anything heavy. It'll be enough for you, won't it?" Leona asked.

"Yes, it certainly will." Ellen smiled. Eating anything bought by Leona's purse felt like charity, so this way she could feel a little less beholden. She asked Leona to order first and then matched it: apple salad and a small but tasty turkey sandwich, only without Leona's chocolate cake. Of course Leona didn't feel it necessary to sacrifice chocolate, but Ellen did.

Back in Leona's dark-blue roadster after both girls changed clothes, Leona started the engine and surveyed the half-full parking lot before pressing the pedal. She left the top down. "That was a delightful morning," she sighed. "You'd like to come again, wouldn't you? Please say yes."

Ellen checked the deserted road they were turning onto to disguise her hesitant answer. "I would, except—" she couldn't bear to be upfront to Leona about money—"I'm afraid I may be too busy to come again. I have plans with other friends, and unfortunately I met you too late to really—"

"Oh, you mustn't let me down, not after we've struck up such a wonderful friendship!" Leona's words rose to a pleading high-pitch, just low of distressed. "Surely you can squeeze me in somewhere?" She dropped a few decibels. "I'm so lonely, you see. I need a friend, desperately, or else I shall go wild with nothing fun to do. Is it a question of money? Because if it is, I shall pay for you each time. We mustn't let money get in the way of our friendship."

Ellen stiffened. So Leona was shrewder than she'd thought. Should Ellen cling to her self-respect and trump up another excuse besides money? Or was it more dignified to acknowledge her real qualms? *I don't want to be forthright with her. She somehow doesn't warrant it; I don't trust her.* "Perhaps sitting and chatting at a park would be a better way of getting to know me," Ellen said finally. "I haven't got much time, but little visits like that I can manage." It was the last thing she wanted—if she had to spend time with Leona she'd far rather be *doing* something than sitting face to face forcing conversation—but it was preferable to receiving charity.

"Well, all right then. But can't you make time for even a little tennis?"

"I'm afraid not."

"You disagreeable girl." Leona pouted but she was not angry. She at last pulled onto the road and continued, "We must think of something fun but fast. Card games? Bowling? Music concerts? Hiking? Oh, Ellen, nothing will do but for you to give me more time! I'll pay for every drop, but I *must* have you."

They argued, civilly, all the way to Canton and Friar's Tool and Die before Ellen capitulated out of sheer weariness. She abhorred rudeness, more so in herself than in others, so it was the only way to evade it. It was awful to be paid for, but if Leona was determined to be a friend, friends did such things. Could Ellen return an equivalent favor someday?

"I shall go in with you," Leona announced as she parked. "I've got time, and I'd love to see my friend. Everett Shepherd —do you know him? He's an old family friend."

An inexplicable misgiving crept over Ellen...but why? It must have stolen in through Leona's tone of voice, but she couldn't lay a finger on why or how it made her uneasy. "Yes, I do. I worked with him for a few weeks before I left Canton." Did she sound short? She was to the point with Leona where she almost didn't care.

"Ah. Did you work closely with him?" Leona shut her door and cast a nervous glance at the assortment of mostly rundown vehicles in the parking lot.

"On occasion," Ellen replied, gazing toward the hulking factory above them.

Leona gave her a searching glance. "I see. Well, he's a nice young man, don't you think? Our families have been friends for years."

"Yes, he is very nice. He's the sort who's great to have at a workplace." Finally, they were at the door.

"Ellen! There you are. It's too bad Everett's out to lunch, but you'll stay long enough for him to get back." Frances was sitting—out of place—at Ellen's old desk in the front room. Besides that, the building felt the same—a dull office area at the rim of the weary, day-in, day-out hum of machinery. But it was a breath of familiarity Ellen sorely needed. The routine of two years of her life stood there, welcoming her, assuring her things proceeded normally just on the other side of a curtain. It took her a moment to recall the curtain was forbidden her.

Hilda emerged from the bookkeeping office on her way out for lunch and greeted Ellen like a friend.

"I'm still full from that wonderful breakfast you made me," Frances informed Ellen as Hilda departed. "I can't touch the sandwich yet. Is this your new friend?" She arose and skirted the desk.

"Yes. This is Leona Bingham. Leona, my friend Miss Frances Lundberg."

Leona stepped forward slowly and mincingly and extended her hand to Frances with the gesture of a princess, though it resulted in a typical handshake. *She apparently doesn't consider Frances and me in the same class, the working class. Perhaps because I'm cousin to her brother-in-law?*

"Where did you work, Ellen?" Leona asked, her voice inflecting with the curl on her upper lip.

"Behind this very desk." Ellen allowed her voice a hint of pride. She chuckled. "Those filing cabinets were my jurisdiction and handiwork. Aren't they nifty? I'm glad you and Hilda have kept everything up so well, Frances."

"Oh my, how tedious it must be," said Leona. "You poor women."

"It's less tedious than starving to death," Frances said, curving back around to the work side of the desk.

Leona's eyes widened.

Ellen hurried to say, "Don't feel too sorry for us working women. It's oddly satisfying to work for pay. I confess I was rather anxious until I got a job in Cardinal Bush."

"Strange, but I guess if that's what you're used to…" Leona murmured, lifting a surreptitious, defiant look at Frances.

"Everett left about fifteen minutes ago, so he should be back soon," Frances said. "Remember when he would eat in? He never does that now, with you gone. He brings a lunch but eats it elsewhere."

Once again Ellen felt the uneasy sensation that her and Everett's friendship mustn't be spotlighted in Leona's presence. Perhaps it was only because her relationship with Everett was a delicate thing, and she did not trust Leona. She couldn't even feel safe or justified telling Marion her fondness for Everett was growing. A girl had to be careful, especially around other girls...especially girls like Leona.

"And you, do you always eat in now?" asked Ellen.

"I'm so plagued with tasks that I have the short end of the half hour to eat lunch," Frances complained. "I'm allowing myself a teensy holiday today because you're here, but if you were to return tomorrow, I'd ignore you as if you were a halfwit bystander at a crime scene. Everett, however, would become one unproductive young fella."

Everett again. "I'm glad you're not staying later than normal, though," Ellen said. "Is it because you're hosting us right now?"

"No, I refuse to stay late. I have my life, even if it just consists of movies and detective novels. Everett stays late whenever he can, though. I suppose the work keeps him occupied, because he misses a certain coworker."

Ellen was ready to throw up her hands in defeat. Leona's gaze hovered between Ellen and Frances with partly concealed suspicion.

"Did you say you couldn't stay long?" Frances asked, granting Leona an intent but smiling look.

"Why—I don't believe I said that, no." Leona glared at the wall clock. One o'clock...she would be late for her mother's engagement. Why was she lingering? She probably wanted to see Everett. Her right-hand fingers wandered to her mouth and she began to nibble at them behind cherry-red lips. She started and flushed when she noticed Ellen's politely questioning stare. "However, I rather think I should leave now, because I do hate being late for things...of course I have somewhere to be after this. I have no reason to stay, after all. Good day, Ellen. I had a lovely morning with you, and we must do it again. Did you say you were free tomorrow morning?"

They had discussed it in the car. "Yes, Friday morning will be fine."

"For tennis?" Leona sighed as if tennis were drudgery now instead of the ecstasy it had been fifteen minutes ago.

"Whatever you wish. Ten o'clock?"

"Done. I shall see you then. It'll be tennis." Leona shook hands with her and, with a final glare at Frances and the clock, scurried out of the building.

"Did you have a nice morning?" Frances asked with a smirk.

"It was fine. I really enjoyed the tennis." Ellen traced the empty top of her former desk. "And Leona is nice; something was eating her just now. Perhaps her next engagement."

"She was a fidgety little floozy," Frances remarked. "Well, since she takes you to play tennis I'll accept her right to be your friend. I know how you adore that sport. Now, if only Everett would get back quickly, before the others, you'll have the chance for a chat without Hilda or Joe, heaven forbid, thinking anything of how long you talk."

"Oh, Frances…"

"Don't 'oh, Frances' me. I'm your old, crotchety friend and I can tease you any way I like. Others daren't cross lines with you, but there are no lines where I step. Am I right or not?"

Ellen couldn't restrain a chuckle. "You're right, Frances. Only you."

The look on Everett's face when he opened the front door would stick long in Ellen's mind: she had never seen him so surprised or so pleased. A bursting silence hung in the room, but no one wanted to speak first. Frances, merely waiting out of courtesy, was predictably the first to break it.

"Well, Everett, I bet you weren't expecting to see this young lady at Friar's today."

"Uh…no," Everett managed, looking past Ellen to Frances.

"You mean you didn't tell him I was coming?" Ellen asked, shifting her eyes off the dark-haired young man as she realized she'd been staring at him since he'd arrived.

"Nope. You know I adore surprises. But—go have a swell chat in the office, why don't you? Ellen, I'll talk to you more once Hilda and Joe come back."

Everett and Ellen took their time getting to the accounting room—the boggy, restraining awkwardness Ellen felt must have been mutual. Once they were alone, their conversation stayed on the surface. Ellen tried not to mind the superficiality;

it was simply nice to be in his company. But something felt off…perhaps Leona was still bothering her, somehow.

Maybe ten minutes later, Frances nipped into the room, busy and official with papers in hand. "Joe is here," she mouthed, spreading her papers on Everett's desk.

Ellen felt unexpectedly thwarted. *Don't,* she told herself. *He probably wasn't going to say anything important.* But the look in Everett's eyes seemed to reveal the disappointment she masked. She wondered… *Don't, you'll only tease yourself. It was nothing. If he needs to say something, there's time and opportunity right now.*

Joe strode in, and that was that. The four of them chatted for a while, and then Frances whisked her off to tour the building, both men giving her an equally cordial farewell.

Just my imagination. Ellen's mind meandered as she rode to Frances's home on the bus. *So why am I dissatisfied? What did I hope he would say?* Her mind attempted to take a trail, but she held it back until she could see clearly where the trail would lead.

Did I hope he would ask me out on a real date? She paused, waiting, her hands figuratively folded. Yes, those were the words she had hoped to hear.

He had not spoken them. *That's all right, you know. Perfectly all right. He has to decide what he wants. What is there to recommend me romantically anyway? I have no reason to expect his interest. We're just friends. I don't even know if I want his interest. A date would be perfectly ridiculous at this point in our friendship.*

Overall, then, she was relieved. Wasn't she?

ᘐ☉ᕟ Chapter Sixteen ᕐ☉ᖋ

LEONA PLAYED MUCH MORE SKILLFULLY THE NEXT MORNING—focused, energetic, even aggressive. It was almost as good as the sport of Ellen's high school years. During their breaks, Leona alternated between lively chatter and pensive silence. They played longer than on Thursday, so when they finally stopped for the day, Leona sat at their glass table limply mopping her forehead and staring at the water pitcher.

"Pour me some water, won't you, dear?" she asked.

Ellen set down her own tumbler and obliged. Holding out Leona's, she said, "You were great today."

"Thanks. So were you. You really make it worth paying your way."

She probably did not intend that as a jab, so Ellen waved it off.

Leona downed her water in several gulps and placed the empty tumbler on the table with a delicate clink. Slowly spinning it, she murmured, "Ellen," as if she were half awake. Ellen listened for her to continue, but the only sound was racket and tennis ball *boings* on the courts.

Leona withdrew her hand to her lap and straightened her spine. "Ellen, you're my friend, aren't you? I know we've only just met, but I feel as if I've known you for ages. You're so kind and you listen so wonderfully. And you have a very good head on your shoulders. And…there may be another reason why you're perfect to confide in, I think. I may confide in you, mayn't I? You won't tell a soul what I'm about to tell you?"

Ellen's heart plummeted to her stomach, but her face didn't reflect the dismay gurgling inside her. She had been afraid of this—of Leona telling her an uncomfortable secret, swearing her to guard it at all costs. Leona was that sort of clinging vine.

Perhaps it won't be so terrible. The only people from whom she'd need to keep secrets are her family, and I'm hardly intimate with them. I just hope she's not looking for advice.

Ellen plunked her tumbler onto the table deliberately. The two girls sat almost knee to knee, the table beside them. "I—I honestly don't know if I'm the right person. I don't know much about you, and I'm no older than you are, so I will be no good for advice. And really, I'm not sure you can trust me...my loyalty to you doesn't extend as far as keeping a dangerous secret."

Leona smiled strangely. "You are so modest and...sincere. I feel even more confidence in you."

"Are you certain this is a secret I should hear? You don't really know me that well."

"Don't you understand? I have to tell *someone*. I'm desperate for advice, and you know about life. You're swell. You're Louis's cousin, and he's the only person in my family who's at all nice to me. Niceness runs in families."

Ellen hesitated, searching for a fresh reason Leona shouldn't unburden her heart to her.

"You see," Leona bent forward, pressing in over the pause, "I have a problem...it's torn me for years now. It's a great, great comfort that I met you—you'll understand, because you know the other person this is about."

Ellen opened her mouth in one more attempt, but Leona dashed on. "No doubt later I'll feel some regret telling you, but that's what a girl's heart is like...it wavers back and forth. But I know I need to confide in you. It's for my own peace of mind; I can't bear holding it in any longer."

Ellen braced herself as if to withstand a huge wave from Lake Erie.

"Would you believe me if I told you I was going to be married?"

Ellen gazed at her coolly, donning her most detached expression. If she had to make eye contact, she at least didn't want to appear eager and encouraging. "I'd believe you, certainly. I think every girl I know will one day be married."

"But I *know* whom I'm marrying, and I could be married any day, if the stars should ever align themselves." Leona paused, awaiting a response. Ellen raised her eyebrows to show appropriate intrigue, but Leona still waited; she desired something verbal. Ellen yielded against her habit.

"Is that so? You are fortunate."

"Sometimes I don't think I am so fortunate." Leona sighed. "To love someone, to know who you want to be your husband...and to be prevented from marrying him because of your family, is simply...*excruciating*. Can you imagine how I must feel?"

Once again Ellen felt forced to reply. She hoped sympathy showed. "It sounds terrible; I'm sorry."

Leona dropped her volume. "Thank you, it is. Now, you must be tired of my being vague. Ellen, I'm engaged, officially engaged, though I have no ring, to your former coworker Everett Shepherd."

Leona was remarkably lucid and specific. For a moment Ellen felt like she was falling, but she couldn't be, not in her chair. She had lost all sense of physicality. Except for the sick, punched sensation in her disembodied stomach.

Leona was looking at her. An inquiring look, or perhaps a feigned inquiring look, but either way, very pointed.

Ellen had to say something. "Engaged? Indeed?" It was all she could do to stabilize her voice.

"You had no idea, did you? Everett is so good at keeping secrets. He *must* be in this case. I'm at stake, you see. As is his happiness, our happiness. If my parents find out they'll forbid me to ever see him again. Social standing is so important to them. His parents aren't too friendly with us either; I don't blame them. Even though our families used to be good friends, ever since his family lost their business and dropped out of our circle, it's been a condescending sort of friendship on our part. I say 'our' but I'm ashamed to be included. On the *Binghams'* part. For me, it's enough that he was born into my class. He's more genteel and darling than young men of my status, I can tell you that."

Was Leona making this up just to perturb her? Leona had known Everett a long time. Everett had mentioned the Binghams on occasion. He was good at keeping secrets, yes, even from hinting at them in his demeanor. But could an engaged, lovelorn fellow be so silent about it? Everett had a subdued temperament, but with Ellen he could be funny and animated and then unguarded about the most surprising things. He'd confided in her about his childhood, his family's business failure, his frustrations with career and familial expectations. Not once did she grasp so much as a suggestion of disappointment in romance. In fact, they virtually avoided speaking of romance altogether. Perhaps…perhaps that was a clue favoring Leona's claim.

"You don't believe me, do you?" One corner of Leona's mouth turned up in a rather disdainful smile, though she surely did not intend it to look that way. "I can tell you exactly how we became engaged."

"Well, I—"

"Let me. It will help, because I've never been able to tell anyone about it. Well, a bosom friend at college knows, but can *you* imagine telling only one person about your engagement? It's awful!" She proceeded with hardly a pause to explain how they'd been friends since childhood and how Everett was always so gentlemanly. She took credit for him finally deciding to become an accountant against his family's wishes—they had wanted him to save the Shepherd name in the business world.

Leona and Everett were eighteen when they realized they loved each other.

Leona wrapped her arms around her middle and stared into space. "If you ever fall in love and are loved in return, you'll understand how marvelous it is. To look into a man's eyes, the man you love, and read in them that he prefers you above anyone else, that you're the prettiest, most desirable girl he's ever known. Being wanted like that is a beautiful feeling. I do hope you get to feel it one day." Her hand dove into her skirt pocket and emerged with an embroidered handkerchief to dab her eyes.

She had to be telling the truth. Ellen's heart had never hurt so much, nor had her breath ever heaved so unwillingly. Desired, wanted, loved. Everett.

Oh God, help me. For once in her life part of her wanted to surrender to hysterics like Marion would. But she battled her way up to sanity and control, like a drowning person to the surface of water. She could never pardon herself if now she lost the restraint that had been her faithful friend whenever she needed it most.

Her stoical face saved her where self-control faltered. Leona looked at her with dry hazel eyes, and she returned the gaze steadfastly. "It sounds like bliss," she said, a stagger in her voice she hoped Leona did not notice.

"It is." Leona twisted her handkerchief around her finger. "But we shall always be kept apart now, and never experience that bliss again, because my family has told me plainly they don't approve of Everett, and they look down on the Shepherds. I'd forfeit everything if they found out. I've no doubt my father would get Everett fired and disinherit me, and then we'd be left with nothing. Sometimes I think…sometimes I think," she dabbed her eyes again, "that we'd be better off if I broke our engagement." She sniffed. "But I didn't tell you how he asked me! Do you know Turkeyfoot Lake? Have you ever been there?"

Ellen nodded.

"Then you know what it's like. My family and Everett went one day that summer we were eighteen. Father was meeting with a new client or business partner or something, so the rest of us had to stay clear of the yacht. Most stayed on the beach, but Everett and I went hiking. When we got tired, we sat down at the water's edge, and you know how the trees grow so close to the water. It's lovely, isn't it? And that's where Everett proposed." A wistful smile drifted onto Leona's face.

Oh, to be loved by Everett…

Leona traced every detail of his proposal, her gaze locked on to Ellen's face—Ellen kept eye contact as much as she could; it wouldn't do to shift and reveal weakness.

She even tried a sentence. "It's—it's good for an engagement to be sweet." She inhaled deeply and silently. "And then I suppose you decided you'd have to wait?"

"Yes." Leona's smile flickered on and off. "We decided right off that we wouldn't tell our families, because everyone was disappointed in him, you remember. We'd wait until he made a success of himself. But time wore on...and now, four years later...no one would be even sympathetic. Everett's mother was never fond of me, peculiarly, and no one in my family approves of how Everett has turned out, and so...we would cast everything to the wind if we were to marry. He doesn't want to do that to me, dear sweet boy, and I don't want to do it to him, and so we are at a dreadful standstill. It's the most awful thing; I hope you never have to experience anything like it."

Ellen could only nod.

"Surely you can feel for us. Everett has said he looks on you and your sisters as the sisters he never had, so you must feel for him as a brother, don't you?"

Thankfully Leona didn't wait for a response. "But, if you could put yourself in my shoes, what *would* you do? Break it off? Tell your family and risk the consequences? I don't want to continue on as we are, miserable and never marrying. My family wants me off their hands, but they're waiting on the right advantageous match. They'll wait forever, because I'm not marrying anyone besides Everett."

"Then you're determined not to break it off?" Ellen asked. When she distanced herself from the scenario, and tried to forget it was Everett of whom they were speaking, she could summon rationality. "Because if it's only him you'll marry, then in a sense you will never break your engagement."

"Well...yes. But, I consider it as freeing him, I guess. So, is that what you would do? Break it off and free him?"

"That isn't what I said." Ellen paused. "I really don't feel I can advise you. I've never been in your situation. It's hard to imagine myself in it, and even harder to think of what is best for *you*. We're different people, and what I should feel comfortable doing is probably quite different from what you'd feel comfortable doing. And I've never thought myself overly skilled at giving advice."

"But surely you have some sort of counsel for me? You won't just leave me to pursue my course in the dark, will you? Really, I have no idea what to do. I'm at the place now where I shall do anything you tell me! Advise me, Ellen."

Everett...Everett she could think for and relate to. Four years was a long engagement, and eighteen was a long way from twenty-two...could Everett actually still be in love with Leona? He did always seem to have a sadness clouding him. So it was not his family affairs...was it then his engagement? Was he sad because he wanted to marry Leona and could not, or because he did not want to marry her but felt obliged to? Either breaking the engagement or marrying under family disownment would be distressing. Everett and Leona each needed to search themselves and find what they really wanted; that was the only way they could make such a difficult choice. Somehow the pain of either of those choices would have to be borne. If indeed there was pain. What if Everett didn't want the engagement anymore? Ellen wasn't thinking wishfully; she'd seen enough of Everett to wonder if he might possibly like *her*.

How could she explain all that to Leona? She couldn't. But she ought to summarize something. She leaned forward to look into Leona's eyes instead of keeping herself stiff and distant. "The only way I see it is that the choice lies with you. I can't tell you what to do, because only *you* can decide which option you can live with."

Leona's lips moved into a pout as she sighed. "Then the decision will have to wait a little longer, because I can't make it." She pressed her fingers to her eyes, her handkerchief bunched up in one hand. "Perhaps Everett may win my parents' approval yet."

Ellen nodded and prayed that would be the end of the confidence. Her prayer was answered when a pair of tennis players left the courts for a rest and realized they were acquainted with Leona. Now, to bide patiently for the time when she could be alone.

ᏬᏬ Chapter Seventeen ᏬᏬ

ELLEN HAD TO ENDURE JUST A FEW STROKES MORE ON THE RIDE home in Leona's roadster. Now that Leona had shared all to do with Everett, she considered every moment between the two girls open for any additional—or repetitive—thought that might occur to her. But nothing could hurt Ellen any worse than the first revelation.

"May I see you this weekend sometime? Mother is having some tiresome old birds on Saturday night to play bridge, and their husbands will play billiards with Father. My siblings are all busy, not that I want to be with them anyway. Come over, won't you?"

Mercy, if only Ellen had a conflict. She would be spending the morning with high school friends and the afternoon with Frances, but the evening was free. It *was* to be a tranquil reading night in Frances's living room.

"Do come! You or I may have new insight into my circumstances."

Leona wrung a commitment from her before they reached Frances's apartment. Ellen couldn't lie about being occupied, and something in her actually hankered for Leona's company, after a respite...perhaps it was the prospect of more revelation about Everett.

Ellen contemplated that as she let herself into the apartment. Wasn't it painful to hear Leona talk about him? Did Leona even describe the real Everett? How could the Everett Ellen knew be drawn to someone like Leona?

Ellen locked the door behind her, deposited her handbag on the coffee table, and kicked off her tennis shoes as she sank flat onto the couch.

How? He had been a shy, sensitive boy, censured by his

family and turning to the only one who seemed to love or appreciate him. Eighteen was a susceptible age. It was the eve of overwhelming changes, and the steady attention of a pretty girl was nearly irresistible comfort. He had never claimed to be wise for his years. And once he engaged himself, he was too much a man of honor to jilt the girl, unless there was something really wrong with her.

A man of honor, yes, to maintain the engagement—but he hadn't carried out the spirit of the thing very well, had he? An engaged man didn't interact with a different girl the way Everett had with Ellen. Her temper rose, and she sat up. Her fingers began to itch for some paper, but she had none and it wouldn't do to tear anything of Frances's. She tamped down the itch and lay back down.

Could Leona create such a story? What would be the motive? Did she perhaps love Everett without being loved in return, and so desired to fend Ellen off as a rival? The facts of her story checked out, so Ellen might as well believe her.

Nothing would really change. Ellen had never flirted with Everett; she never would have unless he…made *his* love plain. So she could continue being his sisterly friend, but prepare to give him up. He and Leona would probably marry. They could get along without family approval. If Ellen were like Leona and detested her family, she would choose Everett. It wasn't reckless, it was reasonable to stick with the person your soul allied with, the one whose love you craved.

But did Everett still love Leona? The way he interacted with Ellen, it was hard to believe. The only explanation was that he wanted Leona no longer. *I can't fault him for that,* Ellen thought. *Leona is someone rational people grow out of quickly.*

So. What were her next steps? She raised her hand and numbered off her fingers. One: talking with Leona on Saturday was actually a good thing. Her veracity needed to be tested, and Ellen needed to know once and for all what to think, what to hope. Two: she needed to show Leona she wasn't disappointed about Everett. She couldn't help her shock when Leona first told her, but now she could calmly sweep away Leona's suspicions of her attraction to Everett. Those suspicions mightn't be based purely on what Frances had said—though it would have been great if Frances hadn't said anything!—but on Everett's opinion of her. He must have spoken highly of her, if Leona felt threatened. So now she had to prove, by acting normally, she was only surprised and interested as a friend. She had to cover her hurt. Leona had no right to know the pain she caused.

And then there was Everett...number three. How ought she to feel toward him? It was tempting to lay him aside for now, but she was anxious to sort it all out. Could she be angry at him for befriending her when Leona might be so unsatisfactory to him? *Why doesn't he break off the engagement then? Is he so concerned with being faithful to her? Or maybe there is more to her than I realize?*

Four—as Leona had requested, she'd tell no one, not even Marion or Mother. They adored Everett, too, and cherished fond hopes for her and him...they wouldn't be able to handle this. Not in the least. And Ellen didn't need the added stress of reconciling them to the situation. She was having a hard enough time with herself.

This would remain between Leona and Ellen. Everett couldn't know she knew. It was too...shameful. And Ellen's true emotions would remain between her and God.

Oh God, she prayed, *can't You split them up? She's not fit for him!* But how could she make that judgment, or know what God intended for them? It would be much better to pray that God would do what was best for Everett.

Some minutes or hours later, Ellen was still lying on the couch, for once too occupied by thoughts to occupy herself with her hands. She sighed. This wouldn't do. Idleness never helped anything. As she dragged herself out of lethargy by sitting up, she dragged her mind out of its whirlwind, to a distance where she could see the whole picture. It showed one thing.

She loved Everett.

The meeting with Leona on Saturday and every meeting thereafter did, indeed, assure Ellen she told the truth about Everett. He was Leona's favorite subject, so whenever Ellen laid a furtive test for veracity, Leona passed without fail.

The rest of Ellen's stay in Canton passed as quickly as if the minutes were mired in a swamp. It was about as miserable, too. Without completely realizing it, she had come to depend on Everett's presence in her life for happiness and hope. When he was taken away, a huge piece of her tore away with him, and though she could keep living to her full capacity, all brightness was gone. Would there be someone else? Perhaps. But he wouldn't be Everett.

First Dad, then Everett. It was surprising how she *could* carry on with her emotions in shambles...she had them mastered, she supposed. Was that the purpose behind all the hurt God had seen fit to allow into her life? To show her life could be lived with hardship and nothing mattered but one's faith in Him? That life could continue without the people one loved? That emotions had to be ignored so that one could bear living? Maybe she hadn't known that as well as she thought she did. Thus, to prove the point, taking Dad wasn't enough; God had to take another loved man after him. So be it. She still had things to live for. There was God to serve. Her family was intact. Dad would be restored to them, perhaps changed, and Ellen might need to be stronger than ever to help him, Mother, and her sisters.

The sole thing missing would be the happiness she had tasted.

Marion, suffering from her own loss, was doing an admirable job of staying busy—but she was not disguising her pain. In their small, shared bed in Frances's guestroom, Ellen heard her sniffles and labored, dreaming breath, felt the dampness of tears on the sheets, and every few nights was kept awake by her thrashing. Sometimes she would come home from a nightly theater practice with swollen eyes and unashamedly admit she'd gone to pieces.

As Canton's two weeks neared their end, Ellen was afraid to

leave her, but Marion assured her she'd be fine. She'd be staying with a girlfriend, and girlfriends gave almost as much support as older sisters. She said on their last Friday together, "Go back to enjoying Cardinal Bush—I can see you're dying to get back to work. Disrupted routine never did agree with you."

Ellen nodded, unconvinced that Marion would be all right. But she *did* need to get back to her job. Mr. Bradley would be there on Monday, and they'd have loads to do. "Telephone me every other evening, won't you? I don't care how late. If you don't, I'll telephone Lillian's family and they'll make you."

"Sure I will. But keep in mind, Ellen dear, the summer stock's coming through next week. That may tie me up and you'll never hear a peep out of me except when I can remember to send a telegram with one word—no, three: 'Alive STOP M.'"

Hope didn't glimmer in Marion's eyes…it would always shine there before when she spoke of theater.

There had been a time—just a few weeks ago, and a few weeks in length—when things had looked up. It wasn't altogether happy; it couldn't be, not with Dad in prison; but it was full of moments that could be enjoyed. Cardinal Bush had created that time. When Ellen returned on Saturday, she might feel slightly better. Leaving behind the coals meant she'd no longer be burnt, though the blisters would still smart.

Except that one of the coals didn't want to be left behind. Leona took her out for lunch on that last Friday and begged to visit. "I should love to see where you live! And your mother is almost like one of my relatives. My brother-in-law's aunt, yes? She sounds nice; I'd love to meet her."

Ellen had learned to be suspicious of Leona's ulterior motives, so she was hesitant to say yes. And of course every moment in her company bore a sting. But Leona had done nothing openly to insult Ellen or otherwise merit snubbing. As much of a relief as not interacting with Leona would be, Ellen would feel worse if she were rude to her.

"It would be a half-hour drive in farm country, or a train ride. Are you up for that?" Ellen asked.

"It's a little frightening alone, but one must inconvenience oneself sometimes, for the sake of a friend." Leona smiled. "And you've been a true, dear friend. How can I ever thank you for all your help and sympathy? I shall ring you up one day soon, and you can give me directions, and then I'll come up and we'll have a grand old time in *your* town."

"Swell." *Don't borrow trouble from the future. She may not follow through.*

When they had finished lunch and were ready to part, Leona exclaimed, "How I'll miss you, Ellen dear!" The gust of her words flew her arms around Ellen's shoulders. "Write to me, won't you? I'll write to you. I wish we could speak of what *really* concerns us on the phone, but of course that must all be done in the privacy of letters or face-to-face tête-à-têtes."

Ellen half-smiled at the redundancy of the English and French and reluctantly agreed to Leona's request.

Lillian Thomas and her father drove the Dashiell girls on Saturday, planning to stay long enough for Marion to hug and kiss Mother and Greta—maybe an hour or two—and get back to Canton in time for an evening rehearsal with the Guild.

"You know, I hadn't realized it before, but this is the longest I've ever been away from Mother and Greta," Marion said as Canton's modern, populous streets melted behind Mr. Thomas's sedan. The pretty, green countryside lay around them.

"You only just realized it?" Ellen half-smiled. Herself, she couldn't wait to get back. "I take it you aren't homesick?"

"Not much, anyhow. I've just been so busy." Marion exchanged a decisive nod with Lillian, in the front seat. "And if I were homesick, I wouldn't be homesick for Cardinal Bush."

Cardinal Bush had been the site of Marion's disappointment; Canton had been the site of Ellen's. Hence the disparity.

"It's Mother and Greta I miss," Marion continued. "I wish I could stay longer, but I'll be back with everyone soon enough."

"I miss them dreadfully, too." Ellen gazed out the window, appreciating a view without any buildings. Fences and cornfields were the only signs of mankind she would tolerate.

She hadn't noticed how much the countryside agreed with her until she had come out of the city again. "It sounds like Greta will have a lot to catch us up on, if her letter is any indication."

During their last, brief telephone conversation the day before, Mother had mentioned that Mr. Bradley had returned early that week—earlier than expected—and had something to tell them. Caution for the party line obviously prevented her from saying more. Would he come today? It must be important.

Greta and Sport ran out from the porch when they pulled into the driveway. Everything looked exaggerated in the intense summer light and the two weeks' absence—the house was grayer and more pocked with imperfections, the trees were fuller and greener, Uncle Melvin's Graham parked in the open barn was a softer maroon with what appeared to be more dents.

"Ellen! Marion! Oh, I missed you so much!" Greta hopped up and down, Sport seated composedly beside her.

"Greta! You look taller," Ellen exclaimed as she folded her into a hug.

"I do? Wonderful! I hope I am." Greta stepped back and looked into Ellen's eyes. "I think I am! I'm right up to your forehead."

Ellen chuckled. "Maybe so, but your head also comes taller than Marion's."

Grinning after they hugged, Marion put her hand on top of Greta's brownish-blond hair. "Goose, you've stretched your neck too far. It's disgraceful for a thirteen-year-old to be so tall."

Sounds clattered from the front porch and Ellen glanced up to see Mother, Aunt Jennie, and Uncle Melvin hurrying toward them. Aunt Jennie and Uncle Melvin were almost more excited to see Mr. Thomas and Lillian than Ellen and Marion, so overjoyed were they to make new acquaintances—no one could ever know enough people, according to both—and Aunt Jennie scolded Lillian for not coming to the spring party.

The air was fresh and the breeze cool, so Aunt Jennie invited everyone onto the porch, which provided just enough seats, with Greta, Marion, and Lillian perched on the railing with the posts for backrests. The porch wasn't in the most laudable condition, but the Thomas family were too good of friends to mind.

"What does your hand find to do in the big city, old boy?" Uncle Melvin asked, characteristically loud, of Mr. Thomas.

Mother, Ellen, Marion, and Greta were on the opposite side of the circle. "Oh, goodness," Mother murmured, scooting closer to Ellen on the porch swing and leaning forward toward Marion. "I'm glad we're way over here." She smiled and held out her palm to Marion; Marion took it and they let their hands rest in the midst. Beside them, Aunt Jennie struck up a conversation with Lillian.

"Well, *I* want to talk with my daughter while her face is in front of me," Mother declared. "So you're rehearsing a play. *Elephant Sunday.* I've never heard of that before. Will you finish in time for the summer stock auditions?"

"Probably not. But that's a price I'm willing to pay for a real theater job," Marion said, lifting her hand from Mother's. "Sorry, I need to get my back up against my post again. Even if I had a really important part—I got in too late for that, you know—I'd give it up for the sake of a paying job. I need to keep my goal in front."

"I understand. Wow. Being parted from you for two weeks has been hard; how shall I ever handle two months? And after that, who knows? Weeks, months, years?" Mother took Ellen's hand into her lap, her smile and bright voice but a mask.

Marion glanced at their joined hands. "It'll be different. You'll have both Ellen and Greta with you this time. Ellen's absence is the one you really felt."

"I felt both of your absences like a gash," Mother responded, still outwardly cheerful. She lowered her volume. "It shouldn't be *so* bad if your father were here. I always knew you'd be going away someday, but just now is not an easy time for me."

"Mother, are you trying to break my heart?" Marion's pout was as masterful as Shirley Temple's.

"No, no! The last thing I want is for you to miss your big chance. I'm just worried about...things. You know what we talked about earlier. I just want you to be prepared. But really, it's because of Dad that being parted from any of you girls is so difficult right now."

"You certainly can't be blamed for your feelings." Ellen squeezed her hand.

"We love you for it, even though you make us feel like stinkers for ever leaving you." Marion grinned; Ellen wished her brown eyes might sparkle, too.

The noise of an approaching motor made everyone look to the driveway. A black Oldsmobile cautiously emerged from the trees. Mr. Bradley?

"Oh ho, girls, look who's here to welcome you!" Aunt Jennie gloried. "Calvin Bradley! Isn't he a lamb?"

Marion turned back into the porch and muttered, "A real pip."

Mr. Bradley parked behind Mr. Thomas's beige sedan and got out slowly.

"Calvin! Hello!" Aunt Jennie waved from her chair.

"I'm sorry, am I early?"

"You oughtn't to be, if it's after eleven." Aunt Jennie's teeth showed in her wide smile.

"Well then, I'm pleased to have the unexpected pleasure of seeing the Miss Dashiells already arrived." Mr. Bradley walked to the porch, briefcase in hand.

"You didn't know they'd be home this early?" Mother asked.

"No—but I must have somehow missed that information. It must be because I've been away so long."

"Calvin, you put me to shame with that perfectly polite, blame-taking tone of yours. I'll 'fess up. I told him to come at eleven, and that you girls would be here at three. He didn't want to intrude on a family reunion, but *I* wanted him to. I wanted him to see *everyone*." Aunt Jennie directed a significant look toward Marion.

Marion sighed just under the surface of Aunt Jennie's hearing, then pivoted herself to face Mr. Bradley as he neared the porch, dangling her feet in the shrubs and greeting him alongside everyone else.

Ellen felt for her; as if missing Wilkie weren't enough, Marion *would* have to be teased about Mr. Bradley. Marion hadn't any right to show exasperation, of course, but Ellen could sympathize with the hurt smarting underneath. The teasing also wasn't fair or respectful to Mr. Bradley, the dignified man that he was. But he would agree Aunt Jennie and Uncle Melvin were due deference and forbearance.

"So it wouldn't be preferable for me to come another time?" he asked after shaking Uncle Melvin's and Mr. Thomas's hands and hovering at the edge of the group, between Ellen and Greta.

"Not at all, old boy! It'd be tragic. Sit on the railing there, by the girls, and join the fun." Uncle Melvin waved his hands in wide gestures.

"I'm sorry, I didn't know you were coming until this evening." Mother looked puzzled. She had said Mr. Bradley had something to tell them. Was she wondering how he could do that now? "But that isn't very courteous of me to tell you that. I apologize."

"No, no—it appears to be nothing we could help," he responded. "And I know you're concerned with what I wanted to accomplish by coming here today. However, it can wait—"

"How long can you stay, Calvin?" Aunt Jennie queried over their undertones.

"I have something to attend to at one thirty. Say, a half-hour after lunch?"

"The cat's meow! That's how long Marion and the Thomases are staying, isn't it?" The latent dance in Aunt Jennie's dark eyes sparked awake.

"Yes, I believe so," Mother replied. As Aunt Jennie went on to talk to Marion and Lillian, Mother continued softly, "I think the Maddoxes will keep everyone else entertained, if you and Ellen and I wanted to slip away to discuss what you have. We have just enough time before we ought to start fixing lunch."

"I'd not be opposed," Mr. Bradley said, giving his briefcase a little swing.

Mother waited for Aunt Jennie to take a long breath. "Would you be so kind as to excuse Mr. Bradley, Ellen, and myself for a few moments? Mr. Bradley wanted to speak to us, you know."

"No trouble at all! Why, take Marion with you. We'll keep your friends happy as clams out here, dear. You ought to go hear what Calvin has to say."

"Oh? Does it concern me?" Marion's voice skipped on the line of nonchalance and something like impudence.

"Yes, but we can always tell you later," Mother said, "if you'd rather stay here."

Marion looked keenly at Mr. Bradley for a moment, then glanced away when he noticed and returned it. "Nothing beats a firsthand account," she said.

Mother led the way inside—to the dining room, because all the house windows were open to welcome in the weather, and the ones in the front of the parlor gaped right behind the shoulders of the circle of talkers on the porch.

They sat around the table and Mr. Bradley swept some documents from his briefcase to the scratched but gleaming surface before him.

"I'll cut right to the chase. I consulted a colleague of mine about Mr. Dashiell's case, as you permitted, and he, too, was surprised by how easily Mr. Dashiell was convicted. It seems he wasn't given a fair hearing. His word and Mr. Green's should at least have balanced each other out, especially considering their equal characters, and the sketchiness of the evidence against Mr. Dashiell. It's as if the possibility that the accountant could have been lying about what he knew was never duly considered. I even suspect corruption on the judge's part—he wanted to wrap up the case quickly and perhaps was even bribed."

Mr. Bradley folded his hands atop the documents and leaned forward in his seat. "I heard from an insider connection of Mr. Green's that Mr. Green recently bought a yacht, and according to the insider, his finances from Friar's shouldn't be enough for that. Some interesting paperwork has also been discovered among Mr. Green's papers, from another bank besides the one that handles Friar's finances. The funds are fairly close to the amount embezzled. Therefore…I suspect Mr. Green is the real embezzler."

Mother and Marion gasped, but Ellen nodded. This matched Everett's account. It wouldn't surprise her if Mr. Green was the culprit and had implicated Dad to cover his own crime. Someone needed to be held responsible for Friar's investors' stolen money, and her former boss saw to it that it wasn't him. Had Everett discovered the paperwork? If it had been Frances, Ellen would have heard of it long ago.

She felt a pang thinking of Everett and snapped her attention back to Mr. Bradley.

"My colleague helped me sift through everything, and while we don't have a firm grasp on an appeal yet, I believe we'll get one soon. What I wanted to ask you, Mrs. Dashiell, was whether there were other character witnesses we could rely upon when the time comes. Not to slight your husband's attorney, but it seems there ought to have been more on hand than there were."

They discussed the case only a few minutes more. Mr. Bradley seemed loath to make the Dashiells dwell on it any longer than necessary. Ellen was grateful, particularly for Mother's sake.

Two and a half hours later, when Mr. Bradley had left and Marion and the Thomases were on the verge of departure, Ellen helped Marion pack a few things from her bedroom. They were alone upstairs.

"Marion, I say this innocent of meaning," Ellen said, "but isn't Mr. Bradley swell to examine the case like this?" She half-smiled. "I'm not asking you to sing his praises. Just acknowledge in your own mind that he's kind."

"I'll make you prouder of me yet. I'll say it out loud: Mr. Bradley is kind." Marion grinned. "But I want nothing more to do with him than that. Now, if you'll excuse me, Mr. Thomas is going to honk his horn any minute." The sisters hugged and kissed and Marion scurried away, all set for her adventure alone in Canton.

ᘓᕉᕗChapter Eighteenᕕᕖᖆᕗ

Monday, Ellen's first day back at Mr. Bradley's office, was the best day she'd had in weeks. The work consumed her from the moment she hurried in the door at eight a.m. to the moment she limped out at five fifteen. She even proofread several of Mr. Bradley's reports from last week while she ate lunch. An avalanche of phone calls, scheduling appointments, taking dictation, filing and typing letters and documents, bookkeeping…it enveloped her, making her forget her troubles in an ecstasy of accomplishment.

By the end of the week the busy, comfortable routine she'd come to love was as fully hers again as if she'd never left. It compensated for the farmhouse's empty mood with Marion gone. Ellen wasn't much susceptible to mood, but Marion had that kind of affect on her.

While Mr. Bradley had occasionally frustrating cases, the only thing to really trouble her was in the books. Several of Mr. Bradley's clients couldn't pay.

Ellen asked him about the accounts on Friday. They discussed it and though Mr. Bradley wasn't worried, she went home that evening concerned enough for both of them. *Things like this happen,* she reassured herself. *Mr. Bradley has enough savings to maintain the practice until it garners money again. We'll just have to tighten the belt.*

At home, she visited the kitchen to say hello to Mother and Aunt Jennie and stow her lunch things. Aunt Jennie whirled from the stove and snatched her wrist with a sweaty, slightly greasy hand.

"Ellen, today the good Lord is smiling on you. On me, too, actually, and Marion, if she'll have it. Do you want to know how I know that wonderful smile is on us?"

Ellen blinked away her surprise. "Why, yes. This is most suspenseful."

"My daughter Gloria wants me to come see her. In New York *City*! I've been there but once, when I was a little girl. She invited both of us, of course—Uncle Melvin and me, I mean—but your uncle doesn't want to leave the office. Understandable. I shouldn't want him to, either, not when I think of the money and people's teeth at stake. Poor dear. Not even in his old age does he get a break! But Gloria's got a rich husband and money to spend on her old mother—her peach of a new husband is indulgent—and she even mentioned us bringing a friend if we wished! So how are your adding skills? You're a secretary—should be sharp. If she invited me and her father and a friend, and if Uncle Melvin can't go, then that's me and two friends—or two relatives. Your mother already said she wouldn't go, but she's given permission for you and Marion...what do *you* say?"

As much as Ellen disliked appearing startled, she couldn't speak or move for several lengthy seconds. Was Aunt Jennie serious? Some people could afford trips like this, but surely not anyone on this side of the family. Unless it was Cousin Gloria's husband...Lawrence Fitzpatrick was a doctor. He and Gloria had been married three years, and from the stories, they sounded well off, with a house in a nice neighborhood in New York, summer trips to Canada, and one or two servants. But why should Lawrence's money pay for two female relatives he'd never met to merely have a good time in New York? That couldn't be expected, even if he was a peachy, indulgent man.

Besides that, Ellen couldn't leave her job, and Marion couldn't leave Canton, not with a summer stock position in reach. Ellen didn't even like the thought of going to New York. Either there were some solid, crystalline benefits Ellen couldn't see, or Aunt Jennie needed to be enlightened.

"It doesn't have to be right away, you know," Mother hastily put in while dividing biscuit dough on a pan. "Marion's so keen on Canton, and you just had time off from your job. And besides, the city will be so hot and unpleasant during the summer, won't it, Aunt Jennie?"

"Well, yes, but that's what the beaches and things are for." Aunt Jennie returned to her stewing pot, which wafted chicken. "Imagine the hustle and bustle and all the people! The amusement parks will be open—I've always wanted to visit those. And my crown of a daughter and son-in-law will pay for it all. Isn't Gloria a lamb? And whatever they won't pay for, I'll pay for, as far as amusements and shopping and things. You needn't spend a penny."

A pile of carrots, celery, onions, and tomatoes awaited chopping for a cold salad on the prep table, so Ellen took up the knife and went after them herself. That and taking a deep breath helped organize her thoughts. "It's very kind of them and you both, and I don't mean to question yours or their generosity, but do they really want to pay for two girls they barely know to come visit, instead of Uncle Melvin?"

Aunt Jennie waved or explained away that and every other question in Ellen's arsenal. By the end Ellen was not persuaded to say yes, but her final bastion was solely loyalty to Mr. Bradley and her job; Aunt Jennie wouldn't touch those. Every other objection had been shot down, even the consideration that Marion wouldn't be persuaded to join.

"Gloria will adore you. She gets along like a caterpillar and a leaf with everyone. Her husband will like you because you're sweet, sensible girls. He'll like you more than he does me! In fact, I think I'm doing him a favor by bringing you two. It'll give him someone else to talk to, an excuse to avoid me. If he feels like talking, that is. The man likes his solitude." She chuckled and shook her head.

"It'll be good for you, whenever you do go," Mother said, scraping and balling up the last of her biscuit dough. "As much as I hate when you're gone, it's good for you to see more of life and good times. And Marion...well, she'd probably find her future in a place like New York, wouldn't she?" She sighed one of her pained, dramatic sighs.

"I suppose so." Ellen didn't trust herself to say more than that in Aunt Jennie's hearing. She could talk to greater effect with Mother in private.

"Mention the scheme to Marion in your next letter, Gussie," Aunt Jennie said, banging her spoon on the edge of the pot. "Or you, Ellen. Whoever writes her next. If anyone's keen on New York, it'd be an aspiring actress like her. Besides, isn't that where Wilkie St. John was going? She'll want to hunt him up, for sure."

Though Aunt Jennie and even Uncle Melvin often talked about New York City in the following weeks, Ellen never seriously considered it. Greta, who nine times out of ten took the Maddoxes' word for everything, was so intrigued that she discussed the city with her friends and "learned" things about it to pass on to Ellen, trying to kindle her interest.

Ellen wasn't impressed. However, she'd pondered one of the reasons Marion might be extra keen on it: Wilkie. If he was still there, she'd find him, maybe discover why he'd left and hadn't stayed in contact, and then…would she and Wilkie go forward in their relationship? Would everything come together? And would that be a good thing?

But two weeks after Aunt Jennie had first sprouted the issue, Ellen had cause to regard it differently for herself.

Mr. Bradley knew about his practice's finances, of course. To make matters worse, several large expenses had come due. She didn't need to bring it up; every day it weighed on both their minds but was left unspoken. After two weeks, though, when she had returned from the bank with the statement after making a deposit, not even her powerful reserve could restrain discussion much longer. *I hope he'll tell me today about what he plans to do. I dread waiting till Monday.*

He was on the phone when she resettled into her desk, but a minute later he hung up and stood in the doorway to his office, observing her. "Now that you're back, I wanted to speak with you." He fell silent and tilted his head while his gaze wandered to the window, full of light and greenery and the white porch columns, such a contrast to her warm-toned, monotonous little workspace. "In fact, would you like to come into my office? It's more comfortable there."

Here it was, the discussion, right in step with her wishes. She and Mr. Bradley worked together almost telepathically. What would it hold? She had scrutinized the financial issues from all angles, and nothing would be a surprise now except for him to do nothing. She'd even...yes, she'd even considered the possibility that he would let her go. It was hateful to think of, but she had faced worse—and would *not* be caught unprepared again.

The offices were different—one a spacious and old-fashioned converted parlor, the other a stark and cluttered room half its size—but it was still the same picture: her, seated in a small chair opposite her employer, enthroned behind an insurmountable desk. She tamped down the fear that rose to her throat. Even if the same thing was to happen, Calvin Bradley was incomparable to Benton Green. He would do everything he could to soften the blow, help her in every way after the fact...

Perhaps he wasn't even firing her. She took a deep breath as he began.

"What do you think of our financial situation, Miss Dashiell? Have you any ideas for cutting back? It must be very, very drastic, whatever we do."

What had she said about the incomparability of her two employers? She offered a couple of suggestions, which he praised as sensible, but ultimately inadequate.

Mr. Bradley put his elbows on his desk and leaned forward. "I hope I don't sound like a rain cloud, but really, I'm at my wits' end. There's nothing that can be helped—people cannot pay and," he added the last bit firmly, "it wouldn't do any good whatsoever to not serve them, because I can't replace them with paying clients."

"You could fire me." Ellen was astonished at the calmness with which she said it, while fear and protests agitated inside her, beyond the focus of her brain. "You *could* do without a secretary—you've done it before. You—"

He interrupted, "No! No, that isn't necessary. I'd sooner sell my car than sack you."

"But you could do without me, just like your car. Only doing without your car would still cost you, because you'd have bus fare, and who knows what you'd do about clients in the country; whereas doing without me would only cost you time."

"I couldn't. Let's not even discuss that." He looked and sounded almost angry, his jaw tense and his dark eyes flickering.

Ellen acquiesced silently with a nod. Relief wanted to dance inside her, but stronger than that was worry over the future of the practice. If it went under, she'd be without a job anyway. Shouldn't she be sacrificed so Mr. Bradley could still help these people?

They talked a little more, but arrived at nothing. Then they parted and resumed work.

She began typing a letter from shorthand dictation. Would misfortune always dog her steps? Would she never again be secure in a job? Must she, this time, insist on her own dismissal, knot her own rope? *God, help, please.*

What was she typing? *Thisreprot wil l sreiousl un—* She stopped. This wouldn't do. She ripped out the sheet and restarted, except this time she made a mistake on the very first line. Her hands dropped to her lap.

God's helped before. He gave you this job. He's always protected you. No one in your family is starving. No one is without clothes. You'll see Dad again, even if it won't be for months yet. Things could be much, much worse.

Even if things got worse, she could still trust Him to protect her. Everyone else might fail her, whether through deceit or powerlessness, but He never would. What had Dad said sometimes? God let one go through bad circumstances so that one would seek Him? She ought to be doing that more earnestly. Dad…her job…the move…Marion…Everett…this job…everything that had gone wrong in her life ought to have brought her to her knees, utterly submitted to God. She should have the faith of an apostle. Even in the bleakest circumstances, He was with her.

The idea came an hour later, as a natural trail end of her thoughts: a way to save Mr. Bradley money without making him feel awful for doing something to her. It was extreme, but so was its antithesis. It called for sacrifice, but sacrificing herself was far easier than allowing bad to happen to anyone else. Especially since she was assured of God's protection and guidance. In fact, she had prayed about the decision and felt peace…maybe He had even led her to it. God did that, didn't He? Step in and lead one to the correct path?

She would go to New York. Take herself out of the way for a time.

If Mr. Bradley vetoed the plan, she would submit of course, feel relief tempered with anxiety for the practice. At least going to New York she'd be doing something to help, and it wouldn't be altogether unpleasant, either. Though New York did not attract her, the prospect of seeing new places did. She'd never been out of Ohio. The distraction would be welcome; it might help ease her pain over Everett.

She presented it to Mr. Bradley right before she left for the day. Not vehemently against it, which told her he was more worried than he let on, he thanked her meditatively and said he'd think about it over the weekend. And that was that. She wouldn't say anything to Aunt Jennie until she heard from him.

Monday came. Mr. Bradley trudged in and stood before her desk early in the day. She started to rise but he motioned downward for her to remain sitting. Then he put his hands behind his back.

"After mulling it over, I think you should go. Whenever it suits you, you can go as long as you like—or however long Mrs. Maddox likes. When you come back, providing there is still an office, your place will be here waiting for you."

She gazed at him and nodded unblinkingly.

"I don't know how I can thank you adequately," he continued. "You're doing a very noble thing; I'm humbled by it. You have my unending gratitude."

"Thank you." She was grateful he thought so highly of her and her plan, but it made her sorrowful. If only Everett thought that way about her. Every thought, even the worries that shouldn't have anything to do with him, was tied up with Everett these days.

And then, there it was. Leaving again. Would she never be settled? Traveling suddenly lost the luster she had polished up over the last two days. It was awful to leave home when one had to.

"Is your sister going with you?" Mr. Bradley asked softly, hands still behind his back. He seemed younger in that posture, almost boyish. "New York is a fine place for actors and actresses."

"I don't know yet. Aunt Jennie begged us to ask her, but my mother refused because she didn't want Marion going there without me." That had been the result of her and Mother's private conversation. Marion unleashed alone—that is, with only Aunt Jennie—in New York City boded ill. "Now that I'm going, we'll ask her and see. You're right; New York *is* very promising for actors and actresses. But as you know, she has a job now with the summer stock theater. That may keep her."

"Have you heard more of how she likes it?"

"No." Ellen tried to smile, but couldn't. "We don't hear much from her these days." Hence affirming their decision not to let her go by herself to New York. At least the summer stock company could be easily traced.

"Which probably means she's enjoying herself a great deal," Mr. Bradley said. "One gets lost in what one loves."

"Yes." Like with her own work, and with Everett; but both were being taken away. *Stop.* It was Marion they were discussing now. "I'm sure she's having the time of her life. I hear stock is pretty rigorous—a new play every week—but she always wished she could spend all her time in theater."

"So she's traveling. Have you heard where she is now?"

"Mansfield. But she's getting ready to move soon to the next place."

"I'm sure you miss her. Do you wish you could see her in

something they put on?"

"Oh, yes; I miss her and I miss seeing her act. She is talented."

"Her singing is splendid as well." He spoke the slightest bit wistfully, but returned to himself in a heartbeat. "I'm glad to hear she has a job she can love. I can't see her buckling down into something she abhors just to earn a living."

"She's often declared she'll never do that, even if she has to starve." Ellen managed a half-smile.

Mr. Bradley nodded and smiled his small smile, then his expression straightened into sober lines. "It takes the sting out of hard times to think of someone who's doing well, doesn't it? Well, I'd better get back to work. Thank you again for what you're doing. Remember, you have a job while you're here, and if our luck holds, you'll have it when you come back." He turned and took a step toward his office. "On second thought, it isn't a question of luck." He swept his gaze to Ellen. "We're both church people. It's a matter of God's will."

Chapter Nineteen

"NEW YORK! WHY, OF COURSE! ARE YOU CRAZY? I'D AS SOON miss that as heaven!" Marion exclaimed. Wilkie was in New York! Her heart leaped, nearly bringing his dear name to her lips. But she needed to impress Ellen with her career-mindedness. She was talking to Ellen on a public phone after receiving a telegram urging her to ring up the Maddoxes. "Summer stock is good training and all, but there's not much of a future. And it's hard work! Hard, hard, hard. I've never been so tired in my life. But it's a good kind of tired." My, it was swell to pour things out to Ellen again! It had been far too long. "They say I've got the goods, and I'm sure they'll give me a reference to take with me to New York." She paused. "I'm going to look for something there, you know."

Ellen paused, too. "I figured you would."

"Yes, you know me too well. The directors here can help me —tell me where to go and who to find. A whole bucketful of tips." Wilkie would help, too, once she found him. And once they were reunited, he'd be so in love with her that he'd bring her to all sorts of people he knew, influential friends who'd see her talent and ignite the engine of her career. But most importantly, she and Wilkie would *never* have to part again. "Oh, Ellen, how can I ever thank Aunt Jennie? And that cousin of ours…she's the top."

She gushed about New York and her work in the company for a while before Ellen reminded her the telephone would cut them off any moment.

"Oh, Ellen, I'm so abominable not to have asked about you and Mother and Greta and everyone! How are you? Fine? I'll see you soon, so we can catch up then. I'll come home as soon as possible. I need to finish out this week, of course, but I'll notify them today. That will give them oodles of time to find a replacement. Some girl will think herself lucky, but I know who's luckier!" The phone went dead. Rats, she hadn't had a chance to give her love to Ellen and the rest. Well, she'd see them in a week, and she could cascade her love all over them.

Leaving her position in the company was risky, because she was giving up a livelihood, but Wilkie and the possibilities New York offered far outweighed a run-of-the-mill summer stock theater. She wasn't naïve enough to think there was any dreamy glamor in cheap staging and props, hot, nonstop commotion, and mediocrely acted plays that died like moths at the end of every week.

Going to New York was the opportunity she had yearned for, the big break on which she'd set her longing eyes even before she thought of Hollywood all those years ago.

And Wilkie would be there. How fitting. The lovely thing was, choosing him was the same as choosing acting. In fact she'd send him a telegram at once.

Cardinal Bush and New York couldn't come quickly enough.

"I can't believe you're going to New York!" Leona said to Ellen on the telephone. "Do you know, I think I shall visit you there? Father likes us to take cultured trips every summer, not just outdoorsy vacations at the lake and so forth, and it's high time for us to go to New York again. It's been ages, and I do love it. The only thorny thing is that Everett's family is there, and we'll see them, and I haven't seen them since I've been—" She gasped, probably recalling the perils of the party line. "You know what I mean. But I shall love seeing you there! I miss you so much. Do you know your address? Telegram me as soon as you know."

Ellen promised, and after a few more parting pleasantries, hung up.

Leona in New York…that was all right. The city was big enough for both of them. Surely her family wouldn't shunt her off onto Ellen as they had in Canton. No, families like that needed all their ducklings making first-rate appearances at all the proper places. Everett's family there, too…that wouldn't be a problem; they had no reason to know she even existed unless Everett was in the city, and he wouldn't be. No, she and Aunt Jennie and Marion could keep on their own. Which meant, since she had nothing better to do, Ellen would be following Marion around like a mother horse.

The train pulled out of the red-bricked Pennsylvania Station, spiriting them on a full day's run to New York City. Ellen, Marion, and Aunt Jennie had taken the train from Cardinal Bush early that morning and changed lines in Canton. As Canton fell away, Marion nestled into her seat and drummed white-gloved hands in her lap. "Wow, just over a week ago I'd no clue I'd be heading to New York. Now, bang! At the end of all my busy insanity, I'm en route to my dream. This is the pace I like living life—no hemming and hawing, no waiting…" She smiled and sighed.

"No time to figure out what you're doing or consider if it's what you really want." Ellen let a smile toy with her lips.

The sisters had had little time to talk between Marion's homecoming from Canton and when they left four days later. They sat together in the Pullman car—Aunt Jennie was happy to allow them that while she made a new friend across the aisle, a petite, elderly woman crowned with a large, feathered hat.

Marion aimed a starlet's irresistible twinkling brown gaze at Ellen. "I've had it figured out for ages. I'm hightailing it to the Theater District, I'm hitting up the casting agencies and movie studios, I'm scouring Broadway for jobs. I'm going to put so many pans into the fire, something will cook."

"You did bring enough money, for train fare back and forth every day? That's going to take days."

"I know, I know. You hammered that into me so much I brought my entire savings."

Ellen paused and the silence weighed. "I thought that was in the bank."

"I got nervous and withdrew it before I left Canton. I was going to leave some with Mother, but you got me thinking...I don't even know for sure if I'm coming back. Hadn't I better have all my money with me?"

Ellen put her finger to her lips and gave Marion a pointed look. Crazy girl; once she did foolish things, she couldn't stop. Could not even hush up about it. She'd better never let Marion out of her sight. "Of course you're coming back. Not forever, but you left so abruptly..."

"I said my goodbyes; what more do I need to do? I can't see Dad until he gets out. I'll come back when he does."

Not long ago Marion would have quieted when she referred to Dad's location, so as not to feed eavesdroppers, but she had altered during the month with the theaters. Hopefully their car companions weren't listening, or they thought of a hospital or sanitarium, but still, Marion's wider lack of proper reserve was...unsettling. Why did her personality have to change with a lifestyle change?

Ellen might as well face it head on: Marion might come to the point of no return. Her obsession with acting had been leading to this all along. Ellen and her parents should never have pretended it wasn't. There was no place in show business for a perfectly decorous young lady. *My only hope is that she retains what propriety she can, and that she never falls from her virtue.* It was too late to deny Marion New York's land of opportunity. Debating her concerns with Mother hadn't canned this trip. Ellen should never have agreed to go.

Marion would have gone eventually, regardless. She's been lost to me in this dream of hers for years. One I couldn't share, couldn't wholly approve of. I couldn't find my way into it. There was nothing I could have done. Or had there been, years back, when she thought it didn't matter?

And now Marion was probably wondering at her silence.

"I know I've left things behind, but I don't need them right away," Marion continued, lifting her favorite pink summer hat off her head and inspecting it. "I'll want them eventually, but if I do stay, there probably isn't room for them where I'll be living. My music, the rest of my books and clothes...I'll send for them or come for them another time."

"You never spoke of this to Mother." Ellen kept her voice hushed, but even she could hear the steel in it.

"Well...not exactly, no. But once I've found a place in a production, how can I be expected to leave it to come home? Perhaps Mother didn't think of that—evidently you didn't, either—but I can't be blamed for that."

"Marion, if you had wanted to discuss this in an adult manner instead of acting like a runaway child, you would have been above board on every detail, no matter how small."

Marion watched nature's green blur outside the window. Then she whipped her head back around to Ellen, curls swinging. "You can believe me or not, but I had no intention of deceiving Mother or you and running away in New York." Her voice at last cut under the threshold of general audibility.

"I didn't say you would run away. I said you were acting like a runaway."

"You seem to think I'm one step from running away."

Ellen exhaled mutely. "Well I don't. But even if you stay with Mother's blessing, it will be a reluctantly given one, and I'm concerned about what you'll make of it. You're going to be an actress, we're not stopping you, but think of how Mother will feel if you don't come home this time; and then decide if that's what you really want."

"I'll negotiate until everyone is as satisfied for me to have my way as I am." Marion smirked. "I love you and Mother and everyone, but this is my life and my future, and no one can live it but me." She drove her gaze deeper into Ellen's eyes. "I love you all to pieces."

Ellen nodded almost imperceptibly. Marion's avowed love soothed her, but Marion's iron desire for her own future, which Ellen had long perceived, meant no argument would avail. At least not one that had yet appeared.

The conductor was squeezing his large frame down the aisle. The fears and sensations of a lifetime—half past, half future—had coursed through her in the minutes it took for the train to start and the conductor to come for their tickets. She would not leave it at that, however. She would find something to do for Marion, something to solidify her safe future. But Ellen couldn't do it in her limited strength... *Lord, please work everything out for Your purposes. Please watch over her. Please help me trust You.*

Marion alternated between staring out the window, pensively silent, forgetting the book in her lap, and bubbling over with two weeks' worth of stories. She never spoke of Wilkie, but surely he was her mind's companion in those silent, brooding hours. Ellen longed to know how she expected to find him and what she would do if or when she did. But the train was not the place for that sort of conversation; the first discussion had been pushing privacy and propriety enough. Marion usually surfaced everything on her heart, so what should Ellen make of her reticence on the Wilkie subject? If Marion had given him up, she'd not have been quiet on a thing like that. But why wasn't she talking about him then? Was she planning an elopement? *Suspicion is beneath our relationship,* Ellen thought with a pang, *or at least I believe it is. Nevertheless, I'm watching her and asking about him once we get a safe hour to ourselves.*

"Oh, Ellen, isn't this wonderful? Canton is no mean village, but this—this is more people in one place than I've ever seen before." Marion stood gaping, a suitcase weighing down both arms, feeling like the scales in Lady Justice's grip. But without the load she might have levitated, so full of excitement as she was. New York! "Look at them all! Like ants or bees. Cliché, yes, but so apt. And just think—we're three of them."

Ellen nodded, eyes darting every which way searching for the sign that would point out their next destination. Marion couldn't help her hunt; this train station put on too good a show to let her limit her observation to the signs. She'd forgotten where they needed to go anyway. It appeared Aunt Jennie was just as useless, as she rotated slowly, her black eyes glazed and her mouth yawning like a cavern. Marion pulled up her lower lip—gaping looked ridiculous, even if *her* gape was only a small parting of the lips.

Aunt Jennie found her voice. It came out quaveringly. "Oh, yes, Marion, so many little ants and bees. And this is only a regular train station. Imagine the Grand Central Station! Times Square! Broadway! Coney Island!" Her shoulders heaved upward and her suitcases swung as she breathed in and let it gush out with a huge smile. "I've always wanted to revisit New York. All the people, all the stories. My dream has come true. I'm here, I'm really here!"

Dear, absurd Aunt Jennie. New York was to her the place of childhood—a spinning, glorious mythological world she'd only tasted when she was nine or ten. To Marion, it was the future, solid and real. It defined the future. Aunt Jennie might be disappointed when things turned out uglier or more troublesome than she remembered, but Marion was prepared for anything. She'd do the adapting, whatever the future demanded.

Only Ellen approached New York stolid and fixed. She wasn't excited about the city…she was going just to keep an eye on her little sister. The suspected runaway. No, Ellen would enter the gates and leave exactly the same.

That was okay. During her stint with the summer stock company, Marion sometimes felt adrift in her lonesome moments, with Ellen the brick not there to return to at the end of a harried day. It would no doubt help her life as an actress having Ellen for a sister. Phone calls, letters, visits…every contact with her would be therapy.

"The subway. That's what we need." Ellen had walked away a few steps, then clipped back. "I found where we're going. Let's be off, shall we?"

Perhaps she could be my agent, Marion thought only semi-wryly. Her naïveté in travel might wear off eventually, but she'd get lost or abducted before then if she didn't have someone watching out for her and making all the plans.

"The subway. We *must* ride the El sometime, don't forget," Marion said.

"Oh, yes! The views will be ten times better!" Aunt Jennie chuckled. "Actually the subway won't have any views at all."

The station was a stunning specimen of Art Deco. The high, sculptured ceiling drew one's eyes up away from the crowds, giving the illusion that it possessed all the space in the world. It alleviated the feeling of congestion. Chandeliers added to the opulence, as did the colorfully patterned tile on the floor. It was one of the most spectacular places Marion had ever been.

They descended the stairs to the subway, but you wouldn't know you were going underground, since there weren't windows in this part of the terminal. Voices and footsteps created a deafening noise, drowning out the announcements on loudspeakers fighting to be heard. Marion drank it all in, too wound up to distinguish any one tidbit of intrigue, and hurried after Ellen.

This was only the beginning. The fringe of New York.

The subway train was something out of a motion picture. Not a mode of transport for a modern day gangster flick, but a silver monster rumbling in a pitch-black tunnel, who shattered the deep, ominous stillness and emerged screaming with what seemed a great rush of wings that tore at your clothes and hair. Marion held on to her hat and grinned. The whooshing air was almost refreshing, the platform was so stuffy.

Ellen, Marion, and Aunt Jennie joined the crowds in the oven of the monster's belly. There was just enough room to drop their suitcases, which they gratefully did. Marion hadn't thought anything could be hotter and denser than backstage in a summer play or in line for a ride at Meyers Lake, but surely the underground train cars took the prize. People, shoulder to shoulder bowling pins, stood gripping whatever they could. The heat of so many bodies held the smell of sweat and grime and cheap perfume to Marion's nose like a chloroformed handkerchief. Was she going to faint? She dipped once, but Ellen grabbed and shuttled her arm to a pole stacked with ten other hands.

"Hold on!" she muttered.

The train jolted forward and Marion stumbled backward into the wall of bowling pin people. They pushed her to her footing, but she couldn't stay steady until she found a grip on the hand-jammed pole. The monster was indifferent to its passengers, rattling and shaking them as it boiled onward. This was better than a Meyers Lake ride. New York was more thrilling than aimless, giddy twists and turns and heights.

Nevertheless, Marion was quite ready to reach their destination when they finally did so. The train's slowing, stopping, and starting had seemed endless. "Ah, here at last!" she said in Ellen's ear.

They surged out of the car with a dozen other people— Marion didn't catch the name of the stop until they were on the platform flowing with the stream toward some steps. Nostrand Avenue. Was that where Aunt Jennie's daughter lived? Or maybe it would take them there? Either way, she'd have to get the exact address so she could write it to Wilkie.

She'd telegrammed him again a day before they left, asking him to respond and assure her he'd be ready and waiting for a Marion whirlwind. Nothing had come. She couldn't help fretting it had missed her. She chewed her lip. Well, she'd send him one more telegram as soon as she got a chance, and the first day she might just have to venture to the theaters and studios without him.

When they surfaced to a blast of hot but mercifully mobile air, they faced a huge intersection, seemingly wider than anything in Canton. Had that been streaking over their heads this whole journey? And Marion hadn't a clue! The noise of vehicles billowed at her ears. Large buildings loomed on all four corners, on the one diagonal to them a Romanesque bank as beautiful as anything in Canton. Activity surrounded the three women; they stood on a median, a side street behind them. Shockingly, trees marched down the median away from the intersection. Out of place—but they made Marion fall more deeply in love. New York wasn't just a concrete jungle, it had heart.

"Ellen, that's Eastern Parkway in front of us?" Marion asked when they rotated slowly on the sidewalk to get their bearings.

Ellen nodded. "Yes. And Nostrand Avenue to our right."

"I imagine we'll know our way around eventually," Aunt

Jennie said, a quiver in her voice and a smile on her face. "Isn't it exciting?"

Down Nostrand there looked to be shops, bedizened with colorful signs and ads. Striking row houses stood along the parkway. At first glance it wasn't too different than downtown Canton, except perhaps dingier and more closely crowded. There weren't any skyscrapers, at least not the gargantuan ones that gave New York its skyline. But that was okay…this was Brooklyn, principally residential. Those types of skyscrapers were in the big business districts. In Canton everything was together, small shops and department stores, offices and apartments and puny brick skyscrapers, with stately homes only blocks from the central point of the courthouse. Here everything was so vast each borough had its own character. Why, each borough—Brooklyn, Manhattan, the Bronx, the others—was bigger than Canton by itself!

The lanes of zooming cars, the imposing buildings forming unbroken walls, the hot wind—they entered and stirred Marion's blood. Excitement filled her whole body. She would have unbelievable escapades in this city. These streets, Nostrand Avenue and Eastern Parkway, welcomed her to the grand adventure.

"We're supposed to get a taxi," Ellen reminded them. She set down one of her suitcases and went to the curb, scanning the roads.

"You've never hailed a taxi, have you?" Marion asked, dropping her luggage.

"No. But all you do is wave at it when you see it," Ellen responded.

"Do you need a handkerchief?" asked Aunt Jennie.

Marion couldn't restrain a snort. "No, she doesn't. Here, I'll watch Nostrand."

"You know what you're doing, Marion?" Aunt Jennie looked at her with slight concern, though, with amusement in her eyes, she was ready to laugh.

"Yes, Aunt Jennie. I've done it in a play before. Plays really expand horizons," Marion replied with a straight face. She smiled to herself as she crossed the side street and approached the intersecting avenue.

In no time she had one pulling aside to the curb, not far past the stoplight. The window nearest her rolled down as the middle-aged driver leaned across the seat. "You betta get in quick, I don't usually stop dis close to the light. But yo're a dish you don't see every day. You a movie star or something?"

Marion laughed. "Not yet." She couldn't tell him how much he'd gratified her. "Okay, let me get the others."

After Ellen and Aunt Jennie hurried over, the driver hopped out and took charge of stowing four of the suitcases in the taxi's trunk. "No more room. You gotta take two with you inside. And one of you hafta sit up front with me." He eyed Marion. "C'mon, let's go, ladies." He circled the cab, opening the passenger-side doors, and darted into his place.

Before Ellen could stop her, Marion obliged him and settled in with a fast-beating heart. Her first ride in a New York taxicab, and in the front no less!

"Where to?"

That accent! The purest, most nasally New York accent she'd heard in person yet.

"What was it, Ellen, dear? I'm so flustery I'm forgetting it." Aunt Jennie rocked upward, downward, right, and left as she got comfortable and tried to fit her suitcase somewhere.

"Eight forty-one Park Place." Ellen, taking up much less room on her side of the seat, quietly tugged the suitcase so it rested on its edge between them and laid her arm atop it.

Marion repeated the address to herself three times and tucked it away.

The cabby's head lifted and dropped with a nod as he shot the taxi forward. At the next intersection he turned left, followed the road, then turned left again, and soon re-crossed Eastern Parkway. After that Marion lost track; the threading roads became a tangled mess in her mind—she never did have a great sense of direction.

A few minutes into their rapid, bouncing ride through streets so crowded it was a wonder they didn't scrape anyone, the taxi parked in front of a stretch of fancy brownstone and limestone row houses.

"A doctor lives here?" Marion asked incredulously before she thought. The houses looked small and narrow.

"I'm sure it's as posh a place as any," Aunt Jennie said with a good-humored sniff. "New York must be quite expensive to live in."

"Got dat right. You want to know the fare?"

"For the transport?"

"Yeah. *Ma'am.*" The driver didn't seem to think he sounded rude; his lean, leathery face and beady eyes were smooth of any malice. It must just be his manner.

"My daughter's paying that," Aunt Jennie said with a nod of triumph. "Stay here and I'll get her."

"Would you mind helping us unload?" Ellen asked while Aunt Jennie got out, paused to pinpoint the actual house, and trotted up the steps.

"Sure." The driver was out like lightning and opened Ellen's door as he passed it on his way to the trunk. He piled out the luggage as a short, plump lady in a scarlet floral dress came down the steps of eight forty-one, preceding Aunt Jennie. She paid the driver and waved him off.

"Oh, Mother, I hope that drive was okay. What I wouldn't give for my Larry to have been home to pick you up!" So this round-faced, big-eyed, brown-haired woman with her clasped hands tucked beneath her faintly defined chin was Cousin Gloria. She spoke in a plain Ohio accent, comforting yet boring.

"No trouble at all, my dear! Not in the least little bit. Why, it was exciting, wasn't it, girls?" Aunt Jennie said.

"Oh, you're such a good sport, Mother dearest." Gloria threw her arms around her. "There's another hug for you. Now, to hug these two!" She grabbed and embraced Ellen, who was closer, and kissed her on the cheek with a resounding "mwah!" and then did the same to Marion. She left them sticky spots of red from her lips.

"Oh, I do wish my Larry were here to carry those in for

you!" Gloria's gaze rested on the suitcases. "But I could have Rosetta come get them. She's busy with supper just now, but she'd surely appreciate the break—"

"Who's Rosetta, dear?" Aunt Jennie asked at the same time Ellen questioned, "Can we just take them?"

Gloria broke into a stronger gale of laughter than called for, doubling over in a most undignified manner. "Oh, I've gotten like you, Mother, in my old age. One question at a time, please, if you want them answered!"

"Old age? Old age, my eye! Why, Gloria, you're thirty-five if I'm not mistaken." Aunt Jennie patted her arm and grinned.

No spring chicken, either, Marion commented inwardly. *And no wonder she got married only three years ago.*

"Why, Mother, I've got aches and pains like anything. It's a swell thing my Larry is a doctor!"

"You remember the convenience of having a dentist for a father." Aunt Jennie pinched Gloria's spherical cheek. "That's why you married into the medical profession."

Marion glanced at Ellen. When would Ellen have enough and ask to go inside? Marion was about ready to run to the corner where a busy avenue rushed by, river-like, just to give her buzzing nerves something to do.

Ellen bent her knees and took up her two pieces of luggage. When that failed to attract the attention of their gabbling hostess and her mother, Marion did the same. That failed as well. As did mutely waiting for a full minute.

The row houses were rather picturesque. Limestone formed the first floor and framed all the windows while brownstone covered the second and third. The little pilasters in the main window of the Fitzpatricks' ration were adorably classy. Once again, trees on both sides of the street were a nice addition. *Nothing grand, but "Park Place" rings like an uptown bell. I won't have to hide my face in my hands giving the address to Wilkie.*

"Oh yes, being a doctor, he needs a stylish black car. He makes house calls at all sorts of wealthy homes! He's got a nice bit of money laid by, but he's so conservative. I felt like I was asking for the moon when I asked him to pay for you to come, but he was shockingly agreeable to the idea. What a perfect kitten, don't you think, Mother dear?"

"A lamb is what I would say," Aunt Jennie replied with a pretend sniff, then guffawed and put her hand on Gloria's shoulder, who joined in the cackling.

"What a swell street this is," Marion said loudly. "Do you often stand here admiring it?" Ellen shot her a look. Marion hid her chuckles with an utterly polite smile.

"Oh, it is a lovely street! I've been so happy here. So happy! My Larry inherited it from his father, also an Irish doctor, but not nearly so...witty and romantic. My Larry lived in it as a boy. Isn't that sweet? His childhood home! And they always had an Italian maid, too, just like we do. I think the traditions are just delightful!"

"And what traditions have you carried in from our home?" Aunt Jennie asked with an expectant smile.

Marion sighed—dramatically as possible.

"Please excuse me, Aunt, but I think we're all anxious to see the inside of the Fitzpatricks' house. Might we carry in our luggage now?" Ellen asked.

"Yes, a thousand times! Why Gloria, why didn't you show us in before? I've been dying all these weeks to finally see your house, and here we are!"

"Oh yes!" Gloria let out a burst of giggles. "Here you are!"

✺✺Chapter Twenty✺✺

GLORIA'S LARRY STOMPED IN JUST AS GLORIA DESPAIRED OF waiting supper on him. Luckily their cousin liked to eat, so she had provided everyone cheese, crackers, and coffee as six o'clock came and went and the girls needed to either A) snack or B) faint.

Rosetta was a glowering, square-shaped, mid-forties housekeeper-type with thin black hair tied off in a low bun. She worked tirelessly and efficiently and didn't talk *at all*. Well, perhaps two words when Aunt Jennie asked what she was preparing—"chicken pasta"—but that was it. She nodded when she met the guests, grunted affirmatives to Gloria's requests, and dropped into a deeper glower when anyone laughed in her kitchen. All in all a pleasant opposite to Gloria. Maybe Gloria's Larry had hired Rosetta to counterbalance his wife.

Gloria's Larry wasn't warm and fuzzy like her. From the things Aunt Jennie had said, Marion wasn't expecting him to be. True, he could have used a bit of sunshine, but he wasn't disagreeable. He didn't talk much—not that he had opportunity to—and he didn't smile, either, but he shook hands and asked his mother-in-law and first cousins once removed-in-law how they were and how their journey went. In addition to a calm, very doctorly appearance, minus the glasses, he had reddish-blond hair, bushy eyebrows, blue eyes, and a chin as clefted as Cary Grant's.

Once the delicious supper was over and they could spread out from the mid-sized oval table, mother and daughter carried on their own chatter side by side on the living room couch while he sat in a wingchair in the corner, nose to nose with a newspaper. Ellen and Marion were left to themselves and two other armchairs by the ornate front window.

Though the house was small, it was richly and nostalgically decorated, probably thanks to Larry's father's steady doctor profession. It was also scrupulously clean, probably thanks to Rosetta and the weekly hired girl Gloria had mentioned.

"I'm tired and limp as a rag doll, how about you?" Marion said to Ellen.

Ellen's nod was wearily short. "Me, too. I'm sure we can go upstairs as soon as it's polite."

"What time will that be?"

"Oh, fifteen minutes or so. Enough time to show we wish we could stay up and talk." Normally Ellen would accompany something like that with a half-smile.

Marion glanced out the window at the sunset-glowing street, where Larry's black sedan was parked under the nearest tree. "I'd almost rather sit out there, wouldn't you?"

Ellen shrugged.

"Tomorrow we ought to go first thing to the Theater District," Marion said. "There; that's our excuse to turn in early. I *will* be rested and in good shape when I make my first appearance."

"*First* we need to see if our hosts have any plans."

"That can wait! Or rather, that's what you can do after you get me settled in the Theater District. You can participate in their schemes for the both of us." Marion grinned.

Ellen raised an eyebrow at her. "I hope you aren't serious."

Marion huffed. "I suppose I'm not. Say, have we sat here long enough? Oughtn't we to write Mother and Greta a decidedly long account of our journey? That telegram we sent at the station won't cut it."

Ellen agreed, so Marion swept up without further ado and announced their intentions to the room.

In their third-floor bedroom, Marion sat gazing out the front window on the sea of city. It was beautiful and awe-inspiring in a strange, what-man-has-done sort of way. Within that puzzle-piece sea brimmed millions of lives, rubbing together hurriedly, purposefully. Poverty and despondency were in there, but you couldn't see it from this window, and if you kept the right attitude, it wouldn't get you down anywhere in the city. Streetlights like gigantic stars hung between the day and the night.

Marion turned away. The view actually wasn't that great. One day she'd see a *real* oceanic cityscape, complete with countless, brilliant, electric stars—the view from a skyscraper.

Ellen sat on one of the beds and listlessly pulled off her stockings. Her shoes sat where she had removed them. "Marion," she said quietly. "I know we're both tired, but I need to talk with you."

"What'd I do now?"

Ellen rolled up her stockings and put them in her shoes. "Nothing. Yet. But tell me, please, what you intend to do… about Wilkie. Will you look him up?"

"Why so gloomy? You sound like a tragedy's happened." Was Ellen really that worried about him? Did she think everything in New York was a monster waiting to swallow Marion? What would get her to relax?

"I will look him up, sure," Marion continued. "He's such a dear chum he wouldn't forgive me if I didn't." Should she confide her hopes, her expectancies? Ellen more than anyone… but no. She'd hold back for now. Ellen didn't need more to worry about. "You know I'm crazy about him. I've gotta see him, and I'll do my level best to find him. Tomorrow. I've got his address, you know. I telegrammed him ours and asked him to come, but he hasn't replied yet."

She sighed, affection and exasperation in one breath. "I want him to passage me through the theaters and studios, introduce me to folks. In fact, let's make finding him the first thing we do tomorrow. I'd been wanting to, but I didn't know how to get past the gauntlet—Aunt Jennie and Cousin Gloria—without getting bombarded with questions. Any ideas on how we can find Wilkie without letting them in on it?"

Ellen sat up straight. "Not at the moment; but we are *not* traipsing around New York by ourselves. Especially not on our first day." Well, that had put some spirit in her.

"His aunt lives in the Upper East Side. I hear it's a ritzy

neighborhood by Central Park. And it's not much farther than the Theater District. It's got to be the safest—"

"The Upper East Side? Isn't that north Manhattan?" Ellen interrupted. "And we're—very—south of Manhattan. You do realize we don't fly."

Now that was certainly the Ellen Marion knew.

They argued about it until they reached a truce: They'd go tomorrow, provided Gloria or Aunt Jennie had no rigid plans and would come along. Ellen thought a journey would be useless because he'd turn up in Brooklyn to see her after a few days, but Marion couldn't wait. They'd be close by in the Theater District anyway.

"He'll be the making of me," she said, sighing with a contented smile when their cozy, domestic squabble was over. "Or at the very least open the door for my foot."

"You do have that one other contact, though, at the Pearl. Don't you?" Ellen said as they continued readying for bed.

"Yeah; Lloyd Heron. Granted, he's my best bet for getting notice in a regular theater. He might interview me for his next play. Except I don't know when that next play will be. Milton—the guy at summer stock who told Lloyd about me—mentioned some plays I could see about. But he doesn't know where the managers' offices are."

Marion twirled in place, hugging her pajamas. "Oh, there's so many opportunities, I don't know what to do with myself! New York, you're golden, you're a feast. I'll never lack for chances here."

Ellen half-smiled and shook her head. Well, let her mock and doubt; that was her norm. Marion knew better.

Ellen was garbed for the night first and sank into a slouch on the gaily colored quilt on her small bed. A slouch. How unlike her.

"Marion, back at the beginning of our conversation, I was actually wanting to ask you something else specifically. About Wilkie. Do you..." Ellen paused.

"Are you well, Ellen?" Marion lightly brushed her hair.

"Yes, yes." Ellen raised her eyes and took Marion's as if they were a pair of hands taking another pair of hands. "Do you love him, Marion? Do you think there's more to your relationship than friendship?"

Marion took her gaze out of Ellen's and ruffled her curls. "I think there is. But please don't ask me any more right now. I promise I have no intentions of running away with him or doing anything outside of our standards."

Ellen nodded. "That's all I needed to know. For now. Keep me informed, Marion. You take things so hard, you need to keep open doors between us."

"Sure thing." Sooner or later, everyone would know how things would proceed. She had only to see Wilkie again.

Aunt Jennie was every bit as eager as Marion to descend upon the town. Both she and Gloria were thrilled at the idea of accompanying the Dashiells to the Theater District. *That makes three out of four,* Ellen thought.

"Why, what better thing to see first than the theaters? Theater is the life of the city!" exclaimed Aunt Jennie at breakfast.

"Oh, I haven't been to the theaters on Broadway for ever so long!" Gloria added. "There are such nice neighborhood theaters here, you know. I must take you to a picture at the Fox Savoy…it's only a few blocks away, and oh! is it ever a palace. But it'll be positively lovely to go to the big ones in Manhattan. What exactly are we going to do there?"

"We're not seeing a show," Marion spoke up quickly, still chewing. She set down her fork, though half her eggs and toast lay on her plate. "It's pure business. I'm investigating acting opportunities and it will be frightfully dull for you. I don't want to drag you and my aunt around in circles."

"But it will be so interesting to see the life of an actor!" Aunt Jennie countered, waving her fork. "So intriguing. I've always wondered how one becomes an actor or actress. I wouldn't miss your 'business' for the world. This is New York, after all. I'll not stay cooped up in one borough, no, not I. And it's about time Gloria gets out and about. Isn't that right, dearest?"

"That's right. I never get out of Brooklyn anymore. Oh, I am sooo excited!"

Ellen felt for Marion. The last thing a seeking actress needed was overenthusiastic relatives. And if Ellen was stuck keeping them out of Marion's way, she might be distracted from her main purpose of watching over her sister.

"Oh! Speaking of theater, I must read you an article in the *Times* by my favorite writer, Jane Watson." Gloria shifted her plump form in her chair, scanning the room for a newspaper. "You'll like it, Marion, because it's about a church in Chicago that puts on Christian plays for their community. Jane Watson writes such intriguing human interest stories!"

Marion twined a leg around her chair. "It sounds charming. I'd adore hearing it, but could you clip it out and read it to me later? I'm afraid I'd better finish getting ready. I have to look my absolute best." Her tone was grave as she shoved her chair from the table. She caught Ellen's eye. "Ellen can tell you what we'll be doing first."

"Goodness, are you done eating?" Aunt Jennie called after her.

"Yes!" Marion called back in the space of two footfalls on the stair.

"It's very good," Ellen said, swallowing the last of her fluffy eggs. "Please give my compliments to Rosetta."

Gloria beamed. "I don't know how we'd fare if I had to cook instead of Rosetta!"

"Speaking of food, what shall we do for lunch? Will you have Rosetta pack us a picnic?" asked Aunt Jennie.

"Not on your life, Mother dear! We're going to Broadway— and that's where we'll get our delicious grub. My treat."

"Wow! You've grown far from your roots, haven't you?" Aunt Jennie gave her daughter a proud smile. "Not that we weren't generous, Ellen—we were just frugal. You know us, we *never* eat out at a restaurant."

Ellen smiled, nodded, and explained Marion's other plans.

Fortunately Aunt Jennie required little enlightenment; she even filled Gloria in on everything she ought to know and more about Wilkie.

Ellen should try to be excited about today, this whole, novel trip, she really should…but that was easier said than done. New York was an overwhelming, potentially dangerous place, and she didn't trust the judgment and abilities of any of the party, not even her own.

Marion had been torn between going to Broadway or to the movie studios first. "I know mostly stage actors, of course, so they all assure me my future's onstage with them," she had told Ellen on the train. "They say it's tough to change your acting style from stage to screen. But Wilkie always encouraged me toward the movies. What I'll do is scout out the theaters first, see what their jobs are like—I could do costuming, too—and then tour the studios. If I get hired at a studio, bingo! But if not, I can always keep my skills up and build connections with an acting company." What she hadn't said then, but what Ellen could infer now, was that her direction largely depended on Wilkie. If he could introduce her to some film producer, her future could quite possibly be decided.

This time, to Marion's and Aunt Jennie's delight, they took the elevated train. And even Ellen found herself impressed—thrilled was too strong a word—when they glided across the Brooklyn Bridge. Before them, Manhattan was a crowd of gray skyscrapers under a cloudless sky. By craning to their left, they glimpsed the Statue of Liberty, far over choppy blue water crawling with boats and ships.

"'Give me your tired, your poor, your huddled masses yearning to be free,'" Marion uttered, enraptured as she gazed. "I knew I'd see it one day. And here it is, on my own road to freedom."

Did Marion think acting as a profession was freedom? Surely she'd been disillusioned of that by the summer stock. But then again, in a way, doing what one loved *was* freedom.

But freedom also meant being entrapped by nothing, because anything could turn into handcuffs. As Ellen had been so lately—and blessedly—realizing, true freedom only came from God.

Unbidden and silent as a puff of wind, thoughts of Everett and Leona arose. Ellen's own snare, what dug into her soul and stole any bit of happiness she might have had left after Dad's and Marion's troubles. If only she knew whether Everett was happy or not, she could know just what to think of him, and just what to do. It was hard to squelch the emotions, but squelch them she must if she was ever going to find joy again.

Ellen's senses had never experienced so much activity. If she could block out half the sights, sounds, and smells, it would be tolerable. The skyscrapers were breathtaking, and some of the architecture of the smaller buildings was picturesque, but that was all she could wholly appreciate. The infinite people and shops of the street had yet to impress her. At least traveling as she was above them, she was not in the thick of it.

Things don't look much like a depression here. I wonder how frenzied everything would be in completely prosperous times?

Marion, sitting beside her, fidgeted worse the closer the El brought them to Central Park. Ah, Wilkie. Even he seemed sane compared to this inscrutable city. *It's got the same brand of overwhelming madness that landed Dad in jail.* Chaos and things that didn't make sense had always frightened Ellen.

They passed some theaters, and Marion seemed like she would bite her fingers off as she followed them with a turn of her eyes, then her head, then her whole body. The Great White Way was calling.

After that, they arrived at Central Park in no time; it was the northern border of the Theater District.

"Central Park! What a magical place! I was here as a child," Aunt Jennie gushed as the four ladies approached it on the bustling sidewalks.

"Oh, isn't it beautiful? I haven't been here in ever so long. My Larry brought me here several times when we were first married," Gloria said. "It wasn't so beautiful then—there even used to be a Hooverville!—but they are always doing work on it now, so I'm curious to see what's new."

"The green certainly is refreshing," Ellen remarked. It almost felt cooler here near the trees. The city was so disconcerting, but the park promised a measure of peace, a reminder that sanity still existed in the world. Ugly, shiny gray towers surrounded it like a fence, but she'd heard it was extensive; perhaps deep in the interior you would finally shake the buildings from looking over your shoulder.

"Wilkie is lucky to live so near the theaters *and* the park." Marion tapped her purse on her hip. She wore a smart blue dress in the latest fashion, the one Mother had let her splurge on at Sears in Canton for the occasion. "Shall we be going?"

"Sixty-eight East 81st Street. We don't know how many blocks away that is. We may need a taxi," Ellen said.

It's a swell thing Gloria likes showing off her money, Marion thought as they careened down stately, genteel Fifth Avenue in a cab to their destination. They might have walked, sure, but it would have taken a whole lot longer. Though the mansion-townhouses were gorgeous, today was not the day for a leisurely stroll.

The taxi turned onto another luxurious street, where the unbroken line of huge, sculptured homes towered over the rows of shade trees on either side. It was just the place where Aunt Bertha Parrington of the grand country palace would stake her claim. Marion shivered with excitement. Wilkie was near.

The taxi stopped in front of a white mansion that took up more street-length than any of its neighbors. Marion was out on the sidewalk in a flash, craning her neck to gulp in all the details. It towered up and up; she couldn't see the sky overhead. Greek columns with ornate capitals framed the rose-red front door, and wrought-iron boxes full of colorful flowers perched beneath every window. A shallow balcony sprouted from the second floor. It was as satisfyingly beautiful a city home as Mrs. Parrington's house in Ohio was as a country home. *Will Wilkie inherit this, too?* Marion found herself thinking. *Mmm. Yes, please!*

She forgot everyone and everything else as she pounded up the stairs to the irresistible red door and shoved in the doorbell. Who would answer? Wilkie himself? A maid? Anyone so long as it wasn't his aunt...

The door opened. A tall old man in a black suit. A butler. There hadn't been a butler in the country. This was the right place, wasn't it?

"Yes?" he asked with the hint of a lyrical accent. French. Too exotic to be snooty.

"Hi, is Wilkie—John Wilkins in?" Was her voice suave? Breathless? She couldn't tell, not in this suspense.

The butler wrinkled his eyebrows. "He ees out, unfortunately. May I convey heem a message?"

Crash. There went her joyous hope, like a glass knocked off a table. She whispered a sigh, then licked her lips and checked her shoulders for sagging. "Well—uh, tell him—no, I'll write a note. Can you wait a moment while I write a note?"

She whirled toward the stairs, opening her mouth to call down to her companions, but the butler said, "Excuse me, but I keep a pen and paper een my pocket. Weel that do?"

"Yes, that'll do." Marion took the proffered materials and scribbled a note in her hand. *Wilkie, I'm here now. Come see me. We got to strut Broadway together. Forgot my address, O forgetful one? 841 Park Place, Brooklyn.* No signature—he'd know her, though his aunt never would. She folded it in half and handed it over to the pole-straight butler. "Thanks." She smiled weakly.

The butler took it solemnly. She almost thought he was going to bow his head to her with its thin, salt-and-pepper thatch of hair. "I shall convey thees as soon as he ees een."

"Thank you," she said again. Good thing he wasn't brusque. His calmness filtered over to her, and boy, did she need all the calmness she could get right now.

He closed the door before Marion had pivoted toward the stairs again. The three on the sidewalk blurred. Aunt Jennie and Gloria...why did they have to be here? To witness her humiliation, to needle it into her like boys poking pins into an interesting insect?

"Well, well, well, someone is playing hard to get!" Aunt Jennie chortled. "Not in, is he? You poor dear. Well, keep after him, I say. We can come every day if we have to!"

"Oh, it is too bad. Your hopes must have been so high! Why, I remember when my Larry was so hard to get in touch with— so busy with his practice—I was always half heartbroken. Do you think he's out acting, Marion?"

It was so tempting to stay on the top of the steps. She couldn't see anything through her tears, and she relished her distance from those meddling cows. If Ellen would come up here…

"Come down now, Marion. It's time to go," came Ellen's flat, gentle command.

Marion took a single step forward without thought.

Must she leave? Wilkie, not where he was supposed to be, again. But if she could wait long enough…

By the time she reached the others and Aunt Jennie and Gloria had given her hugs and Ellen had touched her shoulder, she could think clearly again. It wasn't supposed to be like this, to proceed without Wilkie on her first whole day in New York, but she'd adapt. That's what the acting life was all about. Forging ahead, no matter what.

It would just take a few moments to recollect her determination and enthusiasm after it was scattered by her disappointment. She had counted on Wilkie to make this easier for her, to smooth her path. *I know I'm good, or at least I think I am. But you've got to know someone in this business for them to see your talent, whatever size.*

They returned to the cab, which had waited for them. Marion sat in the front again. She had to be as alone as she could get. As soon as her feet left the pavement and the car door shut her off from the mansion, the defeat weighed more heavily than she could bear, because she felt more rational. *Get a grip on yourself!* She would not break down in front of Aunt Jennie and Gloria. That was far, far worse than holding it in. *You'll see him soon. He just wasn't here now. I could even get the others to come back when it's time to head home. And why didn't he respond to my messages? It's a simple matter of them getting lost. My note will do the trick.*

The driver asked where next, and Ellen answered quickly—she saw Marion was in no condition to. The ache in Marion's throat subsided as he whisked them to their next target, the Pearl Theater. By the time she stepped out the door on that end, she'd buoyed up considerably. She could see over the surface of the water and the boat wasn't too distant after all. Acting was her element. True, she didn't know how to land a position in a cast on Broadway, but she'd figure it out as she went. It was the acting that mattered. And this Lloyd Heron, Milton's college friend, might be able to help her, if he respected her "introduction," Milton's scrabbled note, tucked now in her purse. He had a soft spot for young, aspiring actors. Of course, he wasn't in movies, and he wasn't Wilkie, but in this business, you had to snatch what drifted by.

ᕉᕧ Chapter Twenty-One ᕧᕉ

"MILTON KENNARD, EH? PRECIOUS, YOU'RE NOT ONLY LUCKY I was in when you came, you're lucky about *everything*. I don't remember any dirt on good ole Milton. Now, if certain other old buddies had sent their hopeful little protégés to me, well, those hopeful little protégés might find the *hope* dashed from their description."

Marion sat in the slovenly "office" of Lloyd Heron, manager of the Pearl Theater, a company so well established it inhabited its own theater. She was alone at last with the second best person in New York with whom to be alone, in her case. He held a key, and if fate or God was with her, that key might unlock her dreams.

Lloyd was tall and dark, but his looks would have been bland if not for his beaked nose. A cigar went in and out of his teeth as the mood struck him. With his long legs and gray-blue suit, he mirrored his name too much for Marion to believe the name was real, yet there was no contrary evidence, and not even she would seriously consider asking him. His voice was loud and rough, but when he said certain words, like *precious*, a warmth crept in. It lifted a corner of the cloth of his exterior, revealing what Milton had called his soft spot for young aspirants.

"Milt said you were good, earnest, and obliging. He's got my requirements down pat. So you played a lead in high school and have had plenty of speaking roles. And you sing. You sound promising, but of course they all do. Now, I don't got much time, but I want you to give me a monologue—whatever you've got, cut it in half—and sing me a song. Cut that in half, too. Five minutes is all I need to tell you what I think."

Terror gripped her. Drat, she'd forgotten the monologue! She'd been so jittery and excited it had jittered the monologue

227

right out of her mind. And Milton and the others had warned her to have one ready. She had it with her, on the train, but had she given it a look? No.

He was staring at her…that nose made it look almost like a glare. She was like a fish a heron had pinioned for devouring. "You could come back when you have it. Of course, I might not be available."

Her mind raced. The speech from *Secrets*. Could she remember it? It had been months since she'd spoken it aloud. Lines of it had cycled in her head since she'd had to desert her golden opportunity to play Mary, the lead character, to go to Cardinal Bush. She opened her mouth, but not a word floated into her mind.

*Wilkie, if only you were here…*Judy! The girl opposite Wilkie's character in *Underhanded*. Every Judy line of the play burst into her memory, and she had only to pick the longest—Judy had two speeches that were relatively uninterrupted. The last one would do, the one where she confronted the butler as the thief.

"This is sort of unconventional, but it's the last play I was in where I had a real speech; not exactly a monologue, but that saves the necessity to cut it half, doesn't it?" She smiled and rushed on. "It's a character named Judy who, with her crush, Fred, solve a burglary perpetrated on her rich neighbor. This is where she accuses the butler before he stuffs her into a closet to suffocate."

It was a cheesy play, and she couldn't believe she was going to use it in front of a professional Broadway director, but she wouldn't think about that. She tentatively stood, and seeing no flicker of disapproval behind that nose or the cigar he took to his mouth, she stepped behind her chair and dove into the lines.

"It was you!" She whirled and pointed to the corner of the room. "It was you all along." Her body parts remembered every motion, every expression she had assigned them, with the ease of months ago. "You drugged your mistress so she wouldn't wake up when you dug your dirty, rotten fingers into her jewels. You stole her pearls and her diamonds and even her precious heirloom locket." She backed away, still pointing, careful to keep three-quarters facing the audience. "We should have known; beneath that slick toupee and groomed suit, you had a Chicago look about you. Mrs. Higginbotham was so blind she couldn't see the heel you'd become!"

She ducked a flying paperweight. "Hurt me and you'll have one more crime on your slate!" Her voice rose, but she held it back from shrieking. "Fred knows you're here. You can't escape!" She took a step back and risked a glance to find an object she could use to defend herself. Her eyes widened. "You drugged Mrs. Higginbotham again, didn't you? That's why she can't hear us. You despicable scum! She can't survive another dose like that! You're a—" Half crouched, she froze with her mouth open. "Why, you're a—murderer." The last word she issued with a strangled breath.

She stayed in place a moment, then straightened and dared to make eye contact with the Heron.

A smile played on his cigar-less lips. Amused, not scornful, but Marion's stomach butterflies were so strong she felt nauseated and faint.

"You can sit down." Lloyd seemed the friendly man again as he tipped his nose toward her chair. She obliged and swallowed, which helped her dry mouth not one bit.

"That was good. You've got talent. The play wasn't great, but you actually took Judy up a notch—you made her real, less melodramatic, less hysterical. I got sucked into your illusion when you ducked. And that last line, especially that last word— *murderer*—that could send real chills with the right audience."

He tapped his fingertips together, the cigar trapped between two knuckles. "Most of the lines were ridiculous, but you didn't write them. Considering what you had to work with, you did swell. But please, pick a different monologue next time."

Next time? Marion bit her lip to keep it from trembling.

"Well, you said you can sing." He bit his cigar again and pushed his water glass to her across his desk. "Take a swig, wet your whistle, and give me a song."

After that letdown, did he really expect her to sing? She felt like crying. She'd bungled it. But…perhaps, if she did well on the song, she could make up for her choice of monologue.

"How about 'Smoke Gets in Your Eyes,'" she said. She'd been crazy over it ever since she heard Irene Dunne sing it in *Roberta* just this year, and selecting original Broadway fare was surely smart.

And the lyrics fit how she was feeling about Wilkie at the moment. Tears wet her eyes at the lines lamenting the desertion of her true love.

Heron nodded when she finished. "That song's a little low for you, but you said you just turned eighteen? You might grow into the voice needed for that one. But, precious, that *was* beautiful. You put feeling into it. You convinced me that song was meant for you, young as you are."

Marion exhaled into a cautious smile and reached for another drink of water.

Lloyd lightly slapped his cigar onto the desk. "I want to keep you in mind. I'll keep your telephone number and photograph. One more question. How's your dancing?"

Marion gulped. "Not super. I've had a little training, though, so I think I could learn fast."

"You look like you could. Tell you what. We're negotiating *Diamonds* right now, and with any luck, we'll be casting in a few weeks. Something about you reminds me of one of the little dames we'll need. You might hear from me."

He stood, his cue for Marion to follow suit. Knees weak with joy, she could hardly do it, and between her huge smile and tear-blurred eyes, she could hardly see.

He walked around the desk and went to the door. "If you don't get a role—and I warn you, you've got tough competition —don't give up. Enroll in acting school. You could use a little know-how; it'll take the gaucheness and nervousness out of you. But whatever you do, don't give up. The profession needs artists like you're well on your way to becoming."

"Oh, yes, sir!" Marion nodded vigorously, unable to restrain that last demonstration of her gaucheness and nervousness.

He opened the door, shook her hand, and patted her

shoulder as she floated out.

"Thank you ever so much. You don't know what this means to me!" she said.

"That's what they all say, so I think I do, by now." He grinned and winked. "So long, kid."

Well, I'm glad this is going well for her. It takes her mind off her disappointment about Wilkie. Ellen sat on a bench with Aunt Jennie and Gloria while Marion browsed the list of parts for an upcoming play at the next theater office they visited. As uncertain as Ellen was about Marion's acting career, Marion's happiness made her happiness.

Ellen hadn't expected Marion to take Wilkie's absence so hard. She was lovesick, plain and simple, and she must have also really desired a shot at the movies above the theater. Only a combination would bring her so near to throwing a fit.

What *would* happen if Marion got a part? It meant weeks— even months—of rehearsals and possibly travel if the show went on the road, and there was no doubt now that Marion would stay with it until it was over. And there was equally no doubt Ellen would stick to her like a bur. And then...one wouldn't be enough. Marion might return home to get her things, but she'd be back for more.

What, then, would Ellen do?

Mother wouldn't need her, since Dad would be safely home from the pen. Calvin Bradley could always find another secretary. And Everett...she needed to forget about Everett; distance would help.

Really, she could up and leave Ohio and follow Marion to the ends of the earth. Marion needed her more than anyone else did. New York was awful, but overcoming her feelings was nothing new.

She'd do it if she had to. One thing about a big city, it was chock-full of work.

Marion strode back to them, uttering a sigh. "I wish I knew if I had any hope of a part with a *name* attached to her. But even chorus members get paid—and experience."

"Chorus member? Like a chorus girl? That sounds risqué," Aunt Jennie said, eyebrows raised. "Your mother wouldn't want you to take such a part, I'm sure!"

Marion rolled her eyes to Ellen, as if asking again why Aunt Jennie had to come along. "This is a respectable show; 'chorus member' is just someone who sings only in the chorus parts of a musical."

"I would think singing at all in a Broadway show would thrill you," Ellen said quietly.

Marion smiled. "Oh, it would! I'd be in heaven. But you know me—always grasping after the moon. The moon of a lead in any show—play or film." She sighed again. "But going to the moon will take years, and lots of ladders. Shall we be going?"

"Oh, you do have such a whimsical way of speaking!" Gloria exclaimed as she slowly pushed herself to her feet. "I wonder if there are enough ladders in the world to take you that far. What an awful lot of them it'd take." She giggled. "Is anyone hungry? I'm starved! I noticed a darling little café across the street, at the corner. Do agree; I don't know if I can walk any farther, I'm so famished!" She elbowed Marion. "I bet actors and actresses eat there all the time."

Café Italienne was a tasty little joint with an assortment of Italian-style foods and coffee even Ellen found refreshing—she drank coffee only when she felt weary and stressed.

As they ate, Marion named two secondary characters in an upcoming play she would love to be picked for. "But they're casting now, and I don't know if I have enough time to research the roles. When you want to stand out to a manager, it helps to show him you have what he needs. But maybe I should seize the moment."

"What about working for that nice Mr. Lloyd Heron?" Aunt Jennie demanded. "Don't you owe him any loyalty?"

Marion gave their aunt a withering look; Ellen kicked Marion under the table. Acting like a child deserved a childish reprimand.

"I don't owe anyone loyalty unless I have a contract with them. It would be an immense treat to work with Mr. Heron, but his play is weeks away, and my time is short. I'd be foolish not to try to find something else in the meantime." Marion cupped her hands around her cool glass of Coca-Cola. "When you're an actor seeking employment, you talk to every manager you can grab until you get a job."

"Mr. Heron suggested drama school. Did he recommend one?" Ellen asked.

"No, I was so wild with joy I forgot to ask." Marion frowned and brushed a stray curl from her eye, glinting in the light from a nearby window. "I've heard that the American Academy of Dramatic Arts is the top. The time would be right to enroll, but of course I've got no money. Not enough anyway." She smirked and winked at Ellen. Ellen remembered that she brought everything she'd earned with her, stowing it... somewhere. Should Ellen be worried about not knowing where?

"You could at least visit it and find out more information while you're here," Ellen said.

"I have the address," Marion agreed brightly. "Is everyone about finished? The day is slipping."

"You hardly ate anything! And after that paltry breakfast, too. Don't you ever slow down?" Aunt Jennie asked.

"I've got more energy than I know what to do with. Just look at me!" Marion held out her hand, which was indeed vibrating. "You wanted to come along and see what an actor's life is like—it's moving and rushing nonstop."

"She slows down when she has to do something she doesn't want to do," Ellen remarked. Marion was behaving too close to disrespect and needed reining in; only clever, or halfway clever, admonishments caught her attention.

Marion leveled her a partially annoyed, partially amused glare. "Excuse me while I go pace."

"She's going to wear herself out! Make herself drop with exhaustion." Aunt Jennie lifted her hands and shook her head. "Those emotions really run her around, the poor dear. Ah, well.

I remember what a giddy girl I was when I was her age."

"If she'd only eat more we shouldn't have to worry about her," Gloria said with a fond smile as her fork scraped up the vestiges of her chocolate cake. "I'm convinced that no one who eats enough can drop dead. At least as long as they're not old." She chuckled.

Marion was pacing the sidewalk outside, studying the beehive-like surroundings, when they joined her. This relatively out-of-the-way street was far busier than rush hour in downtown Canton, and hotter. The buildings were so tall, the concrete so prevalent, and the car fumes so thick nothing that could be called decent air was obtainable. The memory of Central Park a few blocks away was like the memory of a desert oasis. It *was* unfortunate they didn't have time to go there today. Perhaps one day soon.

Marion led them to three more managers' offices that afternoon and talked to several people—secretaries, office boys, actors—all the while gleaning knowledge, confidence, and exuberance. No one gave her much encouragement, but it was her first foray; she saw no reason to be daunted. She started planning how she could research the roles she wanted. They ended the tiring trail at the American Academy of the Dramatic Arts, where Marion collected a pamphlet.

It was nearing five o'clock when the four women emerged onto the now shadowed sidewalk. People still streamed past; no surprise there, as they would probably never stop. Here in the Theater District it would only intensify as night came on.

Marion darted to Ellen's side when Aunt Jennie's and Gloria's backs were turned. "One more try at Wilkie's, please? Since it's a different time of day, he may very well be in. I *have* to see him."

"I understand, but it's late, Marion. Think of Aunt Jennie and Gloria—Gloria's husband will be home before we are, and he might worry. We're coming back tomorrow—"

"For the thousandth time, they didn't have to come along. They can go ahead of us. But I've got to see Wilkie."

Ellen was curious herself. It would be wonderful to settle at least one uncertainty, and practically speaking, this hour was more likely to find someone at home than an earlier one. "Well, we'll beg their indulgence, because we are *not* traveling alone."

Aunt Jennie and Gloria were delighted to accommodate; Aunt Jennie thirsted to see Wilkie again, Gloria was desperate to meet him, and they both wanted to have a role in a love story.

Back at the white street-side mansion, Marion ran up the steps and knocked without hesitation while the others waited beside the cab.

The butler responded. "I fear he ees out with hees great-aunt, but I conveyed heem your note, when Mrs. Parrington was absent, as you requested. I have no doubt he will contact you shortly. Perhaps he even sent you a telegram thees afternoon."

"Oh, that'd be lovely." Marion sighed. "Thank you. I sure don't mean to be a bother, but you don't mind, do you? It's part of your job, dealing with annoying little mosquitoes like me."

"It ees my pleasure, rather." The butler bowed.

"You're sweet." Marion started to turn away. Ellen caught a glimpse of her gloomy face. "What's your name, by the way? I should know your handle so I can bless you in my prayers."

"Thoreaux. Thank you, mees."

"You're welcome."

He closed the door and Marion shuffled down the stairs. "That's that."

"Aw, don't give up, Marion! You'll find him—or he'll find you—yet!" Gloria exclaimed.

"The course of true love never did run smooth," Aunt Jennie quoted gaily.

Marion nodded and ducked into the yellow taxi.

ᖰᖰᖰᖰᖰᖰChapter Twenty-Twoᖰᖰᖰᖰᖰᖰ

AS IF THE STRENUOUS DAY HAD NOT BEEN ENOUGH, IT followed Ellen into the evening. At the late supper, which a short-tempered, tight-lipped Rosetta reheated and served with utmost precision, a telegram appeared beside Ellen's plate.

Ellen looked up at Rosetta, clipping back into the kitchen. "Telegram for you," was all the rather obvious explanation the cook gave.

"Ohhh," Aunt Jennie inflected, her mouth curving up into a beam. "Gloria, I neglected to tell you much about Ellen's adventures of the heart. Is that from your Mr. E., dear?"

Ellen blushed, whether from embarrassment, irritation, or pain, she herself couldn't discern. She studied the envelope, which plainly declared Leona Bingham. "It's from a girlfriend in Canton," she said as she sliced it open with her knife. It wouldn't have been Everett, but did it have to be Leona?

Dear Ellen I'll be in NY next Friday and I'll call on you Monday STOP Much love

So all the chaos was piling up in this frantic city. "My friend Leona Bingham is coming to the city next week," she announced quickly, even before Aunt Jennie had opened her mouth to ask. "She wants to call on me."

"How interesting! Your own friend coming to New York, too," Gloria said. Still holding her knife and fork, she leaned from her chair toward the general direction of the living room and shouted, "Larry! Larry, Ellen's having a friend call on her. Next week. Isn't that fun? We'll have to plan something special." She settled back in place with a satisfied smile. "I do hate dining without Larry. We miss out on so much good chat. But he must have his mealtimes prompt whenever possible! Oh, it's so fun being married, girls, learning your sweet husband's little eccentricities and wants. I hope you both get as delightful a man as I did!"

Ellen smiled and nodded, while Marion just went on eating quietly. Marion's movements were sluggish, and she wasn't making much headway with her portion of meat loaf, potatoes, and green beans. Ellen would need to talk with her later about eating more; she was under so much stress, she was liable to fall ill on a diet like that.

Aunt Jennie and Gloria chattered about the day, while Marion kept company with her own mind. Ellen hated to appear moody, so she pushed herself to listen to the others and contribute genial remarks. She couldn't wait for bedtime, when she could be her own occupation, pray, and make sense of what she could, striving for a calm spirit.

She needed that profound inner stillness that only came from God in the following days as she tagged after Marion, Aunt Jennie, and Gloria on their various jaunts. They always went as a foursome.

Marion took them to the Theater District two other days, and to Wilkie's once on each of those days. The fourth time she appeared at the East 81st Street town mansion door, the butler merely gave her one sweeping glance and shook his head with a baleful smile. Marion sobbed in Ellen's lap both those nights, but without saying a word about it.

Gloria and Aunt Jennie led them on shopping trips. They went to the Fox Savoy movie theater several nights. One day they spent in Central Park—Marion begged only to go through the Theater District to find a show to see that weekend and buy tickets—and another day they sweated it out at Coney Island. By that Saturday, they were so exhausted none of them awoke before eleven in the morning.

Marion sat in bed while Ellen dressed for the day. "I can't wait to see *Anything Goes* tonight," Marion said with a yawn. "My first Broadway show. What a momentous occasion."

"You sound flat," Ellen observed, buttoning her light green pleated dress.

"You know what would make me sharp and excited,"

Marion returned. "And apparently I can't have it. My one hope is that I'll see him tonight. I picked a show I thought he'd like, but of course it's a long shot. He could have seen it any other night but this."

"I wish I knew how you could get a hold of him," Ellen said. She herself was getting highly perturbed with Wilkie St. John. No friend could have that good of an excuse to be so hard to find. "Perhaps you should take Aunt Jennie's offer and let her camp out in front of his house until he appears."

Marion managed a half-smile. "It's awfully tempting. But I still want to avoid his aunt. I have a feeling he doesn't think she'd approve of me...and that's maybe why he hasn't been coming after me. She may have her leash on him when they're in the city."

Ellen nodded thoughtfully and turned to the vanity mirror. She would just pin up her hair blandly for now, and have Marion help her concoct something with froth later on. She assumed Broadway-goers dolled up in their best.

"I chose *Anything Goes* because it's so wildly popular," Marion explained as she swung her legs over the side of the bed. "It's run for hundreds of performances, and it's still going strong. I really think Wilkie would adore it, so even if he's seen it, he might see it again. I'm keeping my fingers crossed." She raised her hands, displaying the gesture.

"That show is so popular even I've heard of it," Ellen said, twisting her hair. "You delighted Aunt Jennie and Gloria."

"And even piqued Dr. Larry's interest. I am *that* talented at choosing a musical for the masses." Marion rose gracefully, stretched, and scrunched up her face. "Make sure you sit next to me, will you, Ellen? We were that lucky to get two sets of seats together, and I don't want that to backfire on me by Aunt Jennie or Gloria landing next door instead of you."

Ellen cornered a bobby pin and put it to work. "Don't worry, I think Gloria would much rather sit next to her husband or her mother."

"You never know."

How relieving Marion didn't want the single seat. Because

they bought tickets so late—and cheaply—the seats were scattered; one of their party would have to sit by his or herself. Ellen felt alarm at any sign that Marion wanted to be alone. *I'll loose up soon…as soon as things are more settled. When will that be?* She drifted into a spontaneous prayer. She'd been doing that more lately, as God's help had become more and more perceptible to her. *Lord, please give me wisdom, and get through to Marion so she'll seek Your wisdom, too. I don't want her to get hurt. She needs to be right with You so that she won't go outside of Your will.*

Ellen and Marion relaxed inside the Fitzpatricks' house all day, taking long baths, sorting their room, and reading. The evening came quickly enough for Ellen. She wouldn't admit to Marion the prospect of the Theater District's glaring bedlam made her tremble inside.

The show will be fun. I've enjoyed everything I've seen Marion in, and this is of completely professional quality. Perhaps the story would sweep her away from her own life for a few hours so she could return refreshed. Wasn't that how Marion viewed plays? Except, they *were* her life now. Ellen had heard Marion analyze plays and films she saw for pleasure lately, and she never sounded as wholly lost in them as she used to be.

They took the subway, their first time traveling out of Brooklyn in the evening. The sun was setting in a warm, orange bath when they trekked beneath Eastern Parkway. Ellen could see its light but not its form on the hidden horizon. When they emerged, it was into the dazzling, blinking, multicolored electric lights of Broadway. Somewhere beyond their glare were the stars; had she ever thought she'd miss the stars? She'd never take them for granted again.

Nor trees, nor grass, nor songbirds…

"The Alvin Theatre, did you say?" Dr. Larry asked in his understated manner once they were on the street. He had been nearly silent on the journey, steadfastly avoiding conversation by hiding behind a newspaper. But now he seemed ready to take the lead.

"Yes. West Fifty-second Street," Marion replied, setting her hat jauntily. She swept a glance over the garden of lights all overhead and around them, transforming night into day with a weird, artificial illumination. Ellen didn't have much experience with science fiction, but it felt like something of that sort.

"Everything looks different at night," Ellen said, "but since this is Fiftieth Street, I'm pretty sure Fifty-second is to our right."

Thankfully, she happened to be correct, and they found themselves in a steady stream of people heading in one direction. Dr. Larry started out quickly, but at his wife's cry he slowed and pivoted, rather resignedly, to take her arm—and then hurried her alongside him. Ellen and Marion fell into step behind them, while Aunt Jennie brought up the rear.

"Oh, Larry, do you really think we'll be late?" Gloria asked, her voice high-pitched with fear.

"No, but neither will anyone else," he answered gruffly.

She pondered that for a moment. "Oh!" She giggled. "Yes, it will be hard to find our seats amid the mayhem!"

"We ought to have been there an hour ago," Marion grumbled. Her impatience had been mounting all afternoon and evening. She hadn't been still for two minutes together.

Nevertheless, they arrived in what seemed like no time. Ellen glanced at her watch. *Eight o'clock.* She took a deeper breath. *We made it, a half hour to spare.* An hour would have been better, like Marion said, but this would do.

As they entered the doors, Marion bumped against her and clutched her arm. "I have a confession to make," she whispered. "I'm irrationally believing he'll really be here."

Ellen grasped her hand; it was the best reassurance she knew to give.

Don't look for him, don't look for him. You're here to enjoy the show. Why did she bother? It did no good commanding herself something; her emotions always overwhelmed her obedience to sound judgment. Marion sighed and returned her gaze to the stage. The ground seats far below were promising, but when she had darted to the edge of the balcony to search them, all she'd gained was the painful wish to have a seat here at the edge, where the view of the performance would be fantastic. *You won't see him tonight, whether he is or isn't here. He may as well be relaxing in that dratted East Side mansion.*

What did bursting out of one's skin feel like? As if her Wilkie emotions weren't mammoth enough, heaped up below them was her utter exhilaration to be at the Alvin Theatre. Not exactly on Broadway, but it was filed under the name regardless. She was in New York City waiting for the curtain to rise on a widely acclaimed musical. She was going to live one of her dreams—experiencing a Broadway musical! She could picture herself on that stage, singing and swirling with a close and talented team in front of a star-struck, adoring audience.

The more she had seen and thought of the theater here, the greater her interest grew until she wasn't so sure she wanted to jump right into movies. Not if it meant missing the opportunity to be onstage in a place like this. The Alvin exuded the classical elegance of eighteenth-century London highlife, awash in rich red hues, gilding, and Roman or Grecian motifs decorating the walls. The play was still minutes in the future, and the Alvin's atmosphere had already taken her far away.

Ellen shifted next to her, still studying the program. Remarkably stiff, she had hardly glanced up since they settled in. Was stoical Ellen nervous around all these people? The people's energetic excitement fed into Marion. She could imagine sucking it in before a performance like a plant drinking rain. Surely with an audience like this, she would perform better than ever.

She'd get her chance.

And Wilkie would see her through it.

How *would* she feel if he went off to Hollywood while she pursued a career here in New York, on stage or even in the movie studios? Well, if her future was in movies, she wouldn't bother to stay in New York for *that*. If the stage…that was a convoluted question. She was falling more in love with it every day.

But she was deeper in love with Wilkie. She realized it

increasingly every day here as well, every day she couldn't uncover him. You didn't relinquish a man like him.

Like a trick of the eye, the lights started to dim, and with them faded the chatter. Marion's breath caught and her stomach leaped. This was it. *Anything Goes.*

The performance carried her onto the stage within the first minutes, and then beyond the veil that separated the here and now, and sensible thought, from the fictional story aboard an ocean liner where the rules of storybook held place. The characters were real and funny and delightful, the score and the songs were catchy and glorious, the vast stage was grand and enveloping. She was there, a part of it, yet hovering, a passenger in love with Billy Crocker and wistful to join in the choruses. Perhaps if she were just allowed to open her mouth, she could sing her own number, one that would resonate in the hearts of all who heard it. She knew what being in love meant.

Intermission arrived, a shaking awake from a beautiful dream. Marion was frozen in her chair, her mind still acting and dancing and singing with Billy, Hope, Reno, Moonface, and the others. But the house lights were up. People were standing, moving around. She might be able to see Wilkie now! Act one had revived her belief that he was here and she would see him.

"I'm dying of thirst," she said loudly to Ellen. "I'll be right back. Don't leave till I get back—standing room only folks have been known to steal seats."

Ellen nodded, her face relaxed. Maybe she'd calmed down and was enjoying herself. Marion wasted no more time sidling out of their row to the aisle, where there was a better view of the ground floor. No one there looked like him...but maybe he was out and about. Walking around was the best way to search. She had fifteen minutes.

She saw nothing until she returned to her row in the balcony. And there, in another section, a few rows ahead, was Everett Shepherd.

৩৩৬/৩Chapter Twenty-Three৩\৩৬/৩

ELLEN WAS HAPPY TO REMAIN IN PLACE. ON HER FEET, GETTING the kinks out of her joints, offering a half-smile to whoever glanced her way, but blissfully not obligated to talk.

She couldn't see Aunt Jennie, Gloria, or Dr. Larry. They'd had to separate straightaway to sit in their far-flung balcony seats. As intermission wore on and the faces of the eddying crowd came and went, Ellen took to people-watching. If Wilkie *was* there, as Marion so ardently and—as Marion herself admitted—irrationally believed, he'd be down on ground level, where the prize seats were, and Ellen wasn't about to lean over the railing to scrutinize them like Marion.

Her gaze drifted. It passed a slight young man in a wrinkly black suit standing in the section to her left and up a few rows.

Her eyes zipped back. Everett? What was he doing here? Their eyes met and her mouth went dry. He stared at her as solemnly wide-eyed as she was staring at him, but he looked more shocked. Of course, he had always been more expressive and less self-possessed than she. His dark hair was stylishly slicked, but other than that and the full suit he was wearing he looked the same. His same, endearing self.

Of course he would, she chided herself. *You're acting like a…like a…a Marion.*

And she had to remember: *He's not mine to think of in that way.*

She wanted to go to him, but would he be flustered and embarrassed? *He doesn't know I know about Leona, so why would he?* The better question was, would *she* be flustered and embarrassed? No, but she was already acting like it. She would behave like the friend she truly was to him and approach him like so.

As she stepped forward, Marion darted into view in the aisle, bee-lining for Everett.

"Everett Shepherd! What are you doing at a theater, of all places? All the time I've known you, you never let on that you were fond enough of theater to splurge on a musical on *Broadway*. Well, I've found you out."

If he had had any notion of venturing out to meet Ellen, Marion had frozen his feet. He smiled, however, after his initial shock, and they shook hands while Ellen quickened her pace. The hordes were returning to their chairs, and any minute the room would blacken.

"I've got our address *memorized*," Marion was saying. "Be proud of me. It's eight forty-one Park Place, Brooklyn. Remember that and call on us—shouldn't he, Ellen?"

"Why, uh, yes." Ellen reached them at last and pressed in behind Marion's shoulder.

"Hello, Ellen," Everett said softly, almost hesitantly, his ears turning pink as if on cue. He took a quick look around and held out his hand.

Surprisingly, his mind was more present than hers; he had greeted her first. She smiled a full smile and leaned forward, returning his handshake, as Marion shifted sideways and tilted backward to open the way.

"Hello, Everett. What a surprise to see you in New York!" Ellen said. The seats around them were filling, the noise level heightening, like a flock of seagulls returning to their nests in the cliffs. Someone would tap her shoulder any second, demanding his or her spot.

"Yes, I, uh, hadn't told you when I saw you last because I didn't know for sure yet. My parents live here, you know, and, well, they want me to come visit for a weekend once in a while…and they wired and wanted me to come now, until tomorrow. So I did."

"And here you are. How fantastically fortunate!" Marion exclaimed. "Are you here alone? Or are they with you?"

"They're with me. They're off somewhere…but they should be returning shortly." He glanced around again, his lower lip slipping under his teeth, as if he were nervous.

"Yes, intermission must be over," Ellen said. The lights dimmed in warning.

"You must introduce us!" Marion said. "Don't leave without finding us afterward. You saw where Ellen was. Don't leave. And come calling if you're in town again soon."

Ellen inwardly winced at the invitation. "Yes, do come."

"I'll…do my best."

The room went dark. "Yikes! Ellen, we gotta scram." Marion led the charge back to their seats, where they had to wedge themselves past a line of disgruntled neighbors. Ellen looked back; Everett had plunked into his chair, and two remained empty beside him. That must be where his parents were sitting.

I'm not sure I want to meet his parents, Ellen worried. *They don't know about Leona, and they might think he and I are dating. It will just make things uncomfortable for him.*

Silence fell faster than it had at the beginning of the show. The audience was expectant now, eager to see the conclusion and satisfy their suspense. Ellen was in a tizzy about Everett. A foolish state to be in. She felt like she'd known about Everett and Leona for ages, so why did every occasion seeing him since flutter her nerves anew?

The curtain rose on the world of *Anything Goes.*

Marion's hands flew into an involuntary frenzy of applause. She felt as if the whole audience's applause lifted her somewhere heavenly. She let her tears gather. The show was beautifully madcap—touching and amusing and thoroughly cheering all at once. It could appeal to the masses and delight critics, planting songs and lines in the minds of everyone to flourish there forever. Someday she would know the actual feel of acting in a show like that, and this applause would be for her and her friends.

The applause subsided like a passing storm after the curtain blocked out the bowing cast. The chorus of the song "Anything Goes" played in Marion's mind and murmured out from under her breath as she remained stationed, one of the last to let her clapping die. She wanted to hear and see it all again. There ought to be a way to talk to the actors—wasn't there a way? To thank and congratulate them, to learn their stories of the humorous pandemonium that had gone on behind the scenes? She sensed such a kinship to the cast that she felt left out here in the auditorium.

Did Wilkie know any of the actors or crew? If she found him, could he take her to them, or perhaps introduce her another day? She surveyed the expansive hall again. Hmm...she hadn't peered closely yet into the fancy box seats on the sides of the auditorium, descending level by level from the balcony.

"Ellen, help me look for him," she insisted.

"For Wilkie?" Ellen clarified.

"Yes." She felt a twinge of guilt, because they were supposed to be convening with Everett and his parents in the aisle. Meeting the parents so Ellen could impress them would be auspicious for the pair's future. His parents would adore Ellen and could hustle Everett along. Besides, Everett seemed to need one more boost of encouragement to come visit Park Place.

But she had to find Wilkie.

He's not here, silly fool! she told herself, but it served only to water her hope that indeed he was. Maybe she ought to hightail it to the foyer and watch for him there.

She pressed into Ellen, indicating she was ready to vacate. "I'm going to the foyer—" The auditorium was half empty. How could she shove through this crush of plebeians to reach the foyer in time?

She cased the boxes once more and took a second look at the farthest box on the right. A young blond man slouched behind the edge, surveying the auditorium like a king over his kingdom, his shiny black suit and red bowtie fitting him perfectly with his sumptuous surroundings.

It was Wilkie.

She jumped and waved her arm. She called his name, but it was lost in the tornado of other voices. He turned face on to her, but still oblivious, as someone appeared beside him—an old woman attired in a huddle of dark furs. She wore long black gloves on which a tiny white star of a ring was precocious enough to be discernible from this far. His great-aunt? The great Bertha Parrington?

Now he was giving Marion his back. Why didn't he see her? In this sea she couldn't expect him to, but wasn't their love somehow magnetic, transcending natural ability, able to draw their eyes to one another's? Her love had somehow made him visible to her, though part of her had thought it impossible. Her high view had shown him to her—wonderful high view— but he, though nearly as high, was yet blind to her.

Poor Wilkie. Once they finally reunited, he'd hate himself that he hadn't seen her tonight. But she mustn't give up—there was still a chance she could intercept him in the foyer, if she could just slip through the crowd.

"I saw him just now, Ellen!" she cried as she hurried after her down their row. She pushed against her, urging her faster. "I saw him, and I'm going to the foyer."

"Are you sure it was him? Did he see you?" Ellen obliged and picked up the pace.

"Yes, I'm sure, and no, he didn't see me. But if I can just get to him in time…!" She broke off as she reached the aisle and forged upward.

By the time she breached the foyer, she was almost sure he was gone. She found the mouth of the stairs that led to the boxes and kept an eye there while she scanned the whole area, paying particular attention to the doors. But the foyer was jam-packed, without any vantage point whatsoever.

It was hopeless. She'd missed him.

Ellen came to her side. "Couldn't find him either?" she asked.

Marion's head shook listlessly, automatically. "You looked, too? Thanks."

Ellen's hand crept into her own. "We need to find Aunt Jennie, Gloria, and Dr. Larry. We're to meet them by the balcony stairs, remember."

"But I can't give up yet!" Marion started spinning her head

again, tugging against Ellen's grip.

"You saw him leave ten minutes ago. He's gone."

"Then we'll follow him to his house!"

"How do you know he's not going out to dinner afterward? It's late, sure, but society keeps the hours of an owl."

Marion subsided. One more instance of knocking on Wilkie's door and facing Thoreaux the butler and hearing "He's not here" would be torment. She might be tempted to abandon all hope of him entirely. Would she even hate him? No, never! There had to be some explanation for why he wasn't contacting her.

"You're all in a lather," Ellen said soothingly, venturing an arm around her opposite shoulder. Physical affection from Ellen? That was rare, and its very rarity put more comfort into the touch. "Everything is looking bleaker than it really is right now. We just need to go back to Gloria's as soon as we can."

Marion wasn't thinking coherently, but she gave a short nod. Wilkie *was* in New York, and she had gotten close enough to assure herself of that. She'd seen his dear, devil-may-care face with her own eyes. Her feeling that she would see him here had materialized—surely that meant their hearts and minds were one.

She let Ellen remove her to their party's meeting spot, where Aunt Jennie, Gloria, and Dr. Larry already waited.

"There you are, my dears!" Aunt Jennie trotted forward. "Ellen, I didn't think I could wait one more minute—I do believe I saw Everett Shepherd!"

Marion's hand took wing to her mouth. "Oh, Ellen! I'm so sorry I forgot! Here you should have been talking with Everett and meeting his parents and instead you were—" She cut off, her lips still apart, but stopping the words in her throat. She didn't want to mention Wilkie, and she also must remember Ellen's reservations about speaking of Everett.

"Oh you saw him, did you? Spoke with him? And he had his parents with him, too?" Aunt Jennie threw an ecstatic glance over her shoulder at Gloria. "This is wonderful! What are his parents like? Did you invite them all to our house?"

While Ellen brushed off their female relatives' million questions with polite, uninformative answers, Marion berated herself. *Magnificent, Marion. Not only did you keep Ellen from seeing Everett again, you spilled the beans to Aunt Jennie. Well, it's Ellen's fault, actually—she didn't have to come help me look for Wilkie. I'd rather have done it alone.* Alone—yes, that's what she wanted. To be isolated, even from Ellen, to have time to vent her disappointment without anyone trying to console her.

But what she really wanted, most of all, was to hold Wilkie's hand again.

Everyone had their own agendas on Monday; Aunt Jennie and Gloria wanted a shopping trip, Marion wanted to visit the library to study for one of her coveted roles, and as for Ellen... *Well, it's my agenda to stay here for Leona.* She couldn't pull a Wilkie trick and be out all day when she knew Leona would be calling on her.

Ellen reluctantly gave her blessing for Gloria to show Marion to the library after lunch when Leona didn't appear in the morning, so she and Aunt Jennie sat alone in the living room, listening to the radio. Aunt Jennie paged through catalogs and Ellen knitted. When the doorbell rang, Ellen almost jumped up to answer, but remembered Rosetta guarded the duty jealously, so she sufficed with lowering the radio.

She expected Leona, but a tiny, irrational piece of her hoped she'd be caught unawares by Everett. Which was entirely silly, because of course he was back in Canton.

She and Aunt Jennie rose when Rosetta's frowning, square blue figure filled the living room doorway. "Someone to see Miss Ellen." She left and in her place materialized Leona Bingham.

"Ellen! Oh Ellen, it's been ages!" Leona minced over to Ellen, who spread her arms just in time to catch her quick, delicate embrace. "I'm so happy to see you." Leona stepped back and traveled her gaze up and down Ellen. "New York is agreeing with you." She grinned.

"I'm glad to see you, too," Ellen replied. What had she noticed that made her believe New York agreed with Ellen? "Aunt Jennie, this is Leona Bingham."

"The delightful Cantonian girl I haven't heard nearly enough about." Aunt Jennie chuckled and extended her plump hand. "How do you do? Yes, I see your wonderment. It isn't that Ellen doesn't speak of her friends; she just never gives enough details. It's a puzzle to someone like me, who just adores people and gossip of all sorts. If you ever want a secret kept, tell it to someone like Ellen; if you ever want a secret loose, tell a lady like me."

Leona darted a glance at Ellen, threadlike eyebrows puckered. Ellen could guess: Aunt Jennie's remark too closely resembled a hint and made Leona suspicious.

"Thank you so much for coming." Aunt Jennie returned to her couch and dropped into it with a comfortable huff. "We've kept Ellen busy, but nobody makes a girl happy like a friend; unless it's a *boy*friend."

Once again Leona narrowed her eyes, but the next instant she slid a giggle over the situation and looked for a place to sit.

"The armchairs by the window are a nice spot, I think," Ellen spoke up.

"Yes, don't mind me; have your girlish chatter, and I'll be leafing through these catalogs. In fact, I feel a nap coming on… that's the only occupation that will keep me from eavesdropping and chiming in on your conversation. But first, pray, indulge me a little, Miss Bingham. Tell me about your family. We're distantly—very distantly related, in a way, you know, since my husband's nephew is married to your brother-in-law's aunt, and we share Ellen in the middle. In a way."

Aunt Jennie and Leona talked for a while. Ellen was relieved. Leona's secret wouldn't become the topic of conversation until the girls were alone, and the longer that was delayed, the less time there'd be to discuss it. Leona surely couldn't stay all afternoon.

Finally, though, with a fond farewell to Leona, her "dear, darling new little friend," Aunt Jennie gathered her catalogs and a magazine from the coffee table and left them with a wink. "Time for your gossip fest," she said. "Ellen, tell Leona all about the Broadway musical. I left it for you." She winked again. "Don't forget about your surprise fellow spectator."

When the stairs ceased creaking and a door shut, Leona settled into her chair with a chuckle. "The dear old thing is gone at last. I've wanted to talk with you for ever so long about a new development or two. Tell me, are there other ears here, or are we completely by ourselves now?"

"There's the woman who answered the door, Rosetta, but she's organizing the cellar today. I don't think she can hear anything there."

"Good. So you went to a musical? Swell—I wish I could have gone to one. But I was ill on the night my parents had planned to go. And I felt awful, especially awful, because I was supposed to meet," she reduced her voice to a whisper, "*Everett* there."

A shock punched Ellen's stomach, but she kept it from manifesting on her face. Leona had almost attended *Anything Goes*? "Oh?" She paused to enhance her pretense at surprise. "Were you able to get a message to him?" She had become natural at going along with whatever Leona said about Everett, acting the part of an intrigued confidante. Hopefully God didn't consider that deceit; she felt it was better for everyone if she did so. *Marion isn't the only actress in the family.*

"Alas, no. There wasn't any opportunity. I don't have anyone else to share my secret and assist me but you, Ellen dear. So he went there expecting to see me but was instead sorely disappointed."

That must explain his nervous skimming of the auditorium. He wasn't looking for his parents, as Ellen had assumed, but for Leona—and what a terrible thing, for him, if he had found her.

"My parents still went, however, and they said nothing of seeing him. I had intended to meet him and his parents and orchestrate an 'accidental' reunion between our families." Leona sighed. "I was bitterly disappointed, though. I thought I would cry all night. I guess it'd have been silly to do that, but I *was* quite ill. Food poisoning, I think."

"That sounds dreadful. Are you feeling any effects now?"

"No, thank goodness. Well, perhaps a touch of weakness, because I could eat only since last evening. But no, I'm fine. It's Everett I'm ill about now. Sending him telegrams has been difficult, and I *don't* know how long I can keep it up before I'm discovered. For all I know Mr. and Mrs. Shepherd might know about me now! I can't decide whether that's a good or a bad thing. I don't really know what they think of me."

She sipped her tea. "They may be on our side, but the only way to find out is if I see them again, and my illness completely destroyed that chance. And now I'm at a loss." She gazed pleadingly at Ellen. "Have you any ideas?"

"Not at the moment," Ellen replied, hiding her face with a drink of tea. She wanted to be as honest as she possibly could; it didn't seem dangerous to divulge this…"But tell me, what musical were you supposed to see?"

"*Anything Goes.* I was quite looking forward to it." She studied Ellen. "What musical did you see?"

Ellen half-smiled. "*Anything Goes*, on Saturday night."

Leona dropped her cup and saucer to her lap. "You don't say! Why, I would have seen *you* there, too!" She gasped. "Tell me, did you see Everett?"

"I did." A little twist in her heart gave her pain.

"Wow! Did you speak with him?"

Ellen nodded. "Yes. He said he was in New York for the weekend because his parents wanted him to come."

"Partially true." Leona smiled. "I'm the one who convinced him to come this weekend, though. I had my plans. Because of your encouragement, I really want to move forward with our engagement. I'm trying to find ways to do so."

My encouragement? What exactly did I say? I guess telling her to make her own decision was encouragement…to, uh, make her own decision. Follow her heart.

"Did he act like he was looking for me at the theater?" Leona leaned forward.

"Now that you mention it, I think he did."

Leona's sappy, loving smile sharpened her pointed chin. "Poor boy. Did he look like he had seen my parents? They were there, you know, though I think they sat in a box. Where did Everett sit? Did you see?"

"I really don't know if he saw your parents. He probably didn't, if they were in a box." Ellen considered how persistently Marion had looked for Wilkie before she spotted him, and that was only because he had lounged at the edge. "Everett sat in the balcony, a few rows away from us."

"My parents were too busy mixing with other wealthy people and making new acquaintances to spot him." Leona drained her tea. "Or, if they did spot him, the last thing they'd do is tell me." She shook her head and uttered a petite growl. "Shall I tell you what I suspect? I suspect they're trying to find a match for me. They've been socializing with people who have sons, and even the young men themselves—or not so young, as the case may be. They'd have no qualms pawning me off on an old geezer, so long as he's rich."

A wave of pity splashed over Ellen. Leona's parents surely wouldn't force her to marry an old man, but Ellen had never given proper sympathy to Leona's situation. She had unsupportive parents, and reason to think they didn't have her best interests at heart; so no wonder she wanted to marry Everett, even if her love for him was shallow. He was young, decent, kind, and familiar. *At least I have a family who is compassionate and each other's best friends. Leona doesn't.*

But that didn't replace the fact that Leona wasn't right for Everett.

"So I have to be on my guard," Leona huffed. "It was my idea first to come to New York, but I'm beginning to see why they gave in to me so easily. It's a marriage mart around here." She raised an arched eyebrow at Ellen. "In any circle. Have you or your sister met anyone yet? Anyone, as my parents would put it, *suitable?*"

"We've met a lot of people, yes. As for their suitability— time will tell, I suppose. My sister is spending most of her time looking for acting jobs. She's gotten encouragement from some professionals."

"Well, good for her." Leona's voice was a little too sugary to be sincere. "My parents do like the theater…I imagine we'll go to Broadway every week. And we'll take advantage of the best cinemas, too. The Palace Theatre in Canton is a dazzler, I won't deny it, but it's thrilling to see pictures in New York's best cinemas."

A whim to know Everett's parents' address buzzed through Ellen's mind, but what would that profit? She had no plausible excuse to give for asking Leona, and besides, it was best that Ellen simply kept her distance. Maintaining Everett's friendship was fine, but ordinary friends didn't need to know their friends' family. That's all she was: an ordinary friend.

"I wish I could invite you to do things with me, but my parents are keeping me closer to them here. But if I ever do strictly 'me' things, I'll contact you, because I miss you so sorely!" Leona wandered into thought for a moment, gnawing a fingernail.

"Say, a millionaire friend of ours is throwing a fete in a couple of weeks. Will you come? It'll be so big you won't be noticed. And anyway this friend and his wife are always easy about extra friends their guests want to bring. They like showing off, I guess." Leona smiled. "But you could even bring your sister, so you'd have someone to talk to in case I get called away to meet some *gentleman*. It'd be so swell if you'd come! Hmm. Maybe you could scheme with me on a way to get Everett there?" She winked.

"I don't know…I can't give you a definite yes or no at this moment," Ellen said. "Much depends on our hosts. But thank you for the invitation."

"I only wish I could have you around more. I feel you'd be a great support wherever I am. And being with you somehow makes Everett feel closer. I guess it's because you know him, and you know my secret, and I can openly share with you." Leona reached out a hand to caress Ellen's knee. "Thank you, my friend."

When would Ellen's heart cease to wince every time Leona spoke like that? When would she get over the pain? She hated to think it would be never.

Ellen half-smiled in response. The antique clock on the mantelpiece sweetly chimed three o'clock, breaking the brief silence that might have stretched into awkwardness. "How much longer do I have you for?" Ellen asked, reviving the smile that had just subsided.

"Not nearly long enough," Leona replied, making a face at the clock. "I ought to leave in fifteen minutes or so. My parents will worry after that. They're so fickle; in Ohio they couldn't care a fig where I was, so long as I wasn't required to be anywhere with them."

"It's the city. I'm always nervous to let Marion out of my sight."

"Are you? Funny dear. Well, since I have to go so soon, why don't you amuse me with some of your stories now? Tell me what you thought of *Anything Goes*, and what you and Everett spoke of, and what else you've been doing."

Ellen condensed her narrative, and between that and Leona's interruptions, she left off at three fifteen with, "I guess that's it. We've been having a good time so far. We already have a few plans this week, such as visiting the Statue of Liberty."

"Oh! Take me with you!" Leona exclaimed. "I'm in earnest. I've always wanted to go, and my parents surely can't object to me going with a friend I went around with back in Canton, especially when they hear we'll also be with two respectable old ladies."

Ellen might as well consent.

After Ellen showed Leona to the door, she returned to the living room and curled up in Dr. Larry's big green wingchair; its size and color reminded her of Dad's. She could sit sideways, knees drawn up, and feel embraced. Who had that chair now? Joe from Friar's, if she remembered right.

Oh God, Ellen cried, closing her eyes. *Help me bear up. This is such a small thing, considering what else troubles the world, but my heart hurts every time I think of Everett. I'm giving him over to You, God, him and Leona. I'm trying to handle this in my own strength, and I'm just hurting myself. Help me not to be bitter toward Leona, help me to surrender my affection for Everett, and help me to bear up cheerfully so that Marion doesn't suspect anything. She needs me to be strong and alert so I can always be ready to point her to You, Lord.*

Ellen exhaled silently. *And in regards to Wilkie…please give us answers.*

∽⊚⌇Chapter Twenty-Four⌇⊚∽

MARION COULDN'T BRING HERSELF TO VISIT ANY MOVIE STUDIOS that week, either. They were too sacred to the memory of Wilkie. She'd stick to her Broadway aspirations for now; they were considerably healthier for her state of mind. Movies were a broader, more attainable horizon than stage, but her heart shrugged.

However, what if Wilkie loitered at the studios all day? That was a very real possibility, and one she should explore...but not now. Her mind was too full to risk more frustration. Perhaps after she'd exhausted every manager on Broadway.

The days rolled on. Since they had gone so often they'd worn a path to the Theater District, Marion persuaded Ellen the two of them could start going alone on Marion's hunts.

There were so many actors in New York, all desperate for work! In every office was a crowd like all those other snaking lines of hungry beings who clung to what hope they could dredge from their despairing souls, hope that *they'd* be picked, that *they* could walk home that day with the guarantee of purpose, money, and food.

Marion had only seen such lines, since she'd never needed a job like some people did. Canton, especially earlier in the Depression, had had its portion. And so she had never shared the emotions in such a line as she did now. She needed this work. Even if she didn't have bills to pay, she wanted to have to pay the bills this way, with her acting skills. She wanted to afford school herself if that would help her ultimate dream. She wanted Dad and Mom and Ellen to be proud of her and not have to worry about her anymore. She wanted her dream to come completely, irrevocably true.

The roles she had studied so painstakingly were given away

by the time she hit the office of the manager of that production.

"Can't he interview me and hear what I've got for his play?" Marion asked the snub-nosed office boy. "He might change his mind—"

"He's not seeing anyone without an appointment," he said wearily, as if those words had walked ten miles. He and every other Broadway clerk must have repeated them hundreds of times each day.

Marion puffed out the breath she was holding, thanked him, and left with Ellen beside her. "Those directors' and producers' offices are like the sacred throne room of some king who thinks he's a god," Marion groused on the street. "I haven't gotten in to see *any* of them since Mr. Heron. But I thought this would be different because I actually studied the play!"

"I guess the effort doesn't matter, not like having connections does," Ellen said.

"You got that right. Oh Ellen, no matter what happens, I'm not giving up, and I'm going to enjoy every minute. I *know* this is what I'm supposed to do." Marion's throat ached with tears. "You said God has a plan for my life. Not that I really know God's mind—who does?—but this is as close to it as I can tell." She wasn't sure she completely agreed or even cared, but talking about God would please Ellen.

Ellen half-smiled. "I hope so. I'd like to see your dreams coincide with God's plan."

Marion felt a little stir of anxiety, even resentment, at that, but it was instantly submerged by the busy street and her even busier mind. Her eyelids fended off the threat of tears. "Well, the wind's gone from my sails. I don't know what to do next, do you? I thought I'd be befriending the manager right now. Give me a peck on the forehead, will you, dear? Just like Dad used to do when I was sad about something?"

The sisters went to Central Park to eat their picnic lunch early in a halfway soothing environment. Marion trailed Ellen dejectedly as they fled the main pathways and found a bench under a gigantic elm in a relatively quiet zone.

Maybe, Lord, You don't want her in any play? Ellen asked as she and Marion sat silent for a moment on the bench.

The park was almost cool here. The walkway wound through gently undulating carpet-like grass, shaded almost completely as far as Ellen could see by majestic trees. The breeze could reach her here.

Ellen opened the basket between the girls and smiled inwardly at the letter perched atop the sandwiches. She hadn't told Marion about it yet so as to give her a pleasant surprise in case the interview was a bust.

"Look what came this morning." Ellen held up the letter.

"Wilkie?!" Marion's eyes widened and she snatched it.

"No, Mother."

"Oh, well, that's the next best thing." Marion sighed softly and hugged the envelope. "Dear old Mother. I miss her."

"Aren't you going to open it?"

"Sweet Ellen, cheering me up." Marion gave her a look as if she were Greta, offering Marion candy and a puppy to mend her broken heart. But she sliced it open with the sandwich knife and began to read the treasure within.

"Mostly cheerful news," Marion said, handing it over. "Maybe in time I'll fully appreciate it…right now everything is clouded in disappointment. I'm not even hungry."

"You'd better eat," Ellen commanded, then dug into the letter herself as she took a bite of her corned beef sandwich. Mother, Greta, Uncle Melvin, and Sport were doing well; Dad was doing okay (code word for still alive, but downcast); how serendipitous that Everett and Leona were both in New York (Mother, of course, knew nothing of their connection); it was a very perplexing and frustrating thing that Marion couldn't find Wilkie; and then, after bits of homely news, the last paragraph:

Calvin Bradley believes he may have discovered something that could provide a good foundation for appealing Dad's case. Some things are making Mr. G look more and more like the embezzler. He doesn't want us to get our hopes very high, but he wants us to keep our courage and faith and to pray that this will lead somewhere. He is also tentatively planning to go to New York on business for a client in the near future. The client will be paying his way. That's gossiping, I know, but I don't want you to think he's using his practice's funds for it, after what you so nobly did, Ellen. Perhaps he'll tell you more if he meets you there.

Ellen, for one, would be glad to see Calvin Bradley. She was getting so homesick she'd appreciate any friend from Ohio.

"Eat, Marion; you're insulting me for having Rosetta make you a special chicken sandwich."

Marion rolled her eyes and sighed, but bit into one triangle of her meal.

"What do you think of Mr. Bradley's discovery?" Ellen asked.

"It'd be wonderful if it helped, but he doesn't sound too sure of it. It's strange he told us at all."

"No, I don't think so. He often understates things, you know. The very fact that he's confiding in us means he's nearly positive it will help."

"Well, that does elevate things a little."

Actually, Ellen was glad Marion didn't go ecstatic about the hopeful news. She herself spoke more confidently than she felt to buoy Marion's spirits. God bless Mr. Bradley for encouraging them, but she'd have to see the appeal in process before she'd tempt herself to believe it might succeed.

"I wonder if Mr. Bradley will come to New York while we're here," Ellen remarked, picking up the second half of her sandwich. "I never believed so many of our friends and acquaintances would be here at once."

"I dread what Aunt Jennie will say if he does come." Marion wrinkled her nose. "Especially since Wilkie has temporarily fallen off the stage. Insufferable woman."

"Don't worry about it," Ellen said. "If he does come, don't let her bother you. How would you put it…let her be like water off a duck's back?"

Marion furrowed her eyebrows, then released a flock of giggles. "You need a little help in the quip department. You make me picture Aunt Jennie as a huge duck."

"At least I made you laugh." Ellen smirked.

"But you know, I may be too busy with *working* and *rehearsals* to be around to tease," Marion said. She exhaled in determination. "Even if I missed this play, I have endless opportunities."

"My cheering up did succeed, I see," Ellen said. "Moments ago you were despondent, but now you're talking about trying again."

"They say don't give up until you can imagine yourself doing something else."

Ellen nodded as she shook out her white napkin. "If that's what it takes, you'll probably never quit." Was that a good or a bad thing? Sometimes, like today, Ellen had her brain so full of trying to discern God's will for her own life that she could make no sense of His will for Marion's.

Ellen was returning the letter to the envelope when she noticed another, smaller folded paper inside. "You missed this. Maybe it's a note from Greta." She opened and skimmed it. Mother's handwriting. She went back and read it closely, and her stomach did a somersault.

She glanced up at Marion, who was toying with her sandwich; she'd probably not finish it now. "Well, it's not from Greta. It's an addendum from Mother," Ellen said. "Marion, you might not like what it says, but please, promise me you won't put up a big fuss."

Marion's gaze turned to her, dramatically unhurried. "I always put up a big fuss when I hear something I don't like."

"This is serious." Ellen read it aloud. "'I didn't want to write this, and I didn't have the heart to in my first letter, but my loyalty to Dad and my conscience dictated that I must. Dad has requested that if Marion doesn't get a part in a play in the next two weeks, you girls come home. He's ashamed to have his cousin and her husband, whom we barely know, keep you for so long when there's no way we can repay them. Aunt Jennie can stay if she wishes, but you must come back. Oh girls, I'm so sorry, and I'm sorry to be so plain, but I can't disagree with him. You understand, don't you, Marion? I wish I could sympathize with you more right now, but I've run out of room. Hopefully you will get a job and then none of this will signify.'"

Ellen studied her sister. Marion stared ahead, lips trembling, hands pressed tightly in her lap. The breeze ruffled her hair. Then she whirled on Ellen and burst out, "It can't be! How can he say that? Oh, I love Dad, and...and...oh, Ellen, how could he?"

Marion dropped her face into her hands. She didn't cry, just sat frozen; in a minute, she'd be capable of listening. "This isn't the end," Ellen murmured after a moment. "This isn't your last chance to act. It'd just be a necessary detour, until we or you have money to come back and try again—"

Marion lifted her face. "I want it now! I'm ready now! Ellen, I can't stand it anymore. I want to be an actress, and I want Wilkie, and—and—all I need is more time!"

"Darling," the involuntary word felt foreign, Ellen never used endearments, "I know. Lloyd Heron might still contact you, remember? It's a chance. And after that, if not, you'll come home and get more experience, earn money for acting school, or for returning to New York..."

"I can't put it off any longer," Marion quavered. "Can't you and I get jobs here and board somewhere so I can find a play eventually? What's the difference between earning money through acting and staying and earning through another job and staying? We must write Mother back and explain to her and Dad, and then they'll understand and let us stay."

Ellen was torn. Home, Mother, Greta, Ohio, quiet, familiarity. Her heart ached for them. She felt on her own here, in charge of Marion; her mother, almost. If she didn't have to stay...if Marion was made to go home...but Marion's heart was an arrow flying to a target, fixated on her dream now within her reach. If she were pulled away, living with her would be a challenge none of them would relish. And would she ever be happy again?

Is this Your will for her, Lord? Ellen prayed. *How can we make her come around to accepting it? And if it isn't...well, perhaps You're using our dad to point us in the right direction. You've often done that. If only*

Dad were here with them. He could take care of them, make it so Marion would have a safe place to live while she pursued her career, and Ellen could find a satisfactory position. No, that wouldn't do. The whole family would have to uproot to the city, and none of them wanted that save Marion.

I'm so confounded.

"Marion, let's take the time to think this over. There's a solution somewhere."

"Whose solution? It's my dreams or their ultimatum."

"Not necessarily. We have to consider all angles." Ellen pursed her lips. "I'll pray about it. Would you pray, too, and really try to seek what God wants you to do? He has the best plans of all of us."

Marion's face was chiseled with pain. "What good it'll do, I don't know, but at least it's something. As long as we *do* something, we're not wasting time."

"May I pray aloud now?"

"If you wish."

Self-conscious, Ellen made it quick; she couldn't remember the last time she'd prayed in front of Marion. "Our Father in Heaven, we are Your children and we want to do what You desire. Please show us Your will for our way, and help us to accept it. In Jesus' name, amen."

"Short and sweet," Marion said, gazing into the wide-trunked trees across the path. "This is a blow, but I'm not giving up. I can't imagine doing something else yet."

৩৩৩৩Chapter Twenty-Five৩৩৩৩

THE VERY NEXT DAY MARION RECEIVED A TELEPHONE CALL from Lloyd Heron asking her back to the Pearl Theatre, his domain, for another interview. She was jubilant.

"This is my last chance." Shivers traced Marion's spine. She and Ellen had just arrived at the waiting room outside Heron's office the day after the happy summons. She tunneled her hands into her curls and gave them a thorough fluffing. "If this fails, I'm going to wish I'd shipped to a movie studio instead. The chances of getting hired are more likely there."

The thought of setting foot in one of those without Wilkie still rankled, but she would gladly do so if it meant she could stay.

She sighed. The time in New York had zipped along, and she had absolutely nothing to show for it.

Ellen was probably happy about going home. The poor girl had divided her hours between reading library books and pleasing everyone but herself—Marion and that flimsy Leona, Aunt Jennie and Cousin Gloria. They were all so demanding. Well, Marion tried not to be, but she was probably the worst. Ellen was so patient and resilient it was easy to forget something might be perturbing her. She was abominably nice to Leona, who, as far as Marion was concerned, didn't even deserve Ellen's notice.

Marion *had* to get this part in Heron's production. A salary. A chance on the Great White Way.

"Pray for me, Ellen?" she asked as they regarded the sweltering room crowded with hopefuls who'd heard Heron was casting. No two chairs were together, so the girls would have to split up.

As Marion perched next to a redheaded girl wearing garish

makeup, her thoughts pounded. Should she pray herself? Nah, Ellen was taking care of it. But it wouldn't hurt...*God, please help me. I really need this part. My future depends on it.*

Did God pay attention, or not? Or was it as Ellen said...He had other plans for her? That perhaps He was "saving" her for just the right play? Actors had told her something like that before, only they hadn't invoked God's planning in it. Ellen seemed to believe He had something to do with everything in your life. Yet, for Marion, there was simply no way to be certain God had anything to do with any of this.

The minutes crept like caterpillars. The sisters had arrived early. How different it felt to be waiting because she had that all-important appointment instead of losing a lifetime of hope every hour spent in the same chair without a sign of the manager. But still, she worried. This was only an interview; she wasn't guaranteed a job.

Well, God, maybe You didn't think anything else was worth it, but don't You think this chance is? How else am I supposed to be a professional if I don't get hired here? The prayer felt a lot like thinking, and wishful thinking at that, but He was God; He knew what it was.

Lloyd Heron's praise had chimed sweetly in her ears all day. Surely, surely this would go well!

It had better sprout results, or she was finished. The terror of powerlessness gripped her, almost as harshly as when they were in the battle of Dad's conviction. No! She must be confident! She wasn't powerless—she'd make Mr. Heron realize she was worth his risk. What beautiful days could lie ahead if only she got a role today.

"Are you new here?" asked the redhead beside her.

"No." Marion wasn't feeling communicative.

"Oh. No offense. I just wondered because I haven't seen you before. Been in any shows lately?"

"Not here. Ohio."

"Really? Do they do professional theater there?"

"Ohio isn't all farm country. I come from the industrial part. Have you ever heard of the Players Guild of Canton? It's one of the best amateur companies in the U.S. I got my start there, and then joined a summer stock company."

"Trying to make it big on Broadway, then? That's what we all do." The girl grinned. "You're pretty enough. That will serve you in the most fun parts of being in a show—the fellas and the parties. You'll go on more dates than you have nights for, and of course they're all handsome guys. Say, do you live anywhere? I'm in a boarding house where the inmates are all theater girls, but I've been wanting to rent an apartment, and I need a roommate."

"I—at this moment I'm staying with relatives. But I don't want to stay there forever." Marion's pulse started racing…had she found a solution? If she failed here, and even if she didn't, could she move in with this girl for a better shot at the life she wanted? She didn't care about the "fellas"—she didn't want anyone but Wilkie—but all she needed was a place to stay where she wouldn't feel beholden.

"I'm Stella. Let me give you my card," the redhead offered. "Then you'll know where to find me when you need me." She giggled. "Better make up your mind quick, because I ask every girl I meet. I'm desperate for someone other than the girls at my boarding house. My only real friend disappeared."

"Disappeared? Did she run off?"

"Nope, went home. She got discouraged because she couldn't find a job."

Marion's skin crawled. *That won't be me,* she assured herself. *I won't ever quit for good.*

She watched the hour and minute set for her meeting tick by on the square, blue and gold wall clock. Finally, the door to the office opened and three men came out. One was shaking hands and laughing with Mr. Heron and the third man, who she assumed was an assistant. A moment later, the secretary was calling, "Marion Dashiell," and Heron was gazing at her with that beaked nose. This was it.

"Show him you've got the goods, sister." Stella patted Marion's hand as Marion rose up on wobbly legs. Ellen smiled at her across the room.

God, are You watching me? I'd be ever so grateful for a spot even in the chorus. Make him pick me, please!

"Any telephone calls this morning?" Marion asked the other ladies at the breakfast table as she entered the small dining room three days later.

"No; it's a bit early," Gloria answered. She shared a conspiratorial grin with her mother. "Why…what are you expecting?"

"Don't say *nothing*. That's what your sister always says, and one secretive person per household is quite enough," Aunt Jennie admonished, brows disappearing into the dollop of gray hair hanging over her forehead.

Marion sighed. "If you must be reminded, it's to tell me whether or not I'm selected for *Diamonds*."

"Oh! How exciting. And that will mean whether or not you can stay," Gloria exclaimed. "I hope you get it. You being in a musical…that would be lovely! And you being able to stay… that would be lovelier!" She plucked up a piece of bacon. "I get so lonesome without a friend or relative around when my Larry is out. Do we get free tickets if you're in a show?"

"Perhaps." Marion did *not* feel like saying more. She'd heard nothing since the interview. She felt like she was in a river being swept past a rock that would have saved her.

"You know, we could refuse to let you leave," Aunt Jennie said mischievously. She swallowed some coffee and clinked down her mug. "Kidnap you. It isn't a bother at all to any of us, not even Larry, if you stay on."

"Thank you for your kind offer," Ellen half-smiled, "but we really must honor our father's wishes."

"And I suppose he can't honor his old aunt's. Oh well. He's a noble man, your father, but sometimes…well, I oughtn't to say anything, but he's proud. It's commendable that you're honoring him. So many children nowadays don't give the time of day to their folks. When will you leave—that is, if dear Marion doesn't get her part?"

"As soon as we can, I guess. We haven't any reason to put it off," Ellen replied.

Marion wrinkled her nose. What unpleasant business.

Just then, the telephone's shrill ring on the wall nearest the kitchen made them jolt upright. Marion leaped up and answered.

"Hello, Marion Dashiell?" said a woman's voice. "This is Lloyd Heron's secretary at the Pearl Theatre. He wants you..."

Marion listened to the message breathlessly, made the proper responses as best she could, then whirled around with a cry.

"Ellen! He picked me, he wants me—I'm a professional!" She bounced up and down. "This is it, sister! I'm Leah Mortimer."

The others took off from their chairs like birds, Aunt Jennie's ovation like flapping wings. Gloria joined in as Marion darted to hug Ellen.

"Hooray! You can stay!" Gloria cheered. "Hip, hip, hooray! Hip, hip, hooray!" She raised her fist.

"Why you brilliant girl, you! I knew you had it in you. You're going to be a star yet, you'll see," Aunt Jennie said. Overwhelmed, Marion wrapped her arms around the lady's ample figure and then turned and hugged Gloria.

She twirled to Ellen again. "I'm a character with a name. Lea Mortimer. I sign the contract as soon as I can get to his office." The joyful tears leaked as she whispered, "Ellen, God answered our prayers. I—I didn't think He would, but He did."

Her dream had come true.

Well, God, You know what You're doing. Maybe You did intend Marion for this all along, Ellen prayed as she sat on the El beside Marion. Whenever they had a choice, they always rode the El...Marion craved the view. Today had been Marion's first rehearsal. Ellen dropped her off and continued on to the Binghams' apartment, whence she and Leona left for a shopping trip. Ellen did no more than help Leona look, bringing no money for anything but lunch.

"He's taking a chance on me, and he knows it, but he's so… chivalrous to do it," Marion said, absently pressing her pink handbag to her heart. The El collected itself with squeals and shudders, then chugged up to speed on its way to ferry them home. "I just know he's going to be my favorite director yet. Perhaps of all time—as long as the experience is a good one, people usually have a soft spot for the first of anything." She breathed a sigh as if settling into a hot bath. "My first director on Broadway."

She clapped a gloved hand to Ellen's knee, wrinkling the white fabric of her skirt. "I'll always save Mother's telegram. 'Well done. I'm sure Dad will have no objection. I'm so proud of you! Today was simply the happiest day of my life.' She froze mid-word. "One of the happiest days. And it won't be the happiest for long. Other days will replace it." She nodded emphatically.

"I'm sure they will," Ellen agreed. Was Marion thinking of Wilkie? His elusiveness continually puzzled and dismayed both of them. It was a shadow in the corner of their minds.

"Was this rehearsal much different than your Players Guild rehearsals?" Ellen asked.

"It was busier. It's a bigger building and stage than I've ever rehearsed in before, but more people were there buzzing around like bees. Crewmembers and so forth. The actors don't do any backstage work, like costuming and sets."

"Will you miss that?"

"At times. But I'll be caught up in my own business soon enough. Today I didn't say or sing a word, but just got shuffled around." Marion snickered. "Lloyd was like a girl playing dolls. He did all the talking and moved us where he wanted us." Her gaze shifted as her expression turned thoughtful. "That redheaded girl, Stella, who was so peachy to me at the office, was there, too, in the chorus. I never told you, but we might be able to solve our living situation through her."

Ellen studied Marion. "What do you mean?"

"She's looking for a roommate, or roommates."

The seat back in front of her received the intensity of

Ellen's stare. She thought for a swollen moment. "Marion, we are not moving in with a stranger. We can't afford living like that, nor is it safe. I'll look for a job starting tomorrow, and you and I will earn just enough to pay back the Fitzpatricks for their continued kindness. After the show is over, we'll either return home or reconsider our options."

"But—"

Ellen pinioned her finger into her own knee to accentuate the point. "If, during your stint with the show, you and I have gotten acquainted with Stella enough to be thoroughly impressed with her character, we may consider writing to Dad and Mother to ask their direction. But then, and only then, shall you tell Stella we might take her up on her offer."

"Tchuh. She'll have found a roommate four times over by then."

"That's just the risk we'll have to take, because we aren't doing it any other way."

Marion crossed her arms, but her face turned to stone rather than slumped into a pout. Since being around Broadway, she seemed to be losing some of her surface melodrama. "This isn't the last word on it. I can get acquainted with people at the speed of lightning if I wish. Stella is a nice girl."

"I have to get to know her, too, don't forget, and I get acquainted with people at the speed of molasses." Ellen folded her hands. "I'm not sure I'll ever be convinced girls should live on their own anyway."

"Well, that puts my whole life plan on your list of sins, apparently."

"I didn't say that. Nor does that seem to be your exact life plan." Ellen sighed. "We'll talk about this later. One change at a time, please."

As Marion's life unfolded, the two of them would be traversing increasingly treacherous paths. Would there continue to be room for them to walk side by side?

ᏬᎦᏪ Chapter Twenty-Six ᏬᎦᏪ

"You're sure you won't be lonely until she comes?" Aunt Jennie asked Ellen in a coddling tone, her hand on the front door. It was late Saturday afternoon and she and Gloria were going out to see friends. Marion was at her third rehearsal. Ellen felt like a mother sending her child to school for the first time, knowing she'd be all right but worrying about all the things that could go awry, and also getting smacked by the realization that her baby was growing up.

"Not at all. You know I do well with solitude." Ellen half-smiled.

"You're not in a tizzy about Marion?"

"Not too terribly." Marion had assured Ellen she knew the way perfectly, and that she'd come right home and not speak to any strangers or leave the path to pick flowers in the woods. The Little Red Riding Hood allusion wasn't encouraging, but Ellen did sense enough responsibility in Marion to give her this trial.

Leona would be visiting soon. She wouldn't take "I'm busy" for an answer two days in a row—yesterday, Ellen had accompanied Marion to Manhattan and poked around for jobs while Marion was in rehearsal. So today was Leona's day.

She arrived not long after Aunt Jennie and Gloria left. "Ellen, I have the news I've been waiting to give you," Leona said as Ellen welcomed her to sit in the living room, in the armchairs they always appropriated. She rifled through her white purse.

Ellen's heart plummeted. *Have she and Everett set a wedding date?* No, that couldn't be right. Other things had to happen first, which Leona would have kept Ellen abreast of, like visiting Everett's parents and sensing their approval.

She had herself collected when Leona's attention emerged from the purse. "An invitation to our millionaire friends' house for their party." She transferred it to Ellen's lap. "It's the Rockfords. It's this Saturday. Can you come? You may bring your sister if she likes. The Rockfords always tell us, 'The more, the merrier!' Of course they don't say that to everyone, but they hold our judgment very highly."

Leona smiled and clasped her white-gloved hands over her knee. "I thought you'd appreciate a chance to go to a party at a magnificent house, eat fine food, and, well, just hobnob. You want to have all kinds of new and pleasant experiences in New York, don't you? Well then, you should come!" She shook her head, jangling her brown curls. "I had a terrible time of it, persuading my parents that you were all right. That's why I couldn't invite you until today. Sorry for the late notice."

"Thank you very much for the invitation." Ellen glanced past Leona to the living room doorway, hoping Rosetta would interrupt with tea. "I…don't know if I can accept; I'll have to ask our hosts and Marion…"

"Do you already have plans for that night?"

Ellen wished. "None that I know of. But my aunt and cousin don't tell me everything immediately." Actually, any plans Saturday night went against Ellen's desires, so what difference did it make whose current carried her? *Though Aunt Jennie's and Gloria's wouldn't involve millionaires and a mansion.*

"Well, be sure to let me know as soon as you know you're free. I can't stand the thought of going without a friend." Leona lowered her voice. "I wish with all my heart the Rockfords knew the Shepherds. I haven't been able to see Everett yet. Wouldn't a party be the perfect opportunity to meet one's secret sweetheart? Oh, I miss him. It's been three weeks since I arrived, hoping to see him, and it has never once occurred. It is so frustrating!"

Where was Rosetta's tea? In answer to Ellen's mute demand, the doorbell rang. Ellen caught Leona's surprised eye as her gaze traveled again toward the entryway, which connected to the living room. Muttering, Rosetta clumped through the dining room on the other side of the wall, materializing as she passed the living room.

Though the girls couldn't see the front door from where they sat, Leona shifted to join Ellen in watching for who might appear. Maybe Marion was home early? They heard muffled voices—Rosetta's and a man's. Someone looking for Dr. Larry, perhaps. Ellen was amazed at how often the bell chimed for him.

Rosetta appeared in the doorway. "Someone to see you, Miss Ellen. He didn't want to disturb you, but I insisted you wouldn't mind."

"Thank you," Ellen said as Rosetta receded. Ellen stood and an instant's lull heightened her anticipation, and then Everett took Rosetta's place.

It was a very awkward moment. Awkwardness and shock radiated from all three of them—Everett's ears turned red rather than pink, Leona's fidgets stopped, and Ellen's blood seemed to have halted its course. Everett. How on earth could he have come now, of all hours and days? She had wanted to see him, but...now? Now, when Leona sat in the same room? When Leona could read everything that passed between Ellen and Everett? When Everett had no warning that these two women knew each other?

It was absurd.

Twirling his hat in his hands like a Ferris wheel, Everett's face changed color several times. His left foot pointed sideways like he wanted to bolt. Leona gazed at him with love and tenderness. Ellen didn't know what she did, only that she was standing and had lost all feeling as her mind raced.

Suddenly the situation burst upon her, and her blood exploded as if from a dam. She could move again, she could act and take control of the situation. Everett didn't know that she knew about him and Leona, and Leona might want to keep it that way. Ellen certainly did. So...she must act as if her two friends were themselves merely friends.

"Mr. Shepherd. It is so good to see you." Ellen closed the distance between them, her outstretched hand leading the way.

"Marion will be disappointed to have missed you. How have you been?"

Everett stared at her and shook her hand, then licked his lips, looked beyond at Leona, and still didn't budge.

"Leona has told me your families are old friends and that she knew you were in New York but had been unable to see you," continued Ellen. "Imagine meeting in my cousins' living room in Brooklyn."

"Yes, rather odd." Leona arose and smiled. "How are you, Everett? It has been a long time." She held out her hand as if awaiting him to come kiss it.

Everett gave his head a tiny jiggle and stepped forward to shake Leona's hand. "He-Hello...Leona." He pivoted toward Ellen. "Hello, El-Miss Dashiell."

The silence had been hard to break, and Ellen had to fight to keep it from overtaking them. "I hope Marion comes back early and sees you, if only for a few minutes," she said. Marion lighting on them all might not be the best thing, but transferring attention onto others outside this room seemed wise. Maybe Rosetta would appear with that tea...

Ellen glanced in vain toward the doorway. "I don't believe I told you about Marion, Mr. Shepherd. She's gotten a part in a Broadway musical."

"You don't say?" Everett spoke quietly. His unhappy eyes flitted from the floor to her and back again.

"Can you stay for a while? Would you like to sit down? We can move to the couch and chairs in the inner circle for better conversation." Ellen's voice had become chipper on its own. She felt as if she were watching and evaluating herself on a movie screen. *God, help me, please,* she remembered to pray.

As they sat, Rosetta came bearing the tray laden with three china teacups. The distraction helped, but Ellen still had to struggle to keep conversation flowing. She told Everett many details about their time in New York and all the updates on family members she could think were appropriate.

Everett nodded and answered her careful queries with short, distracted replies. He downed his tea quickly and tipped the empty cup to his lips countless times instead of asking for more. Leona was no help at all, but sat looking as charmingly demure as she could and offering very few words. Now and then she darted suspicious glances toward Ellen, which made Ellen casually cite her and Everett's relationship as coworkers.

Could she find an excuse to leave the room? She didn't want to, but her conscience prodded her. If she had truly surrendered Everett, and truly pitied Leona, she ought to leave them alone to give them a chance of connecting for real, in the way Leona at least longed to do.

"Shall I ask Rosetta if she would allow us a refreshment? Perhaps she also has more tea." Ellen stood.

Everett looked up as if begging her not to go, but Leona said, "By all means. I *am* getting hungry."

There, Ellen thought as she left the room. *They can do what they want with that.* She took her time going to Rosetta, at work on supper in the kitchen.

Rosetta's eyebrows rose halfway to her black hairline when Ellen made her request. She paused her potato-mashing. "Girl, that party don't seem very happy in there. Why are you stretching it out like a goose's neck? Just kick that girl out and enjoy time with your man."

Ellen blanched. "It—it isn't like that. We're…enjoying ourselves as we are."

Rosetta kept her eyebrows elevated and shook her head. "I'll bring cookies and more tea in a jiffy."

"Thank you." Ellen backed out of the kitchen. So much for the safety of Rosetta's taciturnity. Lingering was just as uncomfortable there as outside the living room doorway.

The front door opened as Ellen stepped into the hallway. "Hiya, Ellen!" Marion walked in, looking a picture in her clean-cut pink dress and hat. "I had a wonderful day. We even got off early. But oh, it was so much fun."

It was a rude interruption to pave the way for the Dashiells to reenter the living room, but being unintentional it did the trick nicely. "Marion, Mr. Shepherd and Leona are both here. Come say hello."

"Everett? Long-lost Everett's here, at long last? Splendid!" Marion marched gaily in to meet them. "Ev—I mean, Mr. Shepherd. How are you? How good of you to finally come. We've been expecting you for weeks, friend-starved that we are."

Entirely appropriate thing to say, Marion, Ellen wished she could admonish. After Everett stood and greeted Marion, they all sat down again.

"I hear you're in a play?" Everett said with some buoyancy. He no doubt welcomed Marion's arrival.

"Yes. It's great—it's not even as demanding as some of the other productions I've been in, though I'd better attribute that to its only being rehearsal number three. We also have more time to rehearse—the premiere isn't till September twenty-third. That relieves the early-on pressure." Marion stretched her arms daintily. "But don't let's talk about me…it's been ages since you've had a good chat with Ellen." She aimed a glare at Leona.

This wouldn't do. Would Rosetta bring in tea soon? Everett's face furrowed more with each passing minute, trying but failing to look natural and attentive as the situation beat upon him. Surely he wanted to leave, and Ellen couldn't blame him. If only she could take his arm and pull him into another room, any room, as long as they were alone, and explain. In fact, they could explain this whole mess to each other. But it was not to be—Everett was Leona's, and Ellen had no business being alone with him.

Rosetta did finally bring the tea and cookies, shaking her head at the group of them and leaving as silently as she had come. They chitchatted a bit more, Marion providing ample reinforcements to Ellen's dwindling efforts at keeping silence at bay.

Everett started when the mantel clock chimed five o'clock. "I fear that means I must go," he apologized.

Leona rose as he did and gazed at him fondly. "It was good to see you again, Everett." Her words were nuanced.

"Don't stay away so long next time," Marion urged him,

standing as well.

Leona glared at Marion and punctuated her next words. "You're particularly sensitive to that, aren't you, Marion? Young men staying away too long?"

Marion's eyes widened and Ellen's cheeks heated. How did Leona know enough about Wilkie to make such a pointed reference? How dare she! Had Aunt Jennie told her all when Ellen's back was turned? Hopefully Marion wouldn't think Ellen had blabbed about it…

Ellen stood; as the hostess, she could do nothing less, though she wished she could send all three of these people and their problems down a chute. The young ladies followed Everett to the door in a cluster and saw him off. Marion didn't return to the living room, but huffed upstairs without another word to Leona, while Leona, not long after polishing off the cookies, left as well.

"Don't forget the party, Ellen, dear!" Leona reminded her. "Your sister," her voice dropped all enthusiasm, "is still welcome, too."

Ellen remained in the entryway when the door had closed on Leona. Her heart ached, but shouldn't she feel relieved? The worst had happened, and the ruses were still in place. Leona hadn't confronted Ellen about Ellen loving Everett; Everett hadn't discovered that Ellen knew of their engagement; and Marion was none the wiser about any of it. Success, wasn't it? And they'd all be on guard to keep it from occurring again.

"That girl!" Marion's voice blasted down the stairs. "Horrid thing, what was she thinking, staying on when it was obvious you and Everett would have been happier alone?"

"Not necessarily obvious." Ellen shuffled to the bottom of the staircase and looked to Marion at the top. "Leona is his friend, too, and it's been a longer time since she's seen him. Of course she'd want to stay."

"She hardly said anything! What could she want with him?"

Ellen shrugged, sighed, and let her gaze slide down to the carpeted steps. "I can't read minds."

"You are far, far too self-effacing, Ellen. You have a chance at happiness and you're throwing it away." The last word came out as a squeak, tripped up in emotion. She inhaled deeply and continued, "Everett was here to see *you*. That's why he came to this house. He didn't know that girl would be here. He wants you, and he made an effort to do something about it. Don't be cold, or you'll drive him away!"

Marion's tears streamed as she turned heel and dashed to their bedroom. Ellen stood motionless, staring at the place she had just vacated. Wilkie was still uppermost in Marion's thoughts. Where was he?

Ellen's fingers jerked. She had the itch to write to him herself. Not that it would do any good—unless something she said could get through to him. But what? Threats? Curses? Pleading? Explanation? Counsel, if his great-aunt or something else was barring him?

Everett and Wilkie. Two very different men, the cause of heartache to two very different sisters.

ᎦᏫᏲ Chapter Twenty-Seven ᎦᏫᏲ

ELLEN HAD NO TROUBLE PERSUADING MARION TO GO WITH HER to the Rockfords' party. She knew the reason: it was a millionaire's party; Wilkie might be there.

Gloria was envious, but gaily lent Marion jewelry and Ellen a pair of shiny black high heels. Ellen looked fancy, for certain, but the shoes squeezed and pinched like one of Gloria's hugs. She yielded, however. Millionaire parties required you to appear at your best, not *feel* your best.

Aunt Jennie and Gloria crowed over how gorgeous the sisters looked.

"You exaggerate *my* merits," Ellen said, correcting her balance and wincing in the heels. "But thank you. Marion does look particularly lovely."

Marion's nervous smiles came and went, doubtlessly mirroring her expectations of the evening. "Thank you," she murmured, posing at all angles in front of the vanity mirror.

She wore a white lawn dress spattered with pink roses. It had been a short summer day dress, but she had bought white gauze to sew into a floor-sweeping ruffle and garlands of ruffles around the neckline and sleeves. She cut a triangle from the back to create the dramatic dip so much in fashion, and used the material for rosettes on the sleeves. She tied a pink sash around her waist and decorated her hair and wrists with Gloria's pearl and roses jewelry. None would be the wiser that she hadn't bought the frock from a designer.

Ellen teetered on the verge of feeling ridiculous. For her Gloria and Aunt Jennie had insisted on buying new—except the dress was a reduced sale from last year's fall/winter season. It was navy blue and long, which Ellen liked. It was slim and overlaid with matching lace and cinched at the waist. But to fancy it up, Marion had added dramatic navy lace ruffles draping from the collar to the shoulders, finishing it off with a big ribbon bow in the center of the neckline.

"I don't want to hurt your feelings, but this isn't really my style..." Ellen had protested.

"It's not fancy enough as it is," Marion retorted. "Aren't you satisfied with the elegant, Ellen-like navy? And rejoice that I listened to you and didn't cut away the back any more."

They were to travel to the Binghams' in Manhattan and then to the elite northwest Yonkers, where Victorian mansions overlooked the Hudson River Palisades. The natural beauty of those cliffs was the only thing Ellen looked forward to. Oh, the mansions would be something, too, but the architectural splendor of the city had numbed her.

They'd stay the night at the Binghams' apartment and return to Brooklyn on Sunday. Leona was thrilled, and Mr. and Mrs. Bingham were courteous when required, inattentive when not. Ellen and Marion didn't matter much in their minds, so the girls might as well not have been there.

The drive to Yonkers might have been short if it weren't so convoluted. Thank goodness the Binghams' chauffeur was a safe, methodical driver. After the tight city streets, he ushered them into the winding roads of the spacious, idyllic Lawrence Park West neighborhood, up to what looked like the largest mansion of all in the dusky light. It was built to impress; Ellen could hardly imagine one family living in such vastness. Romanesque and built of gray stone like a castle, it presided atop a hill, crowning the manicured lawns surrounded by a wrought-iron fence. It towered over even the old forest trees that shaded the grounds, as if compelling their veneration, too.

Supposedly one could see the Hudson River and the cliffs from a corner of the back garden. The place was certainly as beautiful as money could buy, and Ellen had to admit it was worth the discomfort to see it.

"At last!" Leona grumbled as the white Cadillac halted before the broad, stone-arched portico, illuminated by countless lantern-like porch lights. The chauffeur opened the doors for all the passengers.

"This is enchanting," Marion murmured.

A short walkway, lit by lights, wound from the drive to the portico. Lush plants, some in flower, lined every pavement. Ellen saturated her lungs with fresher air than she'd smelled in weeks—it was loamy and sweet. Yes, coming here was most definitely worth it.

Cars, both parked and moving, filled the drive. "Hurry, we're late." Leona looked over her shoulder at her parents.

"We are not late." Mr. Bingham spoke in the authoritative voice that Marion had compared to growling thunder. Nothing he said encouraged dispute.

Ellen had met Claude and Mildred Bingham a few times before, the first at Louis and Ida's wedding. But she'd never carried on more than stilted conversation with them.

"Massive" defined Mr. Bingham—massive body, though not overly tall; massive voice; massive money and massive sense of style. His tuxedo tonight was top of the line. He came across as a very shrewd, knowledgeable, and quick-witted man; but common courtesy, true religion, and the arts weren't worth his time. He was a stereotypical industrial monarch.

Mrs. Bingham was small-boned like Leona, as short as Leona but twice as round. Her hair was dyed black and set in mounds of curls, and she wore a glitzy purple gown whose fashionable sleekness was lost on her. She was as clueless to genuine politeness as her husband, and said even less to the Dashiells than he did. Ellen knew she was talkative in her own circles. Her voice was slow and deep like Ida's. She was particular about everything that caught her notice and what words she bothered to use on Leona were all nagging.

Yes, Ellen pitied Leona. The girl needed someone to love her.

Leona lost all bluster around them. Even at her father's commonplace rejoinder she lapsed into moody, drooping silence. She looked charming tonight, dressed in a white chiffon frock nearly as exquisite as Marion's, her dark hair curled to perfection and her face brightened by a touch of makeup. She seemed fidgety, even nervous. Perhaps she dreaded what men would be introduced to her tonight.

The double front doors were like a castle's, tall and arch-shaped, of iron and oak. A butler welcomed the newcomers, opening the doors to a hive of a party that took up multiple rooms. The hum of voices was constant; band music rose and fell against it. The presence of the over one hundred people was palpable in the stuffy, smoky, perfume-laden atmosphere. Light shone everywhere: chandeliers overhead, sconces on the wall, candles on the tabletops. White pillars grew like indoor trees from the marble floors in the entryway and the ballroom.

Ellen battled intimidation. Finery-bedecked guests packed the ballroom, while a buffet of unrecognizable food packed the dining room. She didn't belong here. She glanced at Marion, whose eyes shone with delight, eager to absorb this slice of the glamorous life. If things went her way, this very well might be in her future.

Mr. and Mrs. Bingham attached themselves to their crowd, while both Dashiells stuck to Leona. A dapper serving man approached them with a tray as they stood against a tapestry on a ballroom wall. "Punch or champagne?"

Marion reached for a glass of yellow punch. "Is the punch spiked?" Ellen asked quickly.

"No, miss."

Leona giggled as she reached for champagne. Marion took two glasses of punch and handed one to Ellen, and the girls sipped as they watched the people.

"Will you dance if you're asked?" Leona gestured to the corner of the room where the band had exerted its pull on several couples.

"No, I don't think so; I don't know anyone," Ellen replied. Her feet, smarting in Gloria's high heels, confirmed her decision.

"I shall!" Marion declared. "I need to practice for *Diamonds*, besides the fact I love dancing."

"Well, if we stand here looking pretty, I guess we might get noticed and picked sooner or later," Leona chuckled.

"Or we could mix and mingle and get noticed and picked that way," Marion said mischievously. Her eyes had not ceased to rove since they'd arrived…looking for Wilkie.

If he didn't show up soon, she'd spend her entire life looking for him.

There weren't an overabundance of young men roaming the crowd, but several did glance the girls' way, lingering longest on Marion. But none approached; most were attached to a young lady.

"I'm scooting closer to the band. You can't hear them in this buzz," Marion said after she'd drained her punch.

"Is she looking for a dance partner?" Leona wondered as Marion slipped between two matrons dressed in dazzling gowns and melted into the throng.

I hope not, Ellen thought. The last thing Marion needed was another wealthy admirer. "Perhaps not. She's musically inclined, so she always gravitates to the music."

Leona rolled her eyes and huffed. "One more thing she's good at. Shall we go to the garden? It's stifling in here."

"I agree. Let me tell Marion where I'll be." Ellen's stomach felt cavernous. "I guess we can eat whenever we wish?"

"Yes. I'm not hungry yet, are you?" Leona used her hand to fan herself. "I must get out of here. Come find me outside, won't you?"

Ellen promised and dove toward the music corner. She ought to bring Marion with her to the dining room to make sure she ate—and Ellen needed to hurry, too, for the sun was setting and she wanted to glimpse the Palisades.

Marion swayed on the edge of the open space, doing half the foxtrot in place that the five couples were dancing.

"Marion—"

"Swell music!" Marion snapped her fingers to the beat and stepped to the right, then the left.

"I'm going out to the garden with Leona. Do you want to come?" Ellen raised her voice over the band.

"Nah. Maybe later. When I get tired of this."

"Do you want to get food with me?"

Marion continued rocking. "Well, I am famished, so that'd be sensible." She pivoted and took a frolicking step forward. "I can still hear in the dining room."

The house felt as crowded as the Alvin Theatre, but its ceilings, though high, weren't tall enough to ventilate to Ellen's satisfaction. The hall they entered as they left the ballroom slashed the noises to merciful echoes. A few men in tuxedos and women in jewels and gowns passed them with full plates, on their way to the conservatory right of the ballroom. Hopefully one could also eat outdoors.

The girls rounded the wide archway to the dining room and were greeted by a smaller crowd and the aroma of rich food. Ellen felt almost faint, her need for food, air, and quiet was so intense.

Marion froze. Ellen saw her at the rim of her vision and turned to question the reason.

Marion's face paled white, then instantly flushed red. Her eyes trapped something at the loaded table. She mouthed a single word and her face transformed into a smile. "Wilkie!" she shouted, rushing forward.

Ellen stood still but followed with her gaze. She couldn't believe it—it *was* Wilkie. He paused in mid-motion, a spoonful of something red halfway to his plate, his face plastered in shock. If she didn't know better she'd have thought Marion had conjured him into view with her yearning.

"Wilkie." Marion stopped just short of embracing him and looked up at him, enraptured.

Wilkie didn't speak, simply stared at her as startled and disturbed as if she were a ghost.

"Wilkie, what's wrong?" Marion sounded like a hurt child. "Say something. Aren't you glad to see me? I have so much to tell you!" She smiled again.

A dark-haired young beauty stepped up beside him. She wore movie-star makeup, brilliant jewelry, and a shiny royal-blue dress, cut to devastate. Her black eyes narrowed and her long, thin eyebrows arched even higher into black accusations. "Who's this, John?"

"Uh, why, an old acquaintance." Wilkie couldn't take his eyes off Marion. "One I haven't seen in ten thousand ages. That's why I'm so surprised." He laughed.

Marion gaped at him. "Didn't you receive my telegrams and messages? Surely you knew I was in New York!"

"Ask her how she is and let's get moving. That music is calling." The girl's voice was flat; she wouldn't have a pleasing voice even if she were cordial.

"Of course." Wilkie relaxed to all appearances—except Ellen, and certainly Marion, could read his distress through his transparent green eyes. "It's nice to see you, Miss Dashiell. Here of all places!" He freed his gaze to travel, and it lighted on Ellen. A flash of worry crossed and was gone. "And your sister, too. How have you been? Well, I hope you enjoy the rest of the party."

He tipped his head toward the dark girl and attempted a quirky grin. "We've gotta wolf down this grub and then get to dancing."

Marion backed away. Ellen couldn't see her face, but she was at her side in an instant, gripping her hand and murmuring, "Come, Marion."

"No…" Marion whispered, a decibel above a puff of air.

Ellen risked one level look at Wilkie. She was too unprepared for this moment, this occurrence, to know just what she did or what she should do, but Marion needed to be whisked from here, to a quiet, out-of-the-way place. If only Leona weren't outside. Maybe they could go out the front door; the back patio and garden would be too full anyway.

Ellen tugged her sister from the dining room, aware of all the eyes upon them and holding her head high because of it. She would not be ashamed. Wilkie was in the wrong, and he refused to blush, so why should they who were innocent do so?

"Ellen," Marion rasped, "what is wrong with him?"

"I don't know," Ellen said evenly, leading Marion toward the front hall.

"Go get him and bring him to me so we can demand an explanation!" She was tearfully adamant.

"No, that won't do," Ellen replied.

The puzzled butler met them at the grand doors. "Going out, misses?"

"Yes, please, just for a moment. The back garden is too crowded," Ellen responded.

"There's a place to sit—a bench under a tree—to the left down the hill," the butler told them.

Once outside, Ellen spotted the bench in the heavy dusk. After navigating the narrow path descending through the landscape's flowers and bushes, the sisters dropped into the seat.

"Ellen, what does it mean?" Sweat and tears streaked Marion's face. "I feel like I'm going to faint."

"Compose yourself." Ellen did her best to sound soothing. "A party is no place to lose control like that."

"Compose myself! Ellen, my own Wilkie denies me to my face. How can I compose myself? I must talk to him, not sit by like a dazed sap." She half stood; Ellen grabbed her arm. "My chance is stealing by. I have to go to him!"

"Not until you've calmed down. You won't get anywhere if you don't confront him calmly."

"He won't see my pain if I'm calm!" Marion pulled weakly against Ellen's grasp. "Let me go."

"You look like you're about to swoon. I'm not letting you go until you can show me you're calm. Sit down and take deep breaths."

"You're off your nut." Marion wrenched her arm and scurried up the path.

Ellen sighed. So much for thinking it over and determining the right course of action. She wasn't about to physically fight her sister. She followed her to the house.

Indoors again, they entered the ballroom side by side and jammed through to the dancing corner. More couples were there, including Wilkie and his dark-haired dame.

Marion lunged into the musical fray and skidded to a halt at Wilkie's shoulder. Ellen watched from the sidelines. "Hey! Wilkie, I *need* to talk to you. It's urgent!"

His partner fixed her with a snake-like glare. They rotated in the dance so that Wilkie faced Marion. "Can't it wait, toots?"

"It's been waiting for weeks." Marion didn't sound angry, just pleading.

"Let us finish the dance, won't you?"

"Okay. But I'm claiming you on the last bar."

The dark-haired girl wrinkled her nose so high her teeth bared like a snarl as she and Wilkie whirled again. Marion backed away, dodging the other couples, and joined Ellen to fidget until the song ended.

It seemed like forever. Wilkie posed with the girl in his arms at the finish, then released her with a mutual laugh before twirling her in again and kissing her forehead. Marion gasped and clutched Ellen's hand.

"There's gotta be an explanation," she moaned.

Wilkie gazed into the girl's eyes, his hands on her waist, speaking for a moment; then he turned away slowly and approached the Dashiells.

"What is it?" he nipped.

"Wilkie, what happened?" Marion returned, her lip trembling.

"I've got no clue what you're talking about." He slipped into a more polite tone. With the music's cessation, the crowd's gabble escalated, but plenty of people were close enough to eavesdrop.

"You know what I'm talking about. I telegrammed you hundreds of times. I came to your house. I left notes with your butler. Didn't you get any of them? Is it your aunt?"

Wilkie's eyes rose and swept over the room. "Look, nothing's wrong. I should have replied to you, sure. But I had other things to do."

Marion breathed more quickly. "I—don't know—for once I'm speechless. Wilkie, there has to be more—"

"There isn't anything more to say." He made as if to step away.

"I think there is," Ellen said quietly. "You owe her an immense explanation."

Tears glistened in Marion's eyes. She looked heartbreakingly beautiful, like a starlet in a tragic scene. "Wilkie," she whispered.

He returned his attention to her face, and that was his undoing. He glanced away again, then down, but it was too late. He finally met her gaze. "Look, I'll meet you…at a restaurant, later. You pick. No, how 'bout the Café Italienne near Broadway. West Fiftieth Street. Theater District; you'd like that, huh? Monday? Eleven?" He peeked over his shoulder. The dark-haired girl had nudged nearer. "That's all I can give you, okay? Now let me have my night, will you?"

He spun and sidestepped to the girl, gallantly looping her arm and leading her toward the open French doors of the conservatory.

Marion suddenly doubled over and cradled her stomach. Ellen held her. "Let's go sit down. You need to be outside again."

"I feel sick," Marion whimpered.

Some of the guests eyed them. One old gentleman took Marion's hand and helped her to a chair along the wall, offering punch or champagne.

"Water, please, if you can get it," Ellen requested. She sat beside Marion and put her hand on her shoulder.

"I want to go home." Marion's elbows were planted on her knees, her face planted in her palms.

"As soon as you're feeling a bit better I'll find Leona and ask if we can arrange that," Ellen said.

"*Home* home," Marion mumbled.

Ellen paused. "That'd be swell, but we'll have to wait some for that. At least we can get to the Binghams'."

Dear God, Ellen prayed, sitting back against the chair. *Could this have gone any worse?*

Chapter Twenty-Eight

"HOW IS THE POOR DEAR? COULD SHE USE SOME CHEERING UP? I have principles against movies on Sundays, but for her, I'll make an exception. She needs a distraction. Or how about coming down and listening to the radio?"

Aunt Jennie spoke as Ellen's hand curled around the banister, ready to slide upward on her way to check Marion.

Aunt Jennie, Gloria, and Dr. Larry had just returned from evening church. The Dashiells had stayed home. They'd gotten to the Binghams' apartment from the party well after midnight on Saturday. Ellen couldn't influence them to depart any sooner, so she and Marion had spent the evening tucked away in the darkest part of the Rockfords' back garden, removed and oblivious to the commotion of the party.

Marion had tossed all night in their shared bedroom and woken up before it was light, itching to leave for Brooklyn. Ellen persuaded her to eat breakfast and bid their hosts a proper thank-you and goodbye. Then they hurried to the place next nearest home, and the nearest they'd get for some time.

"Thank you, but she's sleeping now," Ellen answered Aunt Jennie. "She didn't sleep last night, nor since we got back. She dropped off not long after you left."

"Ah! Attagirl." Aunt Jennie nodded emphatically. "Has she eaten anything?"

"No."

Aunt Jennie shook her head and clicked her tongue. She faced her daughter, who stood alongside her. "Gloria, what did you eat when you were suffering from heartbreak? You've had your share of callous fellows."

"Oh, Mother." Gloria drew down her brows and tried to sound miffed, but an irrepressible smile escaped. "I *was* always in some sort of heart trouble, wasn't I?" She giggled. "Well, there was nothing like ice cream if the weather was hot, or your hot spiced apple and caramel bread pudding if it was cold. Mmm. But there was that one time when I was particularly bad off after Jerry took another girl to the dance. You gave me spiced wine, and that cheered me up like anything."

"I did that, did I? How old were you?"

"Oh! Maybe it was Dad that did it." Gloria chuckled. "He never did know what to do with a weeping girl, but it turns out that was the best of all."

Aunt Jennie laughed with her. "Well, well, do you keep any wine?"

"As a matter of fact, yes!"

"I'm not sure—" Ellen protested. Her parents had supported Prohibition, and they didn't even entirely approve of wine.

"It will be just the thing!" Gloria exclaimed, aiming her steps for the kitchen.

"No, don't trouble yourself," Ellen said. "Please, she's sleeping, and food or drink won't help her."

"You say she's going to see that fellow tomorrow. How does she expect to hold up without something in her stomach?" Aunt Jennie turned to Gloria. "Get the wine; we'll let her sleep, but as soon's she's awake, we're plying her with as much victuals as we can. Do you have any chocolate?"

Ellen watched them amble to the kitchen. When Marion had arrived teary-eyed and haggard, they'd demanded the whole explanation of last night and extorted it from Ellen piece by piece. Marion had locked herself in the bedroom. Aunt Jennie couldn't believe Wilkie had treated her in such a way, and Gloria stopped just short of rubbing her hands with excitement over the drama and intrigue.

Ellen took the first stair step. Mother would be wonderful right about now.

"I'm talking to him alone. You're not even going into the café with me," Marion said stiffly as she sat fixing her hair in front of the vanity Monday morning. "It's going to be like old times, and heaven knows how often we've talked alone." Her stomach churned. Couldn't she get sick and unable to go? Couldn't Wilkie come on his knees bearing flowers and clear it all up?

Her hands crashed to her lap as she stared into the mirror. "I'm sure not looking good. The spark's deserted my eyes."

"You look beautiful. Don't worry about your appearance anyway," Ellen said from her bed, where she pulled on her stockings. "Just worry about keeping a clear head. You can't put on any displays in a café, and you have to always keep your wits about you in the city."

"That's why you're coming with me," Marion responded.

"Where should I wait since you don't want me in the same building?" Ellen knelt and collected her black Oxfords from under her bed.

"I don't know. Outside. Across the street. Go for a walk. Just wait for me to come out, and don't go in."

If Ellen had asked why she was so adamant about Ellen staying out, she couldn't have said. She only knew she wanted to face him alone, hear his explanation without influence from anyone else. He could be one-hundred percent candid with her like he could with no other person. And if a reconciliation was coming that day, as she so hoped it was, she didn't want Ellen to see them kiss; because after a separation like this, kiss they would.

"What are you going to talk about first?" Ellen asked hesitantly as they waited for the El to touch at their station. Monday morning was marching on. She was setting aside all qualms of nosiness. She was the only parent Marion had access to, and she needed to know all she could to advise all she could.

"How should I know? The words will come of their own accord when we sit across from each other," Marion replied, biting her lip and peering down the track for the train.

"Marion." Ellen inhaled. "Marion, you're prepared for the

possibility that he might…stand you up?"

Marion's head whipped to face Ellen. "Wilkie wouldn't do that."

He's done it to you for a month, Ellen wanted to say. *What makes this different?* Aloud, she settled on, "You never know. Just be prepared for the worst; that helps ease pain."

"I know all about pain. I'm ready to put it behind me." Marion gripped her purse tighter as the El's whistle and rumble reached their ears. "All this time of missing him will be as if it hadn't happened, for the joy we'll have at our reunion. It'll be like I pictured, ever since I came to New York." She smiled sweetly.

Ellen shivered. She couldn't help but fear Marion was in for an earthquake. How could she still trust Wilkie? It was like trusting something broken would all of a sudden, without repair, work.

Lord God, I wish there was something I could say to warn her, to change her expectations, but I don't think there is. Only You can reach her. Please let Wilkie show up, and please let them come to some kind of satisfactory understanding.

At the end of their journey, Ellen reached out and squeezed Marion's hand as they halted opposite Café Italienne. The traffic roared on the street between.

"Here we are," Marion announced, returning Ellen's squeeze.

"I'll be here, across the street, where you wanted me." Ellen took care to keep her voice steady, with a little infusion of brightness.

"I'll come get you once everything's square," Marion said, loosening her clutch on Ellen's hand. "Hopefully it won't take ages." She smiled slightly. "Get some lunch if you get hungry, just in case."

Letting Marion go alone through that café door would be one of the hardest things Ellen had had to do yet. As hard as… letting Everett go. No; she mustn't go there, not now. Not when Marion's potential heartbreak was nigh.

Lord, be with her.

Wilkie, here I come! Marion strolled into the café. It would be him and her alone once more, pouring their hearts out to each other, washing away the confusion of the past.

The clock over the counter showed eleven o'clock on the dot. Good; she couldn't possibly miss him. Was he here yet? Apparently not. She took a booth in a corner and forgot to acknowledge the waiter when a menu landed on the table before her. She didn't open it.

She waited five minutes. Kitchen stuff clanged, workers groused at each other, customers gabbed, somebody hummed. During the rare seconds those were silent the traffic noises wafted in and the clock ticked.

Fear clenched her stomach. He wasn't coming.

The bell tinkled over the door. A thin, blond man flashed into the café, as Wilkie as he could be. She half rose and got trapped by the table, but he was already striding toward her.

Marion sat back as he slipped into the booth across from her. She wanted to shout his name, hug him and cry on his shoulder, but he gave her no time.

"I'm here to give you your explanation," he said. "I'm in a rush, so let's make it snappy."

"Wilkie," Marion squeaked, "what is wrong?"

"Nothing, unless it's your understanding."

Marion's eyes widened and grew dry exposed to the air. "*My* understanding? When you left Ohio you gave me your address and fully intended to see me again. What happened? What's going on with that other girl? Why have you been avoiding me?"

"Avoiding you? I didn't intend to. I've been busy, as I've been telling you. 'That other girl' is Belinda Huntington." Wilkie clapped his palms to the tabletop. "Look, I'm all kinds of sorry if I ever made you think there was anything between you and me. I didn't realize you'd take my having another girl so hard." He pursed his lips and closed his eyes, shutting out the hurt and pleading in Marion's gaze. "I need to go now. I wish you all the best." He was up and speed walking to the door faster than her brain could process it.

"Wilkie!" she shrieked. He paused, going ramrod straight just inside the door. The next instant he opened it and was gone.

"Wilkie!" Marion leaped up and ran, heedless of bystanders, heels skidding on the tile. She caught the door before it fully shut and was on the sidewalk in a wink, looking wildly for him.

"Wilkie!" She couldn't see him along the streets, but a fancy black sedan had just sped away from the opposite curb, merging into the traffic. Was that Wilkie in the back seat? It looked like his hat. He must have run across the street and jumped in right as she came out.

She ran into the street toward the fast disappearing car, waving her arms and stumbling over her shoes. Tears blinded her. Horns honked and wheels swooshed. She vaguely heard her name.

She was in the other lane of traffic. A thunderous screech and a blaring horn filled her senses. There was a terrific thump and a whirl of surroundings, as if she were spinning in the air, and then a brief shot of pain that exploded into blackness.

It was the single worst day of Ellen's life. Never would it leave her mind's eye: Marion's body sent spiraling by that blue DeSoto, so like their own. Never would she forget the horror of knowing her sister was dead.

But then, neither would she forget the heaven of realizing she was wrong.

She sat now by Marion's bed in a hospital room, stiff and straight because the moment she allowed her muscles to relax, she would crumple into her own lap and weep.

Everything else about the accident was a blur, the concerned pedestrians, the halted vehicles, the actions she took to get to Marion's side. Marion on the road, her beautiful face white as death, her pink dress ripped and spattered in blood, was another clear image. So were the police and ambulance sirens.

She knew she had answered the questions coherently, but couldn't remember what they were.

It didn't matter now. None of it did. What mattered was Marion was alive. For this day at least.

A nurse entered the room quietly. Ellen saw her out of the corner of her eye as she gazed at Marion.

"Miss Dashiell, your relatives are here. Shall I let them in?" the brunette nurse asked in a subdued voice.

"Yes," Ellen replied.

"It's so sad," the nurse said before she slipped out again. "Your sister's such a lovely girl, and so young. We're all sorry for her. She an actress? They say it was on West Fiftieth near Broadway."

Ellen's throat constricted. "Yes. Yes, she's an actress."

Aunt Jennie and Gloria rushed in after a few minutes. Ellen answered their torrent of questions, wishing she could trust them not to go hysterical while she left to telephone Mother.

The sounds of the emergency ward of the hospital crept in. Marion had already been in surgery, and she lay now under morphine, white-faced, white-blanketed, white-bandaged.

Aunt Jennie leaned against the bars of Marion's bed, teary-eyed. She sniffed and looked up at Ellen, a recollection lightening her eyes. "Ellen, I meant to tell you. You and Marion would have been in for a happy treat when you came home, if you'd come home normally...I'd have had such wonderful news to share with you. Now, maybe it will go a long way to cheering at least one of you up. Calvin Bradley dropped by while you were out!"

"Not long after you left, in fact," Gloria pushed past her choked-up throat. She blew her nose and brightened. "He's gotten to be handsome in such a distinguished way. I remember when he was rather gawky."

"I told him all about Marion's woes. Of course, I didn't know about this." Aunt Jennie waved her hand, fisting a handkerchief, over Marion's still form. "But he knows about that cad Wilkie. He was angry in that quiet way of his—it's frightful if you know him. I can just imagine how livid he'll be

over this, once he hears what that cad Wilkie had to do with it."
She shook her head. "Anyway, I have his hotel address. I
took the liberty of telegramming him as soon as we heard."

Ellen's eyes widened. Did she want yet another person here?
Particularly her boss? No; but then again...he was a good
friend, and it would be great to have a level-headed man to rely
on. He'd also be swell at navigating the potential legal matters
that would come with this accident.

"What a surprise, but thank you," Ellen managed.

The concerned brunette nurse came and went often—
Marion was under high supervision. The third time she
appeared, she told Ellen a man was there to see Marion, but
one of them would have to leave before he could be allowed.
Aunt Jennie out-claimed Gloria and made her head home, so
within five minutes of Gloria's departure, Calvin Bradley was
there at the opening of the door.

He hesitated, surveying the room, acknowledging Ellen, then
riveting his gaze on Marion in the bed. He hadn't altered,
except his usual peaceful, slightly grave expression was creased
with anxiety and his suit didn't hang so tidily. A whim to hug
him whispered over Ellen, but she only stood on her wobbly
legs and greeted him.

He took a few steps forward, his eyes fixed on one object.
"How is she?" It was barely above a groan.

Ellen inhaled and exhaled. "It's a long story, but the short
answer is, she's stable. They've X-rayed her and set her broken
bones, and she doesn't appear to be bleeding internally. They'll
run some more conclusive tests later today. She's...probably
going to be all right."

Mr. Bradley closed his eyes. "Thank God."

"Yes." Ellen slipped her gaze to the floor. "Aunt Jennie
could tell you more of what happened. But I need to go
telephone Mother."

It was a long day and a long night. Hearing and visualizing
Mother's anguish was horrible, but Ellen was comforted and

sustained through the trying days that followed by knowing God was near and that His messenger, Mother, was on her way.

Ellen spent the first night in the hospital, sleeping on a rigid couch in the nearest lobby; a nurse took pity on her and allowed it despite the rules. Mr. Bradley had brought her dinner. The next morning he arrived even earlier than Aunt Jennie, squeezing through the doors the moment they were open for visitors.

He and Ellen stood by Marion's bed. "Has she ever awakened?" he asked after apologizing for being so early. He'd soon need to get to work for his client. He looked rather tired and mussed, wearing the same suit as yesterday.

"Not to any great extent. They're keeping her in morphine because the pain would be too bad if she were awake," Ellen replied. She probably looked terrible after her restless night, but even though he was her boss, she couldn't be embarrassed, not now.

"May I take you out for breakfast? Or fetch some for you?" he asked.

Ellen contemplated Marion, bandaged head, arm, torso, and leg, white and peacefully asleep. "They probably won't let her wake until this afternoon at the earliest, but I can't leave the hospital. You understand?"

"Then I'll bring you breakfast. I haven't eaten yet, either; may I join you?"

"By all means. We ought to eat in the cafeteria, though, I believe."

They ventured through the clean, identical white halls, traipsing downstairs and finding the cafeteria by the signs. Even at this hour the hospital was active; though it was such a large place, it never felt crowded or hectic.

Ellen sighed as they sat down to sterile white plates of half-warm eggs, sausage, and toast. Her heart hurt. The worry and strain begged her to release some of her feelings. Mother couldn't come soon enough; she wished she could talk to Dad or Everett. But Mr. Bradley was the next best.

"She will be all right," Ellen reassured herself after Mr.

Bradley said grace. "She was hit hard, and the car was going fast, but…if she's lived this long beyond it…"

"I know," Mr. Bradley said, staring at his food. Like Ellen, he hadn't touched his fork or knife. "I've been there. Not to minimize your pain, but I've…lost someone very dear to me through a car accident."

Ellen looked at him, concern etching her face. "No! I'm so sorry. This must bring back terrible memories for you."

Mr. Bradley nodded slightly. "She hung on for a little while before…passing away."

Ellen felt sick. No—this wasn't Marion they were talking about; it was a friend of Mr. Bradley's.

He met her eyes. "You…may have noticed that I think very highly of your sister. She reminds me of that young lady—my fiancée. It happened five years ago."

The equivalent of a gasp welled up, confined inside her. This revelation—it explained so much! Even his fondness for Marion! However, she'd have to meditate on it later, because his feelings for Marion didn't seem limited to a friendly reminiscence.

"That's even worse, that she was *so* dear to you," Ellen murmured. "I'm surprised the Maddoxes never told us."

"They were honoring my request. They care deeply enough for me to have that much discretion." Mr. Bradley stared at the empty tables nearby. They'd picked an isolated spot. "There's more. I don't like spreading conjecture, but I think you're a good enough friend that I can share this candidly with you."

"Yes; friendship helps unload one's burdens." Ellen trusted Mr. Bradley's comradeship far above Leona's. He wouldn't overburden her.

"Exactly." Mr. Bradley returned his gaze to her. "Well, before John Wilkins was Wilkie St. John, he was just John, a wild teenager who occasionally visited his great-aunt near Cardinal Bush. At sixteen she gave him a car. He'd been in a couple of smash-ups in the area, though never involving another person or automobile. He drove a green roadster. He'd been seen driving around drunkenly on the day—" Mr. Bradley paused. "On the day and near the time and place Helen was hit by a car alongside the road out of town. It was a hit-and-run. John's car was investigated, but damage was difficult to determine because he'd hit a fence the week before, while he was drunk."

Mr. Bradley maintained Ellen's eye contact. He acted like he probably did in court—cool, convincing, relentless. "When confronted, he said he knew nothing about it, but he acted uneasy. He may have been uneasy simply because he was suspected. He was also underage; he could be in deep waters if convicted of drinking. Also, he couldn't be sure what he did while drunk, so perhaps he wasn't completely positive he was innocent. All quite probable. But the driver of the automobile that killed Helen was never found."

Mr. Bradley shook his head. "John never reformed his ways that summer he was in Cardinal Bush. His aunt had been influencing the police to overlook him, but she finally allowed him to be arrested for drunk driving and to spend a few days locked up. After that he left, but he's been back almost every year."

"Has he ever gotten in trouble again?" Ellen asked.

"A few times while still a teenager. I don't remember hearing about anything lately. But honestly and unfortunately, it wouldn't surprise me if he had."

Ellen studied her unappetizing and now cold breakfast. "So he's always been irresponsible. And we let Marion drive with him, date him."

Mr. Bradley cleared his throat. "That's why I never seemed overly friendly to him. I knew he was bad news, but I didn't feel it was my place to warn off any potential friends of his...and I didn't really know how intimate you were with him. I thought —I don't wish to sound like I'm blaming them—but I thought you might have been cautioned by other sources, and had decided he was all right. I'm sorry."

"You didn't know. It's okay. And...he didn't really cause any harm, until now, and that not in the way anyone would have expected." Ellen picked up her fork and touched it to her scrambled egg, then gave up the effort. "Did he have a reputation with girls? I guess we ought to have known. How could we have trusted a Hollywood actor with Marion?" She shuddered. "This whole thing could have been avoided—"

"Don't blame yourself. You didn't know. None of us did; the only one who can be blamed is the man himself." Mr. Bradley pulled his coffee toward him. "And now the only one who isn't suffering is him."

Ellen contemplated that for a while. "I guess he'll get his deserts sooner or later. It's the way things are; God sees to it. And then maybe I'll pity him."

"Perhaps I will, too." He sipped his coffee.

The two finally ate their food, silent until finished. Then Mr. Bradley said he'd better go attend to his work.

"How long will you be here?" Ellen asked.

"Five days. I need to be absolutely certain I collect every piece we need for my client's case. If you don't mind, I'd like to keep coming to check on her and you."

"Of course. Do you need a secretary while you're here?" Ellen half-smiled, then wished she hadn't said anything. She didn't want to seem desparate.

But he took it as the joke she intended. "Would be nice, but I could hardly pry you from your sister's bed for a meal. What makes me think I could get you out of this hospital?"

ᏣᎦᎦᎦᎦ Chapter Twenty-Nine ᎦᎦᎦᎦᏣ

MOTHER HOMED IN TO MARION'S HOSPITAL ROOM LIKE A maternal robin on Wednesday morning. Never, even as a child, had Ellen been more relieved to see her. They fell into each other's arms beside Marion's bed as if years had sliced between them instead of weeks.

"Mother," Ellen whispered. "You can be Mother again, and I don't have to anymore."

Mother's tears induced Ellen's, and together they woke Marion from her stupor.

The doctor had been reducing her morphine, but she was still groggy and sedated to fend off the pain. "Hey, it's Mother, i'n't it?" she mumbled while Mother and Ellen hugged.

"Marion! You're awake!" Mother cried, lunging to her bedside and leaning on the bar.

"Sure. Ellen'd tell ya I'd been before. What day is it?"

Mother bent over Marion, gingerly squeezed her shoulders, and kissed her forehead and cheek. "Wednesday. I came as soon as I could."

After the emotional reunion, Marion drifted off again, so Ellen debriefed Mother. "No internal bleeding, thank God," she concluded. "But she'll be here for quite some time, healing up. The pain in her leg and ribs will be unbearable without morphine. They'll keep shrinking the dose, but they expect to keep her at least a week. They'll move her out of the emergency ward to another room tonight."

Mother rubbed her hands over her arms as if she were cold, though the room was stuffy. "I thank the Lord it wasn't worse, that she's still with us." Tears dewed her eyes. "I wasn't always that meek about it. I spent the time on the train wrestling with it before I came to realize He'd been merciful. She's...still with us."

She dabbed her eyes and twisted her handkerchief. "I need to get better at that, Ellen. At trusting God."

"So do I," Ellen said matter-of-factly. She'd known that of herself for months, and she acknowledged it freely.

"I always thought you were good at it, being so calm and assured all the time." Mother managed a smile. "I was struggling with how the Lord seemed to have taken first my husband, then my home and finances, then my daughter, never dwelling on…on the blessing that none of these people or things were gone completely. That though misfortune beset our family, we were still alive, still united, and that's much more than some can say in these hard times." She drew a shaky breath. "I have nothing to complain about. I have been blessed."

Ellen was silent. Mother's trust had grown deeper roots than hers. Ellen trusted God that everything would be all right in the end, though that end be heaven, and that suffering was to be expected and borne with His help. But she had never considered herself *blessed*—blessed that things were not worse.

"We're always supposed to count our blessings rather than our woes, aren't we?" Ellen mused. "Like the hymn—'Count your blessings, name them one by one.'"

"Yes. And it's wonderful how it succeeds. It gives me the heart of trust and gratitude that I need to make it through," Mother said. She smiled softly. "Pastor Griggs has given several swell sermons lately, and Dad and I have had good talks."

"Dad is doing better?"

"Yes, he is."

"And how is Greta taking all this?"

"She was hysterical at first, but she calmed down by the time I left on Tuesday. She's staying with Violet and Mrs. Cavendish. Uncle Melvin isn't cut out for comforting." Mother shook her head, her brown hair waving. "I'd never have thought my older girls would need me so much I'd have to leave little Greta to go tend to them."

"New York proved too much for us, I guess."

Time passed more swiftly now that Mother was here and Marion was awake. Calvin Bradley and Aunt Jennie came often, and Mother spent every night at the hospital so Ellen could retire to the Fitzpatricks' in the evening.

On Friday night Gloria handed her a telegram from Leona, which politely inquired where she had been and informed her Leona was very impatient to see her, so she'd better come calling on Saturday.

She hasn't heard about Marion. But that won't be a good enough excuse, so I'd better visit her and get it over with. At least her apartment and the hospital are both in Manhattan. Ellen rubbed her forehead as she stared blearily at the message. *I wonder what drama* she'll *have for me.* She was too tired to speculate or even worry.

"You'll never be an actress now!" Lloyd Heron taunted. *His nose, a sharp, pointed beak, jabbed at her.*

Wilkie grinned at her devilishly. "I'll never want you. You're crippled!"

"No!" Marion screamed and jerked. A shadowy white ceiling confronted her flung-open eyes. Pain crept over her entire body as she quivered tensely.

"Marion," a deep, quiet voice resonated. Dad? Was that Dad? "Relax; you're safe now. You're fine."

No, it sounded like him, but it wasn't. She turned her head but could see no one, only yellow lamplight glowing from a corner of the dark room.

"Who are you?" She ought to know; this voice had been in her room before. Comforting, soothing. Why wouldn't her brain work? She knew the man, for Pete's sake! She spoke to him. "Dumb question. But I'm pretty dazed right now. Take my time waking up."

"It's okay." Hesitation. "A bad dream?"

"I'll say. Awful. Just awful." The words sloshed in her head like drunken sailors in a storm-tossed ship. Whoever this man was, he was a friend, so she sure felt like confiding in him. "Terrible. It always comes. Ever since I realized what's happened to me, and that I won't be getting off a bed for weeks." Tears pooled up and trickled out, chilling her temples. She nudged her good left arm free of the bed clothes and swiped them before they could torment her ears.

"Which means no acting. My big break—is broken. Busted. So much for all the effort and struggle. So much for this trip. Pointless. Hopeless. A waste." The tears pooled faster; she let them drench her face. It was cathartic.

"Nothing is ever pointless," the man spoke up quietly. "It only seems that way until we discover the point."

Marion was sufficiently alert now for the words to penetrate, but still entranced enough in sleepiness that they sank deep into her consciousness, like the last words of a dream. "What about Wilkie? I loved him. Why did he reject me? For crying out loud, what's the point of that?"

Silence. Was that guy still here? Then, "I don't believe we've discovered it yet."

"Who's we? Who are you?" Marion demanded, her crying stopped.

Silence. "Calvin Bradley. Forgive me for not saying earlier."

Marion started to boil until memories of the recent days tickled her mind. "Oh. Well…you're all right. You've been kind. I don't have a reason to be mad at you." She smirked. "I don't think. Anyhow, I can't remember if I do or not."

He chuckled. "Memory loss has its perks."

"I guess so, if it could just be controlled."

"If you lose something purposefully, you'll never forget where you lost it. I've tried."

"I haven't. I'll try, though. I might succeed where you didn't." Marion's thoughts were bubbling now, and she found herself unable to control them. "What'd you try to lose? Stuff? Memory? Person?"

"A memory…of an event. Fortunately, you can also lose something by accident, but remember it if you try."

"That's handy. Wish I knew what I wanted to remember and what I wanted to forget. Wilkie—" She broke off as an ache surged through her and choked her throat. She couldn't talk about him now, not even in her uninhibited mood. She licked her lips. "Say, can you give me water? Gotta wet my whistle."

A chair creaked as he got out of it, glass clinked and water poured, and then strong arms gently helped her lift her head enough to sip from a straw. Marion looked up at the looming figure as she sank back after her drink, grateful to rest her neck on the pillow again. "Where's my mother?"

"Out eating dinner. I sent her to a nice restaurant so she could have more than hospital cafeteria food and lukewarm meals sent from your cousin's."

Marion stared into his eclipsed face, the lamplight haloing his head. "Thank you." She blinked back sudden tears. "Mr. Bradley, you're swell. You've helped my family so much, and I never appreciated it before."

"Thank you." Mr. Bradley returned her look, intensely. "I care for all of you. You're some of the best people I've ever known."

Marion smiled and mumbled, "Mr. Sour-face."

"What was that?"

"Nothing!" She grinned wider.

He smiled back. It was a nice smile. Handsome in the dramatic, shadowy light.

"It's finally happening, Ellen. We're going to tell my parents. Everett's mustered up the courage, and he's almost certain his parents will support us." Leona still clenched Ellen's hands. They stood in her well-dressed apartment bedroom, Saturday morning sunlight streaming in through the long, sheer drapes.

"I can't wait to be finally married." Leona smiled wistfully. "You'll be my bridesmaid, won't you? I feel closer to you than ever I did to my sisters, and you're Everett's friend, too."

Could it get any worse? Could her heart be pierced any deeper? *You've gotten past this, remember?* Ellen chided herself. *You've given him up. He's in God's hands, and Leona's. Not yours.* But she wouldn't be capable of being in their wedding.

"Of course, we may elope, if my parents aren't...agreeable. But if we do have a proper wedding, I certainly want you in it."

"Where will you have it? I may not be able to come if it's in New York."

"Oh, we'll pay for you to come, wherever it is. We simply must have you." Leona smiled. Not even her expertise at masquerade could disguise the smugness in it.

Yet even now Ellen must keep up appearances. "If they say yes, will you continue living in Canton, where Everett works?" She attempted a smile.

"Yes, though I'd love to live somewhere more exciting." Leona chuckled. "But I guess where we live isn't important, so long as we're together. That's what they say anyway." She released Ellen's hands, sashayed to the double bed, and perched on the puffy white quilt. "It's wonderful to know that it's close. Soon we'll no longer be apart."

Ellen had difficulty supporting her half-smile. *If we ever move back to Canton, I'll be in the same town as them.* "Has he talked to his parents, then, so that he knows they approve?"

"Not yet. He hasn't been in town, but he'll talk to them soon, alone. He won't tell me when because I'll hardly be able to stay away, and he doesn't want me there in case they say no." Leona cupped her hand around her mouth and whispered coquettishly, "He's afraid of how delicate I am and how badly I'll take it." She laughed. "But I'm sure they'll say yes!"

Sobering, she confided, "I hope *my* parents will be agreeable. I'll get an inheritance if they are, and that will give Everett a leg up in the world. He could get more schooling, a better job, anything." She sighed. "I want to give him something by marrying him." She vacillated to a giggle again. "Besides myself, that is."

Ellen nodded and surveyed the bedroom once more; looking away from Leona helped her forbearance. The room radiated Leona's wealth and privilege. True, these things—the bed, the ornate oaken wardrobe, the plush red armchair, the French vanity, the oriental rug in a wealth of colors, the red and white wallpaper—weren't Leona's, but her parents' money had afforded them. She was accustomed to décor like this. Could she be happy living with less, but in marriage to Everett?

Knowing her character, Ellen couldn't say yes. *Oh, Everett, what have you gotten yourself into? Lord God, are You watching over him?*

"Ellen, you can choose to believe this or not, but I miss Mr. Bradley," Marion said as she and Ellen sat in her hospital room after lunch Tuesday afternoon. It had been over a week since the accident, and she needed only local painkillers, so she was no longer, as she termed it, "morphinated." She was still sore and tired, especially when she breathed and her broken ribs twinged, but her brain was fully her own. If only it didn't throb so with excruciating thoughts.

Ellen half-smiled, probably disbelieving. "Really?"

"Yes. You see, he's such a nice fellow, and I could use all the friendly faces I could get right now." Marion had started with a smile but ended with a frown. "I think I may have been more open with him than I intended. It's not really clear to me what I said and what I thought. But oh well. He's an understanding man." She dug her left hand into her hair, her right obediently remaining on her lap where the arm cast required it. "I'm ready to scram. Even Mother and Aunt Jennie's excursion sounds wonderful."

They were out for a jaunt around Central Park and other sights in the area. The only sightseeing Mother had done since arriving had been the inside of this rundown Manhattan hospital and the trackline between here and the Fitzpatricks'. Marion was well enough that Mother felt secure leaving her for more than an hour. Since Mr. Bradley had returned to Ohio, they and Ellen and Gloria had been the only ones to come see her.

"I'd love to look out that window at least. Goodness, the sun's pouring in and calling me."

"It isn't much of a view, I'm afraid."

"Better than what's here." Marion brushed a straggly piece of hair from her eyes; she couldn't call it a curl. Curls were a thing of the past, like so much else. "Say, why hasn't Everett come to see me? Doesn't he know?"

Ellen lowered her eyes. "He's in Canton, of course. And I... haven't told him."

"What? Ellen, how could you? He's practically family!"

"I wouldn't say that."

Marion rolled her eyes. "Enough with the modesty. He's your boyfriend."

Ellen didn't answer. Instead she lobbed the conversation in another direction. "What's the first thing you're going to do when you get home? Three more days and you'll be headed to the Fitzpatricks', and soon after that, home."

Marion stared at the ridges her legs made under the white sheet, the right larger than the left because it was in a cast. This was her lot: broken right arm, broken ribs, broken right hip and leg. The arm and ribs could heal correctly, but the hip and leg...she may never walk evenly again. Her eyes brimmed.

"Ellen, I don't care about going home. I don't care about anything anymore." She sniffled, and Ellen stuck a hankie in her hand. "I just wish none of this had happened. Can't we turn back the clock? Or maybe it's fate, and can't be changed, even if I could go back." She dabbed her eyes as her throat ached. Uh-oh, this was going to be a big, painful cry, a torment to her ribs, if she didn't stem it. "It's lost, Ellen. All lost. Wilkie, acting...my future. What do I care about living if I don't have a future?" She gasped. "If I don't have love." She tried to take a deep breath but winced when her ribs protested.

"Don't work yourself up. The calmer you stay, the quicker you'll heal."

"Yeah, right. Will that help my leg? Will that bring Wilkie back to me? Will that bring back my career, my lost opportunity? I had it, Ellen. I had it in my grasp." Marion stopped heaving simply because it hurt so much. "It was all there. And God snatched it away!" She glared at Ellen. "I was beginning to believe He cared, that He'd given me wonderful things, but then poof! It was gone. Either He hates me, or He has no power."

"It isn't either." Ellen's brown eyes flashed. "You don't understand how God works." She paused. "You've been misinformed, and I'm sorry. But God doesn't hate you, nor is He powerless. The Bible contradicts both those things. When He allows bad things to happen to us, it's to make us turn to Him. Suffering is never pointless, if we know what to do with it. If suffering makes you depend on God when you haven't before, that's worth more than all the beds of roses we think we want." She caught her breath as if a thought had struck her.

Eyes wet, Marion looked away and tensed with anger until a memory drifted in. "Pointless...that sounds like something Mr. Bradley said." She frowned, collecting the exact words. "'Nothing is ever pointless. It only seems that way until we discover the point.'"

"Mr. Bradley said that, did he?" Ellen mused. She fixed a poignant gaze on Marion. "So you've gotten a similar statement twice."

"Yeah, well…" Marion shifted. "He seems like he's been through something. But you, Ellen. Look, I know you've lost Dad just like I have, and you've lost your job. But you never had the ambition I had, and you still have Everett."

"No, I don't," Ellen murmured.

Marion sighed dramatically. "Now what did I *just* tell you about your modesty?"

"Marion, I don't have Everett anymore. He's engaged to someone else."

"*What*?!" Marion's mind braked like a car before a washed-out bridge. "You're joking, aren't you? Everett can't be engaged to someone else. He's practically engaged to you!"

"No, he never was. He's been engaged to another girl for four years."

"*Four years*? The cad! Why, that evil—"

"Don't."

Marion huffed. "He deserves it. Well then, who's the witch that has him under her spell? Do we know her?"

"I don't think we should be discussing this right now, in your condition."

"It's someone we know, isn't it? Who?"

"Marion—"

"I'm already worked up. I'll work myself up even more trying to figure out who she is."

Ellen's placid expression tweaked into one of consternation.

"Tell me. I'll hold my breath if you don't." Marion gave her voice a playful lilt. She used to threaten Ellen with that as a kid; it succeeded when they were five and seven.

"It's Leona Bingham."

"*What!*"

Ellen explained everything in as little detail as she could, each word transferring Marion from the state of heart attack to the land of rage. They hashed it over and over again until Marion felt she was sufficiently calm to think clearly, find Leona, and strangle her effectively. When she declared so, of course Ellen forbade it.

"You can't tell anyone, Marion. Not even Mother. If Mother is to hear, it's to be from me. Leona never swore me to secrecy, but it was implied that it ought never to escape me. I told you only so it would…help you. Besides, it may soon be known to all, as I said."

"Help me?" Marion furrowed her brows. An uncomfortable understanding dug the furrows deeper. "Ellen, you…kept this pain to yourself these two months? And you're only opening up about it because you think it'll help me? And I've been miserable and bellyaching so much about Wilkie and you've never complained about Everett and Leona once. Ellen, how *did* you stand it?"

"It wasn't as difficult as you imagine. It was duty more than anything else…I needed to be quiet about it for their sakes. And for yours and Mother's. I've wanted comfort, yes, but I'd feel awful piling one more disappointment on you two. You'd find out sooner or later, and I had hoped it'd be later, but with Leona and Everett trying to make it official *now*, it was as good a time as any."

"Especially when, as you say, it might help me." Marion plucked her bottom lip with her left fingers, mulling. "What a selfish fool I've been! And you, suffering all this time with your own heartache! While I, boohooing over mine, making sure everyone knew about it, particularly you, and believing no one knew misery except me—I demanded comfort for every little prick. Not only with Wilkie, but with the theater." She shook her head. "You put me to shame."

"I tell you to show you something. I've been disappointed in love—"

"You admit it! You were in love!"

"Of a sort. It certainly had more growing to do—but yes, I did favor him. Anyway, I've been disappointed. You could say I've suffered, if you want to compare it to your own feelings. And yet I've given this over to God. I haven't stopped believing in Him or accused Him of hating me. It doesn't work that way. Bad things happen to teach you something, to make you stronger, or to make you turn to God."

Ellen's chin lifted as she inhaled deeply. Her breath gushed back out with her next words. "On that note, I could go further and say that I've been blessed to 'suffer' these things, since they've brought me closer to God. 'Blessed are those who mourn, for they shall be comforted.' They've shown me that He is all I need."

Marion cocked her head and peered at her. "Really? You say that truthfully? My sister's become a missionary martyr!"

"Hardly. I've just now—as in the past few minutes—realized this and taken it to heart. If Dad hadn't been falsely accused, I'd never have started praying so earnestly for it to be fixed. And if he hadn't been wrongfully jailed and taken from us, I'd never have depended so much on God. If I hadn't lost my job, I'd have still relied on myself. If I hadn't met Everett and loved him and then lost him again, I'd—" She snatched up her breath as if afraid a sob would tumble out. Her chin quivered and she swallowed. "I'd never have known what it was to give the last thing I was holding back from God, my hopes and dreams and Everett, over to Him."

"Oh, Ellen!" Marion cried, then broke into the sobs that Ellen had refused herself. Ellen dashed to the bed and wrapped her arms around Marion as best she could. Marion felt teardrops not her own fall on her forehead.

"Shh, shh, your ribs; you'll hurt yourself," Ellen soothed.

Marion cut off her sobbing as quickly as possible, because it did hurt like the dickens, and her ribs prevented her from dredging very deeply anyway. Crying wasn't the catharsis it usually was.

"Oh Ellen, it isn't fair. You and I, every promise of happiness we've had is crushed. And I don't have the faith you have. So maybe God doesn't hate me, because surely He doesn't hate you, and you have it rotten, too. But what good can come of this? You've rattled off some things, but those are all feelings, and things that have to do with your relationship to God. What good is there for your personal life? You don't have a stupendous job, a stupendous fiancé. What do you have?"

"I have something better. I'm closer to God than I was. I love Him so much now, I can't believe there was a time I didn't really care. I hope...I hope one day you'll realize how important that is for yourself."

Marion couldn't think of anything to say. Could God ever be so important to her that closeness with Him could outshine everything else in her life? That she could dismiss, or at least diminish, the things she suffered in light of that relationship? The brain power to consider it was beyond her at the moment. Her head was starting to ache.

She summoned an ounce of selflessness and told Ellen, "Promise me one thing: that you'll talk about Everett and Leona with me whenever you hurt. I want to do something for you; you've done so much for me."

Ellen gazed at her, gravity, almost sadness, in her eyes. "I shall. Thank you."

To Ellen's relief, she saw Leona only once that week, on Wednesday. The girl effused exhilaration: Everett was back, and they had been meeting at a café; they were going to tell his parents Thursday; with their support, she and Everett would approach her parents. If they couldn't finagle her parents' approval, they'd still have Everett's income and the promise of inheritance from the wealth his father was slowly re-accumulating. Then there was also some money from a grandparents' estate that was supposed to go directly to Everett when he was thirty. All that was enough to get by, surely! And besides, they'd have each other.

Marion was released, complete with casts, crutches, and pain medication, to the Fitzpatricks' on Friday.

"Isn't this exciting? You're leaving those high walls for good!" Mother exclaimed to Marion as she slid into the back seat of Larry Fitzpatrick's car beside her. "You'll get to practice on those crutches more, and you'll be getting around in no time."

Ellen turned to gaze at them from the front with a smile, feeling more joy than she'd felt in weeks. *Thank you, Lord, for this blessing. You've brought Marion through, and she's healing.*

Marion looked out her window. "Not much of a view on this side of the hospital either. My room was on the other side, wasn't it? Nothing around here is anything to write home about —just ugly, blunt sides of buildings and cars jammed up on streets."

"We *are* in the middle of Manhattan." Ellen kept her grin.

"I know. But don't you see? It represents my prospects— I've got nothing. I almost did, but now my future is ended before it even began." Marion sighed. "I guess I'll hear about

313

Diamonds pretty soon and find out who took my place. Maybe it was that redhead Stella. She ought to get it, anyhow."

"Now Marion, it isn't that bleak—" Mother started.

"Yes, it is. I don't want to talk about it."

"Marion." Ellen locked a grave look on her sister. "You could still be in that hospital. Remember the talks we've been having?" Since the first one on Tuesday, they'd had serious, searching conversations every day, and Marion had actually made slight progress in her outlook. "It only looks like there are no blessings because you don't see them. But they are there regardless."

Marion's return glance was withering.

"And feelings aren't the only reality," Ellen added, to which Marion tossed her attention to the window, where the city was now flowing past. At least Ellen knew the thoughts could penetrate; sprinkle them in here and there, careful not to preach, and something was bound to take root.

Marion stayed in Aunt Jennie's room on the second floor, while Mother slept on a cot there and Aunt Jennie moved in with Ellen. Rosetta was strong enough to carry Marion up and down the stairs as needed during the day, and Marion always retired before Rosetta left for the night.

She was no happier there than at the hospital, but she wasn't a difficult patient; just despondent. The others, however, especially Aunt Jennie and Gloria, were optimistic enough to make up for her lack. Ellen thanked God that the two were so positive…even though some of their joviality was unfounded and ridiculous, it cheered her and Mother.

Ellen received a letter from Leona on Monday that rocked her good mood. She carried it to her room to read. Aunt Jennie only trekked the stairs twice in a day, so Ellen had the room securely to herself. For Leona, it could be good news or bad news, but for Ellen, it would only be bad.

Forgive me, Lord. I sorrow for them when their news is bad, but I sorrow for me when their news is good. Will I ever be able to get over my indignation for what Leona is doing to Everett? Will I ever be able to truly forgive her?

She curled up on her bed and slit open the envelope with her nail file.

My Dear Ellen,

I am so distraught I hardly know what to say or think. Everett is comforting, but he is a man, and sometimes a girl needs her best friend to confide in. But for some reason I haven't the heart to see you face to face. Perhaps when you get this letter I'll be feeling up to calling on you.

Everett told his parents Thursday afternoon and they violently expressed their disapproval for our union. It seems they hate my family now and don't want the connection, however much I am willing to break off with my family. I persuaded him to take me to their house that night to use my arguments on them, but that didn't work either. Everett said they were even worse than with him.

That isn't the worst of it. When he said he'd stand by me no matter what, and marry me with or without their approval, they threatened to disown him if he follows through. And do you know what he said? He said, "So be it. I shall not desert her." Now isn't that a knight in shining armor? I could have swooned when he said it, but his arm was around me. It was the proudest moment of my life, though it was also very dreadful, with his parents shouting and fuming at us.

I knew you would want to know. We are going to try my parents soon; we have nothing to lose. It may be that my parents' hearts will soften when they hear about Everett's parents, and they'll give me my inheritance. If they don't, I don't know what we'll do, but I have my hopes they will.

I hope to see you soon when I am feeling calmer. This is so unexpected I am still reeling. But side by side with my dear Everett I shall weather it.
Your friend,
Leona Bingham

Ellen read and analyzed the letter twice to catch all the facts. This was a new twist! Everett's parents the rejecters now? *What would they have thought of me?* she thought wryly, though they did have a worthwhile reason to disapprove of Leona and not necessarily any other prospective girl.

Where did that leave Everett and Leona? It certainly showed

they were in earnest; especially Everett, who, as far as Ellen knew, had never had serious disagreements with his parents. She had doubted his love for Leona. But he was a man of his word; how could she have thought he'd do otherwise? He was like the man in the Psalm she'd just read, the one who swore to his own hurt yet did not change.

The reflection made her admire him more—for his honorable, understated character and his insight into real love, based not on emotion but on faithfulness. Perhaps after meeting Ellen he had wavered and permitted himself to get attached when he shouldn't have; she could allow for that now. No one was perfect.

So they were in earnest. Their attachment thus far had withstood the steady ravages of time and the shaking of an earthquake from Everett's parents. The marriage seemed more imminent than ever. *Dear God, give him happiness somehow. Please.*

Aunt Jennie gusted into the living room, where Ellen was reading that afternoon, waving a telegram. "Calvin is returning to New York! Business for his client again. On Monday. And," she winked, "he plans on staying in Brooklyn this time to be nearby. Of course Gloria and I shall invite him to dinner *every* night. He may win your sister's heart yet!"

"How wonderful he's coming!" Ellen half-smiled. "But please, don't tease Marion about him, Aunt. You know there's nothing there, and she is so sensitive right now. I'd hate for her to lash out on you or him."

"Mm. I disagree with you on there being nothing there, par-ti-cu-lar-ly since that wolfish Wilkie's out of the picture, but you have my word I won't say a word. I'll let true love find its way."

Oh, Aunt Jennie. But Ellen was glad Mr. Bradley was coming again. With Marion confined as she was, Mother and Ellen hardly got out, either, and though Aunt Jennie had made plenty of friends around the neighborhood and beyond, no one had yet latched on to the Dashiells. Even Marion's doctor was in-house, because of course Dr. Larry had assumed the post.

But though the following days were monotonous, with Mr. Bradley's visits all that the Dashiells could look forward to, they were not unhappy. Despite herself, Marion was growing inexorably stronger, and thus each passing day brought the family closer to home. With Dr. Larry as physician, he might discharge Marion early simply to finally be rid of them!

Before Marion got well enough for them to plan their return, however, they had a different visitor than Mr. Bradley.

"Why, hello, Everett," Ellen said, rising from her chair in the Fitzpatricks' living room. Rosetta had just shown him in.

Marion gasped and stared at him over the top of the couch, where she reclined against a thick pillow. Ellen gave her a warning look and pressed on her shoulder as she passed to greet Everett, hoping to remind her to not stir up trouble.

"Hello, Ellen…and Marion." Everett stood in the doorway, dressed in a brown suit and holding his hat. His ears were pink. "I-I can't stay long, I'm afraid."

Though she was shocked to see him, Ellen slipped effortlessly into politeness as they shook hands. "My mother and Aunt Jennie will be sorry they missed you. They're running errands with my cousin."

"Your mother is here? Wow, I'm sorry to miss her—and your aunt—too." Everett's grip was slack and he avoided her eyes. "Er, tell them hello for me." He paused. "I came to ask after Marion. I heard about her accident. What a sorry affair."

"That's so kind of you," Ellen said. "She can't move much, but you're welcome to stay awhile."

"Hello, Everett," Marion said coldly when he stepped into the circle of couch and chairs.

I wish she'd be more charitable, but she is miffed for my sake, Ellen thought. She invited him to sit down, and the three of them talked briefly about the accident and Marion's injuries. Marion didn't say much and her attention to Everett took the form of a glare, so Ellen did her friendliest best to put him at ease. Not that it succeeded. He only grew more uncomfortable the longer he stayed. If only she'd known about his coming, she could have prepared Marion's attitude.

That talk subsided, and then Ellen knew it was time to bring up the other subject. *God saw fit to give him to Leona, not to me,* she exhorted herself. "I understand congratulations are in order."

Marion choked. Ellen paused and went on. "Leona told me about your engagement." She smiled as warmly as she could but felt chilled inside. *Please, God, help me.*

"Oh, yes." Everett's ears turned pink again. "Thanks." He looked at the dark brown fedora in his lap. "And thanks for being a good friend to Leona. She told me how you helped her."

"Of course. She's a sweet girl." *It isn't a lie. She can be sweet.*

Marion groaned. Ellen hoped it was just pain, and that she wouldn't burst out in protest.

"She told me," Everett gulped, "she told me you know everything now."

Ellen burned with pity for him, for her, for the whole situation. If only it had been different.

"Listen, I'm sorry," he blurted. His ears were red now, and he shifted his hat.

"Yes, well…" Ellen stopped because her voice was trembling. She took a deep, silent, steadying breath. "It's in the past."

Everett finally matched her gaze and nodded with a whispered sigh. "Yes."

Silence. Ellen wished Marion weren't there, because at every second she expected her angry outburst.

Everett traced the brim of his hat with a fingertip, shoulders drooping. "I'm ashamed to say anything more about my problems to you, but if you could…pray for me…I'm rather afraid for my job. I think Benton Green is on to me. Suspicious that I've found something out about him."

Ellen was grateful Everett had bravely breached the awkwardness—and was still able to talk to her like a friend. She looked her concern. "Oh no, I'm sorry. On my father's account? Everett, how could I ever thank you—"

"No." Everett stayed downcast. "I don't deserve it. I was

something of a coward the whole time I was investigating, if you want to call it that. Always afraid I'd get caught." His chin dipped toward his collar and he muttered, "Mr. Bradley is the real hero."

"But you investigated anyway—and I do call it that. You were courageous, not cowardly, because you did it despite your fear," Ellen said. "I'll—we will always be grateful. Won't we, Marion?" She spoke her sister's name forcefully.

"Of course." Marion stared at the fireplace.

"Well, I think I've overstayed my welcome." Everett rose.

Ellen wanted to talk more about his job, learn what was going wrong and why Mr. Green seemed suspicious of him, strategize over what he could do to not get sacked like she had; but she acknowledged it was best for him to leave now before anyone lost control...and she didn't necessarily believe it would be Marion.

"Thank you for your steady friendship. It means so much to Leona and me," he said.

"I..." Ellen faltered. What could she say beyond the searing hurt that obliterated all thought of words? "It's my pleasure, Everett," she managed with a constricted throat.

They shook hands. He seemed afraid to go near Marion, so he just tipped his hat at her and said goodbye to both of them. And then he was gone.

৩৬৫৫ Chapter Thirty-One ৫৬৫৫

THE DAY CAME AT LONG LAST. IN LATE AUGUST ELLEN, MARION, Mother, and Aunt Jennie boarded a train; final stop, Canton, Ohio. The very next day the Fitzpatricks themselves were going on their much postponed seaside vacation. Ellen had been right: Dr. Larry hurried Marion's recovery along, finally pronouncing that what she needed was more room to practice walking. She needed to go home to Cardinal Bush.

Greta, Uncle Melvin, and the Cavendishes, Greta's friends whom she had been living with, heralded their homecoming with a small party, not too fanfarish so that Marion was overwhelmed, but with enough special food and decorations to be convivial. The reunion with Greta reduced all the Dashiell women to puddles, especially Greta.

"I've missed you so much, Greta," Ellen whispered as she hugged Greta goodnight after the Cavendishes had gone home and everyone was retiring. Greta was now eye to eye with Ellen, but still as slender as a little girl.

"I missed you so much, too!" Greta exclaimed, squeezing her. They stood between their bedroom doors, just like they always used to at bedtime.

"I thought about you often, but I confess I felt so lonely sometimes I forgot how lonely *you* must have been," Ellen said, still holding Greta. "At least I always had Marion with me; but you, you spent weeks without even Mother."

"It wasn't so bad." Greta's voice tremored despite her firmest efforts. "Writing was fun. I liked hearing about New York."

"And I loved getting your letters," Ellen said. "They made me homesick for Ohio, and for you. I'm so proud of you, Greta, for being brave and letting Mother come to us without a

320

fuss. You're so grown up."

"I think I missed being around Sport all the time as much as I missed you and Marion," Greta said mischievously.

"Oh, you!" Ellen pushed herself off her sister and braced her hands on Greta's shoulders.

"Except I could see him almost whenever I wanted to, and you not at all…so I guess maybe I did miss you lots more." Greta smirked.

"You had better." Ellen leveled a glare at her but couldn't fend off a grin. "Well, off to bed with you. Perhaps you'll appreciate us in the morning."

"I won't much appreciate it if Marion doesn't get in a better mood."

"Hush. She's not asleep yet." Ellen sighed inwardly and pulled Greta into the room Ellen and Mother shared. Mother was downstairs. She turned on the light and shut the door. "It's been a long and wearying day for all of us, and you can't forget she's in pain. Pain makes people crabby. She may be gloomy and irritated for a long while yet, and you just have to be gracious and patient."

"Will she always be that crabby when she's on the stairs?"

Ellen and Uncle Melvin had helped Marion go upstairs; it was as painstaking as scaling a cliff. "No, that was because she was tired. She should get used to it." Ellen paused. "For the first few days, don't pester her with questions. Mother or I can fill you in on everything."

"Okay. I'd probably figure that out myself sooner or later," Greta said. "Do you think Mr. Bradley would make her feel better? You said she enjoyed his visits in New York."

"He might, but I think waiting a few days is best for him, too."

"I am glad he didn't come tonight, though Uncle Melvin and Aunt Jennie wanted him to. I wanted you all to myself."

"As did we." Ellen tiptoed to the door. "Time's marching; your bed is calling."

"I could stay up talking with you all night!"

"You'd be talking to the wall. Now goodnight." Ellen

shooed Greta across to her bedroom and watched until it received her.

Ellen remained there, taking in the dingy, wallpapered hallway, the scuffed floor clouded with dust, and the dim staircase railing. She had housework cut out for her again. Good; she needed work. Desperately. No more aimlessness, thank God—it would be ecstasy to be busy again.

And at "home," too. Comfort and relief were the best words to describe how she felt upon returning to Cardinal Bush and the farmhouse. It wasn't exactly home, but it had welcomed them with open arms all those months ago, like its owners, and it welcomed them now as if they truly belonged. That was a blessing she hadn't fully appreciated: to be embraced by a place and a family that hadn't raised you.

"She hasn't been downstairs yet today," Ellen answered Mr. Bradley's query. He had arrived a few minutes ago to have lunch at the farmhouse, via Uncle Melvin's invitation. It was a weekday, so the two men had slipped out of their respective offices and given themselves a generous lunch hour.

"How did she do yesterday, her first full day back?" Mr. Bradley asked, staying clear of the kitchen activities by stationing himself against the wall beside the swinging door.

"She stayed upstairs then, too," Mother sighed. "All day. She's been having nightmares. I thought they'd go away once she got back to Ohio, but they seem worse."

"Perhaps it's the memories here. She spent most of her time with Wilkie in Cardinal Bush, and in this house," Mr. Bradley said soberly.

"I hadn't thought of that, but yes, it must be." Mother shook her head. "Poor dear. I wish I—or anyone else for that matter —could do something for her."

"Her mind is on fire. She's not at peace with what happened," Ellen said. "I don't blame her, but…only God can give her peace, and she has to allow Him to do that."

Mr. Bradley relaxed his rigid posture and leaned against the doorframe, peering at Ellen. "Has she come around to giving God more thought, as you hoped? Has this experience changed her mind at all?"

"She's...I honestly can't say for sure either way. She talks about Him more, but it's usually accusatory or plaintive, wouldn't you say, Mother?"

"I agree. We've tried talking to her, counseling her, but I'm not sure it's getting through. We're trying to be gentle, of course."

"She wants to control her future, so she's afraid to do what it takes to surrender to God, to cede her will," Mr. Bradley mused. "She ought to realize it doesn't go well when it's in her power. In fact, she's not in control now; unforeseen circumstances are. She might as well be at peace with God."

"Tell her that when you talk with her, which will hopefully be today, if we can get her to come down for lunch." Mother smiled. "It sounds like you and she had good chats in New York. Maybe she'll listen to you."

When Mr. Bradley left after lunch, Ellen's thoughts turned to Everett and Leona as she and Greta washed the dishes. What was happening with those two? Had they approached Leona's parents yet? Could they have even gotten married already? Surely Everett wouldn't rush in...but where it came to Leona, Ellen really couldn't predict what he might do. His very attachment to Leona would always remain a puzzle to her.

Well, I'll find out eventually. Leona will make sure of that.

The weekend was quiet. The ladies spent much of it settling back into the house, getting it used to their presence again—cleaning, organizing, restocking. Marion stayed in her room and hardly touched her tray meals. She unintentionally drove out Greta—her noisy, agitative nightmares sent Greta scurrying to sleep with Ellen and Mother. And during the day she must have repelled her, too, because Greta hardly came in then, either. Oh well; she preferred her room to herself.

It was late Sunday afternoon. She reclined on her

counterpane trying to read, but her gaze went to the sun-bedazzled window.

There just wasn't much to live for anymore. The view from her window flaunted life and nature, but what good was greenery? Music played on the radio downstairs, but why be beguiled by entertainment when you could never make your own again, and could no longer strive to be that good? Piano was out of the question, and why would she even torture the air by playing on that horrid out-of-tune thing? Her hurt ribs stopped her from singing like she used to, so she didn't sing at all. What was the use? She couldn't do anything worthwhile with her voice. She'd lost her chance. She'd lost her chance at everything. She'd failed at eighteen.

She might as well languish in her room. Maybe she'd die soon? It was too much to hope.

Someone knocked on her door. "Come in," she sighed.

It was Ellen. "Mr. Bradley was hoping he could see you. Do you want to come downstairs, or should he come up here?"

Ellen always suggested she come downstairs, but Marion always refused. "Send him in," she directed. Her family was loving and nice, but Mr. Bradley succeeded more than any of them to make her forget her sorry lot. He stirred something in her, piqued her interest in life, drew her attention to things outside the walls—especially outside the walls of her injuries. Before this, she'd never have thought Mr. Sour-face capable of that; but perhaps his sobriety resonated with her now.

He entered the next moment, and Ellen left them alone.

"How are you?" He always started with that, sounding courteous and sincere.

"No different than yesterday. I think I've hit a fence—I haven't felt better for ages."

"Have you tested that hypothesis?"

Marion smirked. "I know what my own body is feeling."

"Your brain can play tricks on you."

"Don't I know it," she moaned.

Mr. Bradley paused. "What if you were to help your brain trick you?"

Marion arched an eyebrow at him. "I don't see how it'd be a trick anymore. Sit down and tell me more."

He pulled up her rickety vanity chair, his light-gray suit incongruous with the feminine piece. "It's called thinking positively. You're not improving because you think you can't, that you're a cripple for the rest of your life. The doctor said you'd be able to walk without crutch or cane."

"But with a limp. And if I can't walk gracefully onstage, I'd rather not walk at all."

Mr. Bradley squinted at her. "That sounds rather…ridiculous to me."

Marion funneled all her expression into the perfect glare. "Acting, singing, even dancing, is my life. That's why I walk. If I do heal, it'll take months, perhaps years, and then I'll be so far behind in everything I'll have to start all over again. And with a limp, too. No one wants a beautiful actress with a limp."

Mr. Bradley was silent for a while. "First of all, your thinking is flawed. Life is so much more than acting, singing, and dancing, even for you. What about walking down the stairs to join your family at the table for a meal? What about going for a stroll with your little sister and the dog? What about walking to a job so you can earn a bit of money? What about having the use of two legs so you can help the needy? You've been so consumed with the stage that you've forgotten what else life includes—the mundane, the time you share with your family, the getting from here to there. I know what it's like to have an all-consuming passion; it's one's lifeblood. My job used to consume me. But since you and your family came along, and your sister started working for me…I've seen that life is more than my job. God didn't make us to idolize one pursuit over everything else, including Him. If your idolized pursuit was taken away for the time being, Marion, it may be because you need to reevaluate your priorities."

"Is your argument finished yet, Mr. Lawyer?"

He smiled slightly. "No; I'll save the rest after I hear yours."

Marion was suddenly too weary to hold up her gaze anymore. It dropped to her lap, covered by a wrinkled blue housedress. "I abstain. You go on."

"How...surprising. Well, by your leave: the second part of my argument rests in you being more capable than you think. You are a very strong and determined young woman, and if anyone is going to defy a doctor's predictions about limping, it'd be you. You're already determined to defy him about walking at all; why not switch your determination to something that will benefit you?

"Then, you have a great deal of talent. Do you really think your talent is so weak it would deteriorate in a few months? *I* doubt it. Soon your ribs will heal, and you can sing. You can use your speaking voice now, as you've so amply demonstrated. Read to your family and friends; entertain them and keep up your training. You have natural grace, and that may overcome the vestige of your injuries. It's easy to disguise a limp on screen, if you can't get rid of it. Hadn't you decided you're going into film?

"I have one more point to make. Months ago, when we first met, I said something about the experience of grief and loss bringing realism to acting." He paused, as if creating a weighty silence. "You've experienced that now twofold. I...didn't want to allude to your other grief, which is very likely the root of your depression. But, if you want to positively regard any of what happened to you, you are now more equipped than you were before to be a skilled actor."

Marion looked up at him, eyes damp, throat aching. "Mr. Bradley, you've hit it right where it hurts most." She couldn't help it; she burst into tears. Her ribs didn't hurt so much anymore, so her sobs welled deep.

She covered her face with her hands, ashamed to be doing this in front of Mr. Bradley. The next thing she knew, however, his warm, broad hands were on her shoulders and a cloth tickled her ear. A handkerchief? She slipped it out of his fingers.

He was silent while she made all her clamor, but when she subsided into shaky breaths, he murmured, "Don't give up, on God or on yourself. What happened to you is terrible, but there is hope. With God there is always hope."

Monday morning, Uncle Melvin was at his office, Greta was at Violet Cavendish's house, and Mother and Aunt Jennie were grocery shopping and calling on friends. Ellen had cleaned deeply during the past days, so today she was on to the lighter dusting and tidying up of the parlor. Décor needed rearranging, and the furniture needed washing or polishing. She'd go back to Mr. Bradley's on Tuesday, since finances had perked up, thank the Lord.

Marion had almost come down this morning, but shied from the notion when one of her crutches caught on the rug in her room and she nearly fell. "I might try this evening, when Uncle Melvin is home," she had hedged. Ellen and the others weren't discouraged, however. That she was interested in leaving her burrow was progress; maybe something Mr. Bradley said yesterday had stirred her. She was asleep now.

Ellen's ears perked at the sound of wheels crunching gravel in the driveway. No one ought to be home yet, so she abandoned her dustrag on the piano and went to the front door. An unfamiliar black roadster had just parked, and a blond young man leaped out.

It was Wilkie.

Ellen stiffened and gulped deep breaths, willing herself away from anger. *God, help me keep calm. Be my peace. Getting angry won't do me any good, though it might do him good.* But what on earth brought him here? Gloating? A sorely delayed apology? Curiosity about Marion's condition?

One thing she knew—he was not setting foot inside this house. She forayed onto the porch and stationed herself at the top of the stairs.

He looked up at her, halfway to the porch, his face grave. He was dressed impeccably in a gray suit, blue tie, and crisp white fedora. "How is she?"

Ellen inhaled. *Don't snap. Speak evenly.* "Why do you want to know?"

His gaze dropped and the toe of his black shoe traced a bow in the dirt. "Please, just tell me. I haven't any right to know, but I *need* to know."

He raised his pleading eyes; he'd used that pleading look on her before when he was being playful, but this time it was different. It was sincere. Maybe. *He's a good actor,* she reminded herself.

"Ever since I heard about the accident from—ever since then, I was dying to hear how she was. What I heard was horribly, maddeningly inexact. Broken legs? Broken neck? A long hospital stay? Crippled?" His voice rose. "Tell me how she is, for goodness' sake!"

"Shhh! The last thing she needs is to know you're here," Ellen hissed. "In fact, I'd rather you left now."

"Not until you tell me what happened and how she is. Please!" He took a step forward and sounded almost as if he would weep.

Marion's bedroom was on the other side of the house. If Ellen kept him quiet, they could converse here and Marion would be none the wiser. "What do you want to hear? About the accident? Her hospitalization?"

"All of it."

"Do you know any of it? I'd rather not—"

"I know none of it. Just rumors, hearsay."

Ellen was struck with a loathing to tell him the story. He didn't deserve it! But if she didn't satisfy him, he wouldn't leave. She gritted her teeth, prayed, then began.

Wilkie closed his eyes while she spoke, whispering, "No. Dear God, no. Not because of me," when she told how Marion was hit.

Oh to say, "Yes, because of you!" but God wanted her to be patient and forbearing. She moved on to Marion's long, painful recovery.

"We've been home for about ten days now," she concluded.

Wilkie nodded, then met her gaze again. "How is she now? Is she walking? Is she...are her spirits up?"

Ellen almost snorted. "No to both those questions."

Wilkie's hands flew to his hair, burying themselves as if to help his mind grasp the knowledge. "How could I expect any different?" He turned a slow circle, his elbows arching from his head.

Ellen waited impatiently. Was this more acting?

Suddenly Wilkie darted to the bottom of the porch steps, banging his shins as he fell to his knees. Ellen jumped back. "You don't believe the agony I'm in, do you?" he moaned. "Oh, Ellen...I'm paying for the agony I caused her. I feel every bit of it. To know that I caused her this pain, I put her where she is now...I can't stand it. Yet I know it's true. Has she given up ambition? Will she ever be well enough to pursue her dream, her heavenly talent?"

Ellen doubted he felt the same pain, but her heart cooled toward him. He...he certainly seemed genuine. "I don't know," she said quietly.

Wilkie uttered a low growl. "How could I have been blind? And now I've robbed her and the world of her talent...Ellen, please, hear my explanation. I don't know if anything I say will fully acquit me, but if some explanation I could give would take away some of the awfulness of how this looks, I'd consider myself blessed."

"All right." She was open to hearing, though she was sure nothing he could say would ever allow him to see Marion again, if Ellen had anything to do with it.

"Where to begin?" Wilkie's hands trenched through his hair. "With my great-aunt. She's at the root of all of this." He nodded. "She's made me her heir, you know. So with that eminent distinction, I must do her bidding in everything. Everything important, that is. She allows the acting though she really doesn't like it; but because of that I absolutely must marry with her approval. Someone wealthy and socially suitable.

"All along, I thought that's what I wanted, too. After all, you don't make big money acting unless you're a big name. If I married money, I could keep acting, maybe even get a leg up in the game. Good plan, huh? I thought I'd fall in love with a girl with money, thought they were more to my taste. But I hadn't reckoned on your sister.

"When I met her, I thought she was one of the prettiest girls I'd ever seen. When I saw her more and more, I thought she was more beautiful than anyone, *anyone*…and then I realized I was in love. I honestly believed it could work out. She was talented, she looked up to me, she was gorgeous, sweet, unspoiled…I *loved* her. You gotta believe I loved her, and I was determined to make it work. Love knows no bounds, you know? I never thought about my great-aunt until it was too late. Somehow she sniffed out your sister, and she whisked me away to New York bent on marrying me off to someone rich.

"I couldn't answer your sister's telegrams because Aunt Bertha knew about them. I had to pretend your sister meant nothing to me. Later I met a swell girl—you saw her, she was a looker—who was rich as gold. I thought I had it made, until I saw you and your sister at the party…you zapped my plans. You shoveled guilt on my head and I wasn't blameless anymore. The girl I was with that night didn't let me live it down, and it wrecked our relationship. Aunt Bertha was sore at me; this girl had a high-class family and big money. I ended it with your sister, and this girl ended it with me, and I was left with no one but a sore great-aunt who was on the verge of cutting my throat and disinheriting me.

"Aunt Bertha introduced me to a family whom she entirely approved of, complete with a marriageable daughter. We were forced together against our wills at first. But when my great-aunt laid down her ultimatum—marry the girl or get cut off—I caved. The girl was rich and rather cute and charming, actually. So I told myself at the time. It seems she was in some sort of disfavor with her parents, too, and marrying me would get her out. She was really adoring once our future seemed inevitable.

"The rest is history. Not the happily ever after kind. Our dictators hurried us to the altar after a few weeks, and we were married last Sunday."

Wilkie sighed. "You'd think I'd be joyful, huh? I got a rich girl, my fortune is secure, I can act to my heart's content and never fret about money again—but the girl is the most irritating little brat. Worse than any Hollywood diva, let me tell you. Oh, she was sweet before I married her—but now she's constantly needling me, constantly pecking my head to get me to do what she wants. We're leaving my great-aunt's for our 'honeymoon' in Niagara Falls tomorrow. I wish I could leave her behind! I'm through with her! Divorce, that saving word, isn't an option, not if I want to go on living. Aunt Bertha would cut me off if I so much as whispered the notion. I'm stuck, and believe me, I'm getting my punishment for what I did to your sister."

He gripped Ellen's gaze. "Am I acquitted in any way? I love your sister, but the world got in the way. If I could go back, I'd marry your sister in a heartbeat. But everything went horribly wrong. In the movies, it's not supposed to happen this way. Stuff gets between a fella and his girl, but despite their mistakes and misunderstandings, they get together in the end and live happily ever after." He looked at the porch steps. "Real life isn't like that, I found out."

He fell silent, and Ellen was left trying to gather up all he said. Speaking just now was out of the question.

The silence stretched on for she didn't know how long. Not long enough, it felt. She needed a solid hour to process this and form a response.

"Say something, please, Ellen. At least assure me you'll tell her. I can't stand the thought of being so despicable in her eyes, though I know I deserve it. But if she knows all the facts, perhaps she won't hate me every time she thinks of me; perhaps there'll be some pity, knowing I, too, suffered, though just a sliver of what she did. I'm shackled like she is, though in a different way. At least she has a chance of recovery."

Ellen weighed his request for a moment. "All right. I'll tell her some of what you said, one day. She'll need closure." In her head, she added, *She'll need to know for certain that you're not coming back.*

Wilkie puffed out some air through slightly puckered lips. "Thanks. That's all I ask." He started to turn, then pivoted back. "Do you think of me a little better?"

Ellen was taken aback. "I...I realize you're not a completely heartless cur, playing with Marion's emotions like you did. You…meant it." Strength filled her voice. "But let me give you some advice. Whoever your wife is, don't speak about her in such a way. Love is more than a whim one feels for another; it's bound up in actions and faithfulness. However you feel about your wife, you're married to her for good, and you ought to respect her, especially to other people like me. You might as well make the best of whom you *are* married to. She deserves that much. If you want to do anything to atone for what you did, respect women more—starting with your wife."

"Ellen Dashiell! You've graced me with one of your gracious, improving lectures. I feel like your friend again. Thank you." He crept up the worn stairs, extending his hand. "Will you honor me with a handshake? With it, I'll not leave in such a cloud, but feel there's yet hope for me to be a better person."

Ellen stared at his hand, then slowly reached out. "Consider this an exhortation to devote yourself to that pursuit of reforming yourself. May I offer one more piece of advice? You'll find the instructions in the Bible."

They shook hands. Wilkie chuckled but stopped when he noticed her expression. "Oh, you're serious. Well, perhaps I ought to. God certainly can't be very pleased with me right now, either."

A neighbor's car rattling down the hidden road reminded Ellen Wilkie should leave before anyone else saw him. "You ought to go."

"Yes, I guess so." He glanced up at the second story. "I wish her, and you, and your family all the best. I'm sorry I wrecked so much of everything. If ever I were free again—"

"Stop that. She's lost to you for good, and you have your wife."

Wilkie licked his lips. "It'd be too much to hope she'd remain free. That lawyer—has he been coming around? He's all wrong for her. I don't want to imagine that."

"You wanted to leave in my good graces, didn't you? Now is most propitious, before you say anything else."

He nodded. "Very well. Thank you, Ellen Dashiell. I shall go to my martyrdom—wait, you said I shouldn't speak that way. Well. I'll take your other advice and leave without another word, except: goodbye."

ᘓᕮᕗ Chapter Thirty-Two ᕬᕮᕗ

ELLEN COLLAPSED ONTO THE PORCH SWING AFTER THE NOISE OF Wilkie's roadster faded. She forced herself to think over everything logically and correctly. *Should I have forgiven him so easily? He worms his way into one's heart so, I couldn't help it! But perhaps the Lord wanted me to leave him with words of forgiveness, when I wanted to condemn?*

She sincerely wanted Wilkie to reform. No matter how much satisfaction she was tempted to feel at his misery, it did her and Marion no good. *But I hope I never see him again!* The pain he had caused was all too sharp, and she knew she would often wonder if she truly had forgiven him. *Wash this from our minds, Lord. Help us to move on. And…help him. Help him find You.*

She sighed and went on rocking in the swing, soaking up much needed serenity from the early autumnal wind that mitigated the warm, sunshiny air. The trees rustled, a bird chirped, insects buzzed. Who was the girl Wilkie married? Was she really that terrible, or was that just how he saw her through his glasses, warped with self-centeredness? Well, Ellen preferred not to know. She also doubted how much of a pawn he had been.

That night, when they were alone in their bedroom, Ellen whispered the story of the morning to Mother. Mother's emotions ran the same gamut as Ellen's, ending with a spirit of forgiveness mixed with a stronger sense of regret for what might have been. But Mother had always been sentimental; doubtless, the next time she talked with Dad about the situation, he'd get her to see it straight: If Wilkie and Marion's relationship had flourished into marriage, the Dashiells could not have trusted Wilkie to be faithful even then. He needed too much reformation, too much sobering and spiritualizing to be suitable for Marion. And letting her go to Hollywood with him? That would have been disastrous. They now knew his true character; it took his betrayal to unmask it.

Ellen broke the news to Marion gently the next day when she was downstairs for the first time, and she received it better than Ellen expected.

"I'll always think of what might have been, but I am glad he's out of my life, now that I see his reality," she said. "I can move on. I'm ready to." She glared at her crutches, leaning on the opposite arm of the parlor couch. "There will be a day, and it will be soon, when I shall toss those away and walk as straight as ever I did before." She lowered her tone. "God will help me if we pray for it, won't He?"

"Yes, of course."

Marion nodded. "Then pray hard. I sure am. This time, I think I'll immediately like His answer. I won't have to deliberate quite so much, like with His other answers." She paused. "I now believe they were good, too."

Ellen actually beamed. "You don't know how happy it makes me to hear you say that."

The days filed into September. Marion pushed herself and grew stronger daily. She read whatever she could get her hands on, including the Bible, which Ellen helped her study. She read aloud, memorized plays, and got Greta and even Bill and Irma, the kids who'd acted with her and Wilkie, to read opposite her. She played the old piano, freshly tuned in exchange for dental work by a patient of Uncle Melvin's. Her nightmares dwindled to one or two a week.

The Saturday after Wilkie's appearance, Mr. Bradley was visiting them all in the parlor. On a whim, Marion mentioned the turret room. "I wonder how it is after all these weeks? I haven't been up there since we came home."

Ellen, perched on the couch with Marion's feet in her lap, peered at her.

"I know, I know. You're thinking I can't handle it," Marion

said. "Not the stairs, or the memories. But...I want to see it again. I want to face it and start shoveling away the memories of—yesterday and put in new ones. The room deserves it." She was proud of her voice for not quivering. She felt composed and strong, like Ellen.

"The stairs won't trouble you," Mr. Bradley spoke up from his chair opposite them. "If you'll allow me, I offer my services to carry you."

Marion looked at him, delight shining out of her face. "Would you? Swell!"

Uncle Melvin and Aunt Jennie shared a wink and a chuckle, but Marion chose not to care. Mr. Bradley was her friend. They could construe what they wanted, but she wouldn't let them bother her out of her friendship.

Ellen brought the crutches while Mr. Bradley carried Marion the whole winding way without a stumble. *Not bad for a lawyer,* Marion thought.

Memories of Wilkie hung like smoke in the round room, clouding over what was really there in the present with what loomed so thick and heavy in the past. Marion was surprised she didn't cry, but that smoke needed to be cleared. *Wilkie, you have no power over me anymore. God, please scrub him and the hurt he caused out of my heart.*

Mr. Bradley set her on the dilapidated couch, and the smell of dust threatened to remind her of Wilkie's woodsy cologne, with which it had mingled so often. She tilted her head back to look up at the high, luminous window. As she did so, she just caught a glimpse that Mr. Bradley shared with Ellen. It seemed meaningful...but you could never tell for sure with those people who hardly ever donned expressions.

"Excuse me for a moment, Miss Marion." Mr. Bradley strode out of sight toward the door. "I'll return shortly; I have to fetch something downstairs."

"Of course," Marion replied. She sighed after he left. "Ellen...do you remember that article Gloria was going to read to me? It was in the *New York Times* and it was a human interest story or something about a church putting on Christian plays. I even remember the author: Jane Watson. Does your elephantine mind recall it, or am I imagining things?"

"I remember it. I don't know what happened to it. Why?"

"I'd like to read it. I want to see how—I'm not sure how to say it, this is such a new thought to me—I want to see how those Christian actors used their acting for the glory of God. I think the Bible puts it that way, doesn't it? 'For the glory of God'?" Marion grinned. "Don't chide me for being so illiterate. I know I ought to know."

Ellen gazed at her for a moment, a half-smile lifting a light to her brown eyes. "Why don't we write to Gloria and ask if she still has it? I saw her clip it out like you'd asked."

After a few minutes of chasing the trail of thoughts that led to theater and Hollywood but didn't quite reach the question Marion was avoiding—her future—Marion asked, "What on earth is taking Mr. Bradley so long? He'd want to be in on this very serious, thought-provoking conversation."

Ellen shrugged. She was sitting on the couch, Marion's outstretched feet once again in her lap.

"You know something, don't you?" Marion wheedled, then jumped as the sound of a clunk on the stairs hit her ears. "Ellen, what was that?"

"You'll see." Ellen slipped out from under Marion's feet and beelined for the door. A minute passed, creaking and clomping stirring Marion's blood into a windstorm of anticipation while she alternately listened and demanded information.

Ellen opened the door. In came Mr. Bradley at the head of a stepladder, followed by Uncle Melvin puffing at the tail. Marion squealed while they lugged it to the wall beneath the high window and set it up.

Mr. Bradley wiped beads of sweat from his high forehead, his dark eyes dancing with a smirk. "You're really giving me my exercise today, Miss Marion. I'm out of shape from too much time in the office."

"Oh, you dear thing! Thanks a million!" Marion positioned herself to spring.

"Wait a moment. I'm helping you climb it. That's the only

way you're doing such a dangerous thing as touching a ladder in your condition."

It was slightly painful, but with Mr. Bradley positioned directly behind her and holding her waist, Marion breached the tip of the window, took one more step, and looked out on the view she had desired for six months.

She could see just above the treetops to a world that was full of blue sky, white cloud balls, and the honeyed greens of nascent fall. The fields were obscured, as was most of Cardinal Bush, but she could see the wide breaks in the trees and the spires of two churches. A spotted black V of early geese flapped their way south, headed for a place that would protect them and allow them to flourish as God intended.

Marion gazed silently until her hip hurt too much. Then she sighed. "Oh, Mr. Bradley, Uncle Melvin. Thank you. I know this sounds cliché, but it's like I'm seeing things with new eyes. It's beautiful. I've got to get down now, but can we leave the ladder here for a while? Say, forever?"

When Ellen returned to work at Mr. Bradley's office, she expected to be inordinately happy. But during lulls, when her mind was not on a task, she was pestered by reminiscences and odd longings whose origins she couldn't trace. Eventually she did discover them, however. When her thoughts rested on Everett she suddenly had focus—every other object left her mind.

Did life have to proceed this way? Did every first romance fail, in such a painful way? Considering the sisters' odds, apparently yes. Despite Ellen's best efforts to protect her heart, it had gotten shattered like Marion's. Not violently, but gradually and tortuously as the truth pierced farther and farther until it could withstand no more.

Like Wilkie, Everett was set to marry someone who couldn't make him happy. Unlike Wilkie, the path he'd chosen was honorable. What did Ellen desire of him? To jilt Leona when they had been engaged for so many years? She couldn't ultimately respect him if he did that. No, it was better this way.

The Sunday almost a week after Wilkie's reappearance, Frances Lundberg came for a visit, primed and ready for a catch-up conversation covering every notable incident of the last two months.

She had much to say about the direction Dad's case was taking. Hers, Mr. Bradley's, and Everett's sleuthing was worthy of a detective novel, judging from the evidence they'd uncovered incriminating Mr. Green. All it would take now was a court investigation to clinch the deal and confirm everything they suspected. The way was paved for Mr. Dashiell's retrial, Frances resolutely declared.

"It sounds wonderful," Mother admitted, brown eyes troubled beneath her furrowed forehead. "But I'm afraid to hope."

"Don't fear something that's perfectly safe." Frances punctuated with a pointed finger. "Hope never hurt anyone. It's a lifeline; it moves you to do things you wouldn't otherwise do. But regardless, I have enough confidence for this entire household, if none of you want to join me."

After Ellen drove Frances to the train station to embark her for Canton shortly before supper, Frances said on the platform, "Ellen, I've got something to tell you."

Ellen smiled. "Something more? Haven't you already told me lots of somethings?" Although she hadn't let on, she'd allowed herself to put one foot, almost two, into Frances's camp of hope, and so she was feeling more optimistic than she had for a while about Dad. Her hope was like a wilted plant perking up after water.

"Ellen." Frances placed her hand on Ellen's shoulder. The call of the incoming train resounded just out of sight. "Everett Shepherd got sacked."

"Oh, no! When? I'm so sorry to hear it. The last time I saw him, he had been afraid that would happen. Have you seen him lately?"

"There's more. I hope I'm not the first one you're hearing this from, but it's going around Canton that Leona Bingham's gotten married to him."

Ellen stared, unfeeling, into Frances's intense hazel eyes. The train was roaring up behind her, but she barely heard it.

"Other people say, however, that they don't really know *whom* she married, just that she's married." Frances bristled and snapped, "And all this time I thought Everett was in love with you!"

Eyeing the other passengers milling around the platform, Ellen put a finger to her lips, let it fall, and nodded feebly. "I did know he wasn't, though I didn't know about the marriage. It's just a rumor?"

"Ida Westwood's housekeeper told my friend about Ida attending her sister Leona's wedding in New York. She didn't say who the groom was, but the name that's circulating is Everett Shepherd. Of course, he's not here to prove or disprove it, but I knew it couldn't be him; he was in love with you. So now you say you knew he wasn't after you? Why on earth did you and he encourage each other like you did?"

"I didn't know he wasn't interested in me until Leona Bingham…" She might as well let it out, now that it was a prevalent almost-fact. "Told me he was engaged to her."

"What?! Oh, Ellen, so the rumors are true! She's married to *Everett Shepherd*! Why, I could wring his scrawny neck! I knew he was trouble. All men are! That cheating, no-good liar, cad, and —"

"Please, Frances, I appreciate your taking up for me, but cursing him won't help me. I've had a lot of time to ponder it, and I don't think he's worthy of that much censure. You see, he had been engaged to Leona Bingham for years, and it might have gone a little stale. He was attracted to me at first, but he stuck by Leona, as he ought to do. Men get tempted, but what really matters is what they do in the end."

Frances looked up at her, eyes and brows narrowed into a legible V. "Yep, you're hurt. Girls like you, when they get hurt, they always defend the fella. Well, I won't defend him. If he dares set foot in my office again, I'll give him a piece of my mind."

"I wish you wouldn't—"

"I will. Now, I really have to go. The train is ready, and it won't wait for me, discourteous thing. I wish I could stay and comfort you, but that's what your mother and sisters are for." Frances patted Ellen's cheek and squeezed her shoulder. "And don't 'forget' to tell them; I know how you are. Farewell, dear. Don't worry—either there will be a worthier man, or you'll be blissfully unhitched all your life, like me."

Frances dashed off into the train car with a final glance back, as sympathetic as she was capable of.

Ellen waved until her car was out of sight, then stood mired in place, feeling like a lead blanket had dropped over her head, down to her feet. A worthier man...perhaps someday. But she wouldn't forget Everett in a hurry.

He was married now, was he? She didn't usually grant credence to rumors, but these were confirmed by Leona herself. She was just surprised that Leona hadn't contacted her as she had promised she'd do, even if they eloped.

So it was final. Everett was lost to her.

Ellen had of course already told Marion, Mother, and Aunt Jennie about their plans to get married, and Uncle Melvin and Greta had been enlightened as well. Telling them all about the inevitable next step once she arrived home nevertheless shocked and sobered everyone to their core.

"I can't believe Everett would be so impetuous and do that." Mother shook her head. "But everything lines up to show that he did. Oh Ellen, I'm so sorry."

"We knew it was coming. Why should we be sorry? I'm relieved that it's finally occurred, and I didn't have to be at the wedding." Ellen managed a weak half-smile. "Now I can move on."

Marion gazed at Ellen with watery eyes. "Oh, Ellen, like me. We can move on together." She spread her arms for an embrace.

Uncle Melvin and Aunt Jennie went to visit some friends in Cardinal Bush after supper, so the four Dashiells curled up in the parlor to the background of the radio and absorbed themselves in reading or handwork.

"What is it, Sport?" Greta asked as the dog raised his elegant head from where he'd been resting on the rug in front of the fireplace. She closed her Nancy Drew book and looked toward the pitch-dark driveway. "Someone's pulling up."

"Aunt Jennie and Uncle Melvin can't be back already." Mother got to her feet. "Maybe they forgot something." She went to the foyer as a car door slammed.

"Ellen, you'd better come here," she called after a moment.

Ellen halted her knitting needles. She was in a good stopping position, so she laid her project aside and followed Greta and Sport out the doorway.

"Thank you for leaving me all alone!" sniffed Marion from the couch.

"Who is it?" Greta asked. Sport poised himself, nose to the front door.

"I think it's Everett," Mother whispered.

"*Who* is it?" Marion asked loudly. "Really, if you were all going to leave, you could have helped me join the welcoming committee, too."

"Do you want me to tell him you're not home?" Mother smoothed her already smooth hair and dress.

"No. We must tell him congratulations," Ellen replied. "He's our friend, after all, and he's not aware his marriage has changed anything. He's probably come to tell us himself." She would pretend she was perfectly unaffected. She'd done that many times over her life, and though this might be the hardest yet, she was up for the challenge.

A knock caused them all to jump. "Greta," Ellen hissed, "tell Marion it's Everett, and tell her to act…like me, not herself. And turn off the radio."

Greta ran to do her bidding while Mother opened the door. "Hello," she said in a firm voice. "What a surprise! It's good to see you."

Everett stepped in looking ashen. He doffed his fedora, revealing rose-pink ears. He clutched a bouquet of red roses. "Hello." His voice was a ghost of its former self. He swallowed and cleared his throat and revised, avoiding Ellen's face with his glance, "Hello. It's good to be here again."

Ellen was disappointed in him. Surely after his display of bravery alongside Leona to their parents, he could have faced her with equal dignity? Flowers and fear were not good companions to confessions.

She greeted him as Mother welcomed him into the parlor, where Greta stood grinning with Sport seated at her side. "Hi, Everett!"

"Everett. Good evening," Marion said like a haughty queen on her divan. "Please forgive my inability to jump up and greet you properly."

"Hello," Everett said. "How is your recovery?"

"Slow, but speeding up," Marion replied, propping her right elbow on the head of the couch. "I couldn't do this the last time you saw me. It hurt my arm too much."

Everett nodded, then fidgety silence reigned.

"Well, may I get you something to eat or drink? Coffee, tea? Cookies?" Mother asked.

Ellen roused herself. "Yes, please sit down."

He sat in an armchair while Ellen sat in another and Greta sank down in front of the fireplace beside Sport.

"I don't want anything, thank you," Everett said, studying the movement of his hands as they rubbed his knees. The roses lay in his lap.

Mother perched in her chair. "How are you, Everett?"

"Well." Everett's quick, affirming nod was too eager.

It was painful to see him so nervous; Ellen should just make him come out with it. But she couldn't.

Mother continued, "And how is Mrs. Shepherd?"

Everett finally gave her a quizzical glance. "She's fine."

Mother shared a look with Ellen. "I understand we are to congratulate you." She smiled.

"Um, thank you." Everett's brows furrowed and his hands ceased moving. "For what, now?"

"Why, for your marriage of course!" Mother chuckled. "I'm sorry to steal your news, but I simply had to speak out when you didn't take the opportunity I offered."

"My...marriage?" Everett's ears flushed redder than before. "I—I don't understand."

"Your marriage to Leona Bingham. We heard from Frances Lundberg the rumor was going around Canton."

"*My* marriage?"

"Yes, yours!" Marion chimed in.

"Well, it was a rumor, but from what Leona told Ellen, we assumed it was true," Mother said.

"I know it's bad form to rely on rumors," Ellen hastened to add. "But..."

"It was only a rumor." A smile inched up the corners of Everett's mouth. "That part of it at least. Leona Bingham *is* married...but not to me."

The drop of a pin could have echoed through the house.

Suddenly Mother stood up. "Greta, help me assist Marion from the couch."

"What? Why?"

"Just do as I say."

Marion's shock changed to a huge smile. "I'll help, too." She scooted around to let her legs down to the floor.

Ellen jumped from her chair and handed Marion's crutches to her.

"No, no, we have this. You stay here...with Everett," Mother admonished.

Everett stood because all the ladies were on their feet, and when everyone but Ellen had left, he turned to gaze at her. Ellen returned his stoical expression—stoical except for the eyes. Both pairs of eyes were a turmoil of emotions—confusion, hope, fear, love.

"I don't know how to ask this," Everett began. "You and Mr. Bradley...you're not..." He gestured helplessly with his left hand. "I mean, there's not, uh, something...is there?"

After a bewildered moment Ellen's eyes widened. "Oh, no! Not—not at all."

Everett's breath hitched. "I thought—I thought perhaps there was. That's why I hesitated...but if there isn't...then I got the right color." He studied his crimson bouquet, spinning it slowly in a mesmerizing circle. Ellen gulped.

Everett looked up, walked forward, and glanced down at his roses, then held them out to her and recaptured her gaze. "I remember you said you liked roses. I think you said white roses, but they don't have the right meaning." He smiled sheepishly.

Ellen's eyes dropped. She reached out a shaky hand and clasped the firm, cool, de-thorned stems. The gauzy white ribbon encircling them tickled her fingers. A faint, sweet scent touched her nose. "Thank you," she whispered as she looked into Everett's face again.

"You...do understand me then?" he asked.

"Perfectly." Ellen burst into tears.

"She married Wilkie St. John," were Everett's words when they had all gathered in the parlor again a half-hour later.

"What?!" Marion squeaked. Ellen pressed her hand. No wonder she had insisted on sitting beside Marion, despite Marion's insistence that she cuddle up next to Everett. Good old Ellen, always putting herself out for Marion's moral support. Everett must have dropped this bombshell on her during their half-hour of seclusion.

"I don't know exactly how it happened, either," Everett said. "I was in New York at the time because I lost my job, you know. I didn't know why, but I didn't hear from her for days after we told her parents about our engagement. They threatened to disown her, so she had been fretting about money; but I didn't think she'd drop me for that. Then, a few days ago, she wrote to me that she had married Wilkie St. John. I came here as soon as I could collect my wits and muster the courage."

"So she was the one in Wilkie's story!" Marion exclaimed. "From what you told me, Ellen, it fits like a glove, down to the Leona-like waffling. She wanted the man with the money. And Wilkie fell for it. Oh, goodness. That *female* ending up with him...no wonder he was so miserable. They rather deserve each other." She giggled and snapped a glance at Everett. "Sorry. You don't feel any attachment anymore, do you?"

"No." Everett smiled slightly. "It was up to her to sever the cords, because I...I cared for her too much as an old friend and a vulnerable lady to jilt her."

"You pitied her, didn't you," Ellen observed.

"Yes. I take it you did, too?"

"And I didn't. That's why you two are a match." Marion shook her head rigorously to make her curls dance—she was back to fixing her hair. "I can't believe she took Wilkie in. And in a way, Ellen, that served *you* because it rescued Everett."

Everett's ears tinged pink while Ellen smiled broadly and glanced down. That girl could never blush.

Marion blew out a dramatic sigh. "I don't know what I think of it. He might have come crawling back to me after that wealthy raven of a girl gave him the boot, and then what would I have done?"

"I don't like thinking about it," Mother piped up. "All I want to reflect on is that God let those two take care of each other while He took care of my daughters."

Marion nodded and sighed again, softer this time. The Wilkie she had loved never existed. He wouldn't have come back to her; it required a mistake like marrying Leona Bingham to pluck the blindfold off his eyes. A mistake that trapped him. Marion's blindfold had been shredded in New York, and she was grateful God had protected her from something far worse than broken bones and setback dreams. Perhaps there was someone better than Wilkie for her...she already knew two young men whose virtues left him in the dust. Surely someone would show up for her.

"My parents will be happy with me again because they'll be so fond of you," Everett told Ellen.

"I hope so. I do regret not meeting them that night at the theater, but I'm sure it won't matter much in the long run," Ellen said.

"Ellen has an uncanny ability to endear people to her," Marion remarked. "In-laws may be the toughest cases of all, but I have utmost confidence in her."

"I do, too." Everett exchanged a sufficiently sappy glance with Ellen. At last those two were acting like lovers, at least as much as they were able.

"Let me get this straight." Greta leaned forward from her chair and tapped her chin. "Did you actually propose to Ellen, Everett?"

"Well…" Everett glanced at Ellen again, "not really. I don't have a ring. And I didn't ask your dad."

"But once he accomplishes those things, he will propose," Ellen stated in her most serious older-sister-instructor tone.

"And you'll say yes?" Greta prodded.

"Of course." Ellen bit her lip and regarded the floor while Mother and Marion giggled. "Not to sound precipitous."

"Knowing Dad as I do," Mother said, "he will certainly give his consent."

"And I will certainly propose once I have it," Everett shyly quipped.

ᐒᕼ᠕ᕲ᠕ Chapter Thirty-Three ᕲᐃᕼᕲ

"Not guilty."

The solemn, thrilling words from the jury foreman's mouth were the crescendo of certainty that had built in the Dashiells' hearts over the past few weeks.

Praise God, throbbed in Ellen's mind as her smile danced with Dad's, Mother's, Marion's, Greta's, and Everett's. Dad was acquitted at last.

A murmur of joyous relief aired the crowded courtroom like a wind resuscitating a stuffy, closed-up house. Everyone at all interested by the eight-month case was convinced that justice had finally arrived this late September day. Benton Green's confession of guilt at his trial, when he could no longer hide from the evidence uncovered by Mr. Bradley, Everett, Frances, and the police, had removed any surprise in the outcome of Oliver Dashiell's retrial.

You did it, Lord. You saved him, Ellen rejoiced. Behind her, Aunt Jennie and Uncle Melvin were applauding and almost shouting. To her left, Mother and Marion were crying happy tears, and they and Greta were wearing grander smiles than they had in months. Standing in front of her with his back to her, Dad bowed his head for a moment, no doubt feeling the same reverence she was feeling that constrained her outward jubilation. Then he turned and grinned at his family once again.

And to her right, squeezing her hand and allowing his small but firm hand to be suffocated back, was Everett. They hadn't talked overmuch today—they were never as chattery together as Marion thought healthy—but their souls always stood in solid alignment, shoulder to shoulder. Ellen didn't need Everett to say that he supported her unreservedly, and he didn't need words to know what she needed and that she appreciated what he gave.

They were caught up enough with the celebration of the courtroom to feel that they, too, were being demonstrative just by gripping each other's hands and beaming. Ellen's heart had never been lighter.

Dad's good name would be restored, all the taint polished away by repentant fellow Cantonians.

His business was to be returned to him. Friar's Tool and Die needed a president, and the only experienced, trustworthy candidate was Oliver Dashiell.

Once all affairs were straightened out, the family could buy back their house, which hadn't been sold, but only mortgaged.

Over the last several weeks Ellen had realized this wonderful lineup of events would happen—it wasn't just wishing; it was sound fact. Their inevitability crashed upon her again, an exhilarating wave of joy. It was almost too perfect to believe that the nightmare web of injustice was to untangle like this, yet untangle it would. The fight was over, God gave them the victory, and only battle cleanup and rebuilding remained.

In another minute the five Dashiells had clasped into a giant hug, smothering Greta in the middle. Their happiness leaped and sparked until Ellen could imagine them all going up as a flame. Dad's left arm wrapped her with crushing strength. He smelled lightly of sweat and generic shaving lotion—but today he was free. He would go back to using his pine-scented aftershave and his leather-scented business jacket, and their aroma would mean all was as it should be.

"Dinner parties are a dime a dozen here at the Maddoxes', but this one is a positive festival!" Uncle Melvin crowed that night from the head of the table. Ten people were feasting in the Maddoxes' dining room. "A regular Fourth of July, Thanksgiving, and Christmas in one bursting package, I tell you."

The table looked like Thanksgiving. Ellen was amazed that Aunt Jennie had pulled off her outrageous plans of roast beef, chicken, gravy, mashed potatoes, corn, beans, biscuits, fruit salad, apple pie, and sweet potato pudding.

"It's because we're all at our absolute happiest," Marion said, forking a bean and exchanging a brilliant smile with Ellen and then Mr. Bradley. She had double reason for ecstasy, because yesterday she had accomplished her first steps without crutches. She couldn't abandon them entirely yet, but the painful, tiny, independent steps across the living room rug were as promising as a baby's.

Everyone—the Dashiells, the Maddoxes, Everett, Mr. Bradley, and Frances Lundberg—heartily agreed with her. Dad's acquittal meant the world to them all.

Aunt Jennie held up one finger while she finished chewing a biscuit. "We're celebrating so many happy occasions!" she exclaimed a little thickly. She swallowed. "Ellen, Everett, you can make your occasion even happier by telling us a wedding date!"

Ellen smiled and fingered her engagement ring—a gold band that gleamed all the brighter for its simplicity. She looked at Everett on her right, and what she'd intended to be a glance became a gaze as their eyes locked and spoke. She knew just what was said. Oh, it was wonderful, the way they could read each other and find their thoughts ran in the same track.

"I'm afraid we don't have a wedding date yet." Ellen transferred her attention to Aunt Jennie. "We were waiting for Dad's good news. But now I guess the time is right to discuss it."

"No pressuring them, Aunt Jennie," Marion admonished with a straight face but laughing eyes. "They don't like being hurried. They're likely to baulk like mules and wait until they're thirty."

"Jeepers, I hope not!" Frances cried, halting her knife and fork's work at some beef. "I'm tired of waiting and guessing their intentions. I've been doing that for seven months. I just want to see them married!"

Everett grinned. "So do I."

Dad cleared his throat and everyone's eyes fixed on him. It

was surreal to have him in their midst again. His blond hair had shaded to silver, and more lines had gathered around the features of his face, but he still held his shoulders straight and spoke in deep, steady tones. "I look forward to working with you, Everett. Friar's is turning into quite the family business, isn't it?"

"Oh, it's a blessing from heaven that your future son-in-law is your accountant!" Aunt Jennie shook her head with a smile. She pointed at Mr. Bradley with a chicken-headed fork. "Speaking of dates and weddings, don't neglect your own."

Ellen captured both Marion and Mr. Bradley quickly enough to witness a blush tinge Marion's cheeks and a curiously mixed expression of happy consternation cross Mr. Bradley's face.

Marion's eyes sparkled. "Aunt Jennie, don't pressure *him*, either."

Across from Marion, Mr. Bradley studied her for a second, riveted by her grin. Ellen knew what he was pondering: Marion had just dropped him a hint. Marion had told Ellen straight out that she was now open to Mr. Bradley's attentions. "He's waited awhile for my opening hour; I think I'm finally ready," she had said. "But, mind you, this will go very slowly, because I just turned eighteen and have lots to figure out about my future. It's a good thing I like to talk and he likes to listen, because that's the only way we'll sort this out."

Ellen was uncomfortable with predictions, but the path she couldn't help but foresee for her vibrant little sister was similarly happy, if perhaps more challenging than her own. But Marion was well on her way to being prepared for it. If things kept on their course, Marion would go to drama school and then discover how she could use her craft for God's glory and not her own. She would wed Mr. Bradley; he would support her and be her earthly rock. Especially lately, he had held a genuine interest in Marion's dreams. His steadfastness brightened by his gentle humor and uncanny insight was entirely suitable for the husband of a talented actress and singer. Particularly one as loving as Marion.

"Dad, can we get a dog when we move back to Canton?"

Greta piped up. Dad was seated next to her, and she gazed at him as if he were the only person in the room. "I've been ever so happy with Sport, and he's Uncle Melvin's dog. I'll be even happier with my own!"

Dad smiled slowly. "Yes. If I can have my job back, Mother can have her house and furniture back, Ellen can have a fiancé, and Marion can return to acting and singing, then you may certainly have a dog."

His right hand disappeared from the table and, sitting beside him, Mother's left arm shifted as her hand no doubt joined her husband's. They gave each other a smile that caused another throb of joy to swell Ellen's heart.

Despite all that the world had done to separate her parents, God had brought them back together. God was faithful—He had brought all the Dashiells to a place of loving and trusting in Him where they had never been before. Ellen prayed her and Everett's union would stand as strong. With God's help, it would. Hadn't He already proven it against the odds?

Acknowledgments

First of all, I want to thank Mark Holland, Archivist, and Tom Haas, research volunteer, at the McKinley Presidential Library and Museum in Canton, Ohio, for being so helpful to my research.

I also want to thank my aunt and uncle in Ohio, my beta readers Sarah S., Elizabeth, Matthew, Deborah, Sarah H., and Crystal, my alpha reader, Gail (my mom), and my omega reader, Tom (my dad), and my cover designer Hannah for all the time and effort they contributed to making this book what it is. I couldn't have done it without you guys!

Most of all, I thank the Lord God of Israel, without whom I am nothing.

About the Author

Since becoming an Austenite as a teenager, Kelsey Bryant has dreamed of writing a book in ode to Jane Austen. *Sense and Sensibility* is one of Kelsey's favorite novels and Elinor Dashwood is her favorite book character, so it's easy to imagine her ecstasy as she was writing *Suit and Suitability*. This is her first published historical fiction work; she has also published two YA contemporary novels.

Kelsey lives in Central Texas with her family, where she's also a copy editor, a martial arts instructor, and an avid student of the Bible.

Visit Kelsey online at kelseybryantauthor.weebly.com or on her blog, kelseysnotebookblog.blogspot.com.